PROFILE DURANGO

"You know I'll do everything in my power to see that nobody hurts you," he said softly as he reached up to stroke her sleek hair.

" I know, but we also both know that if somebody wants me dead badly enough, they'll find a way to accomplish that." Her voice trembled slightly and he could feel the beat of her racing heart against his own.

He cupped her face and forced her to look up at him. When he'd been injured and in the hospital with a raging fever and facing death, it had been a vision of her eyes that had sustained him. The hope that he'd see her once again had kept him fighting for his life.

"Not on my watch." And even though he knew it was a mistake, he couldn't help himself. He bent his head and claimed her mouth with his.

First published in Great Britain 2010
Harlequin Mills & Boon Limited,
Eton House, 18-24 Paradise Road, Richmond, Surrey TW9 1SR

Secrets in Four Corners © Harlequin Books S.A. 2009
Profile Durango © Harlequin Books S.A. 2009

Special thanks and acknowledgement to Debra Webb and Carla Cassidy for their contributions to the Kenner County Crime Unit mini-series.

ISBN: 978 0 263 88246 9

46-0810

Harlequin Mills & Boon policy is to use papers that are natural, renewable and recyclable products and made from wood grown in sustainable forests. The logging and manufacturing processes conform to the legal environmental regulations of the country of origin.

Printed and bound in Spain
by Litografia Rosés S.A., Barcelona

SECRETS IN FOUR CORNERS
BY
DEBRA WEBB

PROFILE DURANGO
BY
CARLA CASSIDY

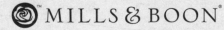
MILLS & BOON

SECRETS IN FOUR CORNERS

BY
DEBRA WEBB

Debra Webb was born in Scottsboro, Alabama, to parents who taught her that anything is possible if you want it badly enough. She began writing at the age of nine. Eventually, she met and married the man of her dreams and tried some other occupations, including selling vacuum cleaners, working in a factory, a day-care centre, a hospital and a department store. With the support of her husband and two beautiful daughters, Debra took up writing again, looking to mysteries and movies for inspiration. You can write to Debra with your comments at PO Box 64, Huntland, Tennessee 37345, USA, or visit her website at www.debrawebb.com to find out exciting news about her next book.

Colorado is a beautiful place. I've been blessed enough to spend time there and I was awed by the natural wonders. Please be advised that Kenner County is a fictional place, although many real towns and areas of interest were used in the creation of this story. As hard as an author works to do all the research necessary, there are times when a little something needs to be added in the best interest of the story. So if you find something missing or where it shouldn't be, please forgive me and please, please enjoy Bree and Patrick's story!

Chapter One

Sabrina Hunter fastened her utility belt around her hips. "Eat up, Peter, or we're gonna be late."

Peter Hunter peered up at his mom, a spoonful of Cheerios halfway to his mouth. "We're always late."

This was definitely nothing to brag about. "But," his mother reminded him, "our New Year's resolution was to make it a point *not* to be late anymore." It was only January twelfth. Surely, they weren't going to break their resolution already.

Chewing his cereal thoughtfully, Peter tilted his dark head and studied her again. "Truth or dare?"

Bree took a deep breath, reached for patience. "Eat. There's no time for games." She tucked her cell phone into her belt. Mondays were always difficult. Especially when Bree had worked the weekend and her son had spent most of that time with his aunt Tabitha. She spoiled the boy outrageously, as did her teenage daughter, Layla. Even so, Bree was glad to have her family support system when duty called, as it had this weekend. She grabbed her mug and downed the last of the coffee that had grown cold during her rush to prepare for the day.

Peter swallowed, then insisted, "Truth. Is my real daddy a jerk just like Big Jack?"

Bree choked. Coughed. She plopped her mug on the counter and stared at her son. "Where did you hear something like that?"

"Cousin Layla said so." He nodded resolutely. "Aunt Tabitha told her to hush 'cause I might hear. Is it true? Is my real daddy a jerk?"

"You must've misunderstood, Peter." *Breathe.* Bree moistened her lips and mentally scrambled for a way to change the subject. "Grab your coat and let's get you to school." Memories tumbled one over the other in her head. Memories she had sworn she would never allow back into her thoughts. That was her other New Year's resolution. After eight years it was past time she'd put *him* out of her head and her heart once and for all.

What the hell was her niece thinking, bringing *him* up? Particularly with Peter anywhere in the vicinity. The kid loved playing hide and seek, loved sneaking up on his mother and aunt even more. His curious nature ensured he missed very little. Tabitha and Layla knew this!

Bree ordered herself to calm down.

"Nope. I didn't misunderstand." Peter pushed back his chair, carefully picked up his cereal bowl and headed for the sink. He rinsed the bowl and placed it just as carefully into the dishwasher. "I heard her."

Bree's pulse rate increased. "Layla was probably talking about…" Bree racked her brain for a name, someone they all knew—anyone besides *him*.

Before she could come up with a name or a logical explanation for her niece's slip, Peter turned to his mother once more, his big blue eyes—the ones so much like his father's and so unlike her brown ones—resolute. "Layla said my real daddy—"

"Okay, okay." Bree held up her hands. "I got that part." How on earth was she supposed to respond? "We can talk on the way to school." Maybe that would at least buy her some time. And if she were really lucky Peter would get distracted and forget all about the subject of his father.

Something Bree herself would very much like to do.

She would be having a serious talk with her sister and niece.

Thankfully her son didn't argue. He tugged on his coat and picked up his backpack. So far, so good. She might just get out of this one after all. Was that selfish of her? Was Peter the one being cheated by her decision to keep the past in the past? Including his father?

Bree pushed the questions aside and shouldered into the navy uniform jacket that sported the logo of the Towaoc Police Department. At the coat closet near her front door, she removed the lockbox from the top shelf, retrieved her service weapon and holstered it. After high school she'd gotten her associate's degree in criminal justice. She hadn't looked back since, spending a decade working in reservation law enforcement. The invitation to join the special homicide task force formed by the Bureau of Indian Affairs and the Ute Mountain Reservation tribal officials had been exactly the opportunity she had been looking for to further her career.

Besides her son and family, her career was primary in her life. Not merely because she was a single parent, either, although that was a compelling enough motive. She wanted to be a part of changing the reservation's unofficial reputation as the murder capital of Colorado. This was her home. Making a difference was important to her. She wanted to do her part for her people.

Not to mention work kept her busy. Kept her head on straight and out of that past she did not want to think about, much less talk about. An idle mind was like idle hands, it got one into trouble more often than not.

Enough trouble had come Bree's way the last few years.

No sooner had she slid behind the wheel of her SUV and closed the door had Peter demanded, "Truth, Mommy." He snapped his safety belt into place.

So much for any hopes of him letting the subject go. Bree glanced over her shoulder to the backseat where her son waited. She could take the easy way out and say his aunt and cousin were right. His curiosity would be satisfied and that would be the end of that—for now anyway. But that would be a lie. There were a lot of things she could say about the man who'd fathered her child, but that he was bad or the kind of jerk her ex, Jack, had turned out to be definitely wasn't one of them.

"Your father was never anything like Big Jack." Even as she said the words, her heart stumbled traitorously.

"So he was a good guy?"

Another question that required a cautiously worded response. "A really good guy."

"Like a superhero?"

Maybe that was a stretch. But her son was into comics lately. "I guess you could say that." Guilt pricked her again for allowing the conversation to remain in past tense…as if his father were deceased. Another selfish gesture on her part.

But life was so much easier that way.

"Am I named after him?"

Tension whipped through Bree. That was a place

she definitely didn't want to go. Her cell phone vibrated. Relief flared. Talk about being saved by the bell, or, in this case, the vibration. "Hold on, honey." Bree withdrew the phone from the case on her belt and opened it. "Hunter."

"Detective Hunter, this is Officer Danny Brewer."

Though she was acquainted with a fair number of local law enforcement members, particularly those on the reservation, the name didn't strike a chord. She couldn't readily associate the name with one department or the other, making it hard to anticipate whether his call was something or nothing. That didn't prevent a new kind of tension from sending her instincts to the next level. "What can I do for you, Officer Brewer?"

"Well, ma'am, we have a situation."

His tone told her far more than his words. *Something.*

When she would have asked for an explanation, he went on, "We have a one eighty-seven."

Adrenaline fired in Bree's veins. Before she could launch the barrage of homicide-related questions that instantly sprang to mind, Brewer tacked on, "My partner said I should call you. He would've called himself but he's been busy puking his guts out ever since we took a look at the…vic."

Damn. Another victim.

Bree blinked, focused on the details she knew so

far. Puking? Had to be Officer Steve Cyrus. She knew him well. Poor Cyrus lost his last meal at every scene involving a body.

One eighty-seven.

Damn.

Another murder.

"Location?" Bree glanced at her son. She would drop him off at school and head straight to the scene. Hell of a way to start a Monday morning. Frustration hit on the heels of the adrenaline. She'd worked a case of rape and attempted murder just this weekend. As hard as her team toiled to prevent as well as solve violent crimes it never seemed to be enough.

"The Tribal Park." Brewer cleared his throat. "In the canyon close to the Two-Story House. One of the guides who checks the trails a couple of times a week during the off-season found the victim."

"Don't let him out of your sight," Bree reminded. She would need to question the guide at length. Chances were he would be the closest thing to a witness, albeit after the fact, she would get. "Did you ID the victim?" She hoped this wasn't another rape as well. Twelve days into the New Year and they'd had two of those already. Both related to drug use.

Bree frowned at the muffled conversation taking place on the other end of the line. It sounded like Brewer was asking his partner what he should say in answer to her question. Weird.

"Ma'am," Brewer said, something different in his voice now, "Steve said just get here as fast as you can. He'll explain the details then."

When the call ended Bree stared at her phone then shook her head.

Damned weird.

"M-o-o-o-m," Peter said, drawing out the single syllable, "you didn't answer my question."

She definitely didn't have time for that now. More of that guilt heaped on her shoulders at just how relieved she was to have an excuse not to go there. "We'll have to talk about it later. That was another police officer who called. I have to get to work."

Peter groaned, but didn't argue with her. He knew that for his mom work meant something bad had happened to someone.

As Bree guided her vehicle into the school's drop-off lane, she considered her little boy. She wanted life on the reservation to continue to improve. For him. For the next generation, period. As hard as she worked, at times it never seemed to be enough.

"Have a good day, sweetie." She smoothed his hair and kissed the top of his head.

His cheeks instantly reddened. "Mom."

Bree smiled as he hopped out of the SUV and headed for Towaoc Elementary's front entrance. Her baby was growing up. Her smile faded. There would be more questions about his father.

She couldn't think about that right now.

Right now she had a homicide to investigate.

ONLY A FEW minutes on Highway 160 were required to reach the Ute Mountain Tribal Park. She turned into the park entrance near the visitor's center, a former gas station that had been repurposed. Getting into the park was easy, reaching the ancient cliff face Ancestral Puebloan dwellings was another story.

A rough dirt road barely wide enough for her SUV was the only way besides making the trek on foot or horseback. The SUV bumped over the rutted dirt road. Twice Bree was forced to maneuver around ottoman-sized boulders from a recent rock slide. The road, which was more of a trail, was definitely better suited for traveling by horse or on foot. Since time was of the essence she would just have to deal with the less than favorable driving conditions. Every minute wasted allowed the possibility of trace evidence contamination or loss of that essential evidence entirely.

The harsh, barren landscape had a character wholly of its own. Basins with scatterings of sage and juniper and pine forests broke up the thousands of acres of desolation. Gray cliffs and brick-red buttes soaked up the scorching sun that even in the dead of winter and cloaked with snow somehow kept the temps comfortable enough most of the time. Not much otherwise in the way of color, but the amazing Colorado sky made up for it with vivid shades of blue broken only by the snow-capped peaks that added another layer of enchantment.

In the distance, providing a dramatic backdrop, was the giant Sleeping Ute Mountain. The name had come from the fact that the mountain's shape gave the appearance of a giant warrior sleeping on his back with arms crossed over his chest. The stories about the cliff dwellings and the great sleeping warrior who'd become a mountain had kept her enthralled as a kid.

At close to fifty degrees, it could have been a nice day. Bree sighed as she caught sight of the official Ute Reservation police SUV. A beat-up old pickup, probably belonging to the guide, was parked next to the SUV.

Another murder.

The idea that Steve Cyrus wanted her on the scene before he passed along any known details nagged at her again. What was with the mystery?

She parked her vehicle, grabbed a pair of latex gloves from her console and climbed out. She headed toward the cliffs where the two-story, sandstone dwelling hung, a proud, crumbling reminder of the residents who built them more than a millennium ago. The dwellings here were every bit as breathtaking as Mesa Verde's, but this park didn't get near the tourist flow. Primarily because no one came in without an official Ute guide. Preservation was far too important to her people.

Both officers as well as the guide waited some fifty yards from the area where during tourist season folks scrambled up the cliff face to check out the condos of the past. The perpetrator apparently hadn't been too concerned with concealing the body, though the location was definitely off the beaten path to some degree, particularly this time of year. Yet, most anyone who might have been out here could have stumbled over the scene. Or the act in progress.

Just another strange element.

As if her instincts had picked up on something in the air, her pulse rate quickened.

"Hunter," Steve Cyrus called out as he headed in her direction. "I need a minute." He hustled over to meet her.

"What's going on?" She glanced to where Brewer and the old man waited. "You got a body or what?"

Cyrus sent an oddly covert glance in that same direction. "Before you take a look there's something you need to know."

This got stranger by the moment. Bree held up her hands. "Wait—have you called the lab? The coroner?" The realization that no one—*no one*—

else had arrived as of yet abruptly cut through all the confusion.

Cyrus shook his head, looked at the ground before meeting her gaze. "To tell you the truth, I didn't know who the hell to call first. This is…complicated. That's why I called you before anyone else."

"What the hell are you talking about, Cyrus?" Good grief, it wasn't like this was the first deceased victim he'd come upon.

"The vic…" He scrubbed a hand over his chin. "She's…"

At least Bree now knew that the victim was female.

"She's a federal agent."

Federal agent? "BIA?" Her first thought was that an agent from the Bureau of Indian Affairs had been murdered. The controversy over who was boss, Tribal Affairs or BIA, was an ongoing issue. Things got complicated and damned hot at times.

Cyrus shook his head. "FBI. Julie Grainger."

Regret hardened to a lump in Bree's gut. She'd only met Julie Grainger once. Nice lady. Young, early thirties, like Bree. Hard worker. Loyal. A damned good agent from all indications.

"I told you this was complicated."

No kidding. "All right." Bree rubbed her forehead, an ache starting there. "I'll take a look and talk to the guide. You call Callie MacBride and get her lab techs over here. Tell her it's Grainger." A mixture of frustration and more of that regret dragged at Bree's shoulders. "Then call the coroner's office." *Think, Bree. This one will be sticky. Protocol has to be followed to the letter.*

"You want me to call Sheriff Martinez?" Cyrus suggested.

A vise clamped around Bree's chest. This was Kenner County...of course the sheriff would need to be involved. Bree heard herself say yes. What else could she say? Then she did an about-face, her movements stiff, and headed to where Brewer and the guide waited.

Patrick Martinez.

No matter that he had been the sheriff of the county for the last six years, somehow she had managed to avoid running into him. They hadn't spoken in nearly eight years.

Eight years!

Focus on the job.

Special Agent Julie Grainger was dead. She deserved Bree's full attention.

Nothing else mattered right now. Determining why she was dead and who killed her was top priority. "Yeah, do that. But call the others first."

"Morning, Detective," Brewer said as she approached.

"Good morning, Officer Brewer."

"This is Burt Hayes." Brewer gestured to the guide.

Hayes was Ute, as all park guides were. Bree's family was Ute, as well. Hayes had that aged, craggy look, the one that said he'd spent almost as much time in the scorching Western sun as the Puebloan dwellings. He wore faded jeans and beneath the matching denim jacket an equally faded khaki shirt, along with leather boots that had seen far better days. His graying hair was pulled into a ponytail that reached the middle of his back.

"Mr. Hayes." Bree extended her hand, gave his a firm shake. "I need to take a look around, then I'd like to ask you a few questions."

Hayes nodded. "You Charlie Hunter's girl?"

Most folks around the Four Corners area knew her father. He'd once been an outspoken advocate for the Ute people and tribal affairs…before a stroke had silenced his deep, strong voice.

"Yes, sir." Bree smiled. "And he's still as ornery as ever." She turned to Officer Brewer. "Why don't you assist Mr. Hayes with filling out his statement while I have a look at the scene?"

Brewer nodded, didn't comment or ask any questions, which meant that neither he nor Cyrus had done that part yet. Learning the victim was a federal agent had shaken them both.

Complicated.

Definitely complicated.

The silence felt deafening as Bree tugged on the

latex gloves and crouched next to the victim nestled amid the rocks ensconced in the desert sand. Grainger's slender body was bloated with the ugliness of death, her skin pale and marbleized. One hand had been ravaged by wildlife, probably coyotes. Bree grimaced. They were damned lucky there wasn't more damage.

Bree visually examined the body for indications of the kind of violence done by man. No blood. Redness and bruising on the throat. No other signs of violence were visible except ligature marks on her throat. Bree leaned as close as possible and studied the marks. A unique pattern...not mere twine, certainly not a particularly thin wire. The longer she looked the more familiar the pattern appeared. Maybe a necklace of some sort. She'd definitely seen something like it before. Though Bree felt fairly certain cause of death was strangulation, the coroner would make the final conclusion.

She sat back on her haunches and inventoried more details. Jeans, blouse, which, on closer inspection, had a tear in one sleeve as if she'd struggled briefly with her attacker. Hiking boots. But no jacket. Though the weather was definitely tolerable, the last couple of days the temps had hovered in the lower forties. Jacket wearing weather for sure.

Bree surveyed the landscape. No vehicle. She wandered wide around the body, careful of every step. No visible shoe imprints. With the dusty terrain and the ever-present wind, that was no real surprise. No purse. No cell phone. Most females carried some sort of purse, even if only a small clutch. And cell phones, hardly anyone left home without them these days.

Had the body been dumped here, making this location the secondary crime scene, or had Grainger met someone here who had taken her personal effects and vehicle after taking her life?

This part of the park's entry and exit possibilities via vehicle were limited to say the least.

The thought drew Bree's gaze to the road. A dust cloud bloomed, announcing that someone was coming...fast. An SUV bucked along the trail-turned-road until it skidded to a halt next to Bree's vehicle. The dust settled and her denial-swaddled brain registered what her eyes had already recognized.

Official vehicle.

Kenner County.

Had Cyrus called the sheriff first? Now that she thought about it, that didn't add up. There was no way the sheriff could have gotten here this fast unless he'd heard already. Before Cyrus called anyone.

The driver's-side door opened and her heart seemed to stall in her chest. A booted foot hit the ground as the trademark white cowboy hat rose above the open door. Broad shoulders followed that same route…then a tall, lean body gloved in jeans and a brown sheriff's department jacket moved aside and the driver's-side door slammed shut.

Patrick Martinez.

Sheriff Patrick Martinez.

Peter's father.

He strode toward her and Bree snapped out of the ridiculous trance she'd slipped into. Focus. She was a professional; he was a professional. There was no need to let personal feelings get in the way of doing the job. She'd considered long and hard what she would do if this situation ever arose. Now was the time to put that plan into action.

"Sheriff," she said, taking the first step.

Vivid blue eyes, ones exactly like her son's, zeroed in on Bree's like a laser hitting its target. Patrick nodded curtly. "Detective."

"The victim's over here." Bree walked back to where Grainger's body lay waiting to reveal the story behind the final moments of her life.

Had Cyrus or Brewer called MacBride yet? Those lab folks should be here. Now.

Patrick crouched to get a closer look. Bree did the same. He pulled a pair of latex gloves from his jacket pocket and tugged them on. "Who found her?"

The pain in his deep voice reflected the ache of finding one of his own murdered. Every victim was a tragedy, but the loss of a colleague was like losing a family member.

"Burt Hayes. Park guide." Hayes was still giving his statement to Brewer. "He checks the trails every couple of days. Found her this morning. Looks like she may have been here a couple of days."

Patrick nodded. Bree tried hard not to stare at his profile. This wasn't the time. No time would be right…not for the two of them. Still, she couldn't look away. Strong, square jaw. He hadn't taken the time to shave that morning, but the stubble looked good on him. Always had. For a man closer to forty than thirty, he looked damned good.

Being so near Patrick after all this time made her even more aware of how very much her son looked like him.

"Coroner on his way?"

Bree blinked. Concentrate. "Officer Cyrus called the coroner and Callie MacBride at the crime lab just before you arrived."

"But he didn't call me." Patrick rose, towered over her before her brain could send the message to her suddenly rubbery legs to stand. He took a long look around the area. "You and your people sure got out here in one hell of a hurry."

The accusation in the sheriff's eyes when his gaze settled on hers once more ticked her off, exiled all the other emotional confusion of seeing him again after eight years…after the discussion with her son not an hour ago…after everything.

"Cyrus was about to call your office when you arrived." She lifted her chin, sent a lead-filled gaze right back at him. "The initial call came into TPD, Cyrus and Brewer got here first, then called me. Obviously someone called you."

"We got a 9-1-1 call," he explained. "The caller didn't identify himself, but there was no question that he was male." Patrick jerked his head toward the guide. "Any idea why he would call your department and report his discovery, then call 9-1-1?"

Bree glanced at the old man. Most of the older folks didn't bother will cell phones. Many didn't even have landlines. Chances were he'd gone to the gas station on Highway 160 and made the call from there since the visitor's center wouldn't have been open so early. But why call twice? She shook her head. That was something she needed to ask him.

Should have already, but she'd only been on the scene a few minutes herself. Still, she felt stupid at the moment. Patrick Martinez somehow always made her feel inept. That had been part of their problem. Here she'd been all caught up in the emotional impact of seeing him again. And he was only concerned with why he didn't get the call first. Not to mention they should both be focused on the investigation, not some petty pissing contest.

Okay, that wasn't exactly true. His point was relevant. Whatever the case, it was past time to cut to the chase here. "As I said, Officers Cyrus and Brewer were the first on the scene. Cyrus called me immediately due to the sensitivity of the situation. We work together. It made sense at the time. It wasn't about leaving you or anyone else out. As for the 9-1-1 call, we'll have to ask Mr. Hayes." She folded her arms over her chest, refused to waver beneath his iron stare. "Bottom line, this is Ute territory first and foremost. Cyrus's decision to call me first was the right one."

The stare-off lasted another eight or ten seconds before Patrick looked away. Bree did a little mental victory dance. It hadn't been her to give this time.

"I'll call my Bureau contact." Patrick shook his head, rested his gaze on hers once more. "There's going to be a firestorm over this," he warned. "There won't be any straightforward lines of jurisdiction beyond the fact that the Bureau will be lead. We'll do what they tell us. But everyone will want a part of this. Unfortunately that includes every damned news network in this part of the country."

He spoke as if she were a rookie straight out of the academy. "Was that announcement for your benefit? 'Cause I sure as hell hope it wasn't for mine. I know how the chain of command works, Martinez. And I also know the full scope of the kind of impact this case will have on the community. I don't need you or anyone else to tell me how to do my job."

With one long, slow sweep of his dark lashes, he looked her up and down. "If working together is going to be a problem for you, perhaps you should step aside and let one of the other detectives on the special task force take this one."

He had to be kidding. Was he trying to piss her off? Fury boiled up inside her. "I don't have a problem. You're the one who appears to have a problem. You rode in here with a chip on your shoulder. I came to do my job. Why don't *you* step aside and assign one of your deputies to this investigation? That way we'll both be happy."

Another ten seconds of dramatic silence elapsed with the two of them staring holes through each other.

"I can leave the past where it belongs," he offered, his tone a little less accusatory but no less bitter.

Enough with this game. "What past?" With that she gave him her back and stalked off to do her job.

This was murder. The murder of a federal agent. It was way bigger than their foolish past.

Time to do more than just talk about it.

Chapter Two

She hadn't changed a bit.

Patrick watched Bree walk away.

Long dark hair always kept in a braid. As a detective she wasn't required to wear the blue uniform, but she did as a matter of pride. She represented her people as well as the police department.

For nearly eight years he had staunchly avoided running into her. Even after the powers that be in Kenner County had persuaded him to come to Colorado and serve as sheriff, in the jurisdiction where she lived, he'd managed to get by without contact. He'd heard that since they'd parted ways she had married a Ute man. It had been fairly easy to pretend he didn't care.

Now here they were…working a case together. And neither one of them was willing to back off.

His gaze settled on the place where the victim lay amid the rocks and dirt of the barren landscape. A scrap of desert grass managed to thrive here and there around her position. Bleak was the word that came to mind…both for the place and the victim.

Julie Grainger.

Patrick hadn't known the agent other than in passing. He'd met her once at a briefing. Professional, compassionate and dedicated.

Now she was dead.

Patrick shook his head. An incredible waste.

Unable to delay the inevitable any longer, he put through a call to Special Agent in Charge Jerry Ortiz of the Federal Bureau of Investigation Durango field office that represented the Four Corners area. Making this kind of call to someone who no doubt knew the victim well was Patrick's least favorite duty.

But someone had to do it.

Ortiz wasn't in the office so Patrick was patched through to his cell phone. Ortiz had already heard the news from Callie MacBride. He was shocked and devastated. He'd called his people to set things in motion. His staff, those who knew Grainger as well as those who didn't, would be stunned as well.

Patrick ended the call, a sickening feeling in the pit of his gut. A damned shame.

He turned all the way around and surveyed the barren land once more. What the hell had Grainger been doing out here? He was certain a highly trained agent wouldn't have met an informant, much less a suspect, in such a secluded setting. Not without compelling motivation. His initial conclusion was that this had to be the secondary crime scene. Meaning she'd been dumped here like a piece of trash.

Fury thundered inside him. As much as he loved the Four Corners area—it was his home—he hated the scum that had recently flocked here. Worse, he despised the lowlifes who were born and bred here. It seemed the harder he worked to clean up the county where he'd been raised, the harder evil worked to worm its way into his territory.

He couldn't stop the spread of drugs and crime; he was, after all, only one man. But he could damned sure do all within his power to slow it down.

Officers Brewer and Cyrus were busy securing the scene, which should have been done immediately upon discovery. Patrick could only assume that the officers had been too overwhelmed by the discovery that the victim was a federal agent to act judiciously. He moved cautiously around the perimeter of the zone now officially designated by yellow tape as the crime scene. No tire tracks other than those of the vehicles parked nearby. No shoe imprints besides the ones belonging to those currently on the scene. The folks from the crime lab would sweep the area for evidence but so far he saw nothing but an abandoned soda can and a cigarette pack wrapper. Both of which would be analyzed just in case.

A cloud of dust announced the arrival of more official vehicles. The crime lab folks, he hoped. The sooner the scene was searched for clues the greater the likelihood that any evidence left behind would be found.

Patrick met the SUV as it skidded to a stop. All four doors opened. Callie MacBride, head forensic scientist at the Kenner County Crime Unit, climbed out of the front passenger-side door. Her face was pale, strained with disbelief and regret.

"Callie, this is a damned shame." Patrick exhaled a heavy breath. There wasn't a hell of a lot more to say. Not at this point. He had no idea what case Grainger had been working any more than he knew any personal contacts that might have brought her to this place.

Callie dipped her head in acknowledgment of his inadequate words. "Patrick, I believe you know most of my team." She indicated her associates who had emerged from the vehicle. "Miguel Acevedo, Bart Fleming and Bobby O'Shea."

Patrick shook the hand of each man in turn and offered his sincere condolences. He'd worked with about every member of the crime unit the past couple of years. The Four Corners area had needed a crime lab for a good long while before the powers

that be finally had the sense to make it a reality.
Times like this were the reason. Every single
member of the team had made Kenner County
home; they knew the land and its people. In the
past, law enforcement had had to rely on state fa-
cilities from as far away as Denver.

These folks would get the job done quickly and
thoroughly with the kind of knowledge only gained
through life experience with the people and the
land. That the victim was one of their own made
their work this morning more than a job.

This was personal.

Faces grim, the team gathered their gear and
donned protective wear. There would be little Patrick
could do until their work was finished. The crime lab
unit was made up of a number of other highly trained
personnel. Though Patrick had worked with each of
them at one time or another, he dealt primary with
Callie on the vast majority of cases.

As personal as this case was, Patrick didn't worry
about those personal feelings getting in the way.
The Kenner County Crime Unit was small in size
and funds were limited for equipment, but the scientists and technicians were top-notch. The best of
the best. Particularly Callie.

Patrick stayed out of the way and let them do
their job. The extended moment of silence as the
group acknowledged their fallen colleague was

painful to watch. Callie MacBride in particular appeared shaken to the very core. Patrick wondered if she'd known the victim personally as well as professionally. That possibility was very likely, considering the whole staff operated as much as a family as a team of colleagues.

While Callie's people did their work, Patrick turned his attention to the Ute guide who had discovered the body. He doubted the man had seen anything but there were questions that needed to be asked. Like why he'd called the Towaoc police and then put in an anonymous call to 9-1-1, evidently some minutes later.

With that in mind, Patrick started in his direction. Bree was interviewing the guide and would no doubt ask those same questions, but it was Patrick's job to ensure every base was covered. Officers Cyrus and Brewer were maintaining the perimeter. If word got out that a federal agent had been murdered the media would flock to the park like vultures ready to pick the kill.

Damn. The reality of what they were doing here hit Patrick all over again.

A federal agent was dead.

Murder was murder and any loss was one too many, but this loss took the act to a higher level. That Grainger, like all in law enforcement, served this community made the business of murder even uglier.

Bree turned to face Patrick as he neared. Judging by her expression there was trouble with the guide's story. "Mr. Hayes only made one call," she said. "That call was to the Towaoc Police Department. Your 9-1-1 caller was not Mr. Hayes."

Patrick's senses moved to a higher state of alert. That meant two things right out of the gate. The recorded 9-1-1 call could very well turn out to be their only tangible evidence. And the caller might just be the killer.

"Mr. Hayes," Patrick addressed the older man, working to keep his composure free of the frustration and impatience despite the anticipation zinging through him. "I'm certain Detective Hunter has already asked, but I need you to think long and hard about the questions I'm going to ask before you answer."

The man nodded, glanced briefly at Bree.

Patrick understood that Hayes was anxious as well. This wasn't a situation anyone wanted to be caught in. Finding a dead Caucasian female on reservation territory was about the last thing a Ute man would want on his plate. The political climate wasn't that different from a few decades ago when Patrick had been in school and distinct cultural lines had been drawn. The undercurrent of racial differences remained a nagging social challenge that played itself out within the criminal element of the area.

"What time did you arrive at the park this morning?"

Hayes looked from Patrick to Bree. He'd already answered this question. Patrick understood that, but he needed the man to think…to be absolutely certain of his answers and to give them again. And maybe again after that. Before this case was solved, Hayes would likely be questioned several times. Patrick and Bree could compare his responses later and analyze any possible discrepancies or suggestions of deception.

Hayes scratched his head. "Before seven o'clock. I stop at Rudy's each morning. Six a.m. From there I come here."

"Rudy's is the service station back at the turnoff to the park entrance," Bree explained.

Patrick knew the place. "Was there a reason you came to this particular place first?" The park was a big place. Patrick needed to know if Hayes had a routine for checking the area.

"I check the dwellings first. This one." He indicated the two-story dwelling. "Then the next. Lately there's been trouble with teenagers using them as hangouts. So I check them first."

"Did you meet anyone as you entered the park this morning? Anything you might have seen could be important," Patrick emphasized. He watched the man's eyes and facial expressions closely. "No matter how unimportant it may seem, there may be something we can learn from the slightest detail. A vehicle parked nearby on the main highway. Anything."

Hayes contemplated the question half a minute before shaking his head. "No one was here except her." He gestured to where the lab folks were methodically working the scene. "It was quiet. Nobody around. Just the dead woman."

"Mr. Hayes," Bree interjected, "believes he returned to Rudy's shortly after seven and made the call to TPD, then he came straight back here and waited for the police to arrive."

That meant the other caller had been here and gone before that since Hayes hadn't encountered anyone and yet the unknown caller hadn't reached out to 9-1-1 immediately. His call hadn't come in until a quarter past eight.

Anytime someone discovered a body and didn't call it in immediately, he was either puking, crying, or he was afraid. Dispatch had indicated the caller sounded male and had no particular accent. Hayes didn't have an accent per se but his speech pattern was somewhat slow, his words not necessarily the first choice to use by those educated in public schools.

Drawing further suspicion, when asked to identify himself the 9-1-1 caller had ended the call—which almost certainly meant he had something to hide. Whether motivated by fear or guilt, the caller had to be found and questioned.

"You're certain you came straight back here," Patrick pressed. "You didn't talk to anyone at the store about what you'd found? Not even the owner? Is there any possibility that perhaps someone overheard you?"

Hayes shook his head resolutely. "I didn't talk to anyone. I don't think anyone heard me. I came back here as fast as my old truck would carry me."

Patrick visually assessed the old truck. Not that fast, he imagined. "What time did you get your call?" he asked Bree.

She checked her cell. "Seven-fifty."

Hayes couldn't have missed the 9-1-1 caller by more than a few minutes.

"Thank you, Mr. Hayes." Patrick wanted to discuss this turn of events with Callie. "We will be in touch with additional questions. This is standard procedure."

Hayes grunted and gave Bree a nod. She thanked the man as well and Officer Cyrus escorted him to his truck to finish his written statement and to obtain pertinent information in terms of how to reach him.

"I know how to question a witness."

Patrick's attention snapped back to Bree. A frown pulled at his brow. "I'm well aware of your abilities as an investigator, Bree." Bree…he hadn't said her name out loud in a long, long time. His gut knotted even now as it echoed through him. He'd loved her....

But that was a long time ago.

Fury etched itself across the delicate lines of her face. A face he'd been hard-pressed to erase from his dreams most every night for nearly eight years now.

"There was no need to reask every single question I'd already posed to Mr. Hayes. What you did undermined my authority and my ability. I don't appreciate it one damned bit."

Patrick didn't have to remind her that he was the county sheriff and this was his jurisdiction the same as it was hers. Doing so would only anger her all the more. "You did your job and I did mine. Mr. Hayes will be asked those same questions and more by numerous others during the course of this investigation. I'm sure you understand how protocol works when jurisdiction crosses the usual boundaries."

Judging by the deeper shade of red that climbed up her neck and across her face, his explanation hadn't been what she'd wanted to hear. If she expected an apology, she could forget it.

"This conversation is pointless." She tugged at the lapels of her jacket. "Callie MacBride needs to know about this. The audio recording of the 9-1-1 call will need to be analyzed in a different light. I, for one, would like to hear it for myself."

He threw up his hands in surrender. "You took the words right out of my mouth."

Lips tight, eyes blazing, Bree executed an about-face and stalked off.

Patrick followed. All these years he'd told himself that if the situation arose he could work with Bree. At this point, there was no logical reason professionalism shouldn't override their personal history.

So much for logic.

Agent Acevedo snapped digital photographs of the scene and the victim. Patrick swallowed hard. Each time he considered Agent Grainger the victim, his gut tightened. Agents O'Shea and Fleming searched the zone within the cordoned-off area and tagged possible evidence. From what Patrick had noted there wasn't much but for now anything and everything had to be ruled out. A time-consuming process to say the least.

Bree approached Callie first. The two stepped aside and Patrick joined the huddle. Bree might not like the fact that he was on this case, but she would simply have to get over it.

Once the facts they had discovered regarding the two calls were passed along, Bree added, "I don't know what we'll learn from the audio recording, but it's worth a shot."

"Absolutely," Callie agreed.

"How soon can you arrange to have the recording at your lab?" Patrick glanced at his watch. "It's almost nine now. I can get the request started while you finish your work here."

When ten or so seconds passed with Callie seemingly lost in thought, he added, "I know the Bureau will be lead on this investigation, but whatever my department can do we're completely at your disposal."

"The same goes for my department," Bree assured her. "The task force is working a couple of other homicides, but I'm certain we can manage some additional personnel to support this investigation."

Patrick recognized that Bree was only doing her job. Still, it felt like they were in competition. That was one issue he had to get under control. Clear the air somehow. Evidently, eight years apart hadn't done the job.

"We'll be here," Callie finally said, her voice as well as her expression distracted, "for several hours." She rubbed her forehead, the gesture uncharacteristic for the hard-nosed, professional lady he knew. "Let's say three o'clock at the lab. I'll put in a call to Olivia. She can cut through the red tape faster than your office and have the recording available sooner." This she directed to Patrick.

"That'll work." Olivia Perez was a go-getter. Like the others on Callie's team, Olivia wouldn't rest until her task was accomplished.

"Meanwhile," Bree offered, "I can begin checking with nearby businesses, like Rudy's, and get a rundown of the customers who come through his station early each morning. Maybe I'll get lucky and find someone who saw something. The locals stay pretty aware of what's going on around them. Any strangers or unfamiliar faces will stick out in their minds. Most will talk to me."

When they might not talk to Patrick or his deputies. She didn't have to say that part. Patrick knew from experience. "I'll go along with you," he said to Bree. The way her eyes widened and her breath caught made him relatively certain she would rather swallow broken glass. "We'll get more done together."

She blinked. "Of course." She turned to Callie then. "I'll keep you posted if we learn anything before the meeting this afternoon."

Callie nodded vaguely, then rejoined her team. Patrick watched her unnatural movements. Stiff. Uncertain. Totally opposite the confident woman he'd seen in action many, many times. Something was troubling her. Something more than the fact that a colleague, and perhaps friend, was dead.

Right now all they had were questions. What had brought Agent Grainger to this desolate place in the dead of winter...all alone? Had she been tailing a suspect? Or meeting with an informant?

There were some signs of a struggle, but not enough to warrant the belief that Grainger had in fact fiercely attempted to defend herself. Whoever her attacker was, he'd moved swiftly and with his victim unaware.

For a skilled agent like Grainger, that was no easy task.

He dragged his thoughts back to the here and now just in time to see Bree settle behind the wheel of her SUV and slam the door.

Damn. She wasn't going to make any part of this easy. He strode to her vehicle, opened the passenger-side door without waiting for an invitation and said, "I guess this means I'm riding with you."

She started the engine, didn't spare him a glance. "Suit yourself. I'm always happy to cooperate fully with the sheriff's department."

Not the slightest bit easy.

Going door-to-door might not garner any information, but right now it was their only option. Until they were briefed—if they were briefed—on Agent Grainger's activities just prior to her death, basic legwork was about the only hand they had to play. As the investigation moved into full swing, the Bureau would lay out the ground rules. Until then, they'd have to play this by the seat of their pants.

Patrick glanced at the driver. Maybe, if he were really, really lucky, he'd get through this without saying or doing anything he would regret the way he regretted so much else that had happened between them.

Like the past eight years.

Chapter Three

He was in her SUV.

Bree covertly scanned the interior of the vehicle. Had her son left anything lying around? A favorite toy or game? Were there indications she had a child? She didn't breathe easy until she felt satisfied that there was nothing for Patrick to notice.

"Where would you suggest we start?"

The deep sound of his voice resonating inside her vehicle almost made her jump. *Stay cool.* Patrick was far too good at picking up on tension. Especially hers. The last thing she needed was for him to start asking personal questions.

"Rudy's." Since the visitor's center wasn't open, Hayes had made his phone call to TPD from the service station just outside the park. Made sense to begin there. To trace his steps, so to speak.

That Patrick didn't argue told her he agreed. She would like to feel flattered that he concurred with her conclusion but the choice was elementary. It wasn't like they had that many.

Rudy's Stop and Go had been around for as long as Bree could remember. The one gas stop for a number of miles in either direction. Outside Rudy's there were a few tourist traps that wouldn't be open before ten. At this time of the morning an employee could be inside stocking shelves and preparing for the business day to begin, but there was little likelihood anyone would have seen the vehicles passing on the highway.

Basically what Bree and Patrick were doing now was going through the motions. Until they knew what cases Grainger may have been working on in the area, or who her enemies were suspected to be, there was no other starting place.

The most primitive of police work.

Bree parked in front of Rudy's and climbed out of her vehicle. She didn't wait for Patrick, the less eye contact and conversation the better. She didn't need him analyzing her every move. And he was a master at scrutinizing and forming conclusions based on nothing more than his suspects' body language.

She felt exactly like that…a suspect.

Perhaps guilt had something to do with her defensiveness.

Inside the store the woman behind the counter glanced up as the bell over the door jingled. Bree flashed the cashier a smile then turned to wait for Patrick, who still lingered in the parking lot. He had paused to survey the parking lot and highway beyond. He walked to the west end of the building and peered toward the turnoff to the Tribal Park. She remembered that he liked to get a feel for the vicinity where a crime had taken place. To form scenarios related to the crime. That obviously hadn't changed.

Frustrating the hell out of her was the fact that her gaze roamed the breadth of his shoulders and the height of his tall frame from the cowboy boots to the familiar hat before she could rein in the reaction to seeing him again. But what really burned her was the way her heart pounded a little harder just watching him move. How could the organ be so mutinous?

This moment had been inevitable. She had contemplated that realization many times. They worked in the same county. It had only been a matter of time before the two of them ended up on a case together.

And still she wasn't ready for this.

When he turned to enter the store, she shifted in the other direction and went in search of Rudy Johnson, the owner.

"Good morning, Mr. Johnson."

"Good morning to you, Detective Hunter." The spry old man hesitated in his inventory duties and shot her a wide smile.

"How's the family?" The instant the words left her lips she could have bitten off her tongue. The bell over the door jingled announcing Patrick's entrance. Rudy would no doubt return the social gesture and ask about her son. Damn! She had to get her act together. The line she walked was precarious enough without tipping the balance unnecessarily.

A wave of uncertainty washed over her. How could she possibly hope to keep this up? Was she making a mistake hiding the truth from Patrick? From Peter? She'd made that decision a long time ago. At a time when her emotions had been particularly raw and she had been terrified of the consequences of telling him he had a son.

Too late to turn back now.

"The wife's arthritis is acting up," Rudy said as he tucked the pencil behind his ear. "But that's to be expected at our age." The smile broadened to a grin and his eyes twinkled. "How's Peter? I still owe him that trip to the cabin."

Patrick came to a stop right beside Bree as if the gods had deemed her guilty as charged and opted to torture her a little as a sneak preview of what was to come. This time the pounding in her chest had nothing to do with his nearness. "He's doing great. We'll have to get together soon and schedule that trip to your cabin." *Change the subject!* "Unfortunately, I'm here this morning on police business.

Sheriff Martinez and I need to ask you a few questions. It'll only take a couple minutes."

Rudy looked from Bree to Patrick and back. Don't say any more about Peter, she urged silently.

"This about Burt Hayes?" Rudy placed his clipboard atop a row of canned goods and gave Bree his full attention. "He rushed back in here this morning to use the phone. The man was acting a mite strange. I asked him if there was trouble but he rushed outta here like the devil himself was on his heels." Rudy raised a speculative eyebrow. "I figured there was trouble at one of the dwellings."

"Did Hayes mention any problem?" Patrick inquired before Bree could.

Rudy shook his head. "Just asked to use the phone. Lizzy was using the one at the counter so I let him use the phone in the office." He hitched his thumb toward the door in the back marked Employees Only. "We had a regular morning rush at the time, so I didn't get to ask him what the problem was."

"Before eight this morning did you notice anyone else behaving strangely?" Bree ventured, unsure just how much Patrick had in mind sharing at this point. "Maybe a little nervous or in a hurry like Mr. Hayes?"

Rudy folded his arms over his chest and rubbed

his chin as he considered the question. "The usual Monday morning crowd came through. And they're all always in a hurry." He shook his head. "I'll never understand why working folks wait until Monday morning to fill up their gas tanks and then they complain because they're running late."

"Did anyone stop in that you didn't recognize?" Patrick asked. "Maybe someone in more of a hurry than the rest?"

Rudy shrugged. "There's always a few strangers passing through. Usually not that many early in the morning. No one at all that I noticed today. Just the regulars."

"If you could provide us with a list of the regulars who were in this morning that would be useful." Patrick slid the request into the conversation, the maneuver slick as glass.

Bree noted the mounting confusion on Rudy's face. "I know that's asking a lot, Mr. Johnson, but we…" she glanced at Patrick, he gave her no indication not to proceed "…discovered a body in the park this morning. We have reason to believe some aspect of the crime was carried out between seven and eight this morning. So anyone you or your regulars might have seen in the area could be a person of interest in the case."

Rudy squared his shoulders and lifted his chin as if ready to do battle. "The regulars who come through my store are good people. Not criminals." The firm set of his jaw warned more so than his words that his hackles were up. "If any one of them had seen or heard anything I would know it."

"That may be," Patrick cut in, his tone firmer this time, "but we'll need that list all the same. Choosing not to provide the names constitutes obstruction of justice."

So much for congeniality. "Anything anyone may have seen could prove immensely helpful to our investigation," Bree explained, hoping to head off a complete lockdown. The Ute people were a proud, stubborn lot.

Despite having been raised here, Patrick apparently didn't understand that as a white man his imposing tone and words could come across the wrong way when dealing with a Ute man.

Rudy glared at Patrick a moment before turning his attention to Bree. "I'll give you the list if it's that important."

Patrick's own hackles visibly reared. His jaw tightened and the rigid set of his shoulders announced this loudly.

"Sheriff Martinez and I are working together," Bree clarified. "Your cooperation with the both of us will make our job a lot easier."

Rudy gave a single curt nod.

Bree pushed a smile into place, relieved. "Great.

I'll pick up the list later today, if that's all right. I know you're busy."

Another tight nod.

"Thank you, Mr. Johnson," Bree offered, understanding that the man's continued cooperation depended a great deal on her keeping the lines of communication on a level that fostered mutual respect. As much as she hated to admit it, that was the very reason she would have no choice but to work directly with Patrick to some degree as long as they were a part of this investigation.

These people knew and trusted her. She was one of them. Patrick represented those who looked down at the Ute people. Unfairly lumped them all in the same category. There was good and bad in all people. No one liked to be judged wrongly because of the actions of others.

Patrick and Rudy exchanged one of those male half-nods that was barely civil.

At the front of the store Lizzy O'Dell was braced against the counter, busily filing her nails. Bree asked her the same questions they'd asked Rudy. Lizzy had been too busy at the register, she claimed, to notice anything out of the ordinary. Bree thanked her as well and made a path toward the door.

If she could get out of here without—

"Say hello to Peter for me," Rudy called after her.

Bree managed a decent stab at a smile and

assured the man she would. She was out the door and climbing into her vehicle two steps ahead of Patrick in hopes of moving on before any related questions could be posed.

"Who's Peter?"

If she hadn't known that it was physically impossible for her heart to completely stop beating while she continued to breathe, Bree would have sworn that it had done just that.

As if luck had opted to show mercy, her cell phone vibrated. Saved by her cell twice in one morning.

"Excuse me." She pulled the phone from her belt and checked the screen.

Her sister. Tabitha.

The heart she'd been certain had stalled rammed into her sternum.

Bree didn't give any excuses to her passenger. She shoved the door open and stepped away from the vehicle for privacy.

"Hunter." Old habits were hard to change. Though she'd known it was her sister calling she answered in cop mode.

"Sis, I have to run some errands today. Do you need me to pick up Peter after school?"

Bree glanced back at her vehicle. Patrick remained in the passenger seat. Though he stared straight ahead she knew better than to believe he wasn't keeping tabs on her movements.

"That would be great. Today's going to be a long one." Bree took a few more steps away from the vehicle. "I don't have much time but we need to talk."

"Uh-oh. What's wrong?"

Her sister knew her well. Another covert glance at her SUV to ensure Patrick was still seated inside with the windows up. Bree lowered her voice to scarcely more than a whisper. "Peter asked me about his father this morning. He wouldn't let it go."

"I've been telling you for years that this conversation—"

"Yeah, yeah, I know," Bree interrupted. She didn't need to hear this right now. Irritation gnawed at her. "I just don't need any help from you and Layla making that happen sooner rather than later. He overheard something Layla said about his father being as bad as Jack."

The silence on the other end of the line told Bree that her sister realized the mistake.

"Oh, Bree, I'm sorry. Layla was complaining about Patrick's deputies singling out teenage drivers. She was off on a *profiling* tangent. She made that remark out of frustration. She didn't mean it and certainly neither of us intended for Peter to overhear."

Bree closed her eyes and let out a weary breath. "It's okay. Just tell Layla to be more careful. I can't deal with that issue—" she snuck another look at the man in question "—not right now."

"Is something going on?"

"We'll talk about it later," Bree promised. Patrick would be growing impatient. "I have to get back to work. Take care of my boy for me, okay?"

"You know I will. And Bree…"

"Yeah."

"Be careful out there. Peter needs you. We all need you."

Bree promised Tabitha she would use caution and ended the call. Her family had worried about her since she'd decided to go into law enforcement, but lately Tabitha had worried a little extra. And it was Bree's fault. She should never have told her sister about the other night. But she'd needed to tell someone.

Bree had been getting those weird feelings…the ones that warned someone was watching her or following her. She would be certain she'd glimpsed someone in her peripheral vision, but she hadn't actually caught anyone yet. It always turned out to be nothing. Then, night before last, she'd been certain someone followed her home. Maybe it was nothing. Coincidence, paranoia, whatever. Yet as a trained cop she knew better than to assume her instincts were completely off the mark.

Ignoring danger, real or imagined, could cost a lot more than she wanted to pay.

Like she'd told Tabitha, Bree didn't have time to

deal with that right now, either. She strode back to the SUV and climbed behind the wheel.

"Sorry 'bout that," she said to Patrick. She almost...*almost* stated out loud that she'd needed to make arrangements for her son. Damn. He was so much a part of her life talking about him was like breathing.

"No problem."

She'd just started the vehicle and shifted into Reverse when he said, "So, who's Peter?"

THE KENNER COUNTY Crime Unit was housed on the top floor of the old city annex building on the outskirts of Kenner City. The building had been used as storage for retired files as long as Bree could remember. When the Bureau finally authorized a crime lab for the Four Corners area the third floor was the only space the city would forfeit. But that didn't stop Callie MacBride and her team from carving out a pretty impressive reputation. Like the little engine that could.

Bree was relieved to be joining the others for the briefing. The better part of six hours spent with Patrick Martinez had her emotions raw. They'd been to her office and to his. They'd stopped at every business within a ten-mile radius of the park entrance. And they'd picked up the list from Rudy Johnson. Bree recognized the majority of the names on the list. Chances were it would be a dead end.

Busywork—that's what they had been doing all day. With next to nothing to go on they'd started with the most elementary procedure: question anyone and everyone in the vicinity of the crime.

Bree was certain that Patrick, as sheriff of Kenner County, had numerous other duties he could have been attending to. Any one of his deputies could have worked with her. But no, he'd stuck close to her all day.

To ferret out information. She was certain. Why did he care what she'd been up to for the past eight years? Her life was none of his business. She'd told him so when he'd pressed the issue of "who's Peter?" and "is that your husband?"

Her nerves were shot.

The entire time her sister's voice had kept echoing in the back of her mind… *You should come clean with both Peter and Patrick. This decision will come back to haunt you.* Although Bree's father had insisted it was her decision, her older sister had staunchly disagreed from the beginning.

Bottom line, Bree couldn't undo the past. She'd made her decision. There was no changing it now. Frustration expanded inside her. So far she'd seen no real reason to regret the decisions she'd made.

Patrick Martinez's nosiness definitely wasn't a good reason.

Inside the annex, Bree and Patrick took the stairs to the third floor. She could feel his gaze on her with every step she took. Or maybe it was her imagination. He'd been dissecting everything she'd done all day. Every word. Every move.

Thank God this day was almost over.

On the third floor, Bree stopped at the receptionist's desk. She dredged up a smile. "We're here for the briefing on the Grainger investigation."

"Detective Hunter?" The receptionist, Elizabeth Reddawn according to the nameplate on her desk, returned Bree's smile.

"That's right." Bree gestured to Patrick. "And Sheriff Martinez."

"Good afternoon, Sheriff." Elizabeth's smile widened. "We've set up a command center in the conference room down the hall," she told Patrick. "You know, the one that used to be a storage room?"

"I know the way," Patrick confirmed. "Thanks, Elizabeth."

Bree should have realized that Patrick worked directly with the lab on a regular basis. He would know the personnel and his way around. Bree, on the other hand, usually got her feedback from the lab through the chain-of-command channels at TPD. She rarely had the opportunity to work directly with anyone at the lab, except, on the rare occasion, Callie MacBride.

Though ten minutes early for the meeting, the conference-room-turned-command-center was crowded with what Bree suspected were FBI agents. She didn't recognize any other local law enforcement personnel.

Special Agent in Charge Jerry Ortiz turned to greet Patrick and Bree as they entered the room.

"Patrick." Ortiz shook his hand. "Detective Hunter, I presume." He reached for Bree's next.

"Ortiz, this is Detective Sabrina Hunter," Patrick said, making the formal introduction, "from Towaoc PD."

"I'm pleased to have you on our team, Detective Hunter," Ortiz said with all the panache of a politician. To Patrick he said, "I decided to come in personally to handle...this." He exhaled a heavy breath. "That's the least I can do."

"Completely understandable," Patrick confirmed.

Bree had heard Ortiz's name on a number of occasions, not to mention she'd seen him in the news on a regular basis. He was assigned to the Bureau field office in Durango.

"Let's take our seats," Ortiz announced to the room at large. He stood behind the chair at the head of the conference table.

Bree put some distance between Patrick and herself. She needed a breather. She settled into a chair next to Callie.

When the room had settled, Ortiz made the necessary introductions. Some of those present Bree recognized from various homicide cases she'd worked. She'd rarely interacted with them, but she was familiar with the faces. Some had been at the crime scene that morning, like O'Shea, Fleming and Miguel Acevedo. Steven Griswold, an older gentleman who was the lab's firearms expert, she hadn't seen before. Ollvia Perez and Jacob Webster. Bree had seen those two around town at lunch together more than once, but she'd never run into either one in the field. She wondered if they were a couple. No wedding rings that she could see, but a definite connection. Every shared glance screamed of that connection.

Three of the field agents present Bree couldn't recall having run into before. FBI agents Tom Ryan, Ben Parrish and Dylan Acevedo. According to Ortiz, Tom Ryan and Dylan Acevedo had flown straight here from their home offices upon hearing the news. That would explain why she didn't recognize any of the three.

Whoa! Dylan Acevedo looked so much like Miguel. Considering they shared the same last name, they had to be brothers.

As if Agent Ortiz had read her mind, he said, "For those of you who don't know, the Acevedo brothers are twins." Ortiz gestured vaguely. "I noted the confusion on some faces so I thought I'd better clear that up before we get started."

Bree hoped she wasn't the only one who'd been confused. Across the table Patrick glanced at her. Oh yeah, she was the only one. Great.

"We all know why we're here," Ortiz said somberly. "Special Agent Julie Grainger will be sorely missed. There are no adequate words to articulate how we all feel about this loss. But anger and regret won't help Agent Grainger and it won't assist us in what we have to do. There is one final thing we can do to support our fallen colleague and that is to ensure her murderer is brought to justice in the speediest possible manner. With that in mind, I'd like to share what I can with all those present regarding her latest case.

"Considering the nature of the investigation in which she was involved, we have good reason to believe that case may be the motive behind her murder."

Tension rifled through Bree. The Bureau wasn't always so forthcoming with local law enforcement, at least not at this level. But everyone present wanted this crime solved—fast.

"This briefing," Ortiz went on, "is need-to-know only. Any leaks could jeopardize the homicide investigation. I don't have to spell it out. Though the Bureau will be handling the main thrust of the investigation, support from the sheriff's department as well as other local police departments will greatly enhance our ability to get the job done under the circumstances."

Around the long conference table the faces remained grim but the determination to do just as Ortiz suggested was thick in the air.

"For several months," Ortiz went on, "Agent Grainger has been investigating the disappearance and whereabouts of Vincent Del Gardo."

Next to Bree, Callie MacBride caught her breath. The sound was so soft Bree was reasonably sure she was the only one to hear it. From the corner of her eye Bree studied Callie. Her face had gone deathly pale, her features even tighter with tension.

Before Bree could analyze the reaction, Ortiz drew her attention once more.

"…based in Las Vegas, Vincent is the head of the Del Gardo crime family. Nearly three years ago he escaped custody and we've been trying to find him ever since. Agent Grainger, after months of intensive work, had tracked him to the Four Corners area."

Bree tried not to let her attention drift back to the woman beside her, but it was hard not to. As Callie reached up to tuck her hair behind her ear, her hand shook. Bree reminded herself that Callie and

Grainger may have been very close friends as well as colleagues. Her reaction might simply be stronger than most due to the personal connection.

"Agent Grainger's investigation had revealed that Del Gardo had purchased a large estate in the area. Unfortunately, before we could close in on him, the estate was sold to a civilian, Griffin Vaughn, who has no ties to Del Gardo. We can only assume, of course, at this point that Agent Grainger's death is somehow related to her investigation. But Del Gardo has a reputation for erasing any presumed nuisance in just this manner."

Ortiz leaned forward, braced his hands on the back of his chair. "We will get this bastard and whoever he hired to take down our agent and friend—one way or another. As badly as we want Del Gardo for many other reasons, right now our primary goal is to determine who murdered Agent Grainger."

The escalating tension seemed to press all the air out of the room. All present wanted to do exactly as Ortiz suggested. To find this killer. Now.

Ortiz briefly reviewed the few details they had on the Grainger investigation already. No real evidence had been discovered at the scene. The hope was that Grainger's body would reveal crucial evidence and lead them to her killer. At last Ortiz got to the 9-1-1 call.

"Are we ready to listen to the call?" he asked Callie.

She stiffened as if she'd been tugged from deep thought, then cleared her throat. "Yes." She gestured to Olivia. "As you may have already heard," the lab's head forensic scientist began as she stood and cleared her throat again, "Burt Hayes, a Ute guide at the Tribal Park, found…the body and made a call to the Towaoc Police Department. During that same time the county's 9-1-1 system received a call as well. This one from a male caller who did not identify himself."

A flurry of movement and muttered words at the other end of the long table drew the room's collective attention there.

Agent Parrish shot to his feet, as did Agent Tom Ryan.

"Sorry. I… I'm all thumbs today," Parrish stammered. He grabbed his overturned coffee cup. Mopped at the spill with a lone napkin.

"It's all right." Ryan waved his hands as if erasing the incident. "We're all out of sorts today. Anyway, you're the one who caught the spill."

Coffee had dripped onto Parrish's khaki slacks.

"Excuse me." He shook his head in disgust. "I'll… I'll be right back. Tom can bring me…up to speed," he said to Ortiz and the room at large as he hurried toward the door.

Ortiz didn't look pleased but carried on. "Let's hear that recording."

Callie nodded to Olivia, who pressed the necessary buttons to play the recorded call.

The 9-1-1 operator's practiced greeting resonated first. A moment of silence. Then, "I need to report a...murder." The voice sounded distant, as if the mouthpiece of the phone was too far away or partially covered. Some muffled sounds and something like, "Oh, God." The male voice continued, "At the Ute Reservation Tribal Park...the body's...oh, God." During the silence that followed, the operator asked the caller to identify himself and that he provide additional details. The caller severed the connection.

As the recording ended the room remained dead silent.

Agent Tom Ryan abruptly pushed out of his chair. "Play that again."

Callie stiffened.

Bree studied first the woman beside her, who seemed suddenly even more flustered, then the man. The cold fury on his face was different than before...had moved to a new level.

Olivia obliged and replayed the recording. Not a single word was uttered by anyone present as the clearly emotional caller's voice filled the air. There was something familiar about his voice, Bree realized this time. The first time she'd been focused on the information relayed. This time she analyzed the voice. Bree knew that voice. Had heard it before.

As the recording ended Agent Parrish reentered the room. That was when Bree recalled where and when she'd heard that voice.

"It was you."

Bree's gaze snapped to the woman next to her.

"You made the call," Callie said, the accusation directed at Agent Ben Parrish.

Agent Ryan stared at the man who'd stalled halfway back to his chair. "What's going on here, Ben?"

All hell broke loose then.

Dylan Acevedo and Parrish almost came to blows. Patrick and Jacob pulled the men apart with Ortiz's assistance.

The already suffocating tension in the room rocketed to a whole other stratosphere even as Ortiz demanded order. The silence that instantly replaced the chaos was even more unnerving.

What was going on here? Bree couldn't believe what she was hearing and seeing. Agent Parrish had discovered the body? Why would he conceal that fact? Why had he left the scene?

"You want to explain this?" Ortiz suggested, his voice hoarse from shouting.

Whatever was going on with the three agents at the other end of the table wasn't good. Bree's first thought was that if Parrish was guilty of something he could have made a run for it as soon as he realized the 9-1-1 recording would be played. But he hadn't. He'd come back into the room knowing what he would face.

"I received a text message," Parrish explained, his tone emotionless, exhausted, "that I should meet Julie this morning." He shrugged, his shoulders rounded with the weight of his confession. "The number the text came from raised my suspicions immediately since it showed up as unknown. Julie's number is on my contact list. And when I sent a text asking her to call me it was ignored." He grabbed the edge of the table to steady himself.

"I hadn't heard from her in weeks and I wasn't about to risk ignoring the request. I was aware that she was deep into her investigation." He heaved a heavy breath. "I figured she needed me and had used whatever means available to contact me. So I went. And…" He dragged a ragged breath into his lungs. "She was dead. Had been for a couple of days."

"And you didn't call it in and stay with her?" Ryan demanded. "What the hell were you thinking? How could you leave her like that?"

"What's the motive?" Dylan demanded. "Why would anyone send you a text to meet her? That doesn't make sense. Why you? You're not involved in the Del Gardo investigation."

More of that consuming silence pressed in on Bree's chest as everyone in the room waited for

Parrish to give a reasonable explanation for his actions.

Parrish shook his head. "I don't know. I can only assume it was a setup." He looked around the room. "One that appears to have worked."

The tension between the three agents erupted into another heated exchange, only this time without the physical tactics.

"Enough!" Ortiz commanded. He held up his hands and waited for silence.

The glare-off between Ryan, Parrish and the visiting Acevedo brother would have cut through steel.

"We will get to the bottom of this," Ortiz promised. His openly suspicious gaze nailed Parrish. "We'll start by having you turn over your cell phone, Agent. If there's any chance we can trace the number where that text came from, we might have a starting place."

Parrish tossed his cell onto the table. "Be my guest. I have nothing to hide." He said the last sentence with considerably less conviction than the first.

"Yeah, right," Dylan muttered.

Ortiz let his glare speak for itself. When the moment had passed, he doled out assignments. "Detective Hunter," he said as his attention rested on Bree, "talk to your contacts among the Ute reservation residents. See if anyone has heard any rumblings regarding the murder of a federal agent. Someone, somewhere will have heard something."

"Yes, sir." Bree could definitely do that. The murder of a federal agent was a major deal, even in Colorado's so-called murder capital. There would be gossip.

Ortiz gave Patrick the same basic order. The agents in the room would attempt to reconstruct Grainger's activities to date. Another briefing would be scheduled in forty-eight hours or sooner if necessary.

As the meeting was dismissed, Bree watched the agents fall into their respective groups. Callie and her lab team huddled to discuss strategy. Agents Tom Ryan and Dylan Acevedo spoke quietly but tensely with Ortiz.

Ben Parrish stood alone, accused and outside the circle of his peers. Bree didn't know the guy, but she couldn't help feeling a little sorry for him. Surely if he was guilty of wrongdoing he'd have made a run for it. To stand here and face all this…it was hard.

But then, she didn't know him. The one thing she did know was that time would tell. If Parrish was involved with Grainger's murder, given time, the investigation would nail him.

The lab folks began to filter from the room. When Callie would have followed her team Tom Ryan stopped her at the door. Callie had been visibly stressed to the max all through the briefing, but her reaction to Ryan was different. The same fierce tension but with another layer. Bree couldn't quite pinpoint it, but there was definite tension between the two that transcended the case.

"I guess you'll have to give me a ride back to my vehicle."

Patrick's voice tugged Bree from her disturbing musings. "Sure." The sooner she was free of his constant analysis the better.

She made her way out of the building and to her SUV. Stopping by the office before going home was essential. She would have messages and she needed to put some of her conclusions into notes. And she wanted to see what she could find on Parrish, if anything.

"I was thinking," Patrick said as they loaded into her SUV.

She could pretend not to hear him but he'd only repeat himself. "Thinking what?" That he couldn't wait to be rid of her? If so, they were on the same page.

"We should coordinate our efforts. There's a lot about this investigation that will fall under Bureau domain and we won't be privy to. But what we can do is put out feelers, follow up on any leads and rattle cages. That effort would be far better served if we work at it jointly."

So much for going her own way.

She'd spent the last eight years attempting to put the past behind her. Now the primary part she'd tried to avoid was smack dab in the middle of her present.

And there wasn't any way to avoid the momentum-gaining collision she felt with every fiber of her being was barreling her way.

Chapter Four

Bree parked in front of her sister's home and shut off the engine. She was exhausted. Mentally more so than physically. She leaned against the headrest and closed her eyes.

How was she going to get through this?

It was bad enough a member of law enforcement was dead, but being joined at the hip with Patrick for the duration of the investigation was nearly more than she could bear.

After eight years she'd hoped the past wasn't going to catch up to her.

Boy, had she been wrong.

She opened her eyes and peered at her sister's home. Her son was waiting for her. She couldn't keep sitting out here trying to pull herself together. She had to go inside and pretend that she hadn't spent the day with the father he didn't know.

That she wasn't lying to him for her own selfish reasons.

And she wasn't...was she?

"No more stalling."

She climbed out of her SUV and trudged up the front walk, then the steps. It was dark and she was so tired. Maybe a long, hot bath and some quality time with her son would rejuvenate her.

Tabitha met her at the door, her face clouded with worry as always. "Are you okay? That federal agent's murder has been all over the news this evening. Is that the case you're working on?"

Bree nodded, hoped her sister didn't ask any more than that. She couldn't talk about the investigation and she didn't want to talk about having to spend time with Patrick.

"I'll bet you haven't eaten all day." Tabitha took hold of Bree's arm and tugged her inside. "I'll warm you up some soup. Peter's already eaten and done his homework. He's watching TV with Layla."

Before Bree could ask, Tabitha tacked on, "And don't worry. Layla and I talked. There won't be any more discussions about you know who."

Bree appreciated that. "Thanks, sis."

The door had scarcely closed behind her when Peter rushed to give his mom a hug. Bree missed her son so when a day dragged on and on like this one.

She mussed his dark hair and kissed the top of his head. "I hope you've been good for your aunt Tabitha."

Peter dragged his mom to the kitchen table and reviewed his day's work with her while Tabitha warmed up the soup. Peter was not only a talented little artist he was a bright pupil. His work ethic and grades continued to make her proud. He was such a good boy.

But he was growing up. Before long he wouldn't want to share his schoolwork with her, much less talk about his day.

Maybe she had made a mistake. He yearned so for a man in his life. His uncle Roy tried to be there for him but Tabitha's husband worked for an oil company and spent more time away from home than not.

When Peter had been a baby and then a toddler, Bree had been totally convinced that her decision was the right one. But after what she'd gone through with Jack and now as she watched her son grow into a young man, she questioned every decision she had made.

By the time Peter had been drawn back to the television by his favorite show, Tabitha had placed a bowl of steaming potato soup along with a glass of chocolate milk in front of Bree.

"Eat," her sister ordered. "And tell me what I can do to clear those worry lines from your face.

You make me worry." She scrubbed at her brow. "And God knows I don't need any more lines."

Bree had to smile, even if only a little. Her sister had taken over the role of mother after their mom had died. Bree had been only fourteen. Four years older, Tabitha had put off going to college to stay home and help their father raise Bree. College had gone by the wayside permanently when Tabitha met Roy. Love at first sight. But Tabitha's had been a good choice. She had a wonderful husband who treated her with respect.

Bree picked up her spoon and stirred her soup. She really had no appetite. Who could eat when she kept thinking about Julie Grainger lying alone in that desolate place for two days before she was found.

"What worry?" Bree countered her sister's suggestion. "I have no worries."

Tabitha rolled her eyes. "Uh-huh, that's right. Denial. They have therapy and drugs for that disorder, little sister."

Bree might as well come clean. Tabitha had ways of prying until she dug up the truth. She was relentless when she picked up the scent of something. Why waste the energy trying to outmaneuver her?

After a quick check to see that Peter was fully occupied with the TV, Bree spilled her guts. She carefully worded each revealing statement so that even if her son did overhear something he'd have no idea who she was talking about.

"You were with him the entire day?"

Bree nodded and forced a spoonful of her favorite soup past her lips. She didn't feel hungry but she recognized the need to refuel her body. The next few days and weeks would require all the strength she could muster.

Tabitha chewed her lip thoughtfully. "You know what this means, don't you?"

Bree wasn't sure she wanted to hear her sister's assessment. "A pain in the butt, that's what I know it means."

Tabitha dismissed that explanation with a wave of her hands. "It means he still has feelings for you." Before Bree could protest that statement, Tabitha went on, "He's using this case as an excuse to get close to you again. To find out what you've been up to all these years. Like you said, he could assign one of his deputies to work with you."

All these years. Bree was sick to death of thinking about all these years. "This isn't an episode of your favorite soap. This is real life and the case is why we're stuck together. My guess is that if he's really as curious as he seems it's only because he wants to hear how miserable my life has been. Men are like that." She licked her spoon and pointed it at her sister. "They want to believe your life is crap without them even if they don't want to be in your life. It's some sort of genetic obsession."

Tabitha arched an eyebrow in objection.

"Okay," Bree allowed, "so Roy is different. He's perfect. But most men are exactly that way. Take Jack—" Bree craned her neck to get a look into the living room "—his goal in life was to make me miserable. Then when I'd had enough he wanted me to be even more miserable without him. He's even had the nerve to try and get me back."

Jack had been her second big mistake. Her father had been certain Bree would be happier with a Ute man as a husband and to raise her young son. Too bad she'd picked one of the bad guys. Giving herself credit, even her family had been fooled at first.

Jackson Raintree had earned his nickname, Big Jack the Bully, many times over. He was an abusive, alcoholic jerk who had no respect for women or people in general. He was nothing but a user. Why, oh, why hadn't she seen that before it was too late? Maybe because she had a young son who needed a father figure? Jack pretended to respect her work…made her think he believed she could do anything. But he'd lied. And she'd fallen for it.

In truth maybe she'd just needed to forget the past. She'd hoped that learning to care about someone else would help erase Patrick Martinez from her heart once and for all.

She'd gotten neither.

"I think you're wrong," Tabitha argued. She

checked her fingernails as if assessing whether or not she needed a manicure. "I've sort of kept up with Patrick over the years."

Bree's head snapped up. "What?" This was the first she'd heard of that. "Why would you do that?"

No longer able to avoid eye contact using her cuticles as an excuse, Tabitha's gaze settled on Bree's. "I didn't want Peter to lose all that time."

"What does that mean?" Bree didn't know whether to be angry or worried.

"Bring your soup," Tabitha order, "and come with me."

Curious or maybe scared of what her sister may have been doing *all these years,* Bree did as she was told. Soup bowl in hand, she followed Tabitha up the stairs and to her bedroom.

"Sit." Tabitha gestured to the bed.

Bree sat and, having forgotten her spoon, sipped her soup straight from the bowl. She had a feeling she was going to need refueling more than she'd thought.

Tabitha dug around on the top shelf of her closet and pulled out a box. She sat on the bed next to Bree and opened it. Inside was a thick, leather-bound album or scrapbook. Bree's heart rate accelerated. This was…unbelievable.

"I started it when Peter was about one."

As Tabitha flipped through the pages each breath

grew more difficult for Bree to draw in. Newspaper clippings from what appeared to be every single time the sheriff had been spotlighted. The dates went all the way back to when he'd first taken the remainder of the former sheriff's term. Patrick had been brought in to clean up the department. He'd gotten the job done and more. The citizens of Kenner County loved him.

Old snapshots of Bree and Patrick together were tucked into pages that included handwritten captions. Emotions Bree couldn't begin to label churned inside her.

"I threw those photos out." Bree's words were scarcely a whisper. "Years ago."

"I—" Tabitha wet her lips "—dug them out of your trash can and kept them."

"My God." Bree shook her head as she moved through more of the pages.

"He never married, Bree. He works all the time. That has to mean something."

Bree met her sister's hopeful gaze. She didn't know how to respond to that.

"Please don't be mad at me. I was so afraid you would regret erasing your past that way. Someday you'll need these mementos. Peter will need them."

Too overwhelmed to speak, Bree didn't know whether to hug her sister or to slug her. She dragged her attention from the old memories. "I honestly don't know how I feel about this, but I understand why you did it."

"I guess that's enough for now," Tabitha offered, tears shining in her eyes. "Remember, no matter how you feel about him, he's still the father of your son and you love your son. The time will come when you can't pretend anymore that Peter's father doesn't exist."

Bree was terrified that that time had come already.

After getting her emotions in check, Bree rounded up her son and his things and headed for her vehicle. Tabitha followed her onto the porch.

"I'll just plan to pick Peter up after school until you tell me different," Tabitha offered.

What would Bree do without her? "Thanks." She hugged her sister, couldn't bring herself to let go for a bit.

"Oh, my God." Tabitha drew back abruptly, her eyes wide with horror.

"What's wrong?" Her sister's gaze was fixed on something behind Bree…something in the street.

"Mommy, what happened to your car?"

Bree jerked around. Several moments were required for her brain to adequately assess what her eyes saw.

The words painted in ugly black across the silver of her SUV shook her, made her knees weak.

I'm watching you.

PATRICK SCRUBBED the towel over his head to dry his hair. He felt a hundred percent better after his shower. The day had been too grating on his senses. Had left them raw and stinging.

Julie Grainger's murder had set the tone, tearing at his soul. But running headlong into Bree on the case had kept his emotions in turmoil all damned day.

He'd told himself a thousand times over that he no longer cared and then he got a glimpse of her in town or on one of those rare, self-defeating occasions when he drove by her house late at night and the lie was revealed.

He'd never gotten over her. Maybe if he'd tried harder...had given any other woman a chance...

When he'd heard Bree had gotten married, he'd thought that was it. He could move on and put that part of his life behind him. Even then he'd still longed for her. Today, watching her, smelling that unique scent of hers and hearing her voice...he'd known for certain he would never stop loving her.

He was a fool. She was married. She belonged to another man. He had no right feeling those emotions. He damned sure had no right allowing her to recognize his feelings. He had a bad feeling he'd let her catch him watching her one time too many.

One way or another he had to keep reminding himself that she belonged to someone else.

But she hadn't been wearing a wedding ring.

And she still used her maiden name. Did that mean she was no longer with the other man?

Damn him for wondering.

Patrick tossed the towel aside and tugged on a T-shirt. He needed to eat and get some sleep. He had work to do at the office first thing in the morning before meeting Bree for lunch to go over any leads either of them had discovered.

He'd picked the Morning Ray Café, his mom's diner, for their meeting. Seemed a safe enough spot to spend time with Bree in neutral territory. He would have the home field advantage and his mom would hover close, ensuring Patrick stayed on his toes.

His cell rattled against the counter and Patrick snatched it up. Getting a call at this time of night was never a good thing.

"Martinez."

"Sheriff, I hope I'm not calling you too late."

Clayton Mitchell, his personal assistant. Clayton preferred to be called a personal assistant rather than a secretary. Patrick couldn't care less what he wanted to be called. Clayton was a man but he was the best damned secretary Patrick had ever had.

"It's never too late to call if you feel the need," Patrick reminded him. "What's up?"

As he waited for his assistant to get to the point

of his call, Patrick padded barefoot into the kitchen to browse the offerings in the fridge.

"When I came to work for you…" Clayton began.

Oh, hell. Patrick sure hoped he wasn't about to lose his assistant. He was pretty sure he couldn't stay on top of things without him. In the five years since Clayton had come on board Patrick's professional life had gone from stressful to organized and reasonably relaxed—for a lawman.

"Clayton, if you're bucking for a raise, you know I'll have to run it by the—"

"Sheriff," Clayton cut him off, his tone testy, "this isn't about a raise."

"Oh." Patrick frowned. "Well, then, go ahead with whatever you were going to say."

He snagged a beer from the fridge and some leftover lasagna his mother had sent home with him.

"Now that you mention it, though," Clayton countered, "I could use a raise."

Patrick shook his head. "Get to the point. Now that you've mentioned it, it is getting late."

The sigh that hissed across the line was completely exaggerated. "Anyway, when you hired me you said there were two things I was never to bring up. Your lack of a social life and Sabrina Hunter."

Damn. Had word that he was working with Bree gotten out around the department already?

"That's right," Patrick confirmed. "I hope you're

not about to fall down on your word after all this time. You do have a job performance evaluation coming up."

Another of those dramatic sighs. "Normally I wouldn't dream of going against your wishes, but I just heard something from a friend that I thought you might need to know since you're working with Detective Hunter on the Grainger homicide."

Friend? Patrick's frown deepened to a scowl, the furrows of frustration dragged at his brow. "What on God's green earth are you talking about?"

"Jesse Phillips, who works dispatch over at Towaoc Police Department, just called and told me a call came in requesting assistance. The call was from Detective Sabrina Hunter."

Adrenaline charged through Patrick's veins. "What address?"

Clayton spouted off the address. Patrick had to think a moment. Tabitha's house. Bree's sister. "What kind of assistance?" Patrick demanded.

"That," Clayton said, "I don't know. But I thought you needed to be aware there might be a problem. Detective Hunter specifically asked that the call not go out over dispatch lines."

Which was code for Bree didn't want anyone to know whatever the hell was going on at her sister's residence. Damn.

"Thanks, Clayton. I'll check it out."

Patrick ended the call and pulled on his shoes. He grabbed his jacket and keys and headed for the door.

His pulse wouldn't slow even as he ordered himself to take deep, controlled breaths. Bree knew how to take care of herself. But her sister could be hurt. There may have been trouble at her house.

Whatever the hell it was, he intended to find out for certain that everyone was all right.

Half an hour later Patrick took the final turn onto the street where Tabitha lived. A small neighborhood in the Towaoc area with neat rows of housing that rose a cut above the norm. She and her husband, Roy, had done well for themselves.

Bree's SUV was parked in front along with two other vehicles. Patrick caught a glimpse of her talking to two men, one wearing a TPD uniform. When Patrick parked next to the curb he could see that the guy wearing civilian clothes was Steve Cyrus from the homicide scene that morning. Patrick didn't recognize the uniformed officer.

That Bree appeared to be all right sent relief gushing through him. Patrick emerged from his SUV and headed across the quiet street.

Bree's gaze collided with his and she looked away. She tucked her cell phone against her ear so he assumed she'd gotten a call.

"Cyrus," Patrick said as he approached the two men, "what's going on?"

Cyrus glanced at Bree before responding. Since she was busy with her call, he gestured to her vehicle. "Someone vandalized Detective Hunter's SUV. We've checked for prints already, but you know how these things go. There are literally dozens. And the chances of catching the perpetrator is not very likely."

Patrick walked to the side of the SUV closest to the house. The oxygen stalled in his chest when he read the words painted there.

I'm watching you.

"Is this the first incident of this nature Detective Hunter has experienced?"

"Yes, sir." Cyrus glanced at Bree once more. She'd put away her cell phone. "To the best of my knowledge it is."

When Bree joined the huddle, Cyrus said, "We've done all we can, Detective Hunter. We'll run this to the lab first thing in the morning and ask them to put a rush on the database comparison."

"Thanks, Cyrus." Bree looked from Cyrus to Patrick. "What're you doing here, Patrick?"

Cyrus hitched a thumb toward what was obviously his vehicle. "I'll talk to you tomorrow."

Bree watched Cyrus and Officer Day leave. Patrick waited until he had her full attention. "What's going on with this?" He indicated her SUV.

Bree looked anywhere but at him. "It's probably

kids. You know how it is around here. Not enough of the right kind of activities to keep them occupied. Mom and Dad both work too many hours and—"

"That's crap," Patrick rebutted. "You won't look me in the eye and we both know that warnings like that don't generally come from restless teenagers. This is personal, Bree. What the hell is going on?"

With obvious reluctance, she met his gaze. "I'm a cop, Patrick. You know how this works. I make enemies every other·day. Sometimes they like getting even." She gestured to her SUV. "This is getting even."

"Has anything else like this happened lately?"

More of that hesitation. "Look, this is none of your business, Patrick. I don't know how you found out about this, but you can go home now. We've got the situation under control."

She had a point there. He couldn't deny it. This was none of his business. But that didn't prevent him from getting mad as hell. If something was going on, he wanted to know what was being done about it besides lifting a few latent prints.

"We're working together on a high priority homicide case," he reminded her. "If something's going on in your personal life that might affect your job performance or my safety when in your presence, I have a right to know." He was reaching but right now he didn't care as long as he got the truth out of her.

"I can't believe this." Bree planted her hands on her hips, her mouth agape with disbelief or something like it. "Are you seriously trying to strong-arm me into telling you my personal business? You should watch your step, Patrick. There are rules against this sort of thing."

He didn't have to think about it. "That's exactly what I'm doing." He matched her stance, hands fixed at his waist. "No more games, Bree. Tell me what's really going on here."

She had the darkest eyes. Standing here beneath the streetlight he couldn't help but notice. He'd noticed way too much today already. But, evidently, in her presence he was helpless not to inventory the details he'd missed so damned much for so damned long.

She peered up at him. He watched the struggle in those dark eyes. She didn't want to tell him. Whatever it was, she didn't want him to know.

Whatever crazy brain cell misfired at that moment he couldn't say but the next thing he knew he'd grabbed her by the shoulders and given her a little shake. "The truth. I want the truth."

That was the moment when he knew that the answers he wanted had nothing to do with her vandalized vehicle and everything to do with their past. Why had she walked away without giving him another chance? Better yet, why had he let her?

"I've gotten a few strange calls," she relented.

"Always from phones in public places." She moistened her lips and his throat ached. "Lately I've felt like someone has been following me, but then there wouldn't be anyone there." She pulled free of his grasp. "It's probably nothing." The vulnerability in her eyes vanished. "Besides, I'm a big girl, Sheriff. I don't need you taking care of me."

And therein lay the rub. Their relationship had ended because he was too protective. Too controlling of her career decisions.

This was different.

He didn't care what she said. He knew the signs. Chances were she had a stalker. Either an admirer or, as she'd said before, an enemy. Neither one was a good thing.

"You have two choices here, Bree." The fury kindled once more. "You can work with me on this or I'll speak to your chief about it. Take your pick."

That was playing dirty. He understood that, but he wasn't about to let her ignore the warning signs. Stalkers, whether admirers or enemies, injured or killed the objects of the obsessions far too often to take the risk.

"Damn, Patrick!" She stopped a moment, visibly attempted to calm herself. Apparently it didn't work. "You haven't changed a bit." She poked him in the chest with her forefinger. "I don't need you taking care of me. Do you hear me? I can take care of myself. You are no longer a part of my life." She blinked, swallowed hard. "So back off!"

He should have listened to her. Should have been ticked off at her insinuation. But all he could do was stare into those deep, deep brown eyes and wonder how he'd ever let this much time pass without touching her...tasting her.

A little voice, growing weaker by the second, kept reminding him that the last he'd heard she was married. That didn't stop him from going temporarily stupid and fulfilling the fantasies that had tortured him every night for eight long years.

He took her face in his hands before she could fathom his intent and kissed her square on the lips.

Inside, he melted, but outside...he hardened like a rock. She tasted like sweet chocolate and hot, tempting woman. He wanted to pull her close and tuck her soft curves into his hard body.

She banged on his chest. Pulled away. "Don't you dare," she warned.

Patrick shuddered with the overdose of emotions. He blinked, once, twice. What the hell was he doing?

He dropped his hands. Took a step back. "I'm..." Damn, how did he excuse such behavior? "I'm sorry. I guess I got carried away and lost my head."

Damned straight he'd lost his head.

He'd gone way too far.

Bree trembled. He cursed himself.

"Just go, Patrick." She sucked in a ragged breath. She squared her shoulders in an attempt to compose herself. "I'll see you at Nora's for lunch tomorrow. We'll…" She shrugged, still visibly struggling to maintain her bearing. He'd shaken her. "We'll review what we have on the case and…"

"Fine." If she let him off the hook this easily he was damned lucky.

He'd definitely crossed the line.

"Well." She backed up another step. "Good night then."

He turned around, read those words scrawled across her vehicle once more and changed his mind.

Patrick faced her once more, met her expectant gaze. "You won't mind if I follow you home? Just to be safe."

He'd kissed her. As crazy as it sounded, he'd put himself at risk for legal action. Had acted like an idiot, basically. Whether it was the kiss or his over-bearing tactics, whatever the reason Bree just stood there staring at him.

"Look." He turned his palms up, tried his best to sound humble. "I shouldn't have kissed you, that was way out of line. It won't happen again. But you've got a serious situation here." He gestured to her vandalized vehicle. "It's not like I'm asking you to invite me into your home."

Still she said nothing, just stared at him.

Well, hell.

"I'll take that as a yes." He started toward his SUV but called over his shoulder. "I'll be standing by. Whenever you're ready to go, I'll be right behind you."

Chapter Five

Bree peered at her reflection in the mirror.

What was she doing?

She'd gotten up this morning, taken her son to school and come to work as if nothing had changed.

From eight-thirty until noon she had worked diligently. She'd touched base with half a dozen reliable informants, called every name on Rudy's list and come up empty-handed. If anyone knew anything, they were too afraid to talk.

Not unusual. Just frustrating.

Now, at half past twelve, she stood in the ladies' room contemplating how she looked.

"This is bad."

One day had changed everything. Put her entire existence into a tailspin. Last night had been the no-turning-back point.

No matter how she lied to herself. No matter how

she lied to her sister. Bree understood with complete
certainty that she could no longer deny the facts.

She still had feelings for Patrick.

She had made a grievous error keeping his son
from him. Though their relationship hadn't worked
out, he would have been a good father.

The problem had been, still was, that he wanted to
run everything. There was no compromise. He took
his lawman tactics home. She hadn't been able to deal
with that. Mutual respect was too important to her.

That wasn't fair. It wasn't that he hadn't respected
her. He just hadn't wanted her doing anything he considered too dangerous for a woman...for his woman.

But none of that meant he wouldn't be a stellar
father.

She had no idea what she was going to do.

Bree had spent nine years in law enforcement.
She had solved the most puzzling cases, had appre-
hended her share of bad guys, including the worst
of the worst—rapist and killers. And she had no idea
how she was going to fix this.

Her life.

Her son's life.

How could she have ever hoped to keep Peter
from knowing his father when they lived in the same
county? Once Patrick moved from Monticello, Utah,
to Kenner County she should have realized
her mistake and corrected it then...before it went

this far. She'd assumed at the time that if Patrick heard she'd had a child that he would probably believe Jack was the father.

"Truly dumb."

Bree should have anticipated the reality that babies grow up to be little boys and girls who ask questions. They then become teenagers who rebel against every perceived offense, real or imagined.

God, she was in trouble.

She took a breath, checked the time on her cell phone. She was also late.

Bree took a breath and walked out the door. If she stalled any longer she would be noticeably late. Nora would notice. Bree didn't want to offend Nora.

Dropping by her desk, she checked her messages before heading for lunch. She had no more excuses.

Making her way through Towaoc's one-level police station, a part of her kept hoping that the chief or one of her colleagues would call her name. If work got in the way, lunch would have to wait. Patrick could brief her by phone. She was fairly certain nothing new had come up on the Grainger case from his end any more than it had hers. Protocol dictated that all involved in the case get notification.

Before climbing into her borrowed SUV, she checked her cell phone once more.

She wasn't going to get a lucky break today.

En route to the Morning Ray Café, Bree replayed last night's close call. Patrick had shown up at her sister's demanding to know what was going on. Bree'd had to covertly call her sister and let her know to keep Peter inside. Not that she would have allowed him outside with what was going on. But Bree hadn't wanted to take any chances. Then Patrick had insisted on following her home, requiring Bree to ask her sister to drive Peter home as soon as Patrick was gone.

She owed her sister big-time.

The drive to Kenner City was spent worrying about facing Patrick after that kiss. Was it possible her sister had been right all along?

That kiss had certainly been…something. She'd melted like a bar of chocolate beneath the scorching desert sun. She shivered even now as she recalled the way his lips had felt pressed against hers. His big, strong hands cradling her face.

Bree had no idea Patrick had never married. That seemed impossible. A man who looked like him. A good, hard-working man.

With whom she'd argued vehemently about her career. She'd been a green recruit assigned to the Ute Reservation when they'd first met. Patrick had been assigned to a special task force in Monticello. They'd worked a nasty hate-crime investigation in Utah territory together. Ended up head over heels in love and sharing an apartment for six months. But Patrick had rigid views on the differences between males and females in law enforcement, particularly the woman he loved. He didn't want her doing the dangerous details. The more intense the relationship had gotten the more protective he'd become.

Bree had felt smothered. She'd needed to be able to pursue her career as far as her abilities would take her. She'd wanted the tough cases, the danger. She hadn't wanted any more of Patrick's grief. So she'd walked. Two months later she'd discovered she was pregnant. Her cycles had never been regular. Missing one hadn't set off any alarms. But the second missed period had gotten her attention. No matter that they'd always practiced safe sex—she was pregnant. And Patrick hadn't come after her or even called in more than a month. Pride and vulnerability, along with her father's urging, had helped make her decision. *Move on.*

She'd been young and full of ambition. After Peter's birth and a hard-learned lesson in bad choices in husbands, she'd realized that risking her life was also risking her son's future. So she'd gone after the rank of detective. Even working homicide was a lot safer than pounding the pavement and cruising the alleyways and streets working in prevention mode.

Then, six years ago Patrick had come back home to Colorado to be sheriff of Kenner County and she'd sweated every single day of every damned year that he would somehow find out about her secret.

He'd called this morning to ensure she was okay, then insisted they needed to talk. Over lunch. God, how would she ever resolve this mess?

The drive down Main Street momentarily tugged Bree from her troubling thoughts. She loved this street. Kenner City was a grand old Western town without the overwhelming crowds of Park City. The refurbished storefronts made her think of the old Western movies she watched as a kid. From the well-maintained sidewalks to the majestic mountains in the distance, there was no place on the planet she'd rather be than here.

The Morning Ray Café sat on the corner of Main and Bridge Street. The perfect location for attracting tourists. But the locals were the mainstay of Nora's customers. Her decadent desserts and wide variety of home-cooked cuisine was known far and wide in these parts. Not to mention her vivacious personality. Everybody loved Nora.

The atmosphere was homey and warm and the diner was filled to capacity as always. From the working cowboys to the polished businessmen of the city's financial district, Nora got them all. The hum of conversation was underscored by the clink of silver and stoneware.

But it was the smell that had Bree's tummy rumbling. She had seriously missed this place. Savoring the delicious smells, she scanned the tables. Patrick sat in one of the only two booths in the diner. This one was near the back. The closest to the kitchen. Most patrons would avoid that booth, but not Patrick. Being close to the kitchen ensured his mother was able to visit with him even during a crowded lunch run like this one.

Patrick waved.

Bree's heart did one of those traitorous flip-flops. Dammit. She headed that way, weaving through the crowded tables.

He stood. Always the gentleman. His ever-present cowboy hat sat on the bench seat.

She'd missed that, too. There was a time when she'd loved to pull that hat off and run her fingers through his thick, dark hair.

Focus, Bree. Don't go there.

"Hey." It was the first word that popped into Bree's sluggish brain. Work. This was about work…not about the pale blue cotton shirt that stretched across his broad shoulders or the softly worn jeans that hugged his lean hips and long legs.

"Hey, yourself." He gestured to the booth. "I took the liberty of ordering for you."

Bree settled into her side of the booth working extra hard at not showing her surprise at the move.

He used to do that all the time. It felt…too fast. Too much like old times.

"Okay," she said hesitantly.

"Mom's meat loaf." Patrick flashed her one of those lopsided grins that sent her heart bumping erratically. Peter smiled exactly like that.

He knew Nora's meatloaf was Bree's favorite.

Even she had to smile. "I do love Nora's meatloaf." She'd missed Nora and her amazing cooking. But coming here had been too risky…too painful.

Patrick slid into the booth and got down to business. "I hope you had better luck running down leads than I did this morning."

Nora's bubbly voice preceded her as she burst through the double doors leading from the kitchen. She settled two glasses of water on the table.

"Bree, sugar, you are truly a sight for sore eyes."

Bree slid from the booth and accepted the hug Nora Martinez was all set to give. The buxom lady was barely five-four, but she made up for her height in personality and voice.

When Bree had settled back into her seat, Nora leaned down and kissed her son's head. "They never get too old or too big for that." She winked at Bree. "You'll find out one of these days."

Bree tensed.

"So, how have you been, sugar?" Nora braced a hip against the side of the booth.

"Good." That was true. "I made detective and I love my job." She thought of the homicide case she was working right now. "Most of the time, anyway."

"Well." Nora pushed away from the booth. "I'd better get hopping. You two enjoy."

Bree didn't realize how much she'd missed Nora until that moment. She had a way of making everything feel all right. She was definitely one of a kind.

Another reality hit Bree then. She had deprived Peter of knowing and loving his grandmother. A woman who would spoil her one and only grandchild to no end. Nora Martinez would be immensely disappointed in Bree for keeping Peter from her.

Bree's heart sank into her belly.

She had made a terrible mistake.

Stop. She had to stop obsessing about this. Whatever was going to happen would happen. She'd deal with the repercussions when it did.

Right now she had to focus.

"No luck with your contacts either?" she asked in answer to his question, steering the conversation to the reason they were here.

Patrick moved his head from side to side, his face grim. "I checked in with Ortiz a couple of hours ago. There's nothing new. They hope to have a preliminary autopsy report by tomorrow's briefing."

"Hopefully we'll learn something from the autopsy." Bree kept thinking about the ligature pattern on the victim's throat. Unusual but somehow familiar. She'd seen it somewhere.

"So," Patrick said, drawing her attention back to him, "how's married life?"

Surprise flared in her chest. Tension followed. Is that what he'd called her here to talk about? "I…I wouldn't know. I'm single."

His brow furrowed in that way that made Bree's heart skip a beat each time she saw Peter do the same thing. He'd never even met his father and yet he was so very much like him.

"I heard you'd gotten married," Patrick countered, not about to let it go.

"I did." She chose her words carefully. "Didn't work out so we divorced."

"When did that happen?"

"About a year ago." They'd been separated for six months before that but she wasn't going into the dirty details.

More of that surprise at just how wrong he'd been flared in his eyes. He shrugged. "I guess I'm way behind on news."

Farther than you know.

"Any hits on the prints from your SUV?"

Something else she'd worked hard at keeping off her mind. "Not unless you count mine and my sister's and my…" She'd almost said her son. "My niece's." Too close.

"You wanna tell me about your anonymous fan?"

If she didn't he would just keep nagging at her. She'd kept the situation to herself until last night. Being a woman in the still predominantly man's world of law enforcement, any sign of weakness was looked upon in a different light. Since she hadn't had any real evidence someone was watching her, she'd let it go. But there was no letting it go now. This was real. She had a stalker. Filing an official report had been necessary.

She toyed with her water glass, mainly to avoid eye contact. "About two weeks ago I started to get this feeling that someone was watching me." She shrugged. "I'd get a glimpse of someone out of the corner of my eye. Notice the same vehicle mirroring my turns. You know. Stuff like that."

Nothing she could put her finger on, more gut instinct than anything.

"What about the phone calls?" Patrick asked.

Oh, yeah. She'd told him about that. "Several hang ups. Always from a public phone. No pattern as far as the time, but a definite pattern in the locations the calls were made from. Kenner City."

Patrick mulled over what she'd told him. "Have you made a list of anyone who might be holding a grudge? Someone you've ticked off in the line of duty or otherwise?"

Actually, her first instinct was to suspect Jack.

But he'd left her alone for the past five or six months. She couldn't see any reason he would suddenly start trouble again now. They were beyond over. She'd seen him around with other women. Clearly he'd moved on.

"What about your ex?" Patrick asked, as if she'd spoken her thoughts.

Bree shook her head. "He's completely out of the picture." In fact, he'd actually been out of the picture all along. She just hadn't realized how much so.

Nora breezed through the kitchen doors. "Here we go, sweet things," she said happily. Her rosy cheeks, vivacious personality and bottled blond hair made her seem far younger than her nearly sixty years. She sat a steaming plate in front of Bree, then Patrick.

The presentation of the food was spectacular. Who knew that there could be such design significance in the way a plate of meat and two vegetables were laid out. Bree never ceased to be amazed at the way the lady could take something as simple as meatloaf and make it look beautiful. That it tasted magnificent as well didn't hurt. The smell was awesome.

Bree picked at her meatloaf. Time to turn the tables. To say at this point that she wasn't curious would be a vast understatement. A flat-out lie. "What about you? Is there a woman waiting at home?" She placed a piece of succulent meatloaf on her tongue. She had to fight the urge to moan.

Patrick picked up his fork and piddled with his food. "Not yet."

Aha. *Not yet.* Did that mean there was someone?

"I suppose you're like me," she suggested, deciding this was the best way out of this subject. She looked directly at him then. Ignored the ping of desire that hit deep beneath her belly button as those vivid blue eyes meshed with hers. "A little too busy for a decent social life?"

"Always." He poked a spoonful of mashed potatoes into his mouth.

She shouldn't have watched. He chewed, swallowed, then licked his lips. Her breath hitched.

Careful, Bree. This is dangerous territory. She was allowing herself to play with fire. Her sister should never have shown her that scrapbook. She hadn't been able to think about anything but what-if since.

She had to remember that any misstep she made now would impact her son.

Patrick had to remember that things hadn't worked out with Bree eight years ago. He could already see that their differences were still the same ones. She liked diving headfirst into intense investigations. Like murder. If he allowed himself to get involved with her again, his protective instincts would make them both miserable. He would only be unhappy.

That was no way to live.

The rest of the meal was eaten in silence, save for the occasional appearance of his mother. Nora had loved Bree. She'd wanted Patrick to settle down and make grandbabies for her.

Seeing them together now would only give her false hope. Patrick had chosen the diner because it represented a safe zone. But maybe he'd been wrong. The environment sure as hell hadn't done anything to slow his need to reach out and touch Bree. Or his burning desire to kiss her again.

Last night he'd dreamed of making love with her. The way they used to, with no inhibitions and with utter trust. At least until those last few weeks. Then the animosity had overridden everything else.

As much as he wanted to stay and learn all he could about her life the past eight years, he had a three o'clock appointment. They'd discussed what little they could do on the Grainger case until the next briefing or until they picked up an additional lead. Trawling for info was about the extent of it. The truth was, sitting here looking at her was pure torture. He needed distance. His upcoming appointment was a blessing.

Before he could voice his need to get back to the office, Bree pushed her coffee cup aside. They'd both declined dessert but no one could pass on his mother's coffee. Her own special blend drew folks from far and wide for a cup of Nora's Good Morning Coffee.

"I have a staff meeting. I need to get back." She glanced at the long counter lined with customers, then toward the kitchen doors. "I should get my check and…go."

"You're kidding, right?" Patrick finished off his coffee, then set his cup aside. "You know Nora's not going to let you pay."

Bree scooted from the booth. "Thank her for me, would you?"

The kitchen's swinging doors flew open and Nora Martinez scurried out. Patrick glanced at Bree as he got to his feet. "I guess we'll both get the chance to thank her."

Nora urged Bree to come again soon, then hugged her twice. Clearly Patrick wasn't the only one who still had feelings for Bree.

Crossing the dining room, Patrick hesitated. Ben Parrish was deep in conversation with a woman. Patrick studied his body language a moment. The two seemed to be arguing or at the very least having an intense exchange. The wavy red hair triggered recognition. Ava Wright, one of the forensic techs at the crime lab. Interesting. The idea that Parrish was currently a person of interest in the Grainger investigation made the fact that the two were having such a tense lunch only a step or two away from suspicious.

"Isn't that Agent Parrish?" Bree asked.

"It is." Patrick opted not to jump to conclusions. He cut through the tables and pushed out the door.

"I'll see you at the briefing tomorrow," Bree said, already moving away from him.

"Just one more thing." He should have done this first. She turned back to him, those wide brown eyes expectant. He rotated his hat in his hands. "I want to apologize again for last night. Like I said, that won't happen again. I don't see why we can't be friends despite the past. Who knows? This may not be the only time we end up working together. It's best that we do this the right way." Okay. Whew. He'd gotten the entire speech out without screwing up.

Bree studied him for two beats, just long enough for him to start to sweat. "You're right. Friends is…good. We should work at that."

Patrick's chest expanded with a deep, relieved breath. "Good."

She glanced at her borrowed SUV. "Gotta go."

Patrick settled his hat into place. "Keep me posted on this stalker business," he urged.

She didn't make any promises. He watched as she moved toward the driver's-side door of an SUV marked with the Towaoc PD logo.

Patrick didn't get into his SUV until he'd watched her drive away. His instincts were hum-

ming. What was she not telling him? Was there
more to this stalker business than she'd let on?

He didn't like the idea that she was taking this
so cavalierly. The warning left on her SUV was
clear and to the point.

Someone was obviously watching her.

Someone who wanted to scare her…or worse.

AFTER HER STAFF MEETING Bree headed for the
parking lot. She called Tabitha as she climbed into
the truck to let her know she would be picking up
her son from school. Once this investigation heated
up, who knew when she'd have the opportunity to
pick him up again.

The press was already badgering anyone they
discovered was involved with the investigation.
Ortiz planned to hold a news conference after the
briefing tomorrow to ease the speculation.

The hounding for information would only get
worse after that.

"How did your day go, son?" she asked Peter as
he climbed in.

He dropped his backpack onto the floorboard
and stretched his safety belt into place. "It wasn't
so good." Those big blue eyes, heavy with frustration, peered up at her. "Robby Benson told me my
daddy must be dead since I've never seen him. Is
that true, Mommy? Is my daddy dead?"

Bree slipped her foot from the brake to the accelerator and rolled out of the pickup lane. Why did kids have to be so cruel?

Why did adults have to lie?

She was no better than Robby Benson. She couldn't keep avoiding the subject and she refused to outright lie to her son about his father. He'd never asked where he was or who he was. He'd never asked much of anything, until recently. Turning seven a couple of months ago had changed everything. "Your daddy doesn't live with us" didn't cut it anymore.

"No, baby, your father is not dead." Did she say he lived far away...that he was too busy? That had worked in the past.

Peter pondered that answer for a moment. Bree braced for what no doubt came next.

"Then why doesn't he ever come to see me? Robby's daddy just bought him the coolest bike ever. Has my daddy ever bought me anything?"

And so it began in earnest.

Just how was she going to do this? She'd already chosen a path...one that was about to bite her in the butt. "Well, sweetie, it's—"

A dark sedan with equally dark windows made the next turn Bree executed. Her instincts went immediately on point. "Hold on a minute, son."

Okay, so that was just one turn...that she'd noted,

anyway. No need to get paranoid just yet. She made another turn, this one unnecessary, just to see if the sedan would follow.

That was an affirmative. Her pulse rate jumped into overdrive.

She glanced at her son. Couldn't risk going cowboy and confronting the driver of the vehicle. If she made any overt moves of aggression her son's life could be put in danger.

The car suddenly lurched forward, got as close to her rear bumper as possible without nudging her.

Her breath caught.

She was barely out of town. She could turn around.

"Lean back hard against your seat, baby." God, if this guy hit her…

The car jerked left, roared forward. She eased closer to the side of the road, let off the accelerator.

The sedan rocketed past her. She squinted, tried to see the license plate but the car was too fast and she was too rattled. If her son hadn't been in the vehicle with her she would have given pursuit.

She could call it in, but she didn't have a handle on the make and model or the license plate number.

But she and Peter were okay and that was what mattered.

Relief struck with such force that her fingers barely managed to keep a grip on the steering wheel as she picked up speed once more.

Calm down. It was over now.

Now she knew one thing for sure. This wasn't going away and it was no teenage prank.

This latest incident was no coincidence. And it damned sure wasn't her imagination.

Someone was following her…watching her.

He wasn't going to stop until he'd accomplished his goal.

To scare her?

Or to kill her?

Chapter Six

Bree arrived at the annex building for the Wednesday afternoon briefing with five minutes to spare. She'd gotten through last night without more questions from her son. Sheer luck. One of his friends from school had needed to sleep over since his mother had gone into labor with her second child.

Bree understood that her luck wouldn't hold out.

The one question Peter had asked was when would he have a little brother or sister.

Now there was a question she sure couldn't answer.

She sat in the borrowed TPD SUV and wondered for the umpteenth time what she was going to do. Last night's tossing and turning had left her sleep deprived and frustrated with herself. And her dreams. She'd dreamed of Patrick…and the way things used to be. Before all the tension and yelling.

"Enough." She had to focus on this case. Dealing

with her personal life would just have to come later. If she were really lucky, a lot later.

Now her stalker…that was something she might just have to deal with sooner than later.

He—assuming it was a he—knew where she lived. Where her son went to school. She'd spoken to Peter's teacher last night and warned her that there was a potential problem. Bree had also spoken with her chief. Two of her colleagues had spent the morning going over her case files for the past couple of years. They'd found nothing that appeared motive enough to prompt retribution.

Until she had more to go on she'd just have to wait it out. That was the thing with stalkers. There was nothing the victim could do until the perp was caught in the act of wrongdoing or had left evidence of his illegal act. There was certainly nothing to be done when the stalker's identity was unknown.

Unfortunately Bree was trapped in that freaky zone where she could do nothing but be aware and be patient. Hope for the best and brace for the worst.

A car parked a couple of spaces over and Ortiz emerged. When he'd gone inside she climbed out and headed that way as well. She didn't see Patrick's SUV. Maybe he was hung up with something else. Had to be something big for him to miss this briefing. He would likely send one of his deputies to cover for him.

Bree took the stairs to the third floor, waved in greeting to the receptionist and for identification purposes, then moved on to the command center. The room was crowded with federal agents already.

Bree took the only available seat and smiled when Callie MacBride looked her way. Callie's return smile was weary. She wore that strained look again. The one that said this case was getting to her. Bree wondered again if she and the victim had been particularly close. There was definitely some aspect of this investigation that was getting to her on a level she couldn't contain. Murder was bad any way you looked at it, but Bree had seen the lady in action before and Callie was as tough as nails. This wasn't her typical reaction.

The scrape of a chair being dragged up next to her drew her attention back to the here and now. Patrick settled into the seat.

Bree's heart reacted instantly with a thump then a stumble. She looked away. Drew in a deep breath.

As if her racing heart wasn't bad enough, her body temperature climbed a few degrees.

Maybe if she hadn't deprived herself of male company for the past eighteen months she wouldn't be so needy.

That had to be the explanation for her reactions to his presence. That or her body was mistaking fear for desire.

She wasn't sure which was worse, being scared to death he would discover her secret or harboring forbidden desire for the man with whom she had a rocky past. Either one was treacherous territory.

"You okay?" Patrick asked for her ears only. The sincere concern in his eyes drew her like a magnet. He'd always been able to do that. To make her want him with just a look.

Bree wished Ortiz would call the briefing to order. Most of the agents were still milling around, talking among themselves...except for Callie and Ben Parrish. Both had already taken their seats and appeared lost in their own thoughts.

"I'm fine." Bree pulled her notepad from her jacket pocket and placed it on the table in preparation for the start of the briefing. Mainly she did it to prevent having to meet Patrick's gaze again. That didn't stop him from watching her. She could feel his eyes probing her, looking for the crack that would let him in.

"Any more trouble with whoever sent you that warning?" He pulled his chair an inch or two closer.

Her pulse raced.

Her first instinct was to tell him no. But he would read the lie in her posture and on her face. He was too good at reading body language to miss the slightest hint of deception.

"There was a car yesterday," she began, but got

distracted by Elizabeth Reddawn hovering at the door. She waved to someone in the room, a large brown envelope in her hand.

Bree scanned the crowd, which was still caught up in conversation. Ben Parrish pointed to his chest and the receptionist nodded. He pushed back his chair and moved wide around the other agents to reach the door. Elizabeth passed him the envelope and hurried back to the lobby to man her desk.

Parrish stared at the envelope for a long moment, glanced back at the other agents, then rushed into the corridor.

"Wonder what that was about?" Patrick whispered to her.

She shivered, hoped like hell he didn't see it. "Don't know."

"I spoke to Ortiz earlier today," Patrick said quietly. "He explained that Parrish, Ryan, Dylan Acevedo and Grainger all attended the Bureau academy together. They've been close friends ever since, despite being assigned to different field offices." Patrick surveyed the assembled group. "There are a lot of intense emotions tangled up in this bunch."

That cleared up a number of questions for Bree. In her experience with federal agents, rigid professionalism were the buzzwords. But this case was, as she suspected, deeply personal.

"You were saying something about a car?" Patrick asked.

Bree had hoped he'd forgotten about that. "I picked up…" Bree froze. She almost said she'd picked her son up from school. This was the second time she'd had a close call like this. She had to pull it together. "I picked up milk on my way home yesterday afternoon." That was true. She had stopped at the Stop and Go. "Anyway, a dark sedan, one with heavily tinted windows, roared up behind me and stayed on my bumper for a bit before barreling around me. It might not have been related." She thought about those moments when she feared the sedan would ram the SUV she was driving. "It felt like an intimidation tactic." She shrugged. "But I was in the TPD vehicle. It could have been someone who just doesn't like cops."

"Bree."

She didn't want to look at him. It was easier to watch the other folks in the room.

"Bree," he said more firmly.

Reluctantly, she met his gaze.

"You have to take this situation seriously. Talk to your chief."

"I already have." God, she needed a distraction here. Anything to move the moment beyond this discussion.

On cue, and much to her relief, Ben Parrish reentered the room. He no longer clutched the envelope the receptionist had given him but judging by the grim expression he wore, whatever had been in that envelope was not good news.

Like her, Patrick watched Parrish take his seat. Bree wished she could read his mind. Obviously he was brutally torn. Was there something he'd done that made him feel somehow responsible for Grainger's death? Bree still didn't believe he was the murderer. She doubted anyone in this room really believed that. But Parrish felt guilty about something. That much was apparent.

"What did your chief say?" Patrick wanted to know.

She didn't want to talk about this with him. She knew to be aware. For now, that was all she could do. Thankfully, before she was forced to respond, Ortiz called the room to order.

Ortiz briefly reviewed their findings thus far, which were pretty much nil. No match had been found for the ligature pattern on the victim's throat. However, the coroner had determined that the item used to strangle Agent Grainger was metal. Silver. The unknown subject, perpetrator in regular cop speak, was suspected to be male due to the depth of the marks. Massive strength had been utilized.

Bree's chest tightened at the idea that Agent

Grainger, although highly trained, hadn't had a chance against such raw brawn.

Acevedo pushed away from the table and walked over to the only window in the room to stare at the mountains in the distance. Ryan exchanged a tense look with Parrish. Ortiz paused only a moment, probably to ensure another physical confrontation wasn't going to break out, before continuing the briefing.

While Ortiz reviewed the details he intended to pass along to the press, Bree watched the people in the room. Acevedo lingered at the window and Parrish remained at the table with his head hung as if in defeat. More tension-filled glances were exchanged, these between Ryan and Callie.

Bree wondered if there was something far more personal than friendship between those two. Then again, she could be reading too much into the turbulent emotions of those involved in this investigation.

Acevedo returned to his seat and he and Ryan spoke quietly. Ryan appeared to be attempting to persuade the other agent to stay calm. Parrish cut a look at his two friends then dropped his head once more.

Again, Bree couldn't help feeling sorry for him. Yes, he'd found the body. Yes, he was male and clearly capable of the necessary strength to strangle the victim in the manner the coroner described. But why not make a run for it? Why keep coming back to face this hostility?

It couldn't be as simple as him being the killer.

Agent Tom Ryan passed out copies of a recent photo of Julie Grainger to all involved with the investigation. Ortiz suggested that local law enforcement continue to prod their contacts. The Bureau remained focused on the Del Gardo connection. Since there was no evidence to indicate otherwise, and likely for other reasons not shared, they were convinced at this point Del Gardo or someone in his organization had something to do with her murder. As he reiterated this conclusion, Ryan and Acevedo stared pointedly at Parrish.

Did his fellow agents believe Parrish was somehow involved with Del Gardo or his activities? If so, no one was saying as much out loud. At least not with Bree and Patrick present.

That would make Parrish a traitor...whether he was a killer or not.

Ortiz had just dismissed the meeting when Bree's cell phone vibrated. She checked the screen. Officer Cyrus. Bree quickly stepped into the corridor to take the call. Maybe he had found something that would determine who was stalking her.

"Hunter."

"Detective, this is Steve Cyrus."

"You have news for me, Cyrus?" It would be damned nice to solve the case of her mystery stalker. She would feel a lot better about her son's safety.

"Yes, ma'am. I got a call from one of the drunks I pick up on a regular basis. He likes building up brownie points so I'll go easy on him when he's on a drinking binge."

Bree understood that strategy. Leverage was a good thing when dealing with informants with criminal tendencies, however minor.

"This guy swears he saw someone matching Sherman Watts's description arguing with Agent Grainger not more than a week ago. He was afraid to ask Sherman if it was him, but he's certain it was."

Sherman Watts? Watts was a local troublemaker. To Bree's knowledge he'd never murdered anyone. Most of his rap sheet consisted of drunk and disorderly charges. He could be a pain in the butt, but so far as she knew he wasn't a killer.

Some part of her was disappointed that the news wasn't related to the jerk who had spray painted her SUV.

But it was about the Grainger case.

"How reliable is this informant?" Adrenaline whipped across Bree's nerve endings. This could in some small way be their first real break.

"He's never failed me before. The best I can tell, he and Watts are occasional drinking buddies. What he saw might mean nothing at all, but I thought it would be worth checking out."

"Thanks, Cyrus." The need to end the call and hunt down Watts charged through her veins. "We're looking at any and all leads. This could give us a definite starting place. I'll talk to Watts and see what he has to say." If she could find him. He had a way of making himself scarce when he was avoiding the law. Which was rather frequently. She mentally ticked off a list of places to start looking, none of them on the Chamber of Commerce's lists of places to visit when in Four Corners.

"I wouldn't go looking for him alone," Cyrus cautioned. "If he's involved in this he might be more desperate than usual."

Bree told herself his warning had nothing to do with her being a woman and everything to do with taking the necessary precautions despite the urgency of the situation. Two days around Patrick and she was already defensive about her physical limitations.

Like Julie Grainger must have felt during those final moments of her life. A shudder rocked Bree. No matter one's training, the element of surprise when combined with lethal intent was a damned near insurmountable opponent. A deadly opponent.

Bree thanked Cyrus and slid her phone back into its holster. At least she had a lead to follow. A

starting place. Knowing Watts's penchant for wom-
anizing it could be a dead end. The incident might
be as simple as Watts making a remark or hitting on
Grainger and Grainger dressing him down in public.

"Ortiz is holding a press conference in one hour."

Startled, Bree turned to face Patrick. She schooled
her expression in the hopes of keeping her reactions
to herself. Hearing his voice again was just something
she hadn't gotten used to yet. Having heard it in her
dreams far too many times didn't count. Nor had it
been necessary to remind her of the way it wrapped
around her and made her want to lean into him. Every
nuance was permanently imprinted in her memory.
The rich, deep timbre was another of those things she
had struggled so diligently, without success, to forget.

"The press conference. Right." She nodded, still
a little distracted by Cyrus's call. And the mere
sound of Patrick's voice.

"Ortiz is heading back to Durango after that," he
continued, seemingly without realizing how he'd
affected her. "He'll be staying on top of the investigation via teleconference unless he's needed back
here. Tom Ryan is in charge of the investigation now."

Focus. She had to find Watts. But Cyrus was
right. She didn't need to go it alone. "I…may have
a lead." She and Patrick were supposed to be
working together on this. A team. Telling him,
taking him along were the right things to do.

"Is that what your call was about?"

Oh, yeah, he was watching her every move. "It was. According to one of Officer Cyrus's contacts, Agent Grainger had a confrontation with Sherman Watts only a couple of days before she was murdered. Considering Watts's obnoxious personality and lecherous ways the confrontation may have been happenstance, but I figure it's worth checking out."

Patrick was familiar with Watts. His wasn't a name Patrick had expected to hear connected with Agent Grainger's murder, but men like Watts were fully capable of the unexpected.

"I was thinking," Bree suggested, "that we should track Watts down and shake him up a little. Get the truth out of him. He runs in some low circles. Even if there's nothing to his confrontation with Grainger, he might know something."

Most of the agents were filtering out of the command center now. There was no reason for the two of them to hang around any longer. Patrick nodded. "Let's do it." He gestured for her to precede him. "I'll drive."

"Fine by me," she tossed over her shoulder as she joined the exodus.

Maybe having her go first wasn't such a good idea, but it was the gentlemanly thing to do. Even if the sway of her slender hips distracted him in a wholly unprofessional way.

They'd made a deal. Friends. Colleagues.

Damn, but that was going to be a hard bargain to keep.

FINDING SHERMAN WATTS wasn't an easy task. Patrick drove to every unsavory hangout he and Bree could think of. It wasn't until they hit the casino in Towaoc that they found a clue as to his whereabouts. One of Patrick's repeat offenders, one with sticky fingers, was happy to report that Watts had been hanging out at a friend's in a trailer park outside the city limits of Towaoc.

"Not exactly uptown," Bree commented, taking in the unsightly conditions of the trailer park as they arrived at the address given.

"Not exactly," Patrick agreed.

The grounds were littered with trash. Most of the vehicles parked next to the dilapidated trailers were equally dilapidated. Music blared through the thin walls of the one closest to the park entrance.

"We're looking for lot ten." Patrick searched the ends of the narrow tin-can homes for the lot numbers. Some were worn nearly beyond the point of legibility. Others were missing entirely.

"Should be the next one on the right." Bree pointed to a rusty box with a broken-down deck leading to its front door.

"His friend must be doing pretty well," Patrick

said, noting the new-looking truck parked in the dirt drive. "Too bad it's likely something illegal."

Bree called in the license plate number. The more information at their disposal, the more power and leverage they possessed.

Patrick emerged from his SUV slowly, scanning the area. There was no way to guess what you could run upon in a dump like this. Better safe than sorry. He rested his hand on the butt of his revolver. Bree did the same.

Patrick climbed the steps of the deck first. Bree hung back to answer her cell. Patrick listened for any sound coming from inside the trailer. Nothing. He stepped to the side of the door, opted not to draw his weapon just yet, then he pounded on the metal door with his fist.

"Sherman Watts, this is Sheriff Martinez. I need to have a word with you."

Bree moved into position on the other side of the door. She drew her weapon and assumed an offense ready stance.

No movement inside.

Patrick pounded harder. "Sherman Watts!"

A bump then a crash inside warned Patrick that someone was up and moving about. He braced. The door swung open, concealing Bree behind it.

"What the hell do you want, Sheriff?"

Watts, half-dressed and looking like he had one

hell of a hangover, swayed in the open doorway. His long, stringy hair didn't look as if it had been washed in a month. Those beady eyes, red from alcohol abuse, glared at Patrick.

The man wasn't armed. Patrick hadn't actually expected him to be, unless he was concealing a weapon in his baggy jeans.

"I need to ask you a few questions. May we come in?"

Watts looked around. "Who's we?"

Bree stepped from behind the door, her weapon holstered now. "Evening, Sherman." She looked the middle-aged man up and down. "Looks like you've been doing a little better at the poker table." She hitched her head toward the truck. "That's a very nice truck you bought last week."

Patrick met her gaze. The vehicle did belong to Watts. A big move up from the rusty old truck he'd been driving for years. If he'd only just registered it last week, then that meant he'd come into some fast money.

Could it be blood money?

"Maybe," Patrick said to Watts, drawing his attention back to him, "you'll share some of your winning secrets with us."

Watts scoffed. "I don't have no secrets." He folded his arms over his skinny chest. "I won that truck fair and square in a private game of chance."

He smirked. "I could give you the names of the fellers I beat, but they'd probably just lie and say they was the ones who won. I don't see where it's any of your business anyway."

"We're not here about the truck," Bree told him.

His smirk faded. "What the hell you want then?"

"May we come in?" Patrick repeated.

Watts allowed his gaze to skim Bree's body. "Why not? I like cops." He said the last with a lecherous grin. "Ain't my place anyhow."

Patrick shouldered him out of the way as he moved through the door. "I'm a cop. You like me?"

Watts backed up a couple of steps. "Don't get your boxers in a wad, Sheriff. I just woke up. I'm not my usual pleasant self yet."

"It's almost six p.m.," Bree informed him as she stepped inside. "What's wrong, Watts? You aren't sleeping well at night?"

He flicked those beady eyes in her direction. "I never sleep at night. Too much happening at night. You know what I mean?" He sniggered.

"Speaking of happenings," Patrick interjected. "Did you hear about the federal agent who was murdered?"

Watts tensed. Only the slightest shift in his posture, but Patrick didn't miss it.

"I don't listen to the news."

Patrick surveyed the trailer's front room. Ragged

furniture. Looked like the place had been tossed but he knew that Watts and his friend were probably just slobs. They would live here until it became completely unbearable and then they'd move to the next dump.

"Julie Grainger." Bree pulled the photo from her jacket pocket. She shoved it in Watts's face. "I understand you knew her."

Watts reared his head back and studied the photo for all of three seconds. "She's a looker. I wish I'd known her."

"The way I heard it—" Patrick walked around the room as if looking for contraband "—the two of you had quite a public disagreement."

Watts followed Patrick's every move, his guard fully in place now. "Well, you heard wrong. If I'd known that bitch, we wouldn't've been arguing."

Bree went toe-to-toe with Watts. "I think maybe you wanted to know her and she took one look at your ugly mug and told you to get lost."

Patrick's pulse skipped. What was she doing getting in this bastard's face like that?

Watts snickered. "Nah, lady cop, you got the wrong man. I don't know nothing about your dead friend. I never seen her before."

Patrick pushed his way between the two. "Why don't we have you come in for questioning just the same," Patrick suggested. "We're just trying to be thorough with our investigation. You know, follow all the leads whether they pan out or not."

Watts searched Patrick's eyes, didn't so much as blink as he met the challenge there. "Name the time and place, Sheriff, and I'll be there."

"I may do that sooner than you think," Patrick countered. "You're a person of interest in this case, Watts. Be sure you're available. I'm certain we'll be talking again very soon."

"You know where to look for me," Watts called as they walked out the door. "Send your pretty squaw on over any time."

Patrick stopped dead in his tracks. For two beats the only thing he could see was rage red. The need to pound Watts into an unrecognizable pulp was a palpable force inside him. It took every ounce of strength he possessed not to turn around and beat the hell out of the guy with his bare hands.

Bree didn't wait. She stamped back to the SUV and climbed in.

Patrick took a deep breath and didn't look back. Getting himself slapped with an assault charge wouldn't help this investigation. But he was sure itching to punch the bastard. Patrick opened the driver's-side door and settled behind the wheel of his SUV. Watts stared directly at Patrick one last time before smirking, then slamming his door shut.

Bastard.

When Patrick had guided his SUV back onto the highway and the trailer park was in the rearview mirror, Bree turned to him.

He'd expected this. He'd opened his mouth prematurely back there. But he was right whether she wanted to hear it or not.

"I don't need you playing the protector when we're interviewing a possible suspect. I had the situation with Watts under control."

She spoke calmly and quietly but the underlying fury in her voice told him she was mad as hell.

"You shouldn't have pushed your luck. You got right in the man's face, Bree. That's a dangerous maneuver if you can't back it up."

Wrong thing to say. Again.

"I can't believe you!" She glared at the highway in front of them. "I'm every bit as well trained as you. I can handle myself. I know how far to go with an interrogation. And it wasn't like I didn't have backup available."

He could argue with her but that would only make bad matters worse. "You're right. I'm wrong. Let's not argue." He told himself that he could see her side, but he didn't. Not really. Was he wrong? "Okay?"

His halfhearted apology didn't help.

She fumed silently, wouldn't give him a response.

"We see things differently on that point," he

offered. "My concern is not an indication of any lack of faith in your ability."

No comment.

Perfect.

Fine. Focus on the investigation. Let her fume. "I'll pass along what we learned about Watts to Agent Ortiz. See if he wants us to follow up with surveillance or additional questioning." The suggestion immediately produced images of him and Bree stuck inside this SUV all night long…in the dark.

More silence.

Great. "What do you want me to say, Bree?" This was just like eight years ago.

"Nothing. You've already said all I needed to hear. Nothing's changed."

And that was what he got for caring.

Chapter Seven

The next morning Bree parked, turned off the engine and stared out at the barren landscape that was the last sight Julie Grainger had laid eyes on before being murdered.

According to the coroner Julie had been dead approximately forty-eight to fifty hours when her body was discovered.

That meant she had possibly died about this time of morning, eight or nine. Five days ago.

Less than a week.

Bree got out of her truck and closed the door. The sound echoed, reminding her she was alone. No work. No family. No Patrick.

She needed to think.

Hand on the butt of her weapon, she walked slowly toward the yellow tape that marked the perimeter of the crime scene. It drooped here and there, a sign of the passage of time.

With no real break in the case.

They were beyond that crucial forty-eight-hour mark. And they had nothing significant to show for it.

Patrick had discussed the Sherman Watts situation with Agent Ortiz. His people were going to take over the follow-up. The press conference hadn't garnered any reaction as far as Bree had heard. Oritz had been brief and to the point. He'd urged anyone with information to come forward. There wasn't really a lot Bree could do at this point except react to new leads, those called in or the ones she drummed up pounding the pavement and rattling the cages of informants.

Bree stopped before reaching the yellow tape. She crouched down and picked up a handful of the sandy dirt. She rubbed it between her fingers, let it drift back to the ground. What was Julie doing out here so early on a Saturday morning?

Had one of her contacts in the Del Gardo investigation asked to meet her in this barren place? Or was her killer someone she'd rubbed the wrong way in a previous investigation? Or just some lowlife who had nothing to do with any of her cases.

In law enforcement there was always that chance. Many times the family of someone you'd helped convict would seek vengeance. Or you'd find yourself at the wrong place at the wrong time.

Had Sherman Watts met Julie here? Was the

drunken weasel capable of killing? More significant, was he smart enough, quick enough to catch
her by surprise and overpower her physically?

Bree blinked away the images her thoughts
evoked. Slowly, she turned all the way around and
surveyed the vast landscape. Rugged and barren, but
beautiful in its own right.

Her own life felt a little like that sometimes. She'd
had her heart broken, her pride battered and her social
skills had taken a hiatus. But she had her beautiful
son.

Unlike Julie Grainger, Bree was alive. As long as
she was alive there was hope for change…for better
things. For smarter decisions.

What, Bree wondered, would Julie have done differently if she'd known her life would end so
suddenly? Were there things left she needed or wanted
to say? Decisions she would have made differently?

Bree would spend more time with her son for sure.

She thought of Peter's excitement about today's
field trip when she'd dropped him off at school this
morning. For the moment he'd forgotten all about
asking questions about his father.

Bree was relieved, but she knew that wasn't fair.
She couldn't carry on this lie much longer. The guilt
was gnawing at her.

But then, at times like yesterday's visit with
Sherman Watts, she wanted to punch Patrick. They

were no longer involved. Hadn't spoken until three days ago in nearly eight years. How could he step into her professional space and treat her as if she were incapable? As if she was still that young, green rookie?

But that was exactly what he had done then and he was doing it again now. That whole macho cowboy thing was driving her crazy.

At least when he wasn't making her wish she'd made different choices. His voice…those eyes… just being near him made her want to reach out and touch him. To be kissed by him.

Again.

And again.

She closed her eyes and dropped her head back. She had tried so hard for so long to pretend she didn't care about him. He damn sure hadn't tried to get her back. Hadn't even called. Her father had insisted that was all the proof Bree needed that Patrick didn't care and certainly didn't deserve her. She belonged with her people. She should make her and her child's life here…where they belonged. She allowed her father to do exactly what she'd sworn she would never permit.

She'd pushed on with her career. She'd stayed busy raising her son. And she'd even allowed herself to get married.

Big fat mistake.

But she'd gone for it.

Seeing Patrick again. Being with his mother even if only for a brief lunch reminded Bree of all she'd walked away from. Of all she'd deprived her son of having. Not once had Bree considered how her decision would impact Nora, Patrick's only family. Or Peter, for that matter, where a paternal grandparent was concerned. He had a whole other family and she had kept him from that part of *his* life. But she'd been so young, so scared.

She couldn't keep pretending that life would go back to the way it was. Pretending Patrick didn't exist or matter was no longer feasible. She simply couldn't do it any longer.

He'd kissed her. He still had feelings for her just as her sister had said. But any feelings he had left would vanish the instant he learned how she had deceived him. He would hate her.

This was no little thing.

"Oh, by the way, Patrick, you have a son?" His age? "Oh, he's seven years old."

Bree groaned.

This was going to be bad.

Peter would be thrilled to have a father. That he was a sheriff would give him that superhero persona he longed for in a male authority figure.

No—in a father. That was what Peter wanted more than anything. A father.

His father.

"Not good. Not good."

Bree scanned the cliff dwelling and the mountains in the distance one last time. There was an emptiness here that mirrored her emotions. She had to find a way to fill that gaping hole.

For her son.

For her.

But what would she lose in the process?

"Just go to work, Bree." There was nothing she could do about any of it this morning.

She trudged back to the SUV. Borrowing trouble wasn't her style. Taking this one step at a time was the key. Talk to her sister. Talk to Peter. Then present the facts to Patrick.

Logical. Rational. Just like her police work. Analyze the situation, present the facts, form a conclusion and take action.

Simple.

"Right."

She reached for the driver's-side door of the SUV and the hair on the back of her neck lifted.

Bree whirled around, her hand instinctively resettled on the butt of her weapon. Her heart rate rushed into rapid fire. She searched the terrain, looking for whatever had set her instincts on point.

She hadn't felt that creepy "being watched" sensation since the day before yesterday. But that sensation was exactly what she was experiencing right now.

As if someone was hiding out there, watching her…waiting for the right moment.

For what?

To do to her what someone had done to Julie Grainger?

The thumping in her chest sped up.

By God, she wasn't going to make it easy.

She checked the interior of the SUV since she hadn't locked it, then climbed in. Keeping an eye on her surroundings, she started the engine and did a one-eighty turnabout.

For the first time in her career she wondered if Patrick was right. Maybe she did take too many chances while ignoring the danger. Otherwise she wouldn't be out here in the middle of nowhere alone knowing that someone was watching her.

It was real. She knew it was. Her vandalized SUV proved that. The car that threatened her with its aggressive driving could have been coincidence.

But not the vandalism.

Yet, she didn't listen.

She pretended the threat didn't exist.

The same way she'd pretended Patrick didn't for all these years.

And now that was coming back to haunt her.

How long before her determination to prove she wasn't afraid of any kind of challenge also came back to haunt her?

FIVE O'CLOCK.

Patrick stared at his phone. He hadn't called Bree today. She damned sure hadn't called him. He'd been playing catch-up all day at the office. Running a sheriff's department wasn't a duty that could be ignored. It was a constant balancing act between the police work and the political side of the job.

The political side was something he could live without but it went with the territory.

His personal life...that was something he'd ignored far too long.

Spending time with Bree again made him all too aware of that seriously neglected aspect of his life.

How in hell could they get along if she was going to be so haphazard with her safety? He couldn't pretend not to be aware of the risks she took. She was in law enforcement. Danger went with the territory.

Why couldn't she understand that he wasn't attempting to control her life? He was trying to protect her.

Because he cared.

Far more deeply than he wanted to admit.

But he wasn't so sure she felt the same way. He'd

noticed tiny reactions when they were together. But not the kind of reactions he felt whenever she was near. Not that he could see, anyway.

If, *major* if, she still had feelings for him, maybe they could start over. Begin back at square one and get to know each other all over again. They could adjust. He could try harder not to smother her.

That was what she had accused him of. She'd sworn that no man would ever control her life the way her father, although she loved him, had controlled her mother's. And he'd done nothing. Just let her walk away. For the first four of five months he'd been certain she would come back. But she hadn't. Then he'd convinced himself it was too late. After that it had been easier not to look back.

Was that why she was single again? Had her husband attempted too much control?

Patrick had never met a woman with a more determined spirit than Bree. Well, maybe his mother was a close match. She'd certainly never allowed a man to control her life, not even Patrick. His father had passed away when he was a kid and his mother had been making it on her own ever since.

But he didn't want Bree to be alone the way his mother was. He'd watched when Nora thought he wasn't looking and he recognized the loneliness.

Truth was, he didn't want to end up alone either.

Time had already proven that he was a one-woman man. No one else had made him feel the way Bree did. He'd even worked hard at a short-term relationship or two. But he just hadn't experienced that magic with anyone else. He was approaching forty. The time to change course was running short.

Only one way to fix this.

He picked up the phone and called Bree's cell. The worst she could do was say no.

She answered and for a moment he couldn't speak. He didn't want her to say no.

"Hello? Patrick?"

She'd recognized his number on her caller ID. "Bree." Suck it up, buddy. "I think it's time we cleared up a few things." Too damned demanding. "I mean…mended some fences." Take a breath. "If you're not busy I'd like to take you to dinner tonight. I mean…if you're available. You do have to eat."

Lame, Patrick. Damned lame.

The silence on the other end of the line had his gut in knots.

"Okay."

Relief surged through him. "Great. So I'll pick you up at seven?"

"Seven," she agreed.

When they'd said their goodbyes, Patrick closed his cell and leaned back in his chair.

He blew out a big, relieved breath.

"Sheriff?"

Patrick's head came up. His assistant loitered in the door. "Yeah, Clayton?"

"I have some information you might find useful."

Confusion furrowed Patrick's brow. He motioned for his assistant to come on in and have a seat. "What sort of information?"

Clayton closed the door behind him, crossed the room and took a seat in front of Patrick's desk. "About Detective Hunter."

Well, hell. How long had the man been standing there listening? When Patrick shot him an accusatory look his assistant seemed to get the point.

"Yes," Clayton admitted, "I overheard your phone call."

When Patrick would have dressed him down for eavesdropping, Clayton held up a hand and insisted, "Hear me out."

At this point, what did Patrick have to lose? His assistant was already eyeball-deep in his personal business.

"I was talking to the receptionist over at TPD."

Great, now the world would know. Patrick rolled his eyes.

"About a report we need from one of their robbery detectives," Clayton said, evidently reading Patrick's mind.

Patrick motioned for him to get on with it.

"Well, according to Mary Jane, the receptionist," he clarified, "Bree's ex-husband was a real piece of work. A total scumbag."

"Explain," Patrick ordered, tension radiating with rapid fire speed.

"His name is Jackson Raintree. He's a bully, a heavy drinker and, again, according to Mary Jane, he roughed Bree up a couple of times during the final days of their relationship."

Patrick sat up straighter. "The bastard hit her?" Fury roared through him.

Clayton nodded. "Mary Jane also said that Bree was afraid his abuse might turn to her son. That was the biggest reason she ended the marriage ASAP after the fool roughed her up."

"Wait, wait, wait." Patrick waved his hands back and forth. "Son? Bree has a son?" This was the first he'd heard of that. Damn. She'd had a kid with this bastard. Why hadn't she mentioned having a kid?

Clayton nodded. "I don't know exactly how old he is, but he goes to school."

Bree had married the guy before Patrick moved to Kenner City to go after the position of sheriff. That was six years ago. For all he knew they could have been together awhile before that. Added up, he supposed. If they had the kid early on in the relationship he would be school-age now. Since her husband's name hadn't been Peter, maybe that was the kid's name.

"Anyway, so take it slow, Sheriff," Clayton advised with a look that said you'd better listen up. "She's had a rocky go of it in the relationship arena."

"Thank you, Dr. Phil," Patrick patronized. He pushed to his feet. "Now, if you'll excuse me, I have places to go."

"Wear that blue shirt all the ladies in the office like so much," Clayton called after him.

Right. Like he was going to worry about what the ladies liked.

This was Bree. He didn't have to impress her with fashion.

Tonight would be about getting to know each other again. And moving forward.

It was a good plan.

"TABITHA, you're really cutting it close." Bree rubbed at her forehead. She had a major headache brewing. "I know. I know. Just drive carefully."

Six-thirty.

Bree reminded herself to breathe.

Patrick would be here in thirty minutes and Peter was still here.

"Oh, God."

Bree left the kitchen and went in search of her son. He was curled up on his bed playing a video game.

"You ready to go?"

"Uh-huh," he said as he simultaneously nodded without taking his eyes off the small screen of the handheld game player.

His backpack was on the bed beside him. He hadn't bothered taking off his shoes. His jacket was close by. He was ready.

But Tabitha wasn't. Layla had run out of gas coming home from a school club meeting.

Roy was out of town with work.

There was no one else to call. Her father couldn't drive anymore. Rarely even left the house.

Of course Layla couldn't be left on the side of the road with an empty gas tank.

Dear Lord.

"Breathe."

Unexpected things came up. Tabitha would get here. She'd already put the gas in Layla's car. She was on her way. It was cool.

Bree walked through the kitchen and living room and looked for signs of her son. Games, books, toys. She'd put everything away.

Like he didn't exist.

She stopped in the middle of the living room and looked around.

"This is ridiculous."

What was she doing?

She would tell Patrick. He deserved to know. More than that, Peter deserved to know. So did Nora. Just not tonight.

She needed a plan. Going about this the right way was extremely important for all concerned. There were many issues she and Patrick had to resolve before this thing went any further.

Her reasons for keeping Peter a secret in the beginning had been solid. Granted her father had had a heavy hand in the decision. But she had respected him, still did.

Even if he was the one to encourage her to marry Big Jack. Bree stopped. Closed her eyes. Her father wasn't responsible for her decisions. True, she had been vulnerable at the time, but, ultimately, she had made the decision. Jack fooled them all.

This was her mess to straighten out. Not her father's. Not even Jack's. She'd heard rumors of his bad-boy reputation before they'd married. But he'd worked overtime wooing her and she'd fallen for it. He hadn't been the answer to her needs or her son's.

The sound of gravel crunching beneath tires signaled that Tabitha had finally made it.

Thank God.

Bree grabbed her sweater and headed for the door. "Come on, sweetie. Your aunt Tabitha is here. You have to get going."

"Coming!" came the answering shout.

Bree felt weak with relief as she opened the door. "Boy, you about gave me a nervous—" Her brain registered what her eyes saw and her mouth snapped shut.

Tabitha wasn't climbing the steps to Bree's porch. Her minivan was just turning into the drive.

Patrick paused on the top step, glanced back at Tabitha's van then turned a questioning gaze on Bree. He wore a blue shirt that made his eyes look even more startlingly blue. "I'm early, I know, but—"

"Who are you?" Peter ducked under Bree's arm and bounded onto the porch.

Bree's heart nearly stopped.

Patrick stared at the boy. He wouldn't know his name or his age, but he would know his own eyes.

"I'm Peter." He pointed to Bree. "Are you here to see my mom?"

"Come inside, son." Bree was shocked that her voice was steady. She'd gone numb all over. Her legs were barely holding her upright.

Peter looked from Patrick to Bree. "But Aunt Tabitha's here."

Bree managed a stiff nod. "Right. Get your things."

Peter rushed through the doorway via the same route beneath her arm. She'd kept it planted in the door to ensure she remained vertical.

"Is everything all right, Bree?" Tabitha stood at

the bottom of the steps. She glanced at Patrick. The worry etched across her face told Bree she was torn between jumping to her sister's defense and taking Peter and running.

"You'll be late for your movie," Bree told her. "Things are fine here."

Peter burst past Bree and jumped off the porch. "Bye, Mom! Bye, mister!"

Tabitha didn't move. She stared at Bree, uncertain what to do.

Bree gestured for her to go. The numbness had abruptly been replaced by staggering emotions she couldn't begin to label. She didn't trust her voice enough to utter a single word.

Tabitha looked back twice before climbing into her van and driving away. Peter waved with both hands. He was completely innocent and oblivious to the tension squeezing the very air from Bree's lungs.

When the van's taillights were out of sight, Bree dared to meet the gaze cutting a hole straight through her heart.

"When did you plan to tell me?"

Patrick's face was hard. Bree had never seen that cold, icy look in his eyes.

"When he graduated from high school?" he demanded.

This was the moment she had dreaded, feared, for nearly eight years. Since the night Peter was born she had mulled over all the things she could or should say to Patrick when the time was right.

None of it would make a difference now.

Nothing she said was going to take that look off his face…or the mixture of disappointment and derision from his eyes.

This wasn't the beginning…it was the end.

Chapter Eight

Patrick settled onto the top step. Standing was no longer possible.

He had a son.

He didn't have to ask the boy's age any more than he had to ask who his father was.

Patrick had stared straight into the same blue eyes he saw in the mirror each morning.

Peter. His son's name was Peter.

Bree had kept this secret for...

Damn. Eight years.

Bree sat down next to him. She braced her arms on her knees. "At the time I thought it was the right thing to do."

Patrick closed his eyes. How could she have ever, ever thought this was the right thing to do?

"I was young. We..." She inhaled a deep, shaky breath. "You and I had parted on bad terms. My father didn't want me involved with...you."

"Since when did you allow your father to dictate your decisions?" Patrick knew better than that. Bree had always complained about how her mother's entire existence had seemed to revolve around her husband. She hadn't worked outside the home, hadn't even finished school. She'd married young and had children. Ignoring the symptoms so she wouldn't have to be away from her family, she'd waited too late to stop the cancer that ended up taking her life.

"I was pregnant." Bree stared out at the street. "I was afraid."

Afraid? Patrick turned his head, stared at her profile. "You? Afraid? I find that damned hard to believe."

"I don't know what to say."

Bree turned to face him. Her eyes were bright with emotion. He refused to feel anything but the anger roiling in his gut. She had stolen seven years of his son's life from him. Those years couldn't be gotten back, couldn't be made up. They were gone.

The rumors about Bree's marriage that Clayton had passed along abruptly slammed in Patrick's chest. Fury detonated again. "Did you let that bastard you were married to lay a hand on him?"

Bree shook her head. "Never. I never left him alone with Jack. And I…" She moistened her trembling lips, blinked back the emotion threatening. "He would have had to go through me to get to him."

The rest of what Clayton had told Patrick poked through his anger and sympathy trickled into his veins. "He hurt you?" Patrick didn't have to spell it out. She knew what he meant. If he'd had any doubts the fact that she looked away confirmed it.

"He did." Bree met his gaze once more. "But only once. I left after that."

Patrick tried to hang on to the idea that she'd already suffered enough to help cool his temper, but the realization of what she'd done, not for a month or a year or even two, but for seven long years pushed him over the edge. He lost the battle with his anger. "How could you keep him from me?"

He just couldn't fathom how she'd let so much time pass.

"I kept telling myself it was the right thing to do. You were in Utah. I was here and it…was easier."

"Out of sight, out of mind, right?" That was no excuse. He wasn't going to accept that answer.

"Maybe."

"I've been in Kenner County for six years, Bree. What's your excuse for that?"

The silence lengthened between them. He was beginning to think she wasn't even going to answer when she finally spoke.

"He was one by the time I saw you again. It was…too late. I didn't want to upset his life."

Too late. Patrick shook his head. "Does he even

know who I am?" Of course he didn't. He'd called Patrick mister.

She didn't have to answer that question. He knew.

Patrick stood. He couldn't talk to her anymore. He had to think. To clear his head and reach some place where reason presided.

"We'll finish this…later. I have to think this through."

He walked to his SUV without looking back. If he said anything else, he would likely say something he would regret. He reached for the door, felt ready to explode with frustration.

"Patrick!"

He took a breath, lifted his gaze to her. "What?"

"Dispatch just got a call about a disturbance at the Saloon. The perp is Sherman Watts."

That would mean Watts was drunk. And just maybe he would talk. "Let's go."

Bree dashed into the house and right back out. She strapped her utility belt and weapon around her hips as she rushed to his SUV.

Patrick started the engine and rammed into reverse. "Just so you know," he said, "I won't let you keep my son from me any longer."

THE KENNER CITY SALOON was a bar designed like an old Western saloon. Not Sherman Watts's typical hangout. Bree knew from the times in the past that she or one of her colleagues had picked him up he generally liked the sleazier joints.

Patrick pulled to the curb at the front entrance. A number of patrons were already milling around on the sidewalk.

"'Bout time the po' got here," someone said loud enough for Bree to hear.

Patrick hesitated at the double entry doors. "No heroics," he warned.

Bree didn't respond, just went inside. Her mind was whirling with this evening's events. She couldn't deal with anything else right now.

At least nothing personal.

Inside most of the remaining patrons were huddled in a corner discussing what was going down.

The saloon's one bouncer, dressed in a black tee that designated him as security, had Watts cornered at one end of the long bar.

"I don't care how many cops you call," Watts shouted at the bouncer. "I'm not going nowhere until I get my drink."

"Mr. Watts, the bartender cut you off. You can either take a taxi home or you can go with the cops when they get here."

Patrick entered Watts's line of sight and propped on the bar. "Maybe the man will settle down if he gets his drink."

The bouncer looked at Patrick as if he'd lost his mind. "You for real, Sheriff?"

Patrick eased onto the closest stool. "Absolutely. I'll make sure Mr. Watts gets home."

The bouncer shrugged and walked away.

Watts swaggered over to the bar and pounded the top. "Give me that JD!"

Bree didn't sit. She crossed her arms over her chest and glared at Watts. "Sounds like your taste in whiskey has changed for the better, Sherman. Since when did you bother with anything that has a reputable label?"

The bartender slapped a glass on the counter. Watts picked it up, lifted it high as if toasting Bree. "That's right. I'm all about moving up."

Bree despised this lowlife. He should be tossed into the pokey and the key be thrown away. "Why don't you do us all a favor and move right on up to Montana or someplace like that?"

Watts laughed. "Maybe I will. This place is going to the dogs." He sneered at her. "Nothing but bitches to pick from."

"Watch yourself, Watts," Patrick cautioned.

Bree had let this guy's name-calling go when they interviewed him at his friend's trailer. Considering what she'd already been through this evening, she wasn't taking any grief from him tonight.

"I guess you thought Julie Grainger was a bitch, too," Bree suggested. She hated that word. Hated scumbags like Watts who just kept repeating the same crimes over and over until they got bored and escalated to something worse. Like rape or murder.

Watts's expression sobered instantly. "I don't know what you're talking about, Detective. I told you I didn't know that fed."

"We have a witness who says you did," Patrick countered. "That you were engaged in a heated exchange with Grainger only a few days before she was murdered. That makes you a person of interest to this case."

Watts shook his head drunkenly. "The only heated exchange I'd like to do is with your sidekick here." He hitched a thumb in Bree's direction. "You nailed that yet, Sheriff?"

The next thing that happened startled Bree so that she could only stand there, stunned.

Patrick jumped off the stool, grabbed Watts by the lapels of his shirt and jerked him close. "How about I nail your ass to the wall for murder? You could make all kinds of friends in prison."

Two Kenner City officers charged into the saloon at that moment. Lucky for Patrick. Bree was pretty sure he was about to cross a line he knew better than to cross. Her emotions were raw, his no doubt were as well. He wasn't thinking rationally.

"Take this piece of crap in for drunk and disorderly conduct," Patrick instructed one of the officers as he shoved Watts toward the other one. He glanced at the bartender. "I guess he won't need that drink after all."

The bartender shrugged and took the glass away.

Watts laughed as the officer cuffed him. "You shouldda slugged me while you had the chance, Sheriff. Maybe you don't have the guts to be a man."

"Come on, Watts." The officer pushed Watts into motion.

The second officer started reading Watts his rights.

"I know my rights," the jerk muttered.

As he was hauled past Bree, Watts stalled. "You come on down to the jail and see me, little girl. I like squaws."

Watts laughed like the idiot he was as the officers hauled him from the saloon. The huddled patrons watched until he was gone then took their places once more. The night was young, they still had drinking and partying and celebrating to do.

Bree walked out of the saloon. She was spent emotionally. She needed to go home and forget this day had happened. She'd had more than enough grief and worry and anger for one day.

She dragged out her cell and called her sister. Gave her location and closed the phone. The last thing she wanted to do was climb back into that vehicle with Patrick. She couldn't take anymore tonight. She couldn't bear the way he looked at her.

"I can take you home." He paused next to her.

She turned to him, looked him square in the eyes. "No. You can't. We both need to think. I can't deal with anything else."

"I'm not leaving you standing out here like this."

Bree threw her hands up. "It's a public street, Patrick. There are lots of lights and people all over the place. My sister will be here in fifteen minutes. Just go home and leave me alone."

She was perfectly capable of taking care of herself. Fury twisted inside her. She just wanted this night to be over. She wanted to hold her son in her arms until she fell asleep and then to forget this day ever happened.

Patrick got into his SUV but didn't drive away until her sister's minivan arrived.

Bree settled into the passenger seat.

"You okay?"

Bree couldn't answer. If she spoke, if she even looked at Tabitha, she would burst into tears.

Because she was not okay.

PATRICK PARKED in front of the Morning Ray Café. He couldn't go home. He'd thought he could, but he couldn't.

He had to talk to someone.

The only person who could possibly understand was his mother.

Nora Martinez lived above the little restaurant that had been her saving grace. She'd been telling Patrick that since he was a kid. After his father had died she'd needed something. Her only child was in school everyday and didn't need so much of her time and attention. Nora had needed this to fill in the gaps.

Patrick had come home from school to his mother's warm hugs and the smell of home-cooked meals and desserts. She'd worked hard to be mother and father. Still did.

She would understand and be able to explain what he was feeling.

The ache in his soul was something he had never experienced before. He kept seeing that little boy with those big blue eyes.

His boy.

The one who didn't even know his name.

He climbed from his SUV and shuffled to the door. Exhaustion clawed at him. Not a physical weariness, but an emotional one.

He pressed the buzzer that let his mother know when after-hours deliveries arrived. He had a key but he didn't want to startle her.

It took a minute or two but soon she was padding across the tiled floor in her robe and house slippers. She worked hard all day being the perfect hostess and chef. The nights were her haven from the noise and the crowd. Though she loved every minute of it, she needed her down time as well.

She shoved the key into the plate glass door, her face puckered in confusion.

"Is something wrong, son?"

Only everything.

But he wasn't a little boy anymore, he was a grown man. Crying was out of the question, though he felt exactly like doing exactly that.

"I need to talk."

"Well, come on in." She took him by the arm and tugged him inside. "You want some coffee?" She locked the door and turned to him. "Something to eat?"

He wasn't sure he could deal with food or even anything to drink. He just needed her to listen and help him make sense of this…this news.

He shook his head.

"Well, come on, let's go upstairs. I'll turn my DVR off. I can watch my soaps another time."

That made him smile. His mother was addicted to the daytime soaps. She had been for as long as he could remember.

Upstairs she settled on the comfy old sofa she'd had forever. "Sit down, Patrick." Her brow furrowed with worry. "It can't be that bad."

He lowered into the chair directly across from her. "It's…not good." That felt like the wrong thing to say. Learning that he had a son wasn't wrong…it was everything else that was not right.

"It's about Bree, isn't it?"

His mother had always been able to read him like a book. "Yeah, it's about Bree."

Nora curled her legs under her and sank deeper into the big cushions. "Start at the beginning, Patrick. You know how I hate it when you leave out parts."

Where exactly was the beginning? Their relationship had ended eight years ago. But Nora knew all about that. No need to start that far back.

"When Bree and I ended our relationship, she was pregnant."

Surprise flared in his mother's eyes. "Oh."

"Yeah. Oh." He scrubbed his hands over his face and wished he knew how to feel about this. Mad. Sick. Disgusted. Anything would be better than this turmoil of emotions playing tug of war inside him.

"Obviously, she didn't tell you," Nora guessed.

He moved his head from side to side. "I found out tonight when I saw my seven-year-old son for the first time."

Her breath caught.

"He…he looks just like I did when I was a kid." Patrick stared at his hands. "Same hair. Same eyes. Everything."

"Did Bree say why she didn't tell you?"

It didn't matter why. It was wrong, no matter the

excuse. "She said she thought, at the time, it was the right thing to do. Her father didn't want me in the picture. Probably because I'm not Ute. She did what he told her."

Nora digested that information for a moment. "And you don't believe that?"

He dropped his head back on the chair. "For as long as I've known Bree she was her own woman. She doesn't take any grief from anyone and she definitely doesn't let anyone tell her how to live her life."

"But," Nora cut in before he could continue, "she was young. Pregnant. And scared."

Bree had said that.

Patrick just couldn't swallow that excuse. "She's the most fearless female I know." He met his mother's gaze. "Besides you. That's a cop-out if I've ever heard one. She just didn't want to tell me. To punish me or something."

Nora shrugged. "Maybe a little, but you don't know how it feels to wake up one day and learn you're carrying another life inside you, Patrick. It's an overwhelming rush of anticipation and excitement and most of all fear. Every decision you make, every move you make, even what you eat and drink affects that tiny life growing inside you. It's a humbling experience, dear. I'm certain she was terrified. Especially considering the two of you had ended your relationship on such bad terms."

How could his mother take her side? "Okay, so maybe she was scared at first. But what about a year later. Or two years later? We're talking more than seven here, Mom, and I still wouldn't have known if I hadn't shown up at her house early tonight."

Nora's face softened. "What's his name?"

Patrick closed his eyes and envisioned his son. "Peter."

Nora repeated the name. "I like that." She settled her gaze onto Patrick's. "There's only one thing to do."

He was all ears.

"You and Bree have to work this out. The important thing here is the boy. He needs both of you and you both deserve to be a part of his life. So, do whatever it takes but work it out."

That was a lot of help. "How am I supposed to do that?"

"Well, that's simple. Patrick, my mother had an old saying about moments like this."

There she went with her mother's sage advice. "Mom—"

"If you're walking down the road and you come upon a mule in the ditch—" she turned her palms up "—you don't ask why the mule is in the ditch, you just get it out."

"What does a mule have to do with the fact that I'm a father and nobody bothered to tell me?" He needed clarification not more confusion.

"You have to get that mule out of the ditch, Patrick. Remember, it doesn't matter why it's in the ditch, you just have to get it out. Wasting time wondering why is just that, a waste. We have a tendency to waste a lot of time wondering why. Why are we too short or too fat? Why are prices so high? Why don't we make enough money? Why does so-and-so have this or that? Don't waste any more time. Get the mule out of the ditch, son."

As if his thoughts and feelings had suddenly all lined up and fell right into place, he knew exactly what he had to do. He smiled weakly at his mother. "You're the smartest woman I know."

"I'm not smart, son. I've just lived a lot more years than you." Nora pressed a hand to her chest. "I have a grandson."

And Patrick was a father.

A father who wanted to be a part of his son's life. All he had to do was get that mule out of the ditch.

He thought about the way he'd reacted tonight. And of how afraid and vulnerable Bree must have been to make the decision she made.

The why didn't matter...all that mattered was his son.

And Bree.

They would work this out.

Tomorrow morning he would call her and make

the first move. He would give her tonight to think about things. Then they would form a plan.

Pride wasn't going to get in the way of doing the right thing.

Patrick was man enough to admit that what happened eight years ago was as much his fault as Bree's. He wouldn't give her another reason to run from him or to avoid him.

Even if they were never anything more than friends, their son had to come first.

He'd been right about needing to mend fences. Tomorrow he would take the first step.

Chapter Nine

Bree stood at the kitchen sink, the coffee she held getting cold.

She stared at nothing in particular. Her son's swing set in the backyard…the picnic table they used so much during the summer months.

In a few minutes it would be time to wake her son to get ready for school. For now she continued to stand there feeling empty and so tired.

Sleep had been impossible. Her sister had brought Peter home around ten-thirty. She'd wanted to talk and to comfort Bree, but Bree hadn't been able to talk. Her emotions had been too raw.

Tabitha had finally, reluctantly gone home. But she'd left Bree with one piece of advice. *"Remember, after every storm comes the calm."*

Bree wasn't so sure about that this time.

This was like a massive earthquake that had hit, ripping open her life and tossing every aspect this way and that. An earthquake she had known for years was coming and still she hadn't been prepared.

Patrick was hurt and angry. She could understand that. He had no intention of being left out of his son's life again. And she understood that, as well. But because of the way he'd found out—no, that wasn't right. Because of what she had done, deceiving him for all these years, their relationship would be strained. He would never trust her again. How could she blame him?

There was absolutely no way to make this right.

Fear and uncertainty had prompted her to make the wrong decision. Selfishness and the feeling of being in too deep to turn back had kept her making those same decisions.

Now everyone would pay the price.

Her cell vibrated and she pulled it from its holster. Dispatch.

"Hunter."

"Detective Hunter, the sheriff's department called. Sheriff Martinez needs you to meet him ASAP."

God, had there been another murder? Bree's first thought was that something had happened to Agent Ben Parrish. He seemed to be high on everyone's suspect list at the moment. If Parrish was somehow involved with the bad guys in this case, she imagined his colleagues at the Bureau were the least of his worries.

"Give me the location." Bree grabbed the pen and pad on the counter and jotted down the directions. "Thanks. I'm on my way."

Bree stared at the location. Pretty much a deserted canyon area. Images from the desolate place where Grainger's body had been found filtered through her mind. *Don't let it be another murder.*

She tucked her phone away and glanced at the clock—6:15 a.m. She would need to get Peter up a few minutes early. Tabitha or Layla would have to take him to school. Bree didn't know what she would do without her family's support. She couldn't fathom how single moms with no network of family or friends survived.

Patrick wouldn't have asked her to meet him like this unless it was important. She supposed he had dispatch call her because he hadn't wanted to speak directly to her. Not that she could blame him. She'd had her reasons for making the decisions she had made. He had his reasons for reacting the way he was now. They were only human and they would both have to come to terms with those feelings.

Bree called her sister who promised to be there in fifteen minutes. Thankfully Tabitha had always been an early riser.

Setting her coffee aside, Bree summoned her missing-in-action courage and pushed away all the uncertainty and niggling fears. It was time to stop whining and fretting about it and face the music. She had a job to do and a life to live.

That was the thing. Agent Grainger had lost her life way too early. She'd been so young. Bree wasn't about to take another moment of hers for granted. This thing with Patrick would work out in time.

Meanwhile she should get her son up and moving. She never liked to leave without giving him a hug and telling him she loved him.

For a moment she stood at the door to his bedroom and watched him sleep. So trusting, so peaceful. His little world was about to change. But it would be for the better. He wanted a father in his life. Now he would have a good one.

One who might never forgive Bree, but Patrick would be an outstanding father.

Further proof she had made the wrong decisions.

Enough. No looking back, only forward.

"Peter." She shook him gently. "Time to get ready for school."

His eyes opened and he frowned. "Not yet."

"Yes, yet," Bree scolded. "Your aunt Tabitha will be here soon and you need to be up and dressed.

Peter frowned. "Do you have to go to work early?"

Bree nodded. "I have to meet the sheriff and I can't be late."

"Okay." Peter got up and dragged himself across the hall to the bathroom.

Bree went back to the kitchen to make his favorite breakfast. Toast and cereal. He preferred picking out his own clothes for the day. Like his father, Peter had very strong ideas about his likes and dislikes.

Five minutes later Tabitha arrived.

Bree was all set to say good morning and get going but Tabitha waylaid her. "There's something I need to tell you."

Bree glanced at the clock. "Make it fast. I really have to go."

"Yesterday after Layla picked Peter up from school they came by here for a couple of hours so he could work on his science project."

The project was due next week. Her son was required to do it all on his own, no help from parents. Bree had no idea what exactly he was doing on his computer but he assured her it was almost finished.

"Did something happen?" Bree didn't like the new kind of worry she saw in her sister's eyes. Bree's problems seemed to be piling up on her sister and that wasn't fair. How would she ever repay Tabitha for all that she'd done?

"Sort of. Layla said it had happened a couple of times before." Tabitha shrugged. "Last week, I think. But last night was different. The phone rang three different times in the space of two hours."

"What do you mean the phone rang? Who called?"

"That's just it, whoever it was kept hanging up when Layla said hello. It was weird. She didn't mention it to me until last night."

"I'll look into it." Bree's instincts warned that it was the same person who was watching her. Who'd left her that warning. She couldn't play off this situation any longer. She had to start taking it a lot more seriously.

"One more thing, Bree."

"Tabitha, honey, I really gotta go."

"I know. I know." Tabitha put her hand on Bree's arm. "Just remember that Patrick is a good man. A really good man. He'll get over his anger and come to terms with the decisions you made."

Bree could only hope.

"Besides—" Tabitha smiled "—Peter is going to be thrilled to have a daddy who's a sheriff. That's pretty cool for a boy, you know."

"That's true." Bree hugged her sister. "Okay, I gotta go. Otherwise the sheriff is going to be mad at me for being late. We don't need to add fuel to the fire."

"Go," Tabitha urged.

Bree called bye to her son and had made it to the porch, hit the button on the remote to unlock the SUV's doors and realized she had better make a bathroom run before heading out. There were no bathrooms in the canyons.

Back in the house, Bree did her business, washed her hands and checked her reflection. She felt calmer now. She could do this. Patrick wasn't a bear. He was a good guy. A man she had once loved…still loved on some level.

This would all work out…eventually.

Bree repeated her goodbyes as she passed through the living room and out the door.

Patrick would be waiting…and maybe another body.

PATRICK PACED the distance between his SUV and the road entering the canyon one more time.

Why had Bree wanted him to meet her here?

If a crime had been committed there was no indication. No official vehicles. No Bree. No victim.

If she wanted to talk to him she'd picked a hell of a place. They certainly wouldn't be interrupted.

He set his hands on his hips and did a three-sixty survey of the canyon. They would definitely have privacy.

There had to be a mistake. He fished his cell phone from his jacket pocket. It was damned chilly to be meeting outside like this for anything other than official business.

He'd just entered Bree's cell number and gotten the no service message when a cloud of dust appeared in the distance.

Now he would find out what was going on. Patrick put his phone away and waited for Bree to reach his position and park.

She climbed out of the SUV, her gaze colliding with his. "What's going on?"

A frown worried his brow. "I was about to ask you the same thing."

Bree stopped a few steps away, turned all the way around to survey their surroundings. "What do you mean?" She searched his face. "You asked me to meet you here."

Wait. "No. You asked me to meet you here."

What the hell was going on?

Patrick took another long look around. The craggy cliffs that surrounded the canyon had snow hanging on the tops. Sprigs of desert grass managed to survive here and there. A couple of old mine shafts were boarded up. One had been vandalized with spray paint and a couple of the boards serving as a barrier to the opening were missing. "I think we've been set up."

"By who?"

Patrick rubbed his hand over his jaw, his instincts moving to the next level. "I don't think we're deep enough into the Grainger case for it to be about that." Sherman Watts crossed his mind. This could be his way of getting even.

No, that couldn't be right. That weasel would

likely still be in jail this morning. Unless one of his buddies had gotten him released. Funny thing was, Watts didn't really have any friends. Not real friends. He had drinking and gambling buddies. Certainly none had the means to post bail.

"I'm calling dispatch to find out what's going on here," Bree said, reaching for her cell phone.

"No service," Patrick warned.

The rear door of Bree's borrowed SUV opened. Patrick's hand was on the butt of his weapon in a heartbeat.

Bree whirled around, her own hand going to her weapon as well.

"Where are we?" Bree's son, Peter, bailed out of the backseat. "I never been here before."

"Peter!" Bree rushed to her son and crouched down to his level. "What were you doing hiding in there? Your aunt Tabitha will be worried sick. You have to go to school."

Bree stood, reached for her cell. Huffed a breath of frustration when she saw that Patrick was right, no service. Bree shook her head. "Tabitha will be scared to death."

Patrick's gaze settled on the boy. His heart started to pound. The child looked like a carbon copy of him at that age.

"Peter." Bree shook her head. "You shouldn't have sneaked off from your aunt Tabitha." She stared at the cell phone in her hand as if she'd forgotten what she was supposed to do next. "I...I need to call dispatch and find out what's going on." But she couldn't...no damned service.

Patrick looked from her to the boy. He couldn't stop staring at him. He was—

"Are you my daddy?"

The impact of the question slammed Patrick square in the chest. He looked from the boy to Bree. What was he supposed to say?

Bree looked as terrified and confused as Patrick.

A snap, then a far too familiar ring echoed through the canyon.

Rifle shot.

"Get down!"

Bree was already flying to the ground, her body shielding her son as she took him down with her.

Patrick hit the dirt.

The next shot sent a puff of dust into the air not two feet from his head.

He'd hoped the first shot was a mistake.

But that wasn't the case.

Someone was shooting at them.

Chapter Ten

Bree tried to roll, with Peter in tow, toward her vehicle. A bullet pinged into the side of her SUV.

Peter wailed. "Mommy!"

Damn. Bree's heart threatened to burst from her chest. She had to do something.

"Head for the rocks," Patrick shouted. "I'll cover you."

"Come on, baby," Bree urged, her throat so dry she could hardly speak. "Crawl with Mommy."

Ensuring Peter stayed beneath her, Bree moved onto all fours and started the slow, treacherous journey toward the base of the mountain. Patrick returned fire. The thundering sounds echoing over and over before fading into the distance.

God, she had to hurry. When he had to reload…

Bree made it to the first pile of boulders.

Thank God.

She pulled Peter into her arms and huddled behind the rock mass.

One second, then two of silence sent a new rush of adrenaline searing through her veins.

Patrick. He'd had to stop firing to reload.

The distinct rifle bursts pierced the air.

She couldn't just sit here. She had to do something.

First, call for backup. Instinctively, she reached for her phone. Wouldn't help. "Damn!"

Okay, okay, think. She had to make sure Peter was safe and then she had to give Patrick backup. Shots from his .40 caliber service weapon popped loudly in punctuation of her reasoning.

Bree surveyed the area behind their hiding place. The base of the mountain. Cracks and crevices. Wait. An old mine shaft. It was boarded up but some of the boards were missing. She visually measured the distance. They could make it.

"Peter, listen to me."

Her son was sobbing. His body shook with fear.

"It's okay, sweetie. We're gonna keep you safe. Now listen to me, okay? It's really important."

Watery blue eyes peered up at her.

"You see that hole over there between the boards?" She pointed to the spot.

Peter nodded. "A cave?"

"Sort of." Gold and silver mining had been rampant in these mountains and canyons during the nineteenth century. Peter had learned about those in school but he was scared right now and not thinking clearly.

"I'm going to hide you in there so I can help the sheriff, okay?"

Peter didn't look to sure of that. "You can't stay with me?"

"I have to help, son."

He nodded. "Okay."

Bree peeked beyond the enormous boulder that protected them from the shooter's view. Patrick had rolled close to his SUV. He couldn't possibly have any more clips handy. There was always one in the weapon and another on the utility belt.

She had to do something. Fast.

"Come on, baby." Bree pulled her son close. "Let's get you to a safe place."

Bree decided on a route that took the most advantage of every boulder and rock between their position and the opening she needed to reach.

"When I start moving," Bree instructed her son, "you stay under Mommy like before." He was getting to be a big boy. But she could shield his body fairly well even if it did make moving difficult. "Remember not to stop unless I stop."

She got a shaky nod in reply.

Bree got into position. "Let's go."

Moving together, they half crawled, half scooted across the cool dirt and rocks. The rifle shots were interspersed between Patrick's louder blasts. If the shooter was still aiming for Patrick that meant he hadn't noticed their movements.

Please, God, let Patrick keep him occupied.

A thud hit the dirt right on her heels. She didn't have to look back to know she and Peter were now targets.

"Faster, baby," she urged as her arms and legs frantically worked to propel them forward.

The last dive for the opening between the boards was accompanied by two pings into the rock right next to the opening.

Damned close.

She urged Peter deep into the darkness.

"It's dark, Mommy."

"Keep going. It'll be all right."

When she felt they were a safe distance inside, she reached for the flashlight on her belt. "You can hold this but don't turn it on unless you absolutely have to. And turn it that way." She wrapped his shaking hands around the flashlight and pointed it away from the opening they'd entered.

She collapsed on her butt. Her arms and legs were trembling.

They were okay.

For now.

Patrick.

She had to make sure he was okay.

"Stay right here, sweetie," she implored. "I'm gonna check on the sheriff."

"No." Peter grabbed her jacket. "Don't go back out there."

Bree hugged her son, fought the tears. "I have to help, baby. You know that. It's my job."

When Peter had calmed a bit, she gave him another tight hug. "Stay right here. Be very quiet. And I'll be back before you know it."

"Okay." His voice was thin and high pitched. He was scared to death.

Bree made her way back to the opening. Though she couldn't see much of anything she was pretty sure this was a shaft that had been used in the early, primitive mining days. Which could mean it wasn't the safest place to hide. But right now she had no choice.

She paused in the shadows near the opening. Listened. Patrick's .40 caliber popped off another round. He was close. He must have sought cover nearer to her location.

Another rifle ping landed near the rocks where she and Peter had first taken refuge. The shooter was coming closer. He likely knew Patrick would soon be out of ammo.

"Patrick!" Normally she wouldn't call out and give her location away, but the shooter already knew exactly where she was.

"Stay where you are!" Patrick commanded.

Could she throw a clip hard enough to reach his position? Bree chewed her lower lip, tried to gauge the distance.

Maybe.

"I'm going to toss you my extra clip," she called out to him.

A ping zapped the edge of the opening. She jerked her head back.

"Stay back!" Patrick shouted, his voice gruff.

Bree ignored his warning. She grabbed the clip from her belt, waited for the next rifle shot.

She thrust her upper body through the opening and threw the clip as hard as she could.

Drawing quickly back inside, she shouted, "I tossed it near the three rocks clustered together."

"Stay out of sight, Bree!"

She'd done all she could.

Now she waited.

Until Patrick nailed the son of a bitch. Or backup arrived. Though they didn't have cell service, Tabitha would be frantic to get in touch with Bree. She would call dispatch and dispatch would send someone to this location.

If neither of those things happened she would be forced to stay put…until the bastard came charging into this shaft.

Bree crawled back to where Peter huddled. She

positioned herself in front of him, braced her arms on her bent knees and took aim at the opening.

If the shooter came through that opening he was a dead man.

PATRICK SCRAMBLED toward the cluster of rocks. Hit the ground on his belly and snatched up the clip.

Two, three bullets rained around him like hail.

He rolled back to take cover behind the larger boulder.

There was no choice at this point but to wait the bastard out. If he thought he'd hit Patrick he might just come closer enough to kill.

Fury tightened Patrick's lips.

He'd only just learned of his son's existence. And Bree. Bree was back in his life, on shaky ground but back nonetheless. No son of a bitch was going to take that from him.

He opened his cell phone again and tried to get a call through.

Not enough service.

Dammit.

The next rifle shot sounded a hell of a lot closer.

Patrick smiled.

"Come on, you bastard," he muttered.

Patrick braced his back against the boulder, knees bent, hands wrapped around his weapon.

A muscle started to flex in his jaw in the ensuing silence.

"Come on."

A rumble echoed in the canyon.

What the hell?

Patrick tensed. Listened hard.

Definitely not a weapon firing. Not vehicles arriving, though that would be nice as hell.

Another thundering rumble.

And then he knew.

The cave or old mine shaft.

His chest seized.

Another fierce rumble reverberated around him.

Dust flew from the opening of the abandoned mine shaft where Bree and Peter had sought refuge.

Terror lit in Patrick's veins.

He shot to his feet, not caring about the danger, and charged toward the opening.

Another dust cloud burst free of the rocks.

Then there was silence.

Patrick stilled.

His heart swelled in his chest until he thought it would explode.

He started forward again.

"Don't move."

Patrick froze.

"One more step and you're dead."

Chapter Eleven

Bree coughed hard. She scrambled up.

Peter?

She shook her baby gently. She'd been lying flat on top of him.

"Baby?"

He whimpered.

Thank God.

"Are you okay, baby?"

"It hurts." He moaned.

Oh, God.

The flashlight. She needed the flashlight!

She felt around where he lay. Where was it?

He moaned softly and started to sob.

"Just let me find the flashlight, sweetie, and Mommy will take care of you." Her heart pounded like a drum inside her rib cage.

"I got it," he mumbled. Peter bumped her with the flashlight.

Relief flooded her. "You did good, baby." Thank God. Thank God.

She clicked on the flashlight and started her examination. Tears spilled from his eyes and his face was contorted with pain but there was no blood. No sign of injury around his head and neck.

"Where do you hurt, baby?" Torso area was also clear of blood. No visible injuries.

"My leg." He cried out. "Oh, my leg!"

The ache that bloomed inside her forced her to swallow a moan.

She guided the light to his legs. "I'm going to touch your legs one at a time, okay?" He moaned but didn't protest further.

She moved her fingers gently down his right leg. No protests. Nothing felt out of the ordinary. Now for the left one.

The instant her fingers touched his left thigh he cried out. "It's okay. I'll be very careful."

Her pulse hammered. All the possibilities, including internal blood loss, if something major was broken badly enough, raced through her mind.

"You tell me if the part I'm touching hurts." She moved slowly down the thigh. Then over the knee. When her fingers eased down his calf, he screamed.

Bree jerked her hand back. "It's okay, it's okay." Tears streamed down her dusty cheeks. She leaned carefully over him and pressed her cheek to his. "It's not so bad," she promised. She tried hard not to allow her voice to shake but she wasn't entirely successful.

She checked him over once more. Hips and pelvis were clear of blood.

She raised up once more. "Okay, baby, I'm going to touch you, starting with your head. You tell me if anything else hurts, okay?"

Please, God, don't let there be any more collapsing in this shaft.

Peter whimpered through the examination but insisted that nothing hurt but his leg. His reflexes appeared fine. Pupils were a little dilated but that could be from the fear. Or the consuming darkness beyond the flashlight's beam.

Hell, she didn't know.

Everything she'd learned in her emergency training course was suddenly out the window.

If she had a knife. Scissors. Anything she could use to remove the pants leg and check out the damage. But she didn't dare move him.

She sat back on her haunches. Tried to think. "I'm going to check your feet. Is that all right? I'll be really careful."

"Don't make it hurt more, Mommy, please."

Why couldn't it have been her? She'd give anything to take away his pain.

"I'll do my best."

She swallowed. Her throat was so dry it hurt. With painstaking care she untied and wiggled off his right shoe. "Everything okay here?" she asked as she palpitated his foot.

"Yes." He moaned.

"Let's try the other one."

Bree untied the left shoe, then held her breath as she slowly removed it. She examined his foot. "Doesn't hurt here?"

He moved his head from side to side.

"Good." She wished she could examine his calf more closely. The best she could tell there might be a compound fracture. There was a significant lump about midway down the length of his calf. Felt like the bone was split completely apart but there was no dampness to indicate it had pierced the skin.

But what did she know? She was a cop!

Stay calm. If Peter sensed she was upset, it would make him more upset. She had to be brave so he could be brave.

"Are we gonna get outta here?" he asked softly.

Fear made her tremble. "Of course we are. Patrick is right outside. I'll bet he's already getting help." If he was still alive.

Bree closed her eyes and forced the images away. Agent Grainger's face kept swimming in front of her eyes.

No. Patrick couldn't be dead.

They were all going to be fine.

Think like a cop, Bree. Don't think like a victim or a mother. Think like a cop.

"I'm going to get as close to the opening as I can and call out to Patrick. Maybe he'll hear me."

Peter's sobs grew frantic. "Don't leave me."

"I'll be right over there. You'll be able to see the flashlight." They weren't more than twelve or fifteen feet from where the opening had been.

"No!" he wailed.

"It's like when you were younger and I'd check your closet," she assured him. "You would be on the bed and you could see me across the room looking in the closet. Okay?"

He nodded jerkily.

Bree took her time, scrambled over the debris. Her senses were ever alert for the slightest sound or filtering of dust that might indicate another collapse was imminent. Thank God she'd recognized what the rumbling meant in time to cover Peter's body. Evidently a falling rock had hit his leg where it lay between hers. She'd pretty much sprawled over him in an effort to protect his trunk and head.

When she'd gone as far as she could, she turned the flashlight beam to the side and looked for any sign of light that might be creeping through.

Nothing.

Did that mean they would run out of oxygen?

Wasn't that the worry when a mine collapsed?

Stop. They weren't underground. This wasn't the same kind of situation. They were going to be fine. Patrick would get them out of here.

Bree took a deep breath, coughed hard. When her lungs had stopped scizing, she took another deep breath and called out, "Patrick!"

She listened for any sound. Nothing. All she could hear was blood roaring in her ears.

"Patrick!"

Still nothing.

There was no way she could dig her way out of here. The rocks were too large. Moving one might start more trouble.

Bree took a moment to calm herself. She couldn't let Peter see her mounting fear.

When she'd pulled herself together again, she crawled over the rocks and debris to where he lay.

"Doing okay?"

He nodded. His eyes were puffy from crying. Bree glanced back at the mass of rocks that lay between them and freedom. For now there was nothing she could do but hope help would reach them soon.

Except... She peered down at her son. She could try to make him feel better.

Bree crept around to his right to lie next to him. It was a lumpy bed but she didn't care. She laid the flashlight between them, letting the beam light up their faces.

"Just think," she said, "when your friends hear about this they're going to be thinking you're a superhero."

Peter made a sound that might have been a laugh.

She swiped the hair from his face, wiped his damp cheeks. "I'll bet none of your friends have ever done this."

He shook his head. "I'll be the only one."

Bree smiled. "You sure will."

Peter licked his lips. "Is that man really my daddy?"

Bree's lashes brimmed with tears once more. "Yes. He's your daddy. His name is Patrick Martinez. He's the sheriff of Kenner County." Dear God, she had made such a tragic mistake.

"He's a good guy then, not like Big Jack."

"Not at all like Jack," Bree agreed.

"He looks like me."

Bree laughed. "Yes, he does." So very, very much.

"Has he caught a lot of bad guys like you?"

"Even more." Pride replaced some of the pain in her chest. "All the good people in Four Corners, especially in Kenner County, love your daddy."

Peter turned his face to hers. "Do you love him like Robby's mom loves his dad?"

The tears won the battle and rolled past her lashes. "Yes, I do."

"Tell me stories about my daddy," Peter said. "It makes me feel better to hear you talk."

"Sure, baby." She wiggled a little closer. "I'll tell you all the stories you want to hear. And the next thing you know help will be here."

Please, God, don't let her be wrong.

"DROP YOUR GUN."

Patrick considered his options. He could toss his weapon and get shot in the back. Or he could make a dive for cover and get shot anyway.

He'd go for Plan C. Even though he didn't exactly have a Plan C.

"If we don't get help," he said slowly, "Bree and her son will die in there. They may be hurt."

The bastard behind him laughed. "Maybe you don't get it yet, but that's the point. I've been planning ways to kill that bitch for months now. I took my time, though. Wanted to give her a good scare first."

"You must be the ex." At least the question of who was harassing Bree was solved.

"That's right. And if I can't have her no one else will. Just knowing she's breathing makes me sick."

Patrick had to make a move. He had to do something. Bree and Peter could be hurt. It would take time for help to get here and time was wasting.

Patrick wasn't about to lose either one of them. "Why don't we talk about this rationally? So far you're only guilty of harassment. You let them die in there and it'll be murder. I don't think you really want to spend the rest of your life in prison."

"Who says I'm going to prison?"

He had moved closer. Patrick braced himself for action.

"Well, since you left your prints all over her SUV," Patrick lied, "it'll be a simple matter to tie you to this."

"But I didn't leave any prints."

He was coming closer.

"Are you sure? The crime lab says differently."

Hesitation.

He was trying to remember if he'd made a mistake. "No way," he finally said. "No way. And I made all those calls from public phones. I wore gloves when I left that message on her SUV. I got friends who'll swear I was with them this morning. No way I can be tied to any of it."

Patrick laughed. Thankfully it didn't sound as nervous as he felt. "I wouldn't count on any of your friends. We've been talking to a few of them and they were only too willing to share what you've been up to." Patrick was taking a risk bluffing like this. But, at this point, he had nothing to lose.

"I said drop your weapon." The business end of the rifle rammed into his back.

Patrick flinched. He had to wrap this up. If Bree or Peter were hurt… "All right. No need to get excited."

"I am excited," he growled, leaning close to the back of Patrick's head. "I want to watch from up on those cliffs as they cart her body out of that damned hole. It would've been more fun to shoot her between the eyes, but this'll work."

Patrick stiffened. The images the bastard's words evoked made his gut clench.

"Now drop it."

Patrick bent at the knees and slowly lowered into a crouch to do as the man said. "I'm putting my weapon down. Just stay cool."

Patrick placed the weapon on the ground.

Uncurled his fingers from around it.

This was it.

Act or die.

Since Patrick had no intention of dying today, he opted to act.

He propelled his body into a spin, crashed into the bastard's legs and twisted.

The impact threw the man off balance. The bastard flew backwards. The rifle discharged into the air.

Patrick got a swing in, an uppercut to his jaw. He grunted but recovered quickly. He rammed a fist into Patrick's chest. Patrick groaned, went for his throat.

They rolled. One minute Patrick was on top, the next the bastard was.

But Patrick had something going for him that this bastard didn't have. Sheer desperation.

Patrick got astride him and punched him in the face. He grunted. Patrick thought of how this bastard had hurt Bree and threatened Peter and he punched him over and over until he was no longer moving.

Patrick couldn't stop. He kept seeing this guy hurt Bree.

Harder and harder he rammed his fist into the bastard's face.

Stop. Patrick hesitated, his fist halfway to the bastard's nose again.

Enough. Getting to Bree and Peter was more important than beating this guy to death.

Patrick retrieved a pair of nylon cuffs from his SUV and secured his prisoner.

For good measure he kicked him in the side. A grunting sound escaped his mouth though he was clearly unconscious.

Patrick left the guy lying there and went in search of his cell phone. He opened it, glowered at the lack of signal bars.

"Dammit!" He'd forgotten. No damned service.

He rushed to the opening that had collapsed and called Bree's name. No answer. He called out to her again, but still nothing.

He pulled away some of the fallen boulders. All the tugging and pulling didn't seem to be getting him anywhere. He needed help.

He raced to his SUV, drove like a bat out of hell to the entrance of the canyon. He checked his phone.

Thankfully every bar was lit up.

He called dispatch, advised them of the situation. He closed the phone and tucked it into his jacket pocket.

A patrol car was already en route based on Bree's sister's frantic call. Dispatch would notify search and rescue. They would be here soon.

But would it be soon enough?

BREE STIRRED.

Was that a scraping sound?

She listened.

Maybe she'd imagined it.

Peter had finally fallen asleep. She touched his forehead. Checked to see that he was breathing steadily.

She shook the flashlight when it tried to go dim.

If Patrick was hurt…

He could be lying out there, dying.

No. She refused to believe that. He would find a way to overtake the shooter and then he would bring help.

She was sure of it.

Her head ached. She reached up and rubbed at her forehead. Something damp and sticky stuck to her fingers.

She looked at her fingers in the light.

Blood.

She shuddered. She was bleeding.

As if she'd only just then become aware of her own injuries, her body ached. Her back. Her right arm. And her head. Her head throbbed like hell.

But she was okay.

More importantly Peter's injury didn't appear to be life-threatening.

Bree reflected on the stories she'd told her son before he'd drifted to sleep. With each one the memories of how very much she had loved Patrick stacked one on top of the other.

She'd been young and impulsive and too career focused. She'd walked away from a relationship that could have been the forever kind.

Worse, she had deprived her son of a complete family unit.

If she made it out of here she would ensure her son knew his father. She couldn't change the past but she could make it right from here on out.

That scraping sound grated against her eardrums again.

Hope bloomed in her chest.

Had Patrick brought help?

She eased carefully away from Peter and scrambled toward where the opening had collapsed.

Putting her head against the pile of rubble, she listened intently.

Voices. More scraping.

Yes! He had brought help.

Her first thought was to wake Peter and tell him but she should let him sleep. As long as he was asleep he wouldn't be suffering from pain.

She wanted to shout Patrick's name but that would awaken Peter.

So she waited. Waited and listened.

The rocks piled between her and freedom suddenly shifted, started to fall this way and that.

She clambered out of the way.

A ray of sunlight pierced the darkness. She held her hand in front of her face and blinked to adjust to the new brightness.

"Bree!"

Patrick.

"Yes! We're here!"

Her heart thumped harder and harder. They were going to be okay. And Patrick was alive.

She repeated a silent mantra thanking God for protecting them.

When enough of the rubble was out of the way

so that she could see Patrick's face among the others working to free her, she wept.

She scrambled over to where Peter lay and gently roused him.

He moaned and agony speared her heart.

"Baby, they're here to help us."

Peter's eyes fluttered open. "My daddy?"

Bree's lips trembled into a smile. "Yes, your daddy and his friends are here to take us out of this place."

Peter licked his lips. "My leg hurts."

"I know, sweetie. We'll make it all better soon."

Everything started to happen at once then. A paramedic came through the opening first.

"What've we got, Detective?"

"I'm okay," she insisted, despite the way the paramedic was looking at her head with his heavy-duty light. "But my son's left leg appears to be broken. The calf area."

The paramedic moved next to Peter. "Hey, little man, let me have a look at you."

Suddenly Patrick was next to her. He hugged her so tight she couldn't breathe. Bree cried against his strong shoulder.

"Thank you," she murmured.

"Mommy!"

Bree pulled away from Patrick and went to her son. The paramedic gave him something for the pain before attempting to move him.

The portable gurney came in next and slowly but surely Peter was transferred onto it. Once the gurney was through the opening, Patrick helped Bree climb out.

Patrick looked at her in the light. "You're hurt."

"It doesn't matter." She looked around. "What about the shooter?"

"It was your ex," Patrick explained, pulling her against his chest. "But I took care of him. They've taken him away already. He was in need of a few stitches."

Bree tried to smile. It hurt. She was glad Jack the Bully had finally gotten his due. A part of her couldn't believe he'd gone so far as to try and kill her and Peter, but the cop in her wasn't really surprised. Violent men like him often escalated. "I should have seen this coming." She shook her head. Puffed out the frustration that tried to build. The cold, hard fact that the bastard could have killed her baby suddenly shook her hard. And she hadn't even seen it coming.

"Don't go there, Bree," Patrick warned. "You couldn't have known he was capable of this." His arm went around her waist. "Now come on. You need medical attention."

Before she could assure him that she was okay, he'd shouted for a paramedic.

The next thing she knew she was in an ambulance

with Peter. He lay still on the gurney but his breathing was slow and steady. The drugs had kicked in.

"I'll be waiting at the hospital," Patrick promised before the paramedic closed the door.

Bree held on to that promise the entire trip. The paramedic cleaned up her head wound. Nothing a little tape couldn't take care of. She probably had a ton of bruises. But she would live. She and her son were safe.

Patrick was safe.

That was all she could ask for.

Chapter Twelve

Patrick paced the corridor outside the treatment room. An orthopedist had been called in to properly set and immobilize Peter's leg.

Patrick closed his eyes and thanked God once more. Bree was a little banged up but it was nothing serious. And Peter would be fine.

Jack Raintree was in jail where he belonged.

Patrick's mother was in the lobby. As were Bree's sister and niece, Callie MacBride, Tom Ryan and Steve Cyrus.

Ryan had let Patrick know that Watts had been released. They had nothing to hold him beyond the drunk and disorderly Kenner City PD had charged him with.

Watts wasn't confessing and the hearsay his drunken friend had passed along wasn't enough. But, Ryan had assured him, Watts was on their watch list.

The door to the treatment room opened and Patrick whirled in that direction.

"He's ready to go home," Doctor Ellis announced.

"Thanks, Doc."

As soon as the doctor had cleared the doorway, Patrick strode into the room.

Bree and a nurse were helping Peter into a wheelchair.

"I'll pull my vehicle into the pickup area," Patrick offered since there didn't appear to be anything else he could do.

"That would be nice." Bree looked totally spent.

"I'll meet you in the lobby."

Patrick hustled out to the parking lot where he'd left his SUV. He rushed around to the pickup point outside the lobby doors. By the time he was back inside Peter was being wheeled into the lobby by the nurse. Bree walked alongside him.

Damn, she looked ready to drop.

Patrick's mother and Bree's family were treating Peter as if he were a prince. Hugs were exchanged between the women. Ryan, MacBride and Cyrus were letting Bree know how happy they were that she and Peter were all right.

Patrick felt a little like an outsider, but he pushed it away. He wasn't allowing his need to be front and center override what his heart was telling him.

Callie hugged Bree. As did Cyrus. Ryan clapped her on the back.

"Let's get this young man headed home," the nurse suggested.

It was hospital policy that all patients left via wheelchair and accompanied by a nurse.

"I'll stay with you tonight," Tabitha offered to Bree.

"You and Layla go home," Bree insisted. "We'll be fine. We'll need you enough the next few weeks as it is."

Tabitha resisted a bit, but then gave in. Goodbyes were exchanged as the entourage following the wheelchair moved toward the door.

Before going through the automatic doors, Patrick glanced back at those who'd come to see that Peter and Bree were safe.

Callie MacBride lingered behind. She had her cell phone in hand. She stared at the screen a moment, then stepped farther away from the others before taking the call.

Judging by the look on her face the caller had relayed some earth-shattering news. She listened for a few moments, made a brief comment and shut her phone. Hard. She shoved it back into her purse.

Between Callie and Parrish, they had the monopoly on strange behavior.

Patrick helped his son into his SUV and drove

him and Bree home. The ride was silent. Everyone was too tired to talk.

When they parked in Bree's drive, she opened the passenger-side door. "I'll get the front door."

Patrick carried Peter to the house. He couldn't begin to describe the amazing feeling of holding his son in his arms.

When Peter had been deposited into his bed and tucked in for the night, Patrick followed Bree to the kitchen. He felt a little like an obedient dog waiting for his next order. There was so much he wanted to say but he didn't know where to begin.

He was just so damned thankful that Bree and Peter were going to be fine.

But he couldn't keep standing here. He had to say something.

"So, how are we going to handle this?" He knew she was exhausted, but he needed some kind of reassurance.

Whatever it took, he would make their relationship work. Even if it turned out to only be one based on friendship.

Bree leaned against the counter. "I talked to Peter a lot while we were trapped. He wants to get to know you and spend time with you." She managed a halfhearted laugh. "Watch out or he'll be taking you to school for show and tell."

Patrick reached up and pushed her dark hair

away from her taped wound. "And you and me, what do we do about that?"

"We take it one day at a time."

Patrick could handle that. "Sounds reasonable."

"But we'll still be a family." She exhaled a weary breath. "We'll do things together, share holidays. Just like any normal family."

"With you working in homicide and me the sheriff of Kenner County, I'm not sure we'll ever be normal."

Bree smiled dimly. "Maybe not, but we'll figure it out as we go."

"You should go to bed."

Bree looked in the direction of the hall leading to the bedrooms. "I don't know. I'm so exhausted. I'm afraid once I fall asleep I won't hear him if he needs me."

"I'll stay." Patrick took her by the elbow and started guiding her toward the hall. Her room had to be one of the two on either side of Peter's. "If he needs anything I'll take care of it."

"Tabitha or Layla could come over."

"Nope. I'm staying. No arguments."

Bree pointed to the bedroom just beyond Peter's. "That's mine."

Patrick ushered her through the door and onto the bed. He tugged off her shoes and spread a blanket over her. "I'll crash on the couch. If you need anything, just give a holler."

When he would have turned away, Bree said, "Patrick?"

He looked back at her. His heart squeezed at how vulnerable she looked. And at the same time she was the most beautiful woman he had ever seen. Her long dark hair was loose from its braid. He yearned to touch it…to touch her.

She patted the bed beside her. "Lay with me."

When he hesitated, she said, "Please. I just want you near me."

Lying next to her without touching her would be one of the hardest things he'd ever done, but he wouldn't deny her that comfort for anything in the world.

He settled on the bed next to her. Took her hand in his.

Just lying there staring at her profile and holding her hand was suddenly enough.

She turned to him. "I've always loved you, Patrick. Somehow it got all tangled up in other things, but it never went away. I'm sorry… I was wrong." She closed her eyes. "So wrong."

"Shh." He touched her lips. "We've both made mistakes. Grown up a lot. We start from here." He smiled. "And it's a good thing you still love me. 'Cause I never stopped loving you."

She reached up, touched his face. Her cool fingertips traced his jaw. "You're right. We are older. We'll take it slow. Do it right this time."

"We'll do it right," he agreed. He kissed her nose. "Sleep. You need the rest. I'll be here when you wake up."

Bree closed her eyes and he watched her drift into slumber.

She didn't ever have to worry again. He would always be here for her...and for his son.

Epilogue

Two weeks later...

Bree walked through the gift shop. Today was Peter's first day back at school since his injury. She wanted to get him a special gift to celebrate how brave he'd been through this entire ordeal.

She couldn't get over how quickly he and Patrick had bonded. It was like they'd always been together.

It made her heart glad.

Her cell phone vibrated. She glanced at the screen. Her lips stretched into a smile. Speak of the devil.

She opened the phone. "What's up, Sheriff?"

"I was thinking you might be available for lunch."

"Definitely. In fact I took the afternoon off."

"What a coincidence. So did I."

Desire swam through her veins. She and Patrick had progressed to long kissing sessions. Making out, as he called it. She was ready for the next step.

"I think I might have just enough time to have a leisurely lunch before it's time to pick up Peter."

"Meet me at my place in half an hour."

"Are you cooking?" Anticipation lit inside her.

"Definitely."

"Half an hour," she promised.

Bree tucked her phone away and moved a little more quickly through the shop. The prospect of finally making love with Patrick again after all these years had her on fire.

She passed a long row of jewelry made by Ute craftsmen. One of the necklaces snagged her attention. She backed up and took a second look.

Her heart bumped against her sternum.

Almost in slow motion, she reached out and touched the chain. Picked it up and examined it more closely. She'd seen it before. It was so familiar.

Everything inside her stilled.

"Oh, my God." The pattern of the silver chain was exactly the same.

A perfect match to the ligature pattern on Julie Grainger's throat.

This, or a chain like this, was the murder weapon.

* * * * *

PROFILE
DURANGO

BY
CARLA CASSIDY

Carla Cassidy is an award-winning author who has written more than fifty novels.

Carla believes the only thing better than curling up with a good book to read is sitting down at the computer with a good story to write. She's looking forward to writing many more books and bringing hours of pleasure to readers.

Chapter One

Blood spatter patterns were fascinating, indicating the force of a blow, the trajectory of a bullet and the truth or lies of witnesses of a crime.

Callista MacBride, head of the Kenner County Crime Unit, liked studying blood spatter because it couldn't lie, because it was a science that had definite answers, predictable results.

It was rare for the Kenner County Crime Unit to be quiet, but on a cold Wednesday night in February, Callie found herself alone. Hunched over a magnifying glass to study the blood spatter left behind at a scene where a young Ute woman had died in what the locals thought was a bear attack, Callie was comforted by the familiar white noise around her—the whoosh of warm air from the furnace, the hum of the various refrigerator units and the sound of her own breathing.

There were times she still couldn't believe she was here in Kenner City, Colorado, running the lab that served the four corner areas of Colorado, Utah, Arizona and New Mexico.

This small operation was a far cry from her previous job as a forensic expert for the FBI in Las Vegas. This lab lacked the high-tech equipment she had grown accustomed to in Las Vegas and it suffered budget issues that occasionally made her want to pull her hair out. Yet she loved the creativity and enthusiasm of her coworkers.

She'd decided to work late because she hadn't wanted to go home and have too many hours to think about Julie. She coughed as her throat tickled and she tried to shove away thoughts of Julie Grainger, the murdered FBI agent who had also been a friend.

Her body had been found nearby on Ute territory and the murder had sparked a massive investigation between the Ute authorities and the Colorado police. The FBI, especially the Durango office, was also involved and the mood at the crime lab had been somber.

She frowned and slid the photo of the blood spatter out from beneath the large magnifier and inserted a photo of the victim and her wounds. She squeezed her burning eyes closed for a minute, then opened them again and studied the wounds.

At first glance they certainly appeared to have been made by giant sharp claws, but there had been no bear scat or tracks found nearby. It was February, certainly not the time of year for any bear to be out and about wandering the area.

In this case it wasn't so much what she was looking at that bothered her, but what was missing that made her leery about the supposed attack. There should have been more evidence of a marauding bear in the area.

Sheriff Patrick Martinez had been troubled by the lack of tracks as well, which was why he had brought the photos and forensic evidence in to be studied before making a final ruling on the case.

She coughed again, the tickle in her throat irritating her. Maybe it was time to call it a night. Her eyes burned and had begun to tear and she was exhausted. She raised her head from the magnifier and a panicked alarm went off in her head.

Smoke!

A faint layer filled the room. And where there was smoke, there was fire. She jumped up from her chair, a new spasm of coughing attacking her. She had to find the source of the smoke.

The hallway just outside the lab, she thought. There was a fire extinguisher in the hallway, along with an alarm that would bring the fire department. With all the smoke, why weren't the alarms ringing?

She crouched low, where the air wasn't quite so thick, and headed in the direction where she thought the smoke was originating. She crawled out of the main lab door and into the hallway where the smoke was thicker, more noxious. It seemed to be coming from beneath a supply closet door.

Her head pounded as she gasped for air. Her vision blurred as her eyes filled with tears. Slowly she crawled toward the door, wondering what might have started the fire.

She finally made it to the supply closet and placed a hand on the door. Although it was warm, it wasn't hot.

She pulled it open and black, lethal smoke rolled out. She fell back, racked with uncontrollable coughing. Air. She needed clean air. She was dizzy. Someplace in the back of her mind she realized that she'd done everything wrong.

She should have gotten out and sounded the alarm. She should have never tried to play the hero. The dizziness grew more intense and she fell to the floor, trying to find a breath of air to fill her lungs.

Stupid, Callie, she thought. *You're smarter than this.*

It was her last conscious thought.

SHE CAME TO with the wintry morning sun shining in her eyes from a nearby window. She winced against the brightness and reached up to touch her face, finding an oxygen mask covering her mouth and nose.

The hospital. She was in the hospital. How had she gotten here? Who had found her? The last thing she remembered was collapsing on the floor in the hallway at the lab. She yanked off the mask as she thought of the lab. Oh, God, had it burned?

"You're supposed to be wearing that mask." The deep, familiar voice came from one side of her and she turned her head to see Sheriff Patrick Martinez seated in a chair next to the bed.

She half rose from the bed. "The lab," she croaked and then coughed to clear her throat.

"Is fine," he assured her. "The hallway outside had a little smoke damage, but the lab itself is okay and the nurse just checked your vitals and you're going to be fine."

Callie breathed a sigh of relief and flopped back against the pillow. She had a pounding headache but other than that she didn't feel too badly. "How did I get here?"

"Bobby O'Shea couldn't sleep last night. He decided to go into the lab and get some extra work done. He found you on the floor in front of the supply closet and dragged you out, then called the fire department."

Patrick's blue eyes were darker than usual as he looked at her. "If he hadn't shown up when he did, you and I wouldn't be having this conversation right now. I'd be talking to you in the morgue."

Callie fought a shiver that threatened to walk up her spine. "It was my fault. The minute I saw the smoke I should have gotten out of the building, but instead I foolishly decided to investigate and see where it was coming from."

"Tell me exactly what happened." Patrick pulled a notepad and pen from his pocket.

It took her only minutes to explain to him the events that had led to her being overcome by the smoke. She explained finding the fire in the supply closet and opening the door to check it out.

When she was finished he leaned back in his chair and stuck the pad and pen back into his pocket. "The fire was intentionally set, Callie. Who knew that you'd be working late last night?"

"Anyone who knows me at all," she replied dryly. "It's not unusual for me to be in the lab late. I'm there most nights until the wee hours of the morning. Surely you don't think this is about me?"

Patrick raised a dark eyebrow. "Wasn't it just a week ago that somebody tried to run you down with a car?"

Callie pulled the sheet tighter around her and averted her gaze from Patrick's. "I still think that was just some dummy on a cell phone not watching where he was going."

"That's two close calls, Callie. And that makes me nervous." He unfolded his long length from the chair and stood. "Needless to say we're investigating the fire, but to be honest I don't feel optimistic about learning who might have set it. I'll keep you posted, okay?"

"Okay. The smoke alarms didn't go off," she added.

"We'll check it all out. You just need to get some rest."

She nodded and then forced a smile. "Are you crazy with wedding preparations yet?" In two weeks Patrick was marrying Sabrina Hunter, a Ute police detective.

"Bree and I have agreed not to get crazy," he replied. "It's just going to be a small wedding without frills or fuss."

"I'm looking forward to it," Callie replied. "Oh, and

Patrick, last night I was studying the photos from the Mary Windsong death. I'm not convinced we have a marauding bear in the area. I think you might be looking for a murderer."

Patrick sighed. "I was afraid you were going to tell me that. We'll talk more later. I'll be in touch," he said and then with a nod of his head he left her room.

Restless energy filled her. She wanted out of here, needed to get back to the lab and assess the damage. Other than the headache and the irritating cough, she felt fine. She found the call button and punched it to get the attention of a nurse or a doctor.

Almost immediately a man wearing a white coat and a nametag reading Dr. Westin entered the room. "Ah, I see my patient is awake."

"And ready to get out of here," she replied.

"Oh, let's not rush things. I'd like to at least keep you through the afternoon for observation and we'll talk about letting you go home this evening if no other symptoms arise through the course of the day. I'll send the nurse in to get vitals and in the meantime it's important that you just rest."

Callie wanted to protest, but she bit her tongue, knowing he was probably right. The doctor left and a nurse came in to take her vitals, then she was once again left alone.

Two close calls in one week. Patrick's words came back to haunt her. Was it merely a case of bad luck or was it something more ominous?

Del Gardo. The name leaped into her head and brought with it a ball of tension that ached in her chest. He was the number one suspect in Julie's murder, but more than that, he was the man that wanted Callie dead as well.

"Hey, boss, how are you doing?" Ava Wright walked into the room, the sunshine from the window shimmering in her wavy red hair.

Callie smiled at the fragile-looking woman who worked as a forensic scientist on Callie's team. Petite Ava might look fragile with her porcelain complexion and big blue eyes, but Callie knew she was tough as nails. She carried with her a bouquet of multi-colored flowers in a glass vase.

"I'm fine," Callie replied. "And ready to get out of here. Those flowers are beautiful."

"I thought they would give you something pretty to look at while you're here." Ava sat in the chair Patrick had recently vacated, a dainty frown creasing her forehead. "Are you sure you're okay? Bobby told us that you were completely unconscious when he carried you out of the building. He was scared to death for you. We all were when we got to work this morning and found out what had happened."

"Please tell everyone I'm fine and should be back to work first thing in the morning," Callie replied.

Abruptly Ava jumped out of the chair. "Be right back," she said, a pale cast to her face. She dashed into the bathroom and Callie could have sworn she heard the sound of retching.

Ava reappeared a moment later, her hand splayed across her stomach. "Sorry, I tried a new breakfast drink this morning and apparently it didn't agree with me."

"I hope you haven't caught the flu bug that's been going around."

"I don't think so. But, I think I'm going to scoot out of here and see if I can find something to soothe my tummy."

"Go on, get out of here and take care of yourself," Callie said. "And thanks for the flowers."

"See you in the morning," Ava said and with a wave of her hand, she left the room.

The morning passed with a number of visitors stopping in from the lab to check on her. After she'd picked at her lunch and the tray had been taken away, she lowered the head of her bed. She was tired. While the steady stream of visitors had been welcome, she now found herself exhausted.

She closed her eyes and tried not to think about the fact that it was possible the fire had been intentionally set, that the goal of the arsonist had been to kill her.

"Hello, Callie."

She froze at the sound of the deep male voice and prayed that she was already asleep and suffering a nightmare. But she knew she wasn't and she opened her eyes and stared at the tall, lean man.

His light brown hair was much longer than when she'd last seen him, but his deep brown eyes still held the brooding darkness that had always been such an integral part of him.

He was the man she cursed on a regular basis and the last person on earth she wanted to see at the moment.

"What in the hell are you doing here?" she asked.

THE FIRST THING that entered Tom Ryan's mind as he gazed at Callie was that at some point over the last three years she'd cut off all her long, luxurious pale hair.

Still, the short and sleek blond cap suited her, emphasizing the elegant bone structure of her face and those amazing blue eyes of hers, eyes that at the moment held all the warmth of an iceberg in glacial waters.

"If you came to make sure that I'm okay, then your question has been answered and you can leave now." She squeezed her eyes closed.

If she was upset at the very sight of him she was really going to go ballistic when she found out why he was here. "It's a little more complicated than that, Callie." He shrugged out of his winter coat, walked over to the chair and sat next to her bed.

"What's more complicated?" she asked as she once again opened her eyes to glare at him.

"The Bureau is concerned about you. With Julie's murder and now the fire, we think you need protection." He watched her features intently. The only sign of her displeasure was her lush lips pressing thinly together.

He'd once believed he knew her thoughts almost before she knew them herself, but that had been a lifetime and many mistakes ago.

"They think it's Del Gardo?" There was a faint weariness to her tone.

He nodded. Vincent Del Gardo was head of the Del Gardo crime family based in Las Vegas. Three years earlier when Del Gardo was on trial for ordering a hit on a competing crime boss, Callie had testified against him. She'd been placed in protective custody and Tom had been assigned to protect her.

The trial had lasted months and eventually he and Callie had become lovers. It was a relationship Tom had ended when he'd taken an assignment working undercover in Mexico.

Del Gardo had been found guilty but had escaped from the courthouse before serving any time. He'd recently been tracked to Kenner City and was now a suspect in Julie Grainger's murder.

"I thought it was over when I left Las Vegas," Callie said more to herself than to him. "I'd hoped he'd gotten out of the country, was living the good life on some foreign soil far away from me."

"But you know Julie had tracked him to that mountain estate not far from here," Tom replied.

She nodded. "I know the man supposedly living there is named Griffin Vaughn, but Julie had discovered that the corporation that owned the property was a front for Del Gardo."

"We're hoping to get inside the place over the next day or two and have a look around. Callie, men like Del Gardo don't forget or forgive. Your testimony helped get him a sentence that would have seen him behind bars for the rest of his life."

"I know." She raised a hand to the side of her head and rubbed her temple as if to ease a headache.

"Sheriff Martinez told me you had a close call last week, too, that you were nearly the victim of a hit-and-run." A rise of emotion shoved against his chest at the thought of how close she'd come to death—not once, but twice.

"It was nothing, just a close call by a driver on his cell phone." Although her eyes remained cool, there was a slight tremor in her voice that let him know she didn't quite believe her own words. "Those things should be outlawed when driving."

Despite the fact that he could smell the smoke that lingered on her skin, in her hair, he could also smell the faint scent of the gardenia skin lotion she'd always used in the place of perfume.

It evoked images of her soft, perfumed skin beneath his hand, of the throaty moans that once escaped her when they made love.

He parked those particular memories in the dark recesses of his mind, knowing that it was useless to dwell on what had once been.

"I'm not here to talk about cell phones. I'm here to talk about the fact that you were almost struck by a car last week and just last night somebody set a fire that might have killed you if a coworker hadn't suffered a bout of insomnia. Has Del Gardo tried in any way to make contact with you recently?" he asked, focusing on duty. "Have you received any strange phone calls or anything like that?"

"No, nothing." Once again she rubbed her temple. "You never answered my question."

He frowned. "What question?"

"What are you doing here, Tom?"

"As I said before, the FBI is concerned about you and they want you back in protective custody. That's why I'm here." He waited for the explosion and she didn't disappoint him.

"You have got to be kidding me." She pressed the button that raised the upper part of her bed so she could glare at him more efficiently. "I'd rather be in the care of a rattlesnake."

Tom winced. "Callie, I know you aren't exactly thrilled to welcome me back into your life again, but I've been assigned to you and you and I just have to figure out how to make the best of it."

She started to say something and then snapped her mouth closed and drew several deep breaths, obviously composing herself. Tom knew from past experience that under most circumstances Callista MacBride was the queen of cool composure.

"Okay, then the way we make the best of it is to do things my way," she finally said.

He got up from the chair and instead leaned against the wall with his hands shoved into his slacks pockets. "And what does that mean?"

"Absolutely no safe house. I stay at my own home and continue my schedule as usual."

"You know that makes it more difficult for me," he replied with a frown. It would be so much easier to keep her safe if she was tucked away in a remote cottage someplace and not going about her normal routine.

"That's not my problem." There was a cold frost of determination in her eyes. "I'm working several important cases right now and I'm not going to be stuck away somewhere until Del Gardo is found."

"What else?" he asked.

She coughed for a moment and then continued. "We keep this strictly professional. You don't pry into my personal life and I certainly don't care about yours."

"Are you through?" He pulled his hands from his pockets and shoved off the wall.

"For now." She closed her eyes and turned her face away from him. "I'm tired now. Go away, Tom."

"I'll go for now, but I'll be back when you're ready to be released from here." She didn't open her eyes or acknowledge him in any way.

Tom grabbed his coat from the chair then walked to the door. He stood for a moment, gazing at the woman he'd walked—no, ran—from almost three years ago.

He'd known that she loved him and yet he'd turned his back on her. It was no wonder that she hated him now. What she couldn't know is just how much Tom hated himself for the choices he had made.

He finally turned and left the room with the taste of rich regret lingering in his mouth.

Chapter Two

There were still times Callie desperately missed her mother, who had been dead for five years. She and her mom, Belinda, had been unusually close. Belinda had been a Las Vegas showgirl, a job she'd continued for years after Callie had been born.

Some of Callie's fondest memories of her mother were of Callie sitting on the bed watching as Belinda applied her stage makeup before going to the casino to perform.

Those had been magical moments between mother and daughter when they'd talked about anything and everything. Nobody had been more proud than Belinda when Callie had told her she wanted to be a forensic scientist.

Although Belinda had enjoyed her share of flashy boyfriends, Callie had never known who her father was. Belinda quit her showgirl job when Callie was in middle school, but money never seemed to be an issue. They certainly didn't live a lavish lifestyle, but they had always been comfortable.

When Callie asked about the money, Belinda had told her that Callie's father had left Belinda enough money so she and Callie would have what they needed. Callie had guessed from that statement that her father was dead.

As she sat on the edge of the hospital bed and waited for the nurse to bring the papers to release her, she wished she could pick up the phone and call her mom. She wished she could tell her that the man who had devastated her was back in her life.

Tom.

His very name brought forth a combination of memories, some filled with joy but others filled with an indescribable pain. And it was the pain that had lingered, that had hardened her heart into a place where no feeling could get in.

"Here we are, honey." The nurse swept into the room with a cheerful smile. "I've got your discharge papers here and a chariot awaiting you." She gestured toward the wheelchair visible in the hallway. "I just need your John Hancock on a couple of these forms, then we'll get you out of here." She handed Callie the papers to sign. "Ah, and here's your handsome prince to escort you home."

Callie looked up to see Tom standing in the doorway and instantly every muscle in her body tensed. "Trust me, that man is not a prince," she muttered. "He's not even on the toad scale."

She would have loved to blow him off, insist that she didn't need to be in protective custody. But Callie had

worked too many crime scenes, seen too often what
people could do to each other, to take her personal
safety for granted. If the FBI thought she needed protection once again, then she probably did.

She'd apparently made a lifelong enemy of Vincent
Del Gardo when she'd testified against him and until he
was in custody, her life was at risk and she'd be a fool
not to accept the protection of the FBI.

"All ready?" Tom asked.

Callie handed the papers back to the nurse, then
nodded. "As ready as I'm going to be."

Tom got the wheelchair from the hallway and pushed
it to the side of the bed. He made no offer to help her
from the bed to the chair and she was glad. She didn't
want him to touch her in any way.

It was the nurse who helped her into the chair. "I've got
my car at the front entrance in the loading area," Tom said.

"Let's go," the nurse exclaimed. As she pushed Callie
out of the room she didn't seem to notice the tension
that rippled in the air between her patient and the tall,
rip-cord lean man walking beside them.

She chatted about the flu bug going around, the pre-
dictions of unusually harsh winter weather set to move
into the area and her plans for the weekend with a boyfriend named Jimmy.

By the time they reached the dark sedan parked at
the curb, Callie was exhausted, both from the tension
of Tom's nearness and the chattiness of the nurse.

She'd had a headache from the moment she'd opened

her eyes that morning. She'd tried to nap off and on throughout the afternoon, but found it impossible. Between the hourly check of vital signs and the visitors who drifted in and out, sleep had been impossible. What she wanted now most of all was the comfort of her own bed and some quiet time.

Tomorrow she'd be back in the lab where she belonged, in a world she understood, a world she found comforting in that there were no shades of gray, only black and white supported by cold, unemotional science.

"Here, take my coat," Tom said when they reached the car. He began to shrug out of the jacket.

"No thanks, I'll be fine once you get the heater going," she replied. The last thing she wanted around her was a coat that smelled of him, that contained the heat from his body.

She slid into the passenger seat, told the nurse good-bye and then watched Tom as he walked around the front of the car to the driver door.

He was thinner than he had been before, although he still radiated with a simmering energy of competence and also a whisper of an edge of danger.

He wasn't a pretty boy. At thirty-six years old, his features were far too rugged, too boldly masculine for pretty. But he was a man who commanded attention, from men who would be slightly wary and from women who would want to dig beneath the forbidding surface to find the soft center. Callie could tell them, there was no soft center in Tom Ryan.

He got into the car, bringing with him a burst of cold wind and the scent she remembered from so long ago, a clean male smell with a hint of lemon and cedar cologne.

The knot of tension in her stomach tightened. It wasn't fair that it was he who once again would be protecting her. But, Callie had learned the hard way that life wasn't fair.

"I can give you directions to my house," she said once he started the engine.

"I know where you live. I've already been by there earlier this afternoon to check things out. Nice place, by the way."

"Thank you. I've been very happy there," she replied with a touch of fervor. She wanted him, needed him to believe that she was happy, that she'd gone on with her life and he'd merely been a small unimportant blip in her history.

He'd never been a big talker and he was silent on the drive. That was fine with her. She had nothing to say to him, nor was she interested in anything he might have to say.

"How are you feeling?" he finally asked.

"Tired and I still have a bit of a headache, but other than that I'm fine." She shivered and sighed gratefully as he turned the heater on full blast and warm air began to fill the car.

"Callie, I know this is a bit awkward, but you know you can trust me to do my job," he said.

A bit awkward? She wanted to laugh. Seeing him

again, being in his company was so much more than a bit awkward. Even now a small shaft of pain attempted to pierce through the protective layers that wrapped her heart, but she shoved it away, refusing to dwell on a past that was empty and dead.

"It never entered my mind not to trust you where the job is concerned. Doing your job has always been your number-one priority." She frowned as she heard the touch of bitterness that crept into her voice. "Hopefully Del Gardo will be behind bars where he belongs in a matter of days and you can move on to the next job."

"Time will tell," he replied.

She needed to believe that this time with Tom would be brief, that she could be strong enough to hold back any emotion that threatened to escape with him back in her life.

She breathed a sigh of relief as he turned into her neighborhood. After the flash and gaudiness of Las Vegas, Callie had been drawn to this neighborhood of adobe pueblo-style homes with their clean, pale colors and simplistic designs.

She lucked into the house. The sellers had been a divorcing couple eager for a quick sale in a depressed marketplace. She'd fallen in love with it and had bought it for a song.

It was the first home she'd ever owned and when she'd moved in she'd told herself it was her new start, her clean slate from the pain that had been a constant since the moment Tom had turned his back on her. Her car was in the driveway. One of her coworkers or Patrick must have gotten her keys from her purse and brought it back here.

As he pulled into her driveway she unbuckled her seat belt. It was only then that the reality of the situation with Tom struck her.

He couldn't very well sleep in his car. In order to do his job properly he would have to be in the house with her. "I have a spare bedroom. I guess you'll be staying there." There was little welcome in her voice.

He turned off the engine and turned to look at her, his eyes gleaming in the deepening shadows of night. "I'll try to be as unobtrusive as possible. I don't want to screw up your life here, Callie. I just want to save it, if it comes to that."

She nodded and opened her door to get out. "Wait," he said sharply. "I'll come around and get you." She sat back as he got out of the car, grabbed a black duffel bag from the backseat, then walked around to her door.

As she got out of the car he used his free hand to pull her close to him. She knew it was a gesture of protectiveness but it still caused a rush of heat to sweep through her.

When they reached the door, he held out his hand for her key. "I need to clear the house before you come in," he said. He scanned the area around the front yard as he pulled a gun from a holster beneath his coat. "Stay here and give me two minutes. If you see anyone approaching, sense anyone nearby, get inside the door and scream."

A new knot of tension balled up in her chest as he

unlocked her front door. She looked up and down the street, wondering if somebody was nearby—watching her—waiting for her to return home. Or was it possible somebody was inside her house, lying in wait?

Tom disappeared into the house and the ball of tension expanded inside her. She would recognize Del Gardo anywhere. The last time she'd seen him he'd been distinctive-looking, with his shiny bald head and white beard. Even if he shaved that beard and grew hair, she thought she'd still recognize him.

What she didn't know was if he'd hired somebody to take her out. A hired killer could look like anyone, a clean-cut young man, a middle-aged businessman, or an attractive woman with manicured nails.

She didn't realize she'd been holding her breath until Tom appeared in the doorway. "You can come in," he said. "There's nobody here."

Her breath whooshed out of her as she stepped into the small entry with its niches carved out of the wall for displaying items. At the moment those niches were empty. In fact, even though the house was beginning to really feel like home to her, the furnishings were simple with almost no personal items displayed to indicate who lived here.

They walked from the entry into the living room where a beehive corner fireplace promised warmth on a cold wintry night and benches protruded from the wall along one side. The furniture was understated earth tones and woven rugs decorated the hardwood floor.

There were only two items in the room that were personal. The first was a photo of her mother on top of the television and the second was a picture of some of the people who worked at the lab and it sat on top of a miniature rolltop desk that held her personal computer.

Tom walked over and picked up the picture. "Maybe you could give me a crash course on the players at the lab," he said.

Reluctantly, she walked closer and tried not to smell that hauntingly familiar scent of him. "The gray-haired man in the back is Jerry Griswold. He's our firearms expert. The tall, dark-haired young guy is Bobby O'Shea. He's the one who pulled me out of the building last night." As she continued to name the people in the picture, her headache became a shooting pain across her forehead.

She knew this headache wasn't from smoke inhalation. It was the band of tension created by Tom. As he placed the photo back on the desktop, she gestured down the hallway. "I'll just show you to your room," she said.

He nodded and picked up the duffel bag he'd dropped on the floor. He followed her down the hallway where she pointed to the first room on her right. "You can use the guest bath. Towels and extra soap are under the sink." She stopped at the first doorway on her left. "You can sleep in here."

The guest room was a nice size, with a king-size bed and a dresser with a mirror. He walked in and set his duffel bag on the multi-colored bedspread. "Thanks, this will be great."

"Feel free to help yourself to anything in the refrigerator, although you'll find the pickings slim. I don't eat here much. And now, I'll just tell you good-night."

There was nothing more she wanted than to escape from him, to get out of the sight of his enigmatic gaze, to go someplace where she didn't have to look at him.

"Then I guess I'll see you in the morning," he said.

She nodded and then hurried down the hallway to the master bedroom. All she wanted was a long, hot shower and the comfort of sleep without dreams.

She didn't want to think about the fact that her life was at risk. She definitely didn't want to think about the new risk that was now living in her house.

Tom was definitely a risk to her well-being, for he brought with him the threat of unearthing memories she'd thought she'd carefully buried, memories too painful to bear.

Tom awoke before dawn was even a promise in the eastern sky. The first thing he did was reach over to touch his gun on the nightstand. It was an automatic gesture, born of years as an FBI agent.

The second thing he did was think of the woman sleeping in the room at the end of the hallway. He'd always believed that he'd made the right decision for both of them when he'd walked away from her.

It had taken the undercover assignment in Mexico and

a near-death experience for him to reexamine the path of his life and think about the successes and the failures.

Certainly his job had been one of the successes. Growing up in the foster care system, it would have been easy for him to have wound up a statistic of failure, either dead at an early age or in prison. It had taken a local cop seeing Tom flirting with trouble to intervene and give Tom a new purpose and drive to succeed.

As he swung his feet to the floor and sat on the edge of the bed, he scratched the ropey red scars that cris-scrossed his chest and belly. Fifteen slashes, that's what he'd received from the members of the drug cartel he'd infiltrated when they found out he was undercover FBI. They hadn't stabbed him to death. That would have been too quick and easy. Instead they had cut him just deep enough to torture him, then had left him to bleed to death.

He'd spent four months in a Texas hospital fighting one infection after another and it was during that time that he'd realized that his personal life was a failure and much of his sense of failure came from his decision to leave Callie.

Water under the bridge, he thought as he got up and grabbed clean clothes from the closet where he'd hung them the night before. He darted across the hall and into the bathroom for a hot shower and once he was dressed for the day, he headed for the kitchen to make some coffee.

Minutes later he sat at the table and watched as the sunrise spilled orange light over the horizon. He heard the sound of water running and knew Callie was not only awake but in the shower.

It was going to be a tough day. Not only did he have to contend with Callie's cool disdain, he also had a memorial service of sorts to attend. He frowned as he thought of Julie Grainger.

She had not only been a fellow agent, she'd also been a good friend. This morning Tom was meeting two other agents at a nearby park to say personal goodbyes to their fallen friend. Although officially Tom wasn't assigned to Julie's murder case, he intended to partici- pate as much as possible unofficially.

Callie came into the kitchen, her features carefully schooled to indicate no emotion. "I see you found the coffee," she said as she moved to the counter to pour herself a cup.

"You weren't kidding about the refrigerator being bare. There wasn't even a single egg in there."

"There's a cafeteria in the building with the lab. You can get breakfast there," she said. "I'd like to leave here in about fifteen minutes and get to the lab."

"Before we go we need to talk about your schedule," he said.

She carried her cup to the table and sat down opposite him. One of her delicate blond eyebrows rose slightly, a gesture he knew indicated a certain level of stress. "What about it?"

"I think it would be in both our interests if there are no more late nights." He held up a hand to still the protest he knew she was about to make. "Personal feelings aside, Callie, you have to work with me here. There's no question that it's more difficult for me to make sure you stay safe in the dark. I'd like you to leave the lab each day by dusk so we can get back here by nightfall. That's the only thing I request of you, that small change in your schedule."

The thinning of her lips as they pressed together let him know she didn't like being reined in, but instead of protesting, she nodded. "Fine. Okay. I'm off the streets at dusk."

Tom released a small relieved sigh. He had a feeling this would be the first of many battles they might have, but at least he'd won this one.

He took a sip of his coffee and eyed her over the rim of his cup. Clad in a long-sleeved white blouse and navy slacks, she looked all business, but the floral scent that emanated from her was all female.

"Callie, maybe it would be a good idea for us to talk, to clear the air between us," he said as he lowered his cup.

Her shoulders straightened. "There's nothing to talk about and the air is fine between us." She got up from the table and took a gulp of her coffee. "I need to get to work." There was a note of finality to her voice that indicated the subject was closed.

He got up from the table and placed his cup next to hers in the sink. "Just let me get my coat and I'll be ready."

He left her in the kitchen and headed to his bedroom. He supposed it had been foolish of him to try to get her to talk about the end of their relationship. And really, what could he say? That he was sorry? That he'd been a fool?

He'd known he'd broken her heart and that would always be between them. He couldn't take back what had been done, so maybe she was right. There was really nothing to talk about.

He strapped on his shoulder holster then pulled on the black suit jacket that matched his pants. He grabbed his winter coat, then left the room and found her waiting at the front door.

Her light-blue ski jacket made her eyes an electric blue and complemented her blond coloring, but those eyes held the same cold frost they'd held the day before when she'd realized for good or for bad, he was back in her life.

They were both silent on the drive to the lab. He was already thinking ahead to the memorial service for Julie and at the same time watching the rearview mirror and their surroundings for any sign of trouble.

The Kenner County Crime Unit was located on the third floor of an old Kenner City annex building. "Don't get out of the car until I come around to get you out," Tom said as he parked the car in the parking space designated for Callie.

He shut off the engine and opened his coat to allow him quick and easy access to his gun, then left the car and walked around to the passenger door.

The air was frigid and held the scent of the possibility of snow. The long-term forecasts were warning of several potential big snowstorms coming into the area in the next couple of weeks.

He opened Callie's door and as she got out of the car he pulled her close against him. He felt her stiffen, but he didn't release his hold on her. This wasn't about emotional baggage between them. This was about her safety.

He didn't release her until they got inside the building. They were early enough that there was nobody standing to wait for the elevators. He pushed the up button and the doors immediately opened.

It was only when they were in the small enclosure that he began to relax. She would be safe here at the lab during the day when the place was filled with both law enforcement officials and coworkers.

"I've got some things to take care of today," he said as they rode up. "Needless to say, I don't want you leaving the lab for any reason until I'm back here to escort you home."

She gave him a dry look. "I might not like what's going on in my life, but I'm also not self-destructive or likely to be stupid. I'm not about to break the rules and get myself killed."

"Good," he said in satisfaction. There was nothing worse than being assigned a protective duty to somebody who didn't really want to be protected or thought it might be fun to try to lose a bodyguard. Those were the people who usually found themselves dead.

The elevator door whooshed open and they stepped out into the hallway. A faint odor of smoke lingered and at the end of the hallway the supply closet was blocked off with bright orange cones that indicated it was a crime scene.

When they stepped into the reception area the dark-haired, dark-eyed receptionist greeted them.

"Oh, Callie, I'm so glad to see you're back here and okay," she exclaimed.

Callie smiled. It was the first genuine smile Tom had seen on her face and it punched a hole in his heart. He'd forgotten how her smile lit up a room, how it not only curved her lips but also warmed her cold blue eyes. "I'm fine. Elizabeth, this is FBI Agent Tom Ryan and Tom, this is Elizabeth Reddawn, receptionist extraordinaire."

"Tom Ryan? Oh, I have a package for you," Elizabeth said. She picked up a manila envelope from her desk and handed it to him.

It had been forwarded to him from FBI headquarters. He turned to look at Callie. "Is there someplace private I can go to open this?" He couldn't imagine what might be inside.

"You can use my office. Follow me." She led him across the lab to a door at the back of the room. The office was small and as impersonal as her home had been. "Feel free to use my desk if you need to," she said as she grabbed a white lab coat that hung on a hook just inside the door and left the room.

"Thanks," he said to her retreating form. He sat at the desk and tore open the manila envelope to reveal a letter-sized envelope inside. It was addressed to him and marked personal. In the return address space were the initials JG.

Julie Grainger? His heart began to pump with a rush of adrenaline. As he ran his fingers across the envelope he felt something hard inside. What the heck?

He carefully tore the top of the envelope open and withdrew the piece of paper that was folded up inside. He opened it and saw that it was a map of some kind. At the top of the map was a strange symbol, like the letters *VDG* entwined with grapes and vines. Vincent Del Gardo?

He shook the envelope and initially he thought it was a coin that dropped out on the desk. He didn't touch it, but instead got up and called to Callie.

When she appeared in the doorway he pointed to the coin. "This coin or whatever it is came in an envelope from Julie Grainger." Callie's eyes opened wide as he continued. "I was wondering if you could check it for fingerprints."

"Let me get a set of tweezers and a fingerprint kit and see what we have." She left the office and returned a moment later. She carefully flipped the item over. "It's not a coin. It's a St. Christopher medal."

"St. Christopher medal?"

"The patron saint of travelers. Legend has it that he once carried an unbearably heavy baby across a wide river and it was later learned that the baby was Jesus Christ."

He looked at her in surprise. "How do you know that?"

"One of my mother's best friends was not only a showgirl, but also a Catholic who had statues of most of the patron saints in her apartment," Callie explained. "She taught me about them whenever she'd babysit me."

Tom watched as she opened the fingerprinting kit then twisted the top of a bottle of metallic powder. Using the ostrich feather duster, she deftly swirled the powder onto the medal. She frowned as no ridges showed up. She flipped it over and dusted the other side with the same disappointing results. "Nothing," she said, stating the obvious. "At least no fingerprints, but there are several numbers etched into the back of the coin."

"Numbers?" He bent closer to take a look and tried to ignore the scent of her, the warmth of her body so close to his own.

"Looks like a seven, a nine and a four. Does that mean anything to you?"

"No." He frowned and stepped back from her. "Can you dust the map?" He pointed to the piece of paper he'd withdrawn from the envelope.

"Sure." She pulled out a bottle of black powder and began the process of dusting the paper. "What is this?" she asked as she worked.

"I don't have a clue," he replied. He was going to have to look at it more closely, see if he could make heads or tails of it.

"VDG," Callie breathed softly, reading the initials at the top of the map. "Maybe this is some kind of a clue as to where Del Gardo might be hiding out?"

"Who knows?" At least for the moment the tension that had existed between them was gone, vanished under the bigger questions of the mystery map and the medal.

He picked up the envelope that he knew had probably been handled by too many people for fingerprinting. "It was mailed the day before her murder."

Callie looked up at him, her eyes wide. "That gives me goose bumps. You think she sensed she was in some kind of danger?"

"I don't know." He watched as she finished fingerprinting the paper. She lifted two prints. Tom figured one was probably Julie's and the other was his own and said that to Callie.

"You're both in the system so we'll be able to quickly rule you in or out," she said as she straightened.

"Do you have a copy machine? I'd like to make a couple of copies of that map, then I want you to put the original in an evidence bag and lock it up."

"I'll get some copies made for you."

Tom looked at his watch. "And then I've got to get out of here. I've got to be someplace in half an hour."

It was just after eight when Tom left the building and got back into his car and headed for the park where he was meeting two other FBI agents for a quiet goodbye to Julie.

Julie, Tom, Dylan Acevedo and Ben Parrish all had gone through FBI training together and even though they didn't often see each other, they'd shared a particularly close friendship that had lasted since their days at the academy. Julie's murder had devastated them all.

He reached the park and got out of his car. The copies of the map he'd received burned hot inside his pocket, as did the St. Christopher medal that now hung on a cheap chain around his neck. Why had Julie sent them to him? What did they mean? What was he supposed to get from them?

He headed toward the gazebo in the center of the park and saw that Ben and Dylan were already there waiting for him. Ben's dark blond hair shone in the early morning sunshine while Dylan's black hair seemed to absorb the sun.

Dylan raised a hand in greeting while Ben merely hunched his shoulders against the cold breeze and kept his hands in his pockets. Ben had always been quiet and brooding, but lately he'd seemed more distant than ever.

"Heard you're on guard duty," Dylan said in greeting. "You think it was Del Gardo who tried to take out Callie last night?"

"Him or one of his minions," Tom replied. "Nothing else makes sense. I've got some information that makes even less sense."

He told the two men about the envelope he'd

received containing the medal and the map, then handed them each a copy of the map.

He watched as they studied the pieces of paper, their confused looks mirroring his own. "I can't get a feel for what's depicted here," Dylan said.

"I can't either," Tom replied. "What about you, Ben?"

He shook his head. "I can't figure out the map, but that makes two medals that she sent. You got the St. Christopher medal and I received a St. Joan of Arc—the patron saint of captives."

"What does it all mean?" Dylan asked. "Why would she send you guys those medals?"

"I don't know, but we all can guess what the initials VDG stand for," Tom said, a simmering rage burning in his gut. If Del Gardo was responsible for Julie's death, Tom would personally like to get the man in a room alone for about ten minutes.

"We need to get that bastard," Dylan exclaimed, his dark eyes burning bright. "We all know she was probably killed because she got too close to finding Del Gardo's whereabouts." He shook the copy of the map Tom had given him. "The answer to where he is might be right here. We just need to figure it out."

"We owe it to Julie," Ben said.

Nobody thought it more important than Tom to get Del Gardo in custody once again. While he mourned for Julie, he knew capturing Del Gardo wouldn't bring her back.

What worried him was that as long as Del Gardo was free, Callie was in danger and he only prayed that when danger reached out for her again he would be in the right place at the right time to make sure she didn't end up like the strangled Julie Grainger.

Chapter Three

Although one of the most important crimes the lab was involved in at the moment was the Julie Grainger murder, that didn't mean all other crime in the area had taken a holiday.

Callie's days were generally spent dividing her time between administrative duties and actual hands-on lab work. Today was no different, except for the fact that she found her thoughts drifting far too often from work to Tom.

It had been difficult to fall asleep the night before knowing he was in her house. Memories of their time together kept drifting through her mind no matter how hard she'd tried to shut them off.

She didn't want to remember the good times, how they'd laughed together, how they'd made love. He'd been the first man, the only man who had ever owned her heart and as their relationship had progressed she'd begun to fantasize the future they'd have together.

She'd been such a fool. If she'd learned anything

living with her mother, it was that love was fleeting and men were temporary.

What she needed to remember was how devastated she'd been when Tom had chosen an assignment over her, when he'd shattered her dreams and walked away without a backward glance.

What she needed to remember was the heartbreak she'd suffered all alone because he was gone and she'd been left to deal with the tragic aftermath all by herself. An edge of grief tried to take hold of her, but she consciously shoved it away, refusing to allow herself to feel.

At five she was seated at her desk when Jerry Griswold ambled through the door and leaned against the wall. "It's official," he said. "The gun used in the robbery of the convenience store on Ash Avenue is the same gun used in the robbery of that gas station on Twelfth Street."

"Patrick suspected it was the same perp," she said.

"Ballistics don't lie," Jerry replied.

Callie smiled at the older man. "And that's why we love them, right?"

"You got that right. I just figured I'd let you know. Have you heard anything about the investigation of the fire?"

Her smile faltered. "Patrick stopped by earlier and said they were trying to identify the accelerant used, but other than that they have nothing to go on. I doubt if we'll ever find out who set that fire."

He frowned and raked a hand through his gray hair.

"We need to tighten up security around here. I can't believe somebody managed to get inside after hours and do something like that."

She nodded. "I've put in a request for some additional money for tighter security measures, but you know how that goes."

He nodded sagely. "Red tape and budget cuts."

"You've got it."

"I'm heading out. Anything you need before I go?"

She smiled at him fondly. He was such a nice man. "No, thanks, I'll be leaving here pretty soon myself."

As Jerry left the office she glanced at her clock and instantly tension twisted in her stomach as she realized Tom would be arriving at any moment.

Last night it had been easy to retreat to the privacy of her bedroom. But tonight she would have to get through dinner and the hours before bedtime with him.

Maybe he would hide out in his bedroom tonight. She couldn't get so lucky, she thought with a grimace.

At precisely six o'clock he arrived at her office door to take her home. "You ready?" he asked. He looked tired, the lines on his face deeper than usual.

Although she didn't want to leave, wasn't accustomed to going home so early, she didn't argue the point. She merely nodded and got up from her desk. It took her only a minute to exchange her lab coat for her ski jacket, then they left the lab and headed for the elevators.

"Tomorrow afternoon I need to go take a look at a site

where a woman was supposedly killed by a bear," she said. She knew he probably wouldn't be pleased by her need to be out and away from the lab, but her job involved other things besides test tubes and lab work. There was a certain amount of field work that was necessary.

"Just tell me where you need to go and I'll get you there," he replied. They rode the elevator down and when they reached the ground floor he grabbed her by the arm and held her tight against his body as they left the building.

Once they were in the car she turned to look at him and again noticed the weary lines on his face. "Bad day?" she asked.

"I met with Dylan Acevedo and Ben Parrish and we had a small memorial service for Julie."

"I'm sorry, that must have been difficult." As she thought of Julie her heart squeezed with pain. "I feel so responsible for what happened to her."

He turned and raised an eyebrow in surprise. "Why should you feel responsible?"

She pulled her coat more tightly around her. "I guess because she was working on the Del Gardo case. She wanted to find him before he found me."

"Callie, Julie wasn't murdered because of you. She was murdered because she was doing her job. We all know the risks when we take on any assignment." He dropped one hand from the steering wheel and rubbed it across his chest, and then frowned and returned his hand to the wheel.

"Julie would be angry with you if she knew you suffered a moment of guilt over her death," he continued. "She died doing what she loved to do—chasing down leads to find bad guys. It wasn't just what she did, it was who she was."

Callie stared out the passenger window and thought about what he'd just said. Yes, that had been the problem three years ago. Being an FBI agent wasn't just what Tom did, it was who he was. He wasn't a husband or a father. He couldn't be because he was already wed to the job and nothing and nobody was more important to him. A trace of familiar bitterness swept through her.

They were silent for the remainder of the drive to her house. When they arrived he escorted her inside where they hung their coats in the closet, then went to the kitchen where the savory scent of spaghetti sauce hung in the air. She knew that smell—Tom's famous sauce—and her mouth began to water in anticipation.

"I took the liberty this afternoon to do a little grocery shopping and made a quick pot of sauce for dinner," he said.

She wanted to be outraged that he'd taken such liberties, had been in her house during the afternoon while she'd been gone. She wanted it to feel like an invasion, a violation, but as he pulled the pot of sauce from the fridge and placed it on the stovetop, all she could muster was the sweet anticipation of a good meal.

"This will take about fifteen or twenty minutes," he

said. "I've got it all under control if you want to go change your clothes or freshen up or anything."

"I think I will go change," she said and left the kitchen. She didn't want to remain and watch him prepare the meal. It was too reminiscent of the times they had shared together.

Most nights when they'd been in the safe house Tom had cooked while she'd sat at the table enjoying a glass of wine. He'd usually cook bare-chested, clad only in a pair of athletic shorts. And there had been times he'd put the meal on the back burner as they'd sated their appetite for each other.

She changed from her work clothes to a pair of navy blue sweatpants and a navy T-shirt, then went into the bathroom and stared at her reflection in the mirror.

The faint pink stain in her cheeks confirmed the rivulet of emotion that fluttered inside her. It felt like excitement, but that was ridiculous. It felt like antici-pation, but she told herself there was nothing she was anticipating where Tom Ryan was concerned.

Sluicing cold water on her face, she focused on the work she'd left back at the lab. The crime scene photos from the bear attack continued to confuse her. There was no question that the wounds that Mary Windsong had suffered looked like those left from a bear attack, but there were pieces of the puzzle that just didn't quite fit.

Maybe seeing the place where the attack had suppos-edly happened would clear up the inconsistencies and tell her definitively if it had been some unusual bear attack or a homicide.

When she left her bedroom she smelled the scent of wood smoke and heard the crackle of a fire. Tom had started a fire in the beehive stove and the flames flickered a warm glow on the pale pink adobe walls.

She heard the sound of him working in the kitchen and stood for a moment with her eyes closed, just listening. She hadn't realized until this moment how lonely she'd been since coming to Kenner City.

Although she worked with a lot of wonderful people at the lab, she was their boss and rarely socialized with anyone. Whenever she was home alone the silence was what so often drove her back to work or into bed.

She gave herself a mental shake, irritated by the faint stir of need for something else, for something more than what she currently had in her life.

"I definitely inhaled enough smoke to addle my brains," she muttered as she walked through the living room and into the kitchen.

"Just in time," Tom said as he lifted a colander of spaghetti and dumped it into a waiting serving bowl. He motioned her toward the table.

"You know all this isn't necessary. You don't have to cook the meals," she said, taking her seat. She kept her voice cool, trying to maintain an emotional distance from the domestic scene, from him.

He shrugged. "It was kind of a matter of survival. As I recall, and unless things have changed, you aren't much of a cook." He ladled the sauce over the noodles and set the bowl on the table.

"When I was growing up, Mom always preferred eating out and in Las Vegas it was almost cheaper to eat out than to cook at home. And things haven't changed. I still don't do much cooking. Most nights I'm working late and just grab something on the run."

He added a tossed salad and a loaf of garlic bread, then joined her at the table. Immediately an awkward silence descended

She didn't want to talk to him, didn't want to engage in the small talk that might somehow be construed as interest or a relationship. After all, she was used to silent meals.

What she wasn't used to was the heady scent of him that filled the room, the brush of his hand against hers as they both reached for a piece of the garlic bread at the same time and the whisper of want that his mere presence evoked in her. How was it possible to want a man she hated?

"Is there somebody special in your life, Callie? Are you dating anyone?" he asked, finally breaking the tense silence that had stretched to endless proportions.

She knew she had two choices. She could either answer his question and indulge in dinnertime small talk or she could be a bitch. As she gazed at him she felt oddly vulnerable.

"I told you before that there was really no reason for us to exchange a bunch of personal information," she said, her voice decidedly cool as she chose option number two.

His brown eyes flashed darkly. "Sorry, for a moment I forgot your rules. Don't worry, it won't happen again."

A twinge of regret edged through her as she stared down at her plate. She knew she was only making things more difficult, but she was afraid to let down her defenses even a little bit where he was concerned.

There was no question that he was under her skin, but what she had to do was keep him out of her heart, because Tom Ryan had as much potential to destroy her as the man who wanted her dead.

TOM CHECKED the rearview mirror as he and Callie drove away from the lab. It was just after three in the afternoon, although it looked more like twilight than midafternoon.

Thick gray clouds hung low in the sky and spat an occasional flurry of snowflakes. The gray of the day fit perfectly with Tom's mood.

To say that things had been tense the evening before with Callie would be a vast understatement. After an uncomfortable dinner he'd sat on the sofa while she'd sat in the chair nearby. She'd grabbed a forensic science tome from the bookshelf and had handed him the television remote control.

She'd read while he'd channel surfed and the tension between them had been palpable. He'd expected this assignment to be somewhat difficult because of the emotional baggage that existed between them. But he hadn't expected her to be so closed off, so unwilling to engage with him on any level.

There was a darkness in her, one that occasionally flashed in her eyes, one that hadn't been there before when he'd known her. It made him wonder just what her life had held over the last three years.

He was relatively certain there wasn't anyone important in her life. The phone had remained silent throughout the evening and she'd made no outgoing calls. Surely if there was a man in her life he would have wanted to talk to her or she would have wanted to check in with him.

She'd finally gone to her bedroom around nine, with scarcely a word exchanged between the two. This morning had been no different. She'd gotten up just in time to take off for work.

While she'd been at the lab throughout the morning, Tom had used the hours studying the map that had been mailed to him, but he was no closer now to figuring out what it depicted than he'd been the day before.

He and Callie were now on their way to the scene where she'd told him a young Ute woman had supposedly been attacked by a bear.

They had entered Ute territory a few miles back. The terrain was rough, the location remote. At least Tom didn't have to worry about being followed. Theirs was the only vehicle on the road.

"I'm surprised you're still doing field work considering your administrative position at the lab," he said. He shot a quick glance at her. Even after all this time the mere sight of her nearly took his breath away.

"I don't do as much as I'd like anymore, but when a particular case catches my interest, I like to get out in the field. Besides, the lab is a small operation and sometimes I'm the only one available to show up at a crime scene."

"What's so interesting about this particular case? A bear attack doesn't sound like something the crime lab would be involved with."

"Normally we wouldn't. The coroner ruled it as an attack, but Patrick had a bad feeling about it and brought us some of the evidence to look at and when I examined the photos and such, more questions than answers jumped into my head. There are some troubling inconsistencies."

Apparently, the secret to getting Callie to talk was to ask about her work, he thought. "So, what kind of inconsistencies?" At the moment the tension between them was gone and he wanted to keep the easy conversation going.

She frowned, the gesture unable to take away from her beauty. "There's no question that the wounds on the victim were made by bear claws. Turn right up here," she said and pointed to a narrow dirt trail, then continued. "Those wounds were lethal in that she bled to death from them."

"Then why the questions?"

"No bear scat or tracks found in the area. While the wound patterns themselves were consistent with claws, the amount of pressure used to inflict those wounds was not. Also, there were no bite marks. When did you ever hear about a bear attack where the bear didn't bite?"

"Never," he replied. "What about DNA analysis. Wouldn't that show you if it was bear?"

She nodded. "And the DNA taken from the wounds was consistent with a black bear."

"What is it you hope to learn at the scene?"

She plucked her lower lip with a finger, a gesture both familiar and endearing. She'd always done that when deep in thought. "I'm not sure," she finally said. "I just wanted to come out here and take a look around before giving my final thoughts to Patrick."

She was good at her job and he'd always admired that about her. She had an attention for details that was absolutely vital in her line of work.

As she guided him over the rough terrain to the site of the supposed attack, he tried not to breathe in the scent of her, knowing that he responded to her scent like a wild animal in heat.

"You should park here," she finally said. "We'll have to walk in the rest of the way."

Tom pulled over as far as he could on the narrow trail, then shut off the engine and looked around. They were in the middle of the Ute tribal park, surrounded by trees and brush.

Although he had seen no cars following them, he didn't intend to take Callie's safety for granted. He unfastened his coat to allow him to access his gun if necessary, then got out of the car.

Snowflakes danced down from the gray skies, but the forecast was only for flurries. As he walked around the car to open Callie's door he sensed no danger in the area.

Callie got out of the car and together they walked toward a grove of trees where a flutter of yellow crime-scene tape still clung to a massive tree trunk.

"The other thing that concerns me is that most bears should be hibernating now," she said as they walked. "It's really too early in the year for them to be active in the area."

"But it's possible one got roused and attacked?" he asked.

She shrugged. "I suppose anything is possible, although it would be highly unusual."

"Tell me about the victim." He wanted to keep their conversation flowing, even if that conversation was about a poor dead woman and bears.

"Mary Windsong, a twenty-four-year-old Ute. She was found there." She pointed to the ground just in front of the tree. "Apparently, the night before the attack she'd been out with friends at a local bar. She left the bar alone at three in the morning and her body was found here just after six. Her blood alcohol level was almost three times the legal limit. She had no defensive wounds and only two bear hairs were found on her."

"Two? How is that possible?" he asked.

She plucked her bottom lip once again as she stared at the place where the woman had been found. "It isn't."

He watched as she walked around the tree, her gaze on the hard, frozen ground. He had no idea what she was looking for, had a feeling she wasn't sure. He'd learned a long time ago that like him, Callie worked with a certain amount of gut instinct.

There was a claw mark on the tree and he watched as she ran her hand across the wounded wood. He remembered how her hands felt caressing his skin, how she'd loved to splay her palms across the smooth expanse of his bare chest.

She wouldn't like that now. Even if she lost her mind and decided to fall into bed with him again, there would be no caress of smooth flesh. He could easily imagine her lip curled back in distaste if she encountered the mess that now decorated his chest and stomach.

She pulled a small tape measure from her coat pocket and measured the marks on the tree, then wrote them down in a small notepad.

"So much of the physical evidence points to a bear," she said, obviously troubled. "And yet, it just isn't right." She looked up at him, her forehead puckered with a frown. "What I think happened is that something of the human variety used bear claws to kill Mary."

"So, you're looking at a homicide."

She nodded. Her cheeks were a bright pink from the cold and the errant snowflakes that fell on her hair looked like a sprinkle of diamonds as they sparkled in a shaft of sunlight that broke through the clouds.

A surge of desire welled up inside him. There was

nothing he'd like to do more than take her back to her house, lay her down in front of the fire and make love to her until she mewled with pleasure.

He mentally shook himself. If he didn't stop thinking like that, the only way he'd be able to cool off would be to strip naked and roll in the snow.

"I guess we can go," she said, giving one last long look to the place where Mary Windsong's body had been found.

A tremendous roar filled the air. Callie screamed as Tom yanked her into him, at the same time grabbing his gun from the holster as the brush ten feet from where they stood rattled and moved as if something big lurked just behind it.

Chapter Four

Callie had told herself that the last man she wanted to be around was Tom Ryan, but as he held her tight and trained his gun on the moving brush, she couldn't think of any other man she'd rather be with at the moment.

She clung to him and felt his heartbeat crashing against her own. He remained in place, his gun trained on the brush, his dark brown eyes narrowed in concentration.

"Is it a bear?" she whispered against his neck.

"That was the puniest bear growl I've ever heard," he whispered back. "It was definitely a bear of the human variety."

Every muscle in his body was tense against her. Not a bear, but the killer who had come back to his ground zero? Or one of Del Gardo's hit men who had somehow managed to track their movements?

For the first time since they'd arrived at the scene she felt the cold. The air frosted any exposed skin, but it was sheer fear that chilled the blood in her veins.

It seemed like they stayed frozen in place for an

eternity. "Whoever it was, I think they're gone," he finally said, but he didn't drop his arm from around her, nor did he lower his gun. "We're going to walk slowly back to the car," he instructed. "I want you to stay behind me."

He moved her behind him and they started the long trek to the car, Tom walking backward with his eye on the brush as Callie faced the direction of the car.

It seemed to take forever before they reached the car. "Lock the doors, I'll be right back," he said as she slid into the passenger seat.

Before she could protest he took off running back to the area where they'd been standing. When he disappeared into the brush that had moved, her breath caught painfully in her chest.

What was going on? What if the person in the brush hadn't left like Tom had thought, what if he'd been waiting for the right opportunity to take out the bodyguard who stood in the way?

"Oh, Tom, be safe," she whispered.

Her heart beat so fast she couldn't catch her breath as she kept her gaze focused on the stand of trees and thick brush.

No matter what her feelings were for Tom now, she didn't want him hurt or worse. Although she was human enough to be concerned for her own safety, at the moment it was worry over his that filled her.

She gasped a sigh of relief as he reappeared and headed back toward her.

His features were taut, his lips a thin slash as they pressed together. She quickly unlocked the doors. "Whoever it was, is gone. I didn't find anything or anyone around," he said as he slid in behind the steering wheel.

"Do you think it might have been Del Gardo or one of his men?" she asked as he started the engine and turned the car around to point it back in the direction of Kenner City.

"Doubtful. Del Gardo or one of his goons wouldn't play games in the woods. We wouldn't have gotten a warning roar before they struck." He frowned and glanced in his rearview mirror. "Dammit, I could have sworn we weren't followed."

"Then it was probably the person who killed Mary Windsong. He must have been hanging around the crime scene. When we get home I need to call Patrick. As sheriff, he needs to know what happened. I also need to let the officials on the reservation know what happened." She frowned thoughtfully. "If there was any question in my mind before about whether this was a homicide or not, the question has now been answered."

"What kind of a person uses bear claws to kill a woman?" Tom asked, his gaze shifting back and forth from the road in front of them to his rearview mirror.

"I don't know. I do know the Ute Indians have a legend about a bear and they have an annual bear dance to celebrate the old legend."

"I don't suppose the legend is about killing young women?" Tom asked.

Callie released a small dry laugh. "Not hardly. The legend of the bear is about two brothers who go hunting and one of them encounters a bear who is dancing and singing. He teaches the song and dance to the younger brother who then takes it back to the tribe and teaches it to them. The songs show respect to the spirit of the bear and showing respect to the bear spirit was supposed to bring strength."

She could tell she'd surprised him and she offered him a small smile. "Detective Sabrina Hunter is Ute and I'm always interested in learning new things. She's told me a lot of things about the Ute tribe and their history." Despite the heat blowing from the vents, she shivered.

"Cold?" he asked and turned the fan up a notch.

"I think it's leftover fear more than cold," she admitted. "When you disappeared into that brush, I was afraid you'd be killed."

He slid her a dark glance and his lips curled up in a half-smile. "Be careful, Callie. If you say things like that, I might get the idea that you actually care."

"Then I will have to be careful because I wouldn't want to give anyone a false impression," she replied thinly.

Drat the man! Why was it so easy for him to get under her skin? It had been almost three years, for goodness sake. Why hadn't time erased or simplified the complexity of emotions he evoked in her?

She stared out the passenger window and tried to ignore the heat of his gaze on her. She finally turned to face him once again. "What?" she asked.

"You've become a hard woman, Callie. You were never that way before. I hope it isn't because of what happened with us."

"Don't flatter yourself," she returned. "It's been a long time since we were together and I've been through all kinds of life experiences since then." In truth, there had been no man since Tom, but there was no way she wanted him to know that.

"If you ever want to talk about those experiences…" He let his voice trail off.

"I won't." Once again she turned her gaze out the window. The only good thing she figured came out of this brief conversation was that the fear had fled, unable to sustain itself beneath the heavier weight of anger.

How dare he want her to share the information of the past three years with him. Not once in the time since he'd left her had he tried to contact her in any way, to check in and see how she was doing, to find out if she were still alive. Now he wanted some sort of bonding experience? She didn't think so.

When they reached her house she went directly to the phone to call Patrick while Tom disappeared into the kitchen.

The conversation with Patrick lasted longer than she'd anticipated as they spoke about several pending cases. He told her that the accelerant used for the fire at the lab was a common brand of lighter fluid and she already knew from the people at the lab that no other forensic evidence had been found.

She hung up the phone but remained on the sofa, her thoughts going to the murder of Julie Grainger. She knew every law enforcement person in the area was working hard to solve the case.

Julie's body had been found in a remote area of the Ute reservation. An object they believed to be a necklace of some kind had strangled her and it had left a distinctive pattern on her neck. They knew the killer was male, but that's all they knew.

Was the map that Tom had received a clue to Del Gardo's whereabouts? How close was Del Gardo? Was he someplace outside now—watching her? Waiting for the perfect opportunity to pay her back for helping to get him convicted?

She glanced toward the window where an early twilight was falling. She suddenly didn't want to be alone. She got up from the sofa and went into the kitchen where Tom sat at the table with the map in front of him.

"Can you make anything out of it?" she asked and sat across from him at the table.

"No. It would help if I could figure out some point of reference, but I can't." He shoved the map away and rubbed his hand across his forehead as if to ease a headache.

"How about I make dinner tonight," she said, and got up from the table.

He eyed her dubiously, a hint of a teasing smile curving his lips. "Will it be edible?"

She felt the answering smile that lifted the corners

of her mouth and it felt good for a change. "I think I can manage to open a soup can and make some grilled cheese sandwiches. Will that work?"

"That will work," he agreed easily and slid the map back in front of him. As he continued to study the map, she got busy on dinner preparations, such as they were.

She didn't have to ask what kind of soup he wanted. She'd learned long ago that Tom was a chicken-noodle kind of man. He also liked pizza, football games with a bowl of popcorn in his lap and high-stakes poker games.

"I'm assuming you gave copies of the map to your FBI friends," she said as she buttered the bread for the grilled cheese.

He reared back in his chair. "I gave one to Ben Parrish and one to Dylan Acevedo. Ben got a medal, too. His is a Joan of Arc medal and it also has numbers on the back, but we can't figure out what they mean. We've twisted and turned them but can't make any sense out of them. We've told our supervisor in the Durango office and they're doing everything they can to try to figure it out."

He squeezed his eyes closed, as if suffering eye strain. "Why don't you put it away for now? Maybe a little distance will illuminate things for you," she said. "Besides, this is about ready and there's nothing worse than cold grilled cheese."

"Except maybe a cold woman," he replied with a sly grin.

She knew it was a not-so-subtle dig at her, but she

let it go. They still had the remainder of the evening to get through and she was tired of the tension that had marked his time with her so far.

The conversation over dinner and after was about the lab and her work. She told him about how the team was challenged by their lack of high-tech equipment, how the very size of the area they served was demanding and how much she absolutely loved it all.

They discussed some of her more recent cases and talked about Julie Grainger and what little evidence they had to point at her killer.

"You like it here in Kenner City," he said.

"I do. It's got the quaintness of an old mining town, but is also close to bigger cities. Even though I've just been here a year, it feels like home."

The feeling of home was something Tom wouldn't know about. "I think I'm going to call it a night," she said as she got out of her chair.

Even though it was early, just after eight, she was ready to escape and be alone. She'd found the easy conversation with him far too appealing.

That's how it had all begun before. Hours of simply talking had eventually led to an intimacy between them and her love for him.

At least she was catching up on her sleep, she thought as she undressed and pulled on her nightgown. She'd been working such long hours at the lab before Tom had insisted on the shorter hours that she hadn't realized how exhausted she'd been.

She decided she'd read for a little while, then turn off the light and go to sleep. What she absolutely, positively refused to do was lie in bed and think about Tom Ryan.

She got into bed before she realized the book she wanted to read was the one she'd been reading the night before and it was in the bookcase in the living room.

Getting up, she grabbed the robe that lay on the end of her bed and pulled it on, then padded out into the hallway.

She was walking by the bathroom door when it flew open and Tom stepped out, colliding with her with a grunt of surprise.

"Sorry," he said as he grabbed her by the shoulders to steady her.

He was bare-chested and she gasped in shock as she saw the angry scars on his chest. Instantly he dropped his hands from her shoulders and stepped back from her, his eyes hooded and dark.

"Oh, Tom, what happened to you?" She fought the impulse to reach out and run her fingers across the raised scars, to somehow take away the pain he must have suffered when the wounds had been inflicted.

A humorless smile curved the corners of his mouth. "Why, Callie, if I tell you that I'd be breaking your rule of no exchange of personal information."

Without waiting for her reply, he went into his room and closed the door behind him.

THE DAWN OF MORNING found Tom seated at the kitchen table and sipping a cup of coffee. He knew Callie was up, but she hadn't made an appearance yet.

His hand tightened around his coffee cup as he thought of their brief encounter in the hallway the night before. The last thing he'd wanted was for Callie to see his scars, to know that he was flawed.

He nearly laughed at this thought, wondering why he cared. She thought he was flawed anyway. She'd just believed his defect was on the inside rather than on the out.

When he'd left her for the assignment in Mexico she'd told him that he was flawed by the fact that he refused to love, was afraid to be loved. He recognized now that there had been a lot of truth to her assessment of his character.

Thank God today was going to be a busy one and hopefully he'd be far too busy to think about Callie MacBride and all that he'd walked away from in the past.

He smelled her before he saw her, that dizzying gardenia scent of her filled the air a moment before she stepped into the kitchen.

"Good morning," she said as she beelined for the coffee.

"Good morning," he replied. She could wear a simple white blouse and slacks better than any woman he'd ever met. The blouse buttoned up the front and the top two buttons were unfastened, exposing her delicate collarbones and creamy skin. The black slacks hugged her in all the right places and a simmer of heat stirred in the pit of his stomach.

"You made the morning paper," he said as she joined him at the table.

"Really?" She pulled the paper in front of her. The headline read Bear Gets Bad Rap. The article basically said that the bear attack was actually a murder, a fact supported by Callista MacBride of the Kenner County Crime Unit.

She finished scanning the article, then took a sip of her coffee. "At least this means there won't be a lot of crazy hunters with guns beating the bushes to find a killer bear. Definitely a good day for the bears." She took another drink of her coffee. "What are your plans for the day?" she asked.

"I'm hoping to join the team that is going to get into the Vaughn estate today," he replied.

"You think Griffin Vaughn is hiding Del Gardo?" she asked.

Tom shrugged. "Who knows. All we really know is that Vaughn bought the place from the corporation that was a front for Del Gardo. On paper Vaughn looks like an ordinary businessman, but who knows how deeply involved he might be with Del Gardo. Mobsters are usually experts at making themselves look like upstanding businessmen."

"Do you have a search warrant?"

"Didn't need one. Although Vaughn is out of town

on business, Patrick contacted him by phone and got his permission for us to go in and search the place."

"I hope you find Del Gardo hiding in a closet or under a bed," she said fervently. "I hope you get him back into custody and then you and I can go back to our normal lives."

"That would be nice," he agreed, although there was a tiny part of him that didn't want to go back to his normal life, that wasn't sure what came next in a life he'd decided to change.

She drained her coffee cup and carried it to the dishwasher. "Ready to go?"

He nodded. There was never any lingering in Callie. The minute she had finished her coffee, she was ready to get to work. *And away from you,* a little voice whispered inside his head.

Minutes later they were in the car and headed to the lab. Tom would meet with the other FBI agents there in a conference room they'd taken over as temporary headquarters until Julie's murderer was brought to justice.

The tension that had been wonderfully gone the night before was back hanging heavy in the air between them. Maybe it was because seeing her in the hallway last night in her short pink robe had stirred a wealth of want in him. And that desire for her hadn't magically disappeared overnight.

He'd thought he could do this, be with her in the role of bodyguard, of protector and not make the mistake again of letting it get personal.

He'd wanted this assignment because he cared about her so much, more than anyone else on the face of the earth and he knew nobody else would guard her better.

He'd only been with her forty-eight hours and already he felt the strain of trying to keep it impersonal. She certainly didn't seem to be having the same problem. Other than her asking what had happened to him when she'd seen the scars on his chest the night before, she hadn't asked or offered any personal information.

When they reached the lab they parted ways. She went to her office and he went on down the hallway to the conference room.

Patrick and Bree Hunter were already there, seated side by side and talking in low, intimate tones. Tom knew the two were getting married in less than two weeks and by the look on their faces as they gazed at one another, it was a match that would definitely last.

For just a moment, a tiny flutter of envy swept through Tom. What would it be like to have that kind of connection with another person?

You had it once, you fool, and you walked away from it.

The couple jumped apart as Tom entered the room. "Hey, Tom, ready to find Del Gardo today?" Bree asked.

She was a beautiful woman, with long black hair, high cheekbones and dark simmering eyes, but her physical beauty didn't touch anything in Tom. He liked his woman cool and blond and prickly. He was such a damned fool.

"I'm definitely ready to get that man back behind bars," he said as he sat in one of the empty chairs at the table.

"I'm sure you're eager to get off babysitting duty," Patrick said with a lazy grin.

Bree nudged her fiancé with her elbow. "Don't let Callie hear you refer to her as babysitting duty or she'll have your hide tanned and made into a jacket."

They all laughed and at that moment Ben Parrish walked in. Greetings were given all around, then the four of them got down to business along with Jerry Ortiz, the FBI supervisor who was on the telephone.

When the briefing was finished, they all got into their individual vehicles to drive to the mountain estate now owned by Griffin Vaughn.

It had taken hours of research to discover the corporation that Del Gardo was behind, the corporation that had initially bought what was now the Vaughn estate.

They still hadn't made a connection between Griffin Vaughn and Vincent Del Gardo, but that didn't mean there wasn't one. Criminals like Del Gardo were smart and cunning and were masters at hiding money and themselves when it was necessary.

As he drove, his thoughts returned to Callie. There was something in her eyes, a whisper of secrets, a darkness of such pain that he couldn't help but wonder what had happened to her since last time he'd seen her.

Had she fallen in love with another man who had also broken her heart? Was that why she'd pulled that icy shell around herself?

Eventually, before he left her life again, he would tell her that he was sorry for what he'd done with her, he would share his regret with her whether she wanted to hear it or not.

He wouldn't burden her with that information now, not while she was afraid of being murdered by Del Gardo. But, once the man was back behind bars and her life was no longer in danger, Tom intended for the first time in his life to bare his heart to her.

As he turned into the drive of the Vaughn place, he shoved thoughts of Callie aside. The best thing he could do for her was focus on the job of getting Del Gardo.

The estate was named Lonesome Lake for the lake at the front of the property. The driveway crossed the lake over a small bridge. The house itself was impressive, huge with lots of windows to enjoy the magnificent view.

Tom parked behind Patrick's car and Ben pulled in next to them. Their cars weren't the only ones in the driveway. Several pickup trucks were parked in front of the house, their tailgates spilling a variety of tools.

"Looks like there's some work going on inside," Tom said as he joined the others on the walkway that led to the front door.

"Destroying evidence?" Bree said, asking nobody in particular.

"It's a good thing we got out here today," Patrick replied, his forehead wrinkled with a frown. "Before any more damage can be done."

They all walked to the front door where Patrick rang

the doorbell. The door opened to reveal an older woman who introduced herself as Gemma, the housekeeper. A tall man stood just behind her who she indicated was her husband, Erik, the handyman on the property.

"Mr. Vaughn told me to expect you," she said as she ushered them into a huge entry. "You'll have to excuse the mess. Mr. Vaughn is having some renovations done."

Tom frowned as he saw the drop cloths that covered the floor in the living room. What evidence might have already been painted over or washed away?

Although this visit was just to perform a cursory search to find some sort of evidence that Del Gardo was either here or had recently been here, the renovations would certainly destroy any forensic evidence they might have wanted to collect.

"Mr. Vaughn said to tell you that you're free to look around. We'll be in the kitchen if you need anything or have any questions," Gemma said.

They split up, Tom heading for the basement area, Patrick and Bree heading upstairs and Ben taking the main floor. This house was the only clue they had to Del Gardo. He'd bought this property for a reason and Tom thought that reason was to be close to Callie.

They met together at the front door almost two hours later with nothing to report. The basement that Tom had searched had been stuffed with junk and covered furniture that had apparently been stored there for the renovations.

They met Perry Long, the contractor doing the work

and had asked him some questions, but all they'd learned from him was that he thought the job was cursed. There had been a high incident of missing tools, accidents and strange noises.

They finally left, all of them dispirited by the lack of success. Del Gardo's whereabouts were still a mystery and as long as he remained on the loose Callie remained in danger.

He didn't realize until he was driving home just how desperately he'd hoped they'd find the man and get him back behind bars.

When he'd taken this assignment he'd thought he would be able to handle being around Callie again, interacting with her on a professional basis without the need for something more.

He'd been wrong.

He felt like a kettle on top of a hot burner, his blood simmering just beneath the whistle level. If he spent enough time with her, he knew that eventually he was going to boil.

Chapter Five

Throughout the day Callie's thoughts had repeatedly drifted to the scars she'd seen on Tom's chest. She wanted to know what had happened to him, knew that whatever had happened must have been serious— perhaps life-threatening—to have left behind those kinds of severe marks.

Her rule to keep things strictly impersonal between them had been dumb. She now stretched her arms overhead to unkink shoulder muscles and recognized that she only thought it was dumb now when she wanted to know something personal about him.

For the first time she wondered what the last three years had been like for him. She knew when he left her he'd been going on a new assignment. Was that when he'd been hurt?

Had he dated other women and never given her a second thought after he'd left? Had he fallen in love with somebody else? Had he ever wondered what had happened to Callie? If she were happy?

Maybe it was time to call a truce with him. Certainly it would ease the tension between them. Although she wasn't interested in rehashing their past, the stress of trying to make conversation and not give away anything personal was a strain for both of them.

There was no question in her mind that Tom would put himself in danger to save her. He would give his own life to make sure she remained safe. For that alone she owed him more than the icy disdain she'd shown him far too often in the last couple of days.

It was just after five when Bree appeared at her door and fell into the chair beside her desk with a tired sigh. "Long day?" Callie asked.

"Lately it seems like they're all long," she replied. "We spent part of the day at the Vaughn estate and the rest of the day I spent chasing down anyone who might have information about the Mary Windsong murder."

"Anything interesting turn up at the Vaughn property?" Callie asked, although she knew if there had been anything she would have heard about it by now.

"Other than the fact that the place is totally awesome? No. There's construction going on but even with the drop cloths and such you could tell that the place and the furnishings are beautiful. There's even a four-room caretaker apartment in the main house."

"Sounds nice," Callie replied, fighting a twinge of disappointment. "But I was hoping you'd find Del Gardo hiding in a closet or behind a secret moving wall."

"Yeah, so were we." Bree's eyes flashed darkly. "Unfortunately we didn't see any signs of him."

"What have you found out about Mary Windsong?"

"No spurned boyfriend, no enemies to speak of, nothing strange or unusual in her life before the murder. Her mother said she wasn't dating anyone in the last four or five months, that she had been in no hurry to find true love. Unless somebody comes forward with some new information, it's not looking good for a quick resolution."

"Too bad there wasn't more physical evidence at the scene or on the body," Callie said. "We can't help you catch criminals unless they leave something of themselves behind."

"I know. Whoever killed her was either incredibly smart or incredibly lucky. She worked as a clerk at the grocery store. According to her boss she was a good worker, always on time and with a cheerful smile." Bree stood.

"You all ready for the big day?" Callie asked, changing the subject to something more pleasant.

The frown that had danced across Bree's features instantly dissipated, replaced by a soft smile. "Ten more days and I'll be Sabrina Martinez. I can't wait."

A wistfulness swelled up in Callie's chest as she saw the happy shine in Bree's eyes. Callie had wanted that, the wedding vows and the married life, but apparently it wasn't meant to be for her.

"I've got to get out of here," Bree said. "I've got a ton of things to do before I can call it a day. You'll let me know if any other thoughts strike you about the Windsong murder?"

"You know I will," Callie replied.

Bree nodded and left the office. Callie returned her attention to her computer screen, where she'd been ordering supplies, a neverending task for the lab, but her mind remained on thoughts of weddings and love.

During the time she'd spent with Tom in the safe house it had been easy to imagine the two of them married. They'd lived like husband and wife. She'd liked waking up in the mornings with him at her side, going to sleep at night in his arms. She'd liked the conversation they'd shared, the easy give and take that had marked their entire relationship.

Callie was a strong woman. She'd never felt as if she needed a man in her life, but during those months she'd spent with Tom she'd realized she liked sharing her life with him.

You can't force people to love you. Her mother used to tell her that whenever she'd break up with one of her flashy Las Vegas boyfriends. "You can love a man to distraction, but that doesn't mean he's going to love you back," Belinda had often said.

And Tom hadn't loved Callie back. It had been that simple and that painful.

What would he do if he knew what had happened after he'd left her? A new sliver of grief sliced through her as she thought of those months after he'd left.

Don't think about it, a little voice whispered in her

head. It was a familiar voice and an equally familiar refrain. She'd become an expert at not thinking about it over the last two years.

She had no idea how long Tom would be back in her life this time, but knew that when Del Gardo was gone and the threat to her had vanished, so would Tom. But just because he hadn't loved her didn't mean she had to continue to be so hateful toward him, she thought.

She didn't know how long she'd been working on the computer when she sensed somebody nearby. She turned to see Tom standing in the doorway. "Oh, you're here," she exclaimed and wondered how long he'd been standing there watching her with his dark brooding eyes.

"I'm here," he agreed.

The intensity of his dark gaze discomfited her as she rose from the desk. "Everything all right?"

"As right as it can be for the moment," he replied.

She grabbed her coat and pulled it on and tried not to notice that his gaze swept slowly down the length of her. It wasn't the gaze of a bodyguard, but rather that of a man checking out a woman he might be interested in.

A whisper of heat swept through her as they left her office and headed for the door that would lead to the hallway.

She said goodbye to the lab techs who were working late, waved to Ava Wright, who had looked up from a microscope, then she and Tom headed for the elevator.

"Bree told me you didn't find anything at the Vaughn estate," she said as they stepped into the small enclosure.

"It was just a cursory search. I imagine when Griffin Vaughn gets back into town we might want to look inside again." He frowned. "Something isn't right in that place. I could feel it in my gut."

"Unfortunately gut feelings won't get you anywhere," Callie said dryly.

The elevator arrived on the ground floor and as the doors whooshed open Tom took her by the elbow to escort her out.

It was another cold, gray day and despite the early hour, night shadows had begun to move in. He got her safely to the car and moments later they were headed back to her house.

"I thought maybe I'd call in a pizza for dinner," she said.

"Fine with me."

"I'll get double pepperoni, just the way you like it."

He turned his head and shot her a quick glance. "Have you been drinking at work today?"

A small burst of laughter escaped her. "No, why?"

"Because you haven't exactly gone out of your way to do anything nice for me since this all began."

Callie studied his profile as he returned his attention to the road. He looked tired. The wrinkles at the corners of his eyes looked deeper than usual and the rugged lines on his face appeared sharper than they had that morning.

"I've decided to call a truce," she said.

Once again he flashed her a quick glance. "What exactly does that mean?"

"It means I know I've been rather difficult with you and I'm going to try to ease up. Tom, I don't want to fight with you. I don't want the tension that's been between us."

"That sounds good to me." He frowned and she had the feeling he wanted to say something. He looked at her once again, then into the rearview mirror. "I just want to say one thing."

She tensed in anticipation. "What's that?"

"What happened between us…when I walked away, I just want you to know that I've had a lot of regrets since then."

She mentally ran for the cover of her hard shell to keep the emotions his words evoked away from her head. "It's over and done," she managed to say briskly. "Regrets are nothing but a waste of energy."

"It doesn't stop you from having them," he replied and then they both fell silent.

Callie stared out the window with a frown. How could a simple sentence from him create such havoc inside her? It didn't make sense. There was no concrete reasoning for it.

That was why she liked science better than emotions. She understood science and she'd never really understood the complications of emotions like love or physical attraction. As far as she could tell there was no definitive reason why she'd once loved Tom. It was even more confusing to realize that she still desired him.

After all she'd been through, after all she'd suffered alone because he'd run out on her, why did he still have the ability to make her heart beat too fast, her pulse race with a sweet anticipation?

He parked in her driveway and she watched as he walked around the front of the car to her door. As usual, his gaze appeared sharp and focused as he scanned the area before opening the door to allow her exit.

As she stood he grabbed her and held her against his side, an arm wrapped around her shoulder to keep her close to him.

For a moment she wanted to melt into him, settle into the safety and warmth of his arms. For just a moment she remembered the taste of him, the texture of his mouth against hers.

Buck up, Callie, she told herself. *A man tells you he has some regrets and all of a sudden you turn into a puddle of goo.*

It was one thing to be nice to Tom, it was quite another to think about kissing him.

They had almost reached her front door when she saw it. Tom must have seen it at the exact same time, for in an instant he tightened his hold on her as his gun filled his hand.

Deep wounds slashed down the wood of her front door, the savage claw marks of a bear.

TOM STOOD just off the front porch next to Patrick Martinez as Callie carefully measured the gouges in the front door. They had set up a bright light to shine on the area where she was working.

"I feel personally responsible for this," Patrick said with a deep frown. "I shouldn't have mentioned her name to that reporter. Now she's not only looking over her shoulder for Del Gardo, but also for some creep who thinks he's a bear."

"Any leads in the Windsong case?" Tom asked as he cast a quick gaze around them. Even though he was standing on the lawn with the sheriff, he was still on guard, filled with the kind of adrenaline that could meet danger head-on.

"Nothing. Bree is questioning some of the victim's friends on the reservation, but so far she hasn't learned anything helpful."

Callie finished up her work and together the three of them went into the house and to the kitchen table. "It looks like the same claw that killed Mary," she said. "I measured the distance between the claws and studied the pattern and they appear to match. I'll know for sure when I get to the lab in the morning and can double-check the evidence from the Windsong case."

She smiled at Patrick, but Tom knew her well enough to recognize that it wasn't a real smile. "Don't look so worried, Patrick." She gestured toward Tom. "I'm in good hands."

"I can't help but think I painted a big target on your

back by allowing that reporter to use your name in the paper this morning," he replied.

"As head of the lab, my name has been in the paper lots of times," she reminded him. "You certainly didn't do anything wrong by mentioning it this time."

She bit down on her lower lip and Tom recognized that despite her words her stress level was through the roof. She was scared and he couldn't blame her.

"I'll check with your neighbors, see if any of them saw anybody suspicious lurking around the house," Patrick said as he rose from the table. "In the meantime, you know the drill. Make sure you don't go out alone. Keep Tom close to you at all times. Aside from the fact that we don't know where Del Gardo might be, we also don't know what this bear character might have in mind for you."

"I was hoping it was something personal with Mary and her death would be the end of it," Callie said. "But this warning, or whatever it was meant to be, left on my door makes me afraid that he might not be finished yet."

Her words hung in the air, and Tom knew they were all wondering if this bear killer might possibly be some sort of serial killer. Too soon to tell, Tom thought. Unfortunately it would take another body killed the same way before they could know exactly what they had on their hands.

Damn, he hoped that didn't happen. The expression on both Patrick's and Callie's face let him know they were hoping the same thing.

Both he and Callie walked Patrick to the front door and it was only when the lawman left that Callie showed the first crack in her composure.

She leaned with her back against the entry wall and looked up at him. Her eyes didn't hold that cold brittleness he'd grown accustomed to in the last couple of days, rather they radiated a soft vulnerability that tugged at his heart.

"I've been scared of Del Gardo for so long I think somehow I'd become numb to that fear. But now, knowing it isn't just him I need to watch out for, but some unsub who has marked my house as his territory, I'm suddenly terrified."

As if she were embarrassed by the confession she pushed herself off the wall and straightened her shoulders. Tom knew he was all kinds of a fool but he couldn't help himself. He reached out to her, surprised when she came willingly into his embrace.

She fit neatly against him, the top of her head just beneath his chin, and he closed his eyes as his body remembered hers, relaxing to accommodate the soft, sexy curves that pressed against him.

"You know I'll do everything in my power to see that nobody hurts you," he said softly. He reached up to stroke her sleek short hair.

"I know, but we also both know that if somebody wants you dead badly enough, they'll find a way to accomplish that." Her voice trembled slightly and he could feel the beat of her racing heart against his own.

He cupped her face with his hands and forced her to look up at him. When he'd been in that hospital bed with a raging fever and facing death, it had been a vision of her eyes that had sustained him. It had been the hope that one day he'd look into those eyes again that had kept him fighting for life.

"Not on my watch," he said. Even though he knew it was a mistake, despite the fact that he knew his action would probably only earn him a new seething rage from her, he couldn't help himself. He bent his head and claimed her mouth with his.

Her lush, pillowy lips were soft as sin and, to his surprise, they opened to him. It was all the encouragement he needed to deepen the kiss. He touched his tongue with hers, heat firing in the pit of his stomach as he pulled her closer against him.

With a soft gasp, she jerked back from him. "That isn't exactly the way to make me feel safe," she said, her voice holding a slight tremble. "Maybe I should go order that pizza."

She turned and quickly left the entry and headed into the living room. Tom remained standing by the front door, waiting for his body to cool. He'd known the kiss was a stupid idea, but it had answered one question for him.

She might act cool and as if she'd firmly put him in her past. But her response to his kiss had told him otherwise. She still wanted him. He'd tasted it, felt it in the quickening of her heartbeat as their lips had touched.

Whatever it was that had been between them before, despite her words to the contrary, it wasn't over.

He walked into the living room as she hung up the phone. "The pizza will be here in about thirty minutes," she said.

"Good, because I'm starving." He could tell by the pink of her cheeks that she knew he wasn't talking about food.

"I'm going to go change my clothes," she said and jumped up from the sofa to escape down the hallway.

With an edge of frustration gnawing at him, Tom wandered back to the front of the house and stared out the window.

He wasn't thrilled with the new turn of events. The idea that Callie was now in the sights of some nut with a pair of bear claws concerned him almost as much as Del Gardo's presence somewhere in Kenner City.

Although he'd played off this new threat as nothing for her to be concerned about, he couldn't help but be worried.

Del Gardo was a known entity, this bear killer wasn't. He could be anyone, and until they had an idea of motive, of what drove him, then he was definitely a threat.

He moved from the front window to the kitchen, where he gazed out at the dark backyard. She was right about one thing. If somebody wanted you dead badly enough, then eventually they'd find a way to accomplish that goal.

Callie had the protection of the FBI now, but that protection wouldn't last forever. Eventually, whether Del

Gardo was caught or not, somebody would scream about budget constraints and decide that it wasn't cost effective to keep an agent on her 24/7.

She could always go into the witness protection program, but that would mean she'd not only have to change her name and location, but also what she did for a living. She'd never agree to that. She lived and breathed her lab and she'd never make a conscious choice to walk away from it.

He reached up and touched his mouth, where the taste of her still lingered. As long as he was on duty he'd do everything in his power to see that no harm came to her. But what happened when he was pulled off this case? Who was going to make sure she was safe then?

Chapter Six

For the last week Callie had thrown herself into her work, trying desperately to forget the unexpected kiss that she and Tom had shared.

The kiss had haunted her, invading her dreams at night and drifting into her head during the day. His mouth had been just as she'd remembered—soft yet commanding and fever-pitch hot. It had taken every ounce of strength she'd had to stop it when all she'd wanted to do was spend the rest of that night kissing Tom.

She now stood in the alley behind the Morning Ray Café, where a member of the staff opening up that morning had found the latest victim of the bear-claw killer.

The young woman had been strangled and then sharp claws had ripped her face and chest. At first glance the marks appeared to be the same as those on Mary Windsong and Callie's door, but it would take further examination at the lab to be certain.

A team of her people, along with Patrick's men, were

busy collecting any evidence that might give a clue to the identity of the killer. Patrick's mother, the owner of the Morning Ray Café, stood at the back door, her characteristic sparkling blue eyes now somber.

Tom stood nearby, dividing his attention between the collection process and Callie and each time his dark gaze found her she remembered that damned kiss. And she hated him for making her remember and hated herself for being so weak.

She tore her gaze from Tom and instead pulled her coat collar up against the frigid February wind. Several techs were collecting trash or debris on the ground and another was dusting for fingerprints around the body. The crime scene photos had already been taken, memorializing where everything was in relation to the body.

"What about this garbage?" Sammy Kincaid, one of Patrick's deputies asked, as he indicated the nearby Dumpster that was about a quarter full.

"Bag it all up," Callie directed. "We'll go through it piece by piece and see if we find anything related to the murder."

The deputy didn't look thrilled at the idea of mucking around in the garbage, but Callie wasn't leaving anything overlooked. It was possible the killer had thrown something in the garbage, a cigarette butt, a drinking cup, something that might yield the DNA that would eventually see him behind bars.

Patrick walked over to where she stood, his frown indicating his foul mood. "I was really hoping that Mary

Windsong was an isolated incident, but this puts a whole new spin on things."

"I know," she replied. "He didn't even try to make this look like a bear attack. Maybe the coroner will be able to tell something about how she was strangled that will help. Do we know her name?"

"Lydia Rose, twenty-four years old. Her purse was found next to the body. Money and credit cards intact, so we know robbery isn't a motive." He raised his hands to his mouth and blew on them. The tips of his ears were red with the cold. "Spring can't come fast enough for me."

He glanced over to where Bree was crouched next to the body. "Hard to believe in two days that woman will be wearing a wedding gown."

"Have you two planned a honeymoon?" Callie asked.

Patrick's frown deepened as he stared at Lydia Rose. "We've both agreed that our honeymoon will be put on hold until this mess is resolved. We're going to sneak away for one night, but that's it."

"Hopefully this time the perp left something of himself behind and we'll be able to get him before any other bodies show up," she replied.

"Let's hope. In the meantime we'll be trying to es-tablish some connection between Mary Windsong and Lydia. Maybe they shopped or got their nails done in the same place. If we can find a point of contact between the two women, maybe we can find a man who was in both of their lives."

He drifted away and Callie returned to the task of making sure everything was collected properly in order to be transported back to the lab for analysis.

The next couple of days would be busy ones for her and her techs and scientists, which wasn't a bad thing. Keeping busy was the only way she could keep her mind off Tom.

The week following the kiss had been another one filled with the simmering tension that seemed to exist between them whenever they were in the same room. Although she wanted to know about the scarring on his chest, she was afraid to ask again about what had happened.

She was afraid that if he told her then she'd care and the last thing she wanted was to care about Tom Ryan again. So for the past week she'd retreated back into her shell of cool reserve to protect herself, to protect her heart.

Unfortunately, it didn't seem to be working. The craziest things could evoke old memories inside her, the same habits she once found endearing in him she still found endearing, like the way he ran a finger across a dark brow when he was deep in thought, or the way he jingled his change in his pocket when he was impatient.

The scent of him had permeated every corner of her home and she wondered how long it would take after he left for her to no longer be aware of that evocative smell.

She focused on the task at hand, ignoring Tom as she

got back to work collecting the evidence that would hopefully help them catch this killer.

They were back at the lab by two and Callie got to work examining some of the evidence that had been collected. Thankfully Tom had left and without his presence she was able to give her complete attention to her work.

While Patrick and all the other detectives would concentrate their efforts on learning more about the victim and her movements before the time of her murder, Callie and her team would work on analyzing any forensic evidence left behind.

The afternoon passed quickly. There was always a frenzied level of activity when new evidence came into the lab and today was no different.

She was exhausted when Tom arrived to get her at six. Instantly she recognized something different in him, a new darkness, an edge of danger simmering just beneath the surface.

"Ready?" he asked, his voice as sharp as a gunshot.

She nodded and grabbed her coat. "Has something happened?"

He shook his head and grabbed her by the elbow to lead her out of the lab. Even though he had indicated that nothing had happened with the shake of his head, she felt the tension rolling off him in waves and her stomach twisted into a knot in response.

What was going on? The muscle in his jaw bunched and pulsed as if he were angry. What had happened in the time since he'd left her at the lab and returned to pick her up?

"Bad afternoon?" she asked tentatively once they were in the car and headed to her house.

"No worse than usual," he replied, his voice deeper than usual.

"You seem upset."

He flashed her a dark look then returned his gaze to the road ahead.

A small laugh escaped her. "You're making me nervous."

"You have something to be nervous about?" There was definitely an edge to his voice.

"Other than the obvious? That a crazy killer with bear claws might have me in his sights and a Las Vegas mobster would like to see me dead? No, nothing else that I can think of." What was wrong with him?

He'd never been an easy man to read. Most of the time he kept his emotions tight inside him. He'd told her once that being raised in the foster system had taught him not to give away too much of himself or his emotions.

He'd explained to her that any display of emotion might be seen as a sign of weakness or as a belligerent challenge. He'd learned at an early age to play things close to his chest.

But there was no question that something was up with him. She knew him well enough to know that he was seething inside.

He didn't speak during the drive home and she didn't

try to pierce through his silence. She had a feeling eventually she'd know what was bothering him.

The minute they got into the house she retreated to her bedroom for a quick shower and a change of clothes. She felt particularly grimy after spending the morning in the alley behind the café. Murder scenes always made you feel as if you needed a shower, not so much to wash off the grime, but rather to banish the evil that hung in the air, that might have seeped into your skin.

As she stood beneath the hot spray of water in her master bath she realized she had no idea what they were going to do for dinner.

Maybe Chinese, she thought. There was a great place in town that delivered and the last thing she felt like doing was cooking.

Maybe Tom's mood had changed by now, she thought as she pulled on a pair of sweatpants and a sweatshirt. She knew that he'd been really close to Julie Grainger. It had to be tough to lose not only a colleague, but also a friend.

Maybe the fact that there were no new leads in her murder was finally getting to him. Maybe that was the source of his bad mood.

She knew he'd spent hours studying the map that he'd received from Julie, but was no closer to figuring it out than the day he'd received it.

She quickly brushed her short damp hair, then left the bedroom. She found Tom in the kitchen seated at the table, his eyes dark and enigmatic as they met her gaze.

"I was thinking maybe if it sounds good to you, we could order some Chinese. There's a place in town that delivers and does terrific cashew chicken," she said. "I know you like cashew chicken."

"Sounds fine to me. Why don't you make the call and I'll go clean up." He pushed back from the table and left the kitchen without another word.

Callie watched him go, the knot of tension still twisted in her stomach. Tom's mood didn't exactly promise a pleasant evening.

She made the call to the restaurant, which promised delivery within forty-five minutes, then she made herself a cup of hot tea and sat at the kitchen table.

She was hungry and she was exhausted and all she wanted was a quiet meal, then her bed and hopefully no dreams of Tom's hot mouth on hers. The mere thought of kissing him again shot a rivulet of warmth through her.

She took a sip of her tea and listened to the wintry wind blowing around the side of the house.

It would be a great cuddle night. All too easily she remembered those nights when she and Tom had cuddled beneath crisp sheets. She'd never felt as safe as when she'd been held in his arms, with his deep voice a rumble in her ear as he talked about anything and nothing.

Sure, she'd missed the hot sex they'd always shared. It had been passionate and wild and always satisfying. She'd also missed their laughter, the way he seemed to know what she was thinking almost before she thought it.

But, more than anything. she'd missed the comfort of his hand splayed across the small of her back, the weight of his lean muscular leg across hers and the rumble of his voice in the middle of the night.

He came back into the kitchen. His hair was still damp and he smelled like minty soap. He walked directly to the table, sat down and set two pale-blue baby booties on top. "You want to tell me about these?" he asked. His voice wasn't a rich rumble, but rather a scratchy rasp of emotion.

The sight of the little blue booties sucked all the air from her lungs and threatened a crashing rise of emotions that she knew, if loosened, would destroy her.

TOM SAW the sharp flash in her eyes and the way all the natural color left her cheeks. She raised her cup to her lips and took a drink, but not before he saw the slight tremble in her hand.

When she set the cup back down, her eyes held that cool composure that masked all her emotions.

"Just because you're a guest in my home, that doesn't give you the right to rummage through my personal belongings," she said.

"I needed some paper before I picked you up and I figured the logical place to find some was in the desk drawers and that's where I found these." His chest felt tight as he looked at her for an answer.

"Who do they belong to?" he asked. Crazy thoughts had flown through his head since the moment he'd found the booties in the back of her top desk drawer.

"A friend, not that it's any of your business." Her gaze didn't quite meet his. "She was visiting me with her little baby and he kicked them off and I didn't find them until after they left. I've been meaning to take them back to her, but I'm sure the baby has probably outgrown them by now."

"Then why not just throw them away?" he asked, not believing a word she said. Tom was an expert in recognizing deception and Callie was showing all the signs at the moment.

"Because they aren't mine to throw away." She got up from the table and grabbed hold of the booties and disappeared from the kitchen.

Tom leaned back in his chair and tried to breathe despite the tight band around his chest. She was lying to him. He knew it in his heart, in his soul. Why would she lie? *Because she has something to hide,* a little voice whispered.

He'd found the booties just before leaving to pick her up from the lab, and when he'd seen them, all kinds of suppositions had jumped into his head.

Certainly when they'd been together three years ago they'd always tried to have protected sex, but toward the end of their relationship they had slipped up more than once. Had one of those slip-ups resulted in a pregnancy she'd never told him about?

She returned to the kitchen, appearing as cool and composed as she had before he'd brought the booties to the table.

"You want something to drink while we wait on the food?" she asked.

What he'd like was a bottle of whisky. At least in drinking it he'd have a reason for the burn in his stomach, and if he drank enough, surely it would banish the haunting questions that now played in his mind.

But he couldn't get drunk and do his job of protecting her effectively. "No thanks, I'm fine."

She returned to sit at the table across from him and wrapped her fingers around her cup, as if seeking the warmth of the hot tea.

He was positive she'd lied to him, but had no idea how to pierce through the lie to discover the truth. She held her chin slightly higher than usual, in a stubborn thrust that told him that, as far as she was concerned, the subject of the booties was finished.

"Don't forget, the day after tomorrow I want to go to Bree and Patrick's wedding," she said in an obvious effort to break the tense silence between them and change the subject.

"We'll go to the ceremony, but not the reception afterward," he replied. "Security will be too difficult at the reception."

She opened her mouth as if to protest, but instead sighed wearily and nodded. "I hate this. I hate having to put limits on what I can and can't do because of Del Gardo."

"Until he's in custody you might as well get used to it," he replied. Callie was the most efficient woman he'd ever known. If somebody had left those booties behind she would have seen that they were returned the very next day. She wouldn't have waited until they no longer fit the baby who had kicked them off.

And still, even suspecting that she'd lied to him, despite the fact that he wondered about the shadow of secrets that occasionally darkened her eyes, he wanted her.

The kiss that they'd shared a week ago had only served to make his desire for her more intense. He went to bed each night with a burn for her inside him and awakened each morning with the same need.

"Tell me how you got your scars, Tom."

He looked at her in surprise. "I thought personal information was off-limits."

She waved a hand in the air dismissively. "Forget that rule. It was childish and stupid."

He had a feeling she'd asked only because she wanted to get his attention on something, anything other than those booties. Still, if she wanted to hear about the almost three years that they'd been apart, then she was going to hear it all.

"I was assigned to work undercover in Mexico and infiltrate a gang that was moving a ton of drugs through Brownsville, Texas. We knew who the gang was, but we hadn't been able to identify the American contacts in Texas. That was my job. For a little over a year I became one of the gang."

He stared out the window at the darkness of night

and felt it closing in around him. It had been the most difficult year of his life. He'd not been able to trust or confide in anyone. He'd befriended men who had been the scum of the earth and throughout it all he'd fought the knowledge that he'd made the biggest mistake of his life in walking away from Callie.

He turned his attention back to her. "Everything was going fine. I'd been accepted as one of their own and I knew I was getting closer to being trusted enough to find out the information I needed. Then one night, two of the men told me to go with them to meet their Texas contacts."

He could still remember the excitement that had filled him as the three had piled into a pickup truck. Finally he was going to learn what he needed to know. Finally he was going to see the end of this particularly nasty assignment and get back to the States.

"I don't know to this day how they figured out that I was a Fed. I didn't think I'd made any mistakes. I never had the feeling that they didn't trust me a hundred percent, but instead of driving me out to meet the contacts, they took me to a field and tied my hands behind my back and my feet together."

Her eyes grew dark as he continued. "They meant for me to die, but they didn't want it to be too quick or too easy. They sliced my chest over and over again, deep enough to scar, deep enough that I should have bled to death, but they didn't deliver a killing stab. When they left me and drove away, I knew I was bleeding to death."

"Then what happened?" she asked softly, a thrum of emotion in her voice.

For a long moment he said nothing, couldn't find the words to explain to her what a man saw when he was staring his own death in the face.

It was true that your life flashed before your eyes and what it revealed in that lightning-quick movie was regrets. All the bad choices, all the things never done, those were the kinds of things Tom had thought about during that agonizing time when he thought he was going to die.

"I drifted in and out of consciousness for what seemed like hours, then a young boy found me. His father owned the field and they took me to the nearest hospital and from there I was flown to a hospital in Dallas. I was there for four months, fighting infections and complications from the wounds, and during those four months all I could think of was you."

He heard her slight intake of breath and saw just a brief flash of joy in her eyes before they turned dark and turbulent.

He didn't give her an opportunity to say anything, but instead leaned forward and gazed at her intently. "You scared the hell out of me, Callie. I didn't know anything about love or family. You had started talking about marriage and children and the whole idea scared me to death. I ran and it was the worst mistake I've ever made in my life."

He wasn't sure what he expected her to say, but he'd

certainly expected her to say something. Instead she raised her teacup to her lips and took a swallow, her gaze not meeting his.

When she looked at him again her features displayed no emotion. "I'm sorry you were hurt, but it's all water under the bridge now." A touch of frost hardened her gaze. "I've moved on and I'm sure you have, too."

The doorbell rang. "That will be dinner," she said and started to rise.

"I'll get it," he replied. As he left the kitchen he realized there were some things you only got one chance to get right. He'd had his chance with Callie and had gotten it all wrong. He could tell by her response that he wouldn't get another.

THE NEXT MORNING, after Tom dropped Callie at the lab, he returned to her house, those little blue booties still playing in his mind.

If her friend's baby had outgrown the footwear, then why had Callie kept them? It didn't make sense and things that didn't make sense made him crazy.

Dinner the night before had been tense. His admission of his mistake in leaving her rather than making things better between them seemed to have made everything worse.

She was closed off, distant and no matter what he did in an attempt to breach her defenses, he'd been unsuccessful.

In addition to what he'd said was the subject of those booties, which hung in the air between them like a white elephant they both refused to acknowledge.

She'd gone to her room early and had been in a hurry to get to the lab that morning.

He walked over to the desk and sat in her chair. He knew what he was about to do was wrong, that he had no right to invade her personal life, but he was compelled to do so by forces beyond his control.

He couldn't get those booties out of his mind. He couldn't get crazy ideas out of his head. He had to do something in an attempt to get some answers.

Callie was anal to a fault. It was what made her excellent at her job and what would make it incredibly easy for him to find out some facts about her life during the three years after he'd left her.

He opened the bottom file drawer where she kept her check registers. They were in chronological order for the last five years. He knew she probably had the very first one she'd ever used packed away someplace in a neatly labeled box.

It took him only a few minutes to find the one he'd been looking for, the register that would show what checks she wrote to whom in the months right after they'd parted ways.

He wasn't sure exactly what he was looking for, but figured he'd know it when he saw it. He began to check the entries in the register.

Rent. Electric. Gas. Checks had been written to all

the places a person would need to pay to live. There were also several checks written to The Best Boutique, which he figured was a clothing store, The Chinese Wok and a pizza place.

As he went down the list of places the checks had been written to, he saw nothing out of the ordinary, nothing that caught his attention.

It wasn't until he looked at the checks written six weeks after he'd left that he found the first entry that sparked a surge of adrenaline through him.

Dr. Roger Weatherby.

There was no notation next to the entry and the amount of the check was obviously a co-pay amount. So, she'd seen a doctor six weeks after he'd left. That didn't mean anything, he told himself.

A month later there was another entry for Dr. Roger Weatherby and a month after that another. Five months of checks written to the doctor and then nothing.

Had she been ill? What kind of illness required a monthly check-in with a doctor? He knew of only one kind and the thought sent a wave of anxiety through him. Was it possible? Blood rushed to his head and for a moment he was dizzy, almost breathless with speculation.

He placed the registers back in the drawer where they belonged, his hands shaking, then he powered up her computer.

There was only one way to make an intelligent guess about what had ailed her during those months after he'd left. He needed to find out what kind of medicine Dr. Weatherby practiced.

Maybe he's a psychologist or a psychiatrist, he told himself as he waited for the computer to get up and running. Certainly she'd been through a difficult situation, first with the testimony against a mobster, then Del Gardo's escape and Tom's defection. He couldn't blame her if she'd needed to see somebody, to talk out everything or maybe be prescribed some medicine to help her cope with everything she'd been through.

Let it be a psychiatrist. Let it be a psychiatrist. The litany played through his head as he typed in the search for Dr. Roger Weatherby in the Las Vegas area.

He held his breath as the search engine did its work, yielding a single result. He clicked on the page and pulled up the official Web site of Dr. Roger Weatherby.

Dozens of pictures of babies filled the screen along with a tagline that read, *Let Dr. Roger Bring Your Baby into the World.*

Tom leaned back in the chair and tried to breathe. Dr. Roger Weatherby was an obstetrician. A baby doctor. Callie had been pregnant when he'd left her. She'd been pregnant with his baby. There could be no other explanation.

His heart pounded with a sick thud that echoed in his ears. If the blue booties were any indication, she'd been pregnant with his son.

A son.

His and Callie's child.

His heart squeezed so tight he gasped as he fought a wave of emotion the likes of which he'd never felt before. Why hadn't she told him? Even though she hadn't known where he was, she could have tried to contact him by leaving a message at his field office.

Beneath the anger, beyond the sense of betrayal that beat in his heart was a single question—where was his son now?

Chapter Seven

It was another quiet, tense meal. They'd left the lab later than usual as Tom had been hung up with a briefing. They hadn't managed to get away until almost eight.

Callie now picked at the cheeseburger and fries from a nearby drive-through and felt an imminent explosion in the air and she was afraid she knew why.

Those booties. Normally she wasn't a sentimental person, but she'd been unable to get rid of them. They had become as much a part of her as her own heartbeat.

"We found two hairs on Lydia Rose's body," she said to break the silence. "Long, black human hair. We're running DNA on them and if the perp has a record we might get lucky and find a match in the system. Even if we don't get a hit in the system, at least it will be evidence to use at trial if and when Patrick arrests somebody for the crime."

She was rambling and suddenly couldn't stop herself. She couldn't stand another minute of his silence and if the only thing available to fill it was her own voice, then so be it.

"Ava has been fighting off some kind of flu bug. Her stomach has been upset for the last two weeks. I'm just hoping none of the rest of us come down with it. We've got so much work piled up right now."

He dragged a french fry through a puddle of ketchup and popped it into his mouth, his gaze not wavering from her face even though he didn't say a word.

"At least the weather is supposed to stay okay through the wedding tomorrow," she continued. "It would be terrible if we got a big snow storm and nobody could attend."

He took the last bite of his cheeseburger and chewed, then chased it down with a sip of his soda. When he was finished he shoved his plate away.

She felt ridiculously nervous as she took another bite of her burger, self-conscious as he watched her chew. He hadn't said more than ten words since he'd picked her up at the lab.

"I guess you haven't figured out anything more about the map Julie sent to you." She continued to fill the dead space with the sound of her own voice. "Maybe it's one of those things that once you stop thinking about it, the answers will just pop into your head."

She finally stopped talking and allowed the uncomfortable silence to descend between them. Unless he decided to share whatever it was that was on his mind, there was nothing she could do about it.

She finally gave up trying to eat and pushed her plate away.

"Tell me about Dr. Roger Weatherby," he finally said.

Callie's heart screeched to a painful stop. What did he know? How had he found out about Dr. Weatherby? Oh God, what did he know? *Bluff,* a little voice whispered. *He couldn't have found out, so bluff your way through this just like you did the booties.*

"What about him?" she asked, trying to keep her voice light and hoping her anxiety didn't show in her voice.

"Why were you seeing him?" Although his voice was calm and measured, she saw the raw, seething emotion that sweltered in the darkness of his eyes.

"I don't think that's any of your business," she replied.

"I think it is," he countered. His jaw muscle worked overtime, knotted with pulsing energy.

"I...I was having some female problems." The lie tasted terrible in her mouth. She kept her gaze riveted to his, refusing to look away despite her desire to the contrary.

"What kind of female problems?" He was deceptively calm, but she knew the kind of anger that could hide beneath that calm. It rolled off him in waves.

"Endometriosis. What difference does it make to you? It was a long time ago." She stiffened her shoulders. "And how did you find out about me seeing Dr. Weatherby anyway?" She grasped for outrage, needing it to keep other emotions at bay.

"It doesn't matter how I found out. Were you pregnant,

Callie? Did you have my baby?" His voice cracked. "Did you have our baby and give him up for adoption?" He pushed back from the table with such force his chair toppled backward. "Tell me, do I have a son someplace out there?"

"No!" She jumped out of her chair, needing to meet him head-on. Oh, God, she didn't want to have this conversation. She needed to put an end to it once and for all. "There was no baby, Tom. There is no son anywhere!"

She felt sick to her stomach and for just a moment she hated him for bringing all this up, for sticking his nose in places where he didn't belong, where he had no right. He'd given up any right when he'd turned his back on her and walked away.

"I don't know what kind of snooping you did to jump to that conclusion, but it's wrong," she exclaimed. "You're wrong." She allowed her anger to overwhelm her, embracing it to keep the darkness of the truth away.

"How dare you come back and pry into my life. You walked away from me without a backward glance. There is no child. Do you hear me?" She shook with the force of her rage.

"If you have questions about what happened to me after you left, then you ask me. Don't you dare sneak around behind my back and pry into matters that don't concern you. Your job here is to protect me. Nothing more and nothing less."

She couldn't say anything else, the wealth of anger and grief twisted her insides so tight she was breathless.

She turned and ran from the kitchen, grateful when he didn't follow her.

When she was inside her bedroom she collapsed across the bed and fought the tears that begged to be released. She couldn't cry. She knew if she started, if she allowed even one teardrop to fall she wouldn't be able to stop. She never cried and she refused to do so now.

Don't think, she commanded herself. There was no going back. Tears accomplished nothing. The past couldn't be changed.

Don't think.

Don't think about Dr. Weatherby or little blue booties and for God's sake, don't cry.

Sleep. That's what she needed. The sweet oblivion of sleep. She got up from the bed and went into the bathroom where she changed into her nightgown, then scrubbed her face and brushed her teeth. Only in sleep could she escape from the heartache that always threatened to grab hold of her.

With the lights out she sank into bed and focused on the work at the lab. Work. That's what had gotten her through the last three years. It was the only thing she could depend on, the only thing that didn't require emotion.

She imagined the spin of the cell-separating machine, the whoosh of the exhaust fan and the white noise that the lab always contained. Within minutes, exhausted by the confrontation with Tom and emotionally spent, she'd drifted off to sleep.

The dream began almost immediately. Tom lay on the ground in the middle of a field, tied up as disembodied bear claws raked down his chest and stomach.

"Where's the baby, Callie?" he screamed with each rip into his flesh. "Where's my son?"

"There is no baby," she cried in return, but he refused to believe her.

The scene changed and instead she stood alone on a hilltop with the wind screaming in a voice that cried of grief and loss. She held a pair of scissors and as the sorrow ripped through her, she cut length after length off her hair.

It was only in her dream world that she wept for Tom and for the loss of the life she'd imagined they might have had together. It was only when asleep that tears seeped from her eyes as she cried over a pair of little blue booties.

Once again the scene changed again and it was Tom again, shouting questions to her about the son he'd never know while his chest was ravaged by a bear, and then the bear began to advance on her.

She had to fight the bear, collect the evidence that he'd left behind. She needed to save Tom.

"Callie!"

The bear roared her name and grabbed her by the shoulders and she realized she had to save herself before she could save Tom.

"Callie, stop!"

Fingers bit into her shoulders and she came awake with

a startled gasp. From the light spilling in from the hallway she realized Tom sat on the edge of her bed, his hands on her shoulders as he shook her from the terrible nightmare.

Recognizing that she was awake, he dropped his hands from her. "You were having a bad dream," he said.

She nodded, her chest tight with the memory. She sat up and slumped forward, her face in her hands as she tried to catch her breath. "I was dreaming about a bear attack," she finally said. "I knew I needed to collect the evidence in order to catch the bear." She shook her head. She didn't tell him what part he'd played in the dream, how he'd cried for answers about a son. "What time is it?"

"Just after two."

She pulled her hands from her face and looked at him in the semidarkness of the room. He wore only a pair of boxers and the clean male scent of him grounded her in the here and now.

"I dreamed the bear was attacking you." Her gaze slid from his face down to his chest, where the skin was puckered and scarred. Without making a conscious decision to do so, she reached out her hand and ran it across the damaged skin.

He sucked in his breath at the soft caress and she felt every muscle in his body tighten. "Callie." Her name was a whisper of warning on his lips.

She didn't stop. Her fingers danced across the broad expanse of his warm chest. She could feel his heartbeat,

a rapid tattoo that told her she was wading into dangerous waters.

The scars didn't bother her. It was skin. Tom's skin,
and rough or smooth, she'd always liked touching him.

Maybe they needed to make love. One last time. A
final bit of closure. There was no doubt that a lot of the
tension between them was sexual. Maybe in indulging
themselves it would clear the air between them.

Even as she thought these things she recognized the
real truth: that she didn't care about clearing the air
between them, that her desire at this moment had
nothing to do with anything other than the fact that she
wanted him to make love to her.

Her caress shifted to his taut lower abdomen and
with another gasp he grabbed her hand. "What are you
doing, Callie?" His eyes glowed in the near darkness.
"Don't start something you don't intend to finish."

"Who said I don't intend to finish?" She heard the
thrum of excitement in her voice.

He let go of her hand and stood. "I'll be right back."
Like a lean shadow he moved out of the room.

She lay back on the bed and drew a deep, steadying
breath. Now was the time for her to change her mind,
she thought. With him out of sight, out of her touch, now
was the chance to cool down.

But she didn't cool down, instead she felt the heat
building, firing through her with an intensity that half
stole her breath away.

It will just be sex, she told herself. Sex was easy and

as long as she didn't get her heart involved with him again there wouldn't be a problem.

He returned to the room a moment later, carrying his gun and a condom package. He placed both items on the nightstand and then stood next to the bed, as if waiting for an invitation.

She could feel his energy, that dark vibe that promised sinful pleasure and she wanted that pleasure. She wanted him. She slid over and pulled the sheet back to welcome him in.

He didn't hesitate. He joined her in the bed and gathered her in his arms as his mouth found hers in a fiery kiss.

His hands moved to the back of her slick nightgown, heating her skin beneath the fabric. She didn't want to think. She just wanted to lose herself in the sensation of his body so intimately close to hers, in the taste of him as he deepened the kiss with his tongue.

She didn't have to love him again in order to love having sex with him. She could still hate him for what he'd done to her three years ago yet love what he was doing to her right now.

She was good at compartmentalizing. It was what made her great at her job. She could take the pleasure he offered without allowing herself to be hurt again.

And there was pleasure. Tom had learned a long time ago how and where she liked to be touched, what intimacy would fire sweet sensation through her body.

A kiss behind her ear, a caress up her smooth inner

thigh, the whisper of her name hot against her neck, each and everything he did electrified her and shot her desire for him higher.

It took only moments before he'd removed her nightgown and his boxers and their naked flesh once again sought each other's heat.

He cupped her breast in his hand and used his thumb to rake over her taut nipple. She shivered with pleasure and then gasped as he drew her nipple into his hot mouth.

Tangling her hands in his hair, she moved beneath him and felt his hard arousal against her thigh. She wanted him hard and fast; not sweet, tender lovemaking, but frenzied, hot sex.

She reached down and took him in her hand, stroked the length of him and he whispered her name against her skin. He seemed to sense her desire for hard and fast, for he slid his hand from her breast to her stomach, then lower still until she cried out with the pleasure at the intimacy of his touch.

Wildly moving her hips to meet his hand, she felt herself climbing higher, the tension twisting tighter inside her.

There was no room for overthinking, no space for thought at all. There was just his touch, his mouth hot against her own and sheer, unadulterated pleasure.

She cried out his name as her orgasm shattered through her. He held her for only a moment then moved away and put on the condom. Then he was back on her, in her, and as they moved in unison Callie felt the rise of that overwhelming tension once again.

She gave herself to it, to him, and someplace in the back of her mind she knew that this was a mistake, that there was absolutely nothing simple about sex with Tom.

TOM SAT in the tiny conference room down the hall from the lab along with Ben Parrish and Dylan Acevedo. They were waiting on a call from their supervisor, Jerry Ortiz.

Jerry wouldn't be happy with their lack of progress in Julie's murder, but they had hit a dead end. The map that Tom had received had been twisted and turned in an attempt to make sense of it. It was the same with the series of numbers that had been on the back of the medals both Tom and Ben had received.

As if his frustration over the case wasn't enough, Tom also had Callie on his mind. Making love to her the night before had been like coming home, and Tom had never had a home before in his life.

She'd fit against him so perfectly, as if their bodies had been made for each other. He'd been lost in her from the moment he'd gotten into bed with her.

But, the moment they'd finished, she'd shut him out. He'd gone back to his bed in the guest room and wondered if she would ever be able to forgive him for his past mistakes.

He had no choice but to believe her when she told

him there was no little boy someplace out there. What had surprised him more than anything was the rush of joy that had swept through him when he thought it might be possible, when he'd believed that she might have had his son.

Maybe it was some sort of female trouble that had prompted those visits to the doctor. After all, the visits hadn't gone on for nine months. He admitted that he might have jumped to a wrong conclusion.

"Let's go over what we know," Dylan said, cutting through Tom's thoughts.

Tom leaned back in the chair with a frown. "We know Julie's body was found on the Ute reservation. We know she was strangled with something that left a pattern on her skin."

"And so far nobody has been able to identify what exactly left that pattern," Dylan added.

"Then we have these." Ben reached up and grabbed the Joan of Arc medal that hung around his neck, then pointed to the one that hung around Tom's neck. "The patron saint of captives and the patron saint of travelers. They have to mean something, otherwise Julie wouldn't have sent them to us."

"Maybe that Del Gardo is traveling around the country? That he's taken a captive that we don't know anything about?" Dylan shook his head, as if aware that his own words made no sense. "Nobody has been able to figure out the numbers on the back, either. It's like we've been given a puzzle, but half the pieces are missing."

"We now know Del Gardo bought that estate a month after Callie took the job here," Tom said. "What I don't understand is why he didn't kill her before we all got involved, before I was assigned to her protection."

"We can't know for sure that he hasn't tried," Ben replied. "Maybe he was being careful to make it look like it was an accident of some kind. Callie admits that there have been two close calls on her life. She was nearly run over, then there was the fire. If it had been allowed to burn out of control it's possible we might not have known the origin. Maybe there were more near misses that she doesn't know about. Maybe she's just been incredibly lucky so far."

"Or maybe Del Gardo didn't want to make his presence here known because he was worried about a member of the Wayne family seeking vengeance. Del Gardo ordered the hit that killed Freddy 'The Gun' Wayne. You know the Wayne mob didn't take that murder lightly. There was obviously a turf war going on between the two families."

Dylan's eyes darkened. "I still believe that Del Gardo killed Julie. We need to find him and the evidence that will tie up this case. We owe it to Julie to get closure."

"I don't believe he's left the area," Tom said. "There's no doubt in my mind that he came here for Callie and until he gets to her he won't leave."

. At that moment the phone rang and it was Jerry and the briefing began.

Even though it was Saturday the work both he and Callie did didn't respect the weekends. He was hoping to keep her home the next day. He could use a day with her safely locked in the house where the level of his readiness to fight any danger that might present itself wasn't quite so high.

It was just before four when Tom went to find Callie. She was knocking off early today to get ready for Patrick and Bree's wedding at six-thirty that evening.

He found her in her office and for a moment he stood at the door and watched her without her knowing he was there.

He'd been in love with her three years ago. He hadn't realized the depths of that love at the time. He'd allowed fear to drive him away. He loved her still. The idea of marrying her, of having a family with her no longer frightened him.

But, how did he get her to forgive him? He didn't know much about women. Before Callie there had been plenty of them in his life, but they had all been transients, passing through on a temporary basis.

She was the only one who had tagged his heart, the only one who had made him not only face his fear of commitment but yearn for it.

So, how *did* he get her to forgive him? The same question continued to play in his mind, a question that had no answer. How did he make her realize that they belonged together, not just for now, but forever?

As if she sensed him standing in the doorway, she whirled around. Her eyes were guarded, as they'd been this morning.

"Time to go?"

He nodded and watched as she stood and reached for her coat. "It's going to be a nice night for a wedding," he said as together they left the lab.

"At least it's not snowing," she replied.

He felt her stiffen slightly as he took hold of her elbow and pulled her closer against him to leave the building.

He'd thought that maybe making love to her would remind her of how good they'd been together, how good they could still be together. But instead of bringing them closer, the act seemed to have cast her further away.

"Tough day?" he asked once they were in the car and headed back to her house.

"No more so than usual." She relaxed back against the seat. "I'm looking forward to the wedding. It will be nice to just get out and relax among other people for a change. It would be nice if we could go to the reception like normal people."

He heard the wistfulness in her voice. He'd said they wouldn't go to the reception because he didn't want to have to worry about her security in the crowd he figured would show up for such an event.

But, he also knew how difficult the last ten days had been on her. They'd gone nowhere but to the lab and back to her house. Hell, they hadn't even acknowledged when Valentine's Day had come and gone.

She'd had no social interaction with anyone other than coworkers and him. Suddenly he wanted—no, needed—to see her smile.

"I guess it wouldn't hurt if we decided to go to the reception," he said.

She turned her head and rewarded him with one of those rare smiles of hers that threatened to curl his toes. "Really?"

"As long as you stick close to me."

She raised her hand. "I promise. Besides, I can't imagine there being any danger. Bree and Patrick have been saying it's going to be a small affair. There will be plenty of law enforcement officials there."

Her eyes shone with the excitement of a night out and his love for her welled up inside him, but he couldn't speak of it now. He didn't want to take away that smile of hers, force the icy shield back into place in her eyes.

Tonight he swore to keep things light, to allow her the night to laugh and to smile with her friends. He wouldn't ask her about forgiveness or a baby that never was, or anything else to dampen her spirits.

Two hours later as Callie came out of her bedroom dressed for the wedding, it was difficult for Tom to think about keeping things light.

The navy dress she wore hugged her curves and the plunging neckline displayed more than a hint of creamy skin. Her slender legs looked long and sexy in a pair of high heels.

He'd never seen her look so softly feminine. He'd grown accustomed to seeing her in her button-down blouses and crisp tailored slacks. "You look amazing," he finally said.

Her cheeks grew pink and she eyed his charcoal gray suit and white shirt with a nod of approval. "You look very nice yourself." She pulled a black dress coat from the hall closet and he helped her into it, trying to keep his fingers from lingering on her bare shoulders, trying not to notice that floral scent that drove him crazy.

As Tom led her out to the car he wondered if maybe he shouldn't pull himself off this assignment. Even though it hadn't been his intention, he'd gotten too close to her again. Only this time he knew it was his heart that was going to get broken.

IF CALLIE WERE a weepy kind of woman, she would have definitely cried at the wedding. Watching Patrick and Bree exchange their vows had stirred all the yearning that Callie usually kept tamped down inside her.

Patrick and Bree had been lovers years ago when they had both worked a series of hate crimes on the reservation. Callie didn't know what had broke them apart, but from what Bree had told her they had parted and Bree had found herself pregnant.

Bree had married a man from the reservation and had her son, Peter, but the marriage hadn't lasted. Then she and Patrick had reunited and the rest was a fairy tale as far as Callie was concerned. The three of them would now live as a happy family.

Bree looked beautiful and Patrick looked as if he was

about to burst with pride as they exchanged the vows that would bind them together as husband and wife.

The ceremony itself was brief and as Callie had guessed, was attended by some of her lab coworkers, Bree's friends from the reservation and some of Patrick's deputies. Patrick's mother, Nora, who was usually a bubbly, giggling woman, wept with obvious happiness. She was not only getting a daughter-in-law, but had gotten a grandson as well.

After the ceremony they all moved to the reception that was to take place at the restaurant Nora owned, the Morning Ray Café. Callie didn't want to think about the last time she'd been there, when the body of Lydia Rose had been found in the alley.

Law enforcement had yet to find a connection between Mary Windsong and Lydia Rose that might point them to the killer, but Callie didn't want to think about murders tonight.

Some of the tables and chairs had been taken down to provide a small dance floor and a three-piece band provided live music.

Nora bustled around, checking the spread of food laid out on the counter, her rich laughter ringing above the din.

Callie and Tom sat at a table and were joined by Deputy Greg Samuel and his wife, Gretchen. The talk was wonderfully normal. The two men talked about football teams and Callie and Gretchen discussed new fashions and home décor.

Tom had relaxed the minute he realized the restaurant

was officially closed and only invited guests were allowed inside. Although Callie knew he'd remain on alert, he seemed to be enjoying the night out as much as Callie.

It was only when Ben brought up the latest bear-claw murder that Tom held his hands up in protest. "Not tonight," he told the tall, thin man. "Callie needs a night off from thinking about work. You can talk about it tomorrow, but tonight is just for fun."

She looked at him with a guarded gratefulness. She was comfortable when he was brooding and surly, but when he did something thoughtful and nice she immediately raised her defenses against him.

In fact, her defenses had been erected again after the night they'd made love. She couldn't allow him back in, not in the way she had done before. She had to hang on to her anger where he was concerned. She needed to remember her sense of betrayal, the agony he'd left behind.

She couldn't let him into her heart again and she couldn't let him know the secret she'd kept from him. There was no point. The past was gone and nothing could be changed or undone.

Yes, she could want him physically again, she could find him breathtakingly attractive and easy to talk to, but she would never, ever allow herself to love him again.

Chapter Eight

She'd drunk too much. Callie didn't realize how much champagne she'd had until she and Tom decided to call it a night and she started to get out of her chair. The alcohol she'd consumed went straight to her head.

"Whoa," Tom exclaimed with a laugh as he grabbed her by the shoulders to steady her.

"Somebody did a little too much celebrating," she exclaimed with an uncharacteristic giggle.

"I think it's time we take that somebody home," Tom replied as he guided her toward the door. As they headed for the exit of the café they said goodbye to all the guests who were left.

Patrick and Bree had left an hour earlier. Their son, Peter, was staying with Nora for the night. As Callie leaned heavily against Tom she was glad they were going home. Another glass of champagne might have been her complete undoing.

"You know I rarely drink," she said to Tom as they left the café and got into his car. "I don't know why I imbibed so much this evening. Imbibed, don't you think that's a funny word?" She laughed again and it felt wonderful to be laughing for a change.

He cast her a lazy, sexy grin, then started the car. "It's a funny word and I think maybe when we get home we should have some coffee."

Callie nodded. "Coffee would be good. You know, I'm not smashed, I'm just highly buzzed."

"You needed to cut loose. I know how tense things have been at the lab not only because of Julie's murder but also the last two young women."

"Things have been tense," Callie agreed. But surely he had to know that work wasn't the only thing she found stressful, that being with him on a daily basis added to her level of stress.

Still, at the moment she didn't feel tense, she felt the floating kind of well-being that came with too much alcohol.

"It was a nice night, wasn't it? Bree looked so beautiful and both she and Patrick looked so happy." Callie leaned her head back and released a wistful sigh.

"Why haven't you married, Callie?" Tom asked softly. "I know you wanted that, the whole picket fence thing with the dog in the yard, a couple of kids underfoot. I figured when I left you'd find some nice guy with a nine-to-five job and be happily married within a year."

She opened her eyes and studied him in the faint light from the dashboard. "I would have liked for that to happen, but it didn't." The conversation was sobering her up quickly. "I have my work, that's all I've really ever needed."

"That's not true, that's never been true," he said as he parked the car in her driveway. He unbuckled his seat belt and turned to look at her. "I knew the minute I met you that you were a woman meant to be a wife, a mother."

Callie opened her car door. She didn't want to have this conversation with him. Just as she knew he would do, he quickly jumped out of the car to escort her into the house.

When they got inside he helped her off with her coat and hung it in the closet, then he shrugged out of his own, yanked his tie free and headed for the kitchen. "I'll put on a pot of coffee," he said. "And you might want to take a couple of aspirins before going to bed."

She followed after him, knowing that coffee and aspirin were probably a good idea if she wanted to ward off a hangover in the morning.

As she sat at the table he took off his suit jacket, unfastened his gun holster and laid it on the counter, then made the coffee.

As they waited for the coffee to brew, they hashed over the night's events. Callie felt more relaxed than she had since the night of the fire in the lab. In fact, she felt more relaxed than she had since the moment Tom had reentered her life.

"Thanks," she said as he placed a cup of the coffee in front of her and then sat next to her with a cup of his own.

"We'll take a day off tomorrow," he said. He raised a hand to still her protest. "Callie, you've been working every day for almost two weeks straight. The lab work will continue without you there for a day. Besides, I could use a day where I don't have to look over your shoulder to see who might be getting too close to you."

She hadn't really realized until that moment how tired he had to be with the day-in-day-out merry-go-round they'd been on.

"Okay," she agreed. "To tell the truth, the idea of sleeping late and just lounging around for a day sounds like heaven."

"How about if I make a big pot of chili?"

"Hmm, sounds good to me. As I remember you make a great chili."

He took a sip of his coffee, his dark brown eyes gazing at her over the rim of his cup. "Why did you cut your hair?"

She reached up and self-consciously ran a hand over her sleek, short hair. She vividly remembered the day she'd taken the scissors to it. Reeling with grief, tormented by what might have been, she'd butchered it to the point she'd had to visit a hair salon the next morning so somebody could repair the damage.

"I just needed a change," she answered.

"I like it. It suits you," he replied. He set the cup down and leaned forward in his chair. "When I was in the hospital recovering from my wounds I had a lot of time to think about my life. I told you years ago that I'd been raised in the foster care system. I never made any real attachments when I was growing up. I learned early on to depend only on myself."

Callie watched him carefully. Tom by nature wasn't a long-winded kind of man. He wasn't given to sharing thoughts or experiences unless it was necessary. She didn't know where he going with this or why a new wave of wariness buoyed up inside her. She took a sip of her coffee even though at the moment she felt stone-cold sober.

"It was while I was lying in that hospital bed that I realized that if I'd died out there in that Mexico field there would be nobody to mourn me, that I'd left nothing of myself behind."

"That's not true," she protested. "You've touched a lot of lives in your work as an FBI agent."

He waved a hand, his eyes growing even darker. "Strangers. People who might appreciate my work for a minute but then get on with their lives, loving their spouses, caring for their kids, doing the kinds of things that really matter in this life."

He reached up and touched the medal that hung around his neck. "The patron saint of travelers. Maybe rather than this being a clue, Julie was making a comment on my life. I'm never in one place for very long. Sometimes I forget exactly where my apartment is because I'm never there. I've been a traveler all my life and now I'm tired of always being on the move, of always being alone." He drew a deep voice and continued, "I've decided that once Del Gardo is back behind bars I'm quitting my job."

Callie stared at him in stunned surprise. "You don't mean that."

"Oh, but I do." He took another sip from his cup. "It's something that I've been thinking about for some time. I want to see the Del Gardo thing to its completion, but after that, I'm out. I've already let my superior know of my decision."

"But, what are you going to do?" She couldn't imagine Tom not being an FBI agent. It wasn't just something he did, it was who he was.

"I don't know. I've never done much of anything with my salary except deposit it in the bank, so I have enough put away that I don't have to make any quick decisions. I was kind of hoping when the time came you'd help me make that decision."

Callie stared at him and a little voice in the back of her head told her to run, to escape from whatever he was going to say. But she remained frozen in her seat with some perverse need to hear whatever he wanted her to hear. "How can I help you make any decision about your future?" she asked.

He turned his head and stared out the window at the dark of night. She studied his profile. He had always appeared to be such a strong man, one who needed nobody. But, there was a softness to his features now, a hint of vulnerability she'd never seen before. When he gazed back at her that vulnerability shone from his eyes.

"Thoughts of you were what made me keep fighting to get well when I was in that hospital bed," he said.

He reached out and took her hand in his. His fingers wrapped around hers, casting a radiating warmth from his touch up her arm and straight to her heart. "As I lay there pumped full of painkillers and antibiotics, all I could think about was what a fool I'd been and how I hoped I got the chance to see you again."

For weeks after he'd left her, Callie had wanted to hear these words from him, she'd ached with the need for him to come running back and tell her he'd made a terrible mistake. But the weeks had turned into months and the months into years without a word from him. Whatever he was about to say, she reminded herself that it was too little too late.

"Tom." She pulled her hand from his as she consciously erected the familiar barrier around her heart.

He must have sensed her need to escape. "Please, let me finish, Callie," he replied hurriedly. "I knew I hurt you when I left you, but I was scared. I knew you wanted a husband, a father for your children and I didn't think I knew how to be either of those things. It was easier to run than to try and then fail."

"It was a long time ago, Tom. It's over and done now," she said, speaking around the lump that had formed in her throat. Couldn't he see that he was killing her softly, tearing her apart as he bared his soul?

"That's the problem, it's not over and done. I knew the minute I saw you again that it wasn't over for me and the other night when we made love I knew it wasn't really over for you, either."

His gaze burned into her, as if attempting to pierce through the protective shell she'd wrapped around her heart. "I want a life with you, Callie. Please, tell me you forgive me for being a fool. Tell me that we can build a life together. For God's sake, please tell me it isn't too late."

Hope shone from his eyes, a hope she wanted to fall into, she wanted to embrace, but she steeled her heart against it.

She'd once entertained that same kind of hope but it had meant nothing to him. He'd heard her tell him how much she loved him, then he'd turned his back on it, on her.

She needed to remember that, she needed to remember that agonizing sense of loss, that raging anger that had sustained her through the worst experience of her life. Without it she'd been empty except for the over-whelming grief she refused to face, she absolutely couldn't face.

"Tom, there's no question that there's a strong physical attraction between us," she began. That was a fact she knew she'd be a fool to try to convince him otherwise.

"But, don't mistake that for anything but what it is. I always liked having sex with you, but there's no do-over with us. You told me before that I'd become a hard woman. Maybe I have, because I can't forgive you for leaving me."

Her heart ached as she watched that hope in his eyes douse and disappear. She needed to escape from the dark shroud that fell over his eyes, from the want that burned inside her heart.

"Good night, Tom." She got up from the table, half-expecting him to stop her, but he didn't. She ran down the hallway and prayed he'd leave her alone.

When she was alone in her bedroom she stripped off her clothes and got into her nightgown, consciously keeping her mind empty of all thoughts.

Before getting into bed she locked her bedroom door. She didn't want him coming in to continue the conversation or for anything else. She was a strong woman, but Tom Ryan had always been her greatest weakness.

She got into bed and squeezed her eyes tightly closed, begging for sleep to take her quickly. She didn't want to think about what she'd just done. She didn't want to reconsider her decision where he was concerned.

No do-overs. She had to cling to that notion because if she didn't she'd have to tell him her secret and that was the last thing she wanted to do.

Thankfully, sleep came quickly. She wasn't sure how long she'd been asleep when some faint noise woke her. She stirred and cold air hit her face. She frowned and then froze as something sharp pressed against the base of her throat.

She opened her eyes and in the moonlight spilling in through the broken window she saw him. A young, dark-haired, black-eyed Ute with red-and-black face paint and bear claws pressed against her neck.

"Don't make a sound," he whispered, his breath a fetid blast of warmth. "I am the spirit of the bear and I've come for you."

TOM REMAINED SEATED at the kitchen table long after Callie had gone to bed. He finally shut off the coffee pot, rinsed it out then grabbed his gun from the counter and went to his room.

But regrets kept sleep at bay. He lay on his back and stared up at the ceiling where the moonlight drifting through the curtains danced eerie shadows.

He'd thought he'd had a chance to make things right. He'd believed that the two of them being together was right. So how had it all gone so wrong?

There had been moments over the last ten days when he'd thought he felt her love for him, thought he'd seen it shining from her eyes. He might not know a lot about women, but he'd thought he knew Callie well. At least he'd once known her well.

He still had the feeling that something had happened to her in the last three years, something traumatic, something that had changed her at her very core.

She'd always been cool and competent at work, reserved with people she didn't know, but there had been a warmth, an irrepressible joy in her that seemed to be missing now.

So, what had happened?

He realized there was no point in lying in the bed and tossing and turning. Thinking about Callie caused an ache in his chest that he'd never felt before.

Work.

He'd always been able to assuage his loneliness with work. With this thought in mind he got out of bed, grabbed the map that had come from Julie and returned to the kitchen table.

Placing his gun and the map on the table in front of him, he stared down at the cryptic message from Julie and willed away any thought of Callie and the conversation they had just shared.

He stared down at the map that appeared to be a sewer-like series of tunnels. They had compared the map to all the underground waterways in Kenner City and it hadn't been a match. So, what did the map depict?

He ran his fingers across the VDG at the top of the map. "Where are you, you bastard?" he murmured aloud.

His head filled with a vision of Vincent Del Gardo. At sixty-eight years old, the man wasn't tall, but gave the appearance of being bigger than life because of the power and confidence that radiated from his brown eyes. He should have been easy to spot with his signature bald head and snow-white beard, but the agents working the case were all aware of the fact that he'd probably changed his appearance.

He'd bought that mountain estate to be close to Callie. There was no way in hell Tom believed that he'd left the area, not with Callie still alive. She was his unfinished business, just like she was Tom's unfinished business.

Why couldn't Callie find forgiveness in her heart for him? What could he do, what could he possibly say to earn her forgiveness and the chance to show her just how much he loved her?

He rubbed his eyes. They felt gritty from lack of sleep. It was a waste of time to sit here staring at the map and apparently it was a waste of time to continue to yearn for a woman who wasn't going to give him her heart again.

He'd abused that heart once. Could he really blame her for not trusting him with it again?

Sighing with a soul-deep weariness, he grabbed the map and his gun and got up from the table, turned out the kitchen light and headed back to his bedroom.

He was about to enter the bedroom when he heard a noise from Callie's room.

A bump.

A rustle.

Noises that didn't belong in a room where a woman was sleeping.

He tensed. Another bump, then a scream that raised the hairs on his arms.

"Callie!" he cried her name. He dropped the map and raced to her bedroom door. He twisted the knob and expelled a curse as he realized it was locked.

Why in the hell had she locked the door?

She screamed again and there were a series of thuds and bumps that sounded like a battle going on behind the locked door. His heart crashed so hard against his ribs he could scarcely catch his breath.

Callie! Her name screamed through his head. He had to get inside the room, knew she was in danger.

Afraid to shoot into the door to get it open, afraid that

the bullet would find her, Tom instead rammed his shoulder into the door.

He slammed into the door once and ignored the excruciating pain that radiated through his shoulder. The door remained solid. He used all his strength to hit the door again. It took four smashes before he managed to get the door open, and when he did, he gasped in surprise.

Callie was held against the chest of a tall, thin man who looked to be in his late teens or early twenties. Red-and-black paint decorated his face and he had one arm around her waist and the other held a bear paw up against her neck. His dark eyes glittered with the wildness of mental illness.

"Don't come any closer," he said, his voice with unmistakable warning.

Tom assessed the situation in the space of a heartbeat. The glass of the window had been removed and cold wintry air poured into the room. Callie's eyes were wide with fear as the bear claws drew several beads of blood on her throat.

He tightened his grip on his gun as a cool calm swept over him, the cool calm of a kill. He swept his gaze to the right, hoping Callie got the nonverbal message.

"I am the spirit of the bear," the young man cried. "The woman is mine."

"And I am the spirit of the bear hunter," Tom said. As Callie threw all her weight to the right, Tom shot the man in his left thigh. "And that woman is mine," Tom added.

The young man screamed and fell to the floor as Callie raced to Tom's side. "He came in through the window," she gasped, choking on a stifled sob. "I didn't hear him until he was on top of me."

His first impulse was to wrap her in his arms, assure himself that she was all right. He needed to hold her against him to still the fear that had roared through him when he'd first heard her scream.

But, he didn't grab her to him. He didn't touch her in any way. He kept his gun carefully trained on the man as he spoke to Callie. "Go call the sheriff's office and tell them we need an ambulance. He's going to need immediate medical treatment."

As she left the room to hurry down the hallway, Tom stared at the spirit of the bear, who lay writhing in pain on the floor.

He fought the shudder of relief that tried to course through him. It had been close. Too damned close. The pain in his shoulder was nothing compared to the pain that clutched his heart as he thought of everything that could have gone wrong.

If Callie hadn't managed to scream when she had, if Tom hadn't managed to get through the locked door, it would have been her lying on the floor strangled to death and wearing the mark of the bear on her body.

Chapter Nine

"I'm sure when I get that thing to the lab and compare it to the marks left on Mary Windsong and Lydia Rose, we'll find out it's the same weapon, so to speak," Callie said to Deputy Greg Samuels as she pointed to the bear paw now in a plastic evidence bag.

"I wonder where he got that thing?" Greg said.

As she stared at the bag she tried not to think about how those sharp claws had felt pressed against the soft skin of her neck. She tried not to dwell on that moment of terror when she'd awakened to find him hovering over her bed.

If she hadn't managed to kick him off her, if she hadn't managed to scream—she fought a shudder at the very thought.

"Who knows," she finally said.

The assailant had identified himself as John Hawk just before the ambulance had left to transport him to the hospital. Once he was well enough he'd be transferred from the hospital to jail.

Callie knew by morning they would learn everything there was to know about the young man, including where he'd gotten the bear paw that he'd used to kill two women and had tried to use to kill her. And why.

Callie and Greg were in the living room and a forensic team from the lab was in the bedroom collecting evidence that would be used for trial, if there was a trial.

In those moments when John Hawk had spoken to her, she'd recognized that the man was obviously mentally unbalanced. He'd spoken of talking to the bears, of a grizzly taking him on a journey and telling him that Mary, Lydia and Callie were bad women, that all women were bad and in killing them he'd become invincible. They were lucky that they'd caught him now before other women had fallen victim to him.

Still, it felt odd for her to be sitting idly by while her team was working. But, she couldn't very well participate in the evidence gathering since she'd been the intended victim.

Somebody had managed to get a large piece of plywood to put over the broken window for the remainder of the night. The slab of wood sat just inside her front door, waiting for the forensic team to finish up in the bedroom.

"Is there anything else you can think of that you think I need to know?" Greg asked.

Callie shook her head. "I can't think of anything." She wrapped her arms around her shoulders, thankful for the robe that covered her slinky nightgown, but still chilled to the very core.

He pointed to her neck. "Sure you don't want somebody to take a look at that?"

"No, it's just a couple of tiny punctures, just skin deep. I've already cleaned them out good and put on some antibiotic cream. I'll keep an eye on it to make sure the area doesn't get infected. I'm fine, Greg. Really."

She forced a smile. Despite her words she didn't feel fine. Her stomach was in a thousand knots and there was a tremble inside her that she couldn't still.

From her vantage point she could see Tom in the hallway just outside her bedroom, watching the activity inside. He leaned with his back against the hall wall, still as a statue as he watched what was going on.

Even though he stood some distance away from her she could see the frown that dug into his features and could almost feel the energy that radiated from him.

Thank God he'd managed to break down her bedroom door. She'd fought John Hawk. She'd kicked him off her and had tried to run for the bedroom door. But he'd been faster, stronger than she. She'd wrestled with him, afraid that he would accomplish what he'd come to do.

If Tom hadn't burst into the bedroom when he had, she'd be another tragic statistic for Kenner City and they'd be no closer to catching the killer than they'd been the day before.

The moment she knew she was safe, it had been instinct to run to Tom, to want him to pull her against his broad chest, to stroke her hair and assure her that everything was all right. But, he hadn't opened his arms to her, he hadn't pulled her to him.

And why would he?

She shouldn't have been surprised or disappointed. Hours before she'd pretty much kicked him to the curb. It wasn't fair for her to want him only when she needed him and it wasn't fair to need him if she didn't want him in her life forever.

She looked up as the team began to file out of the bedroom. There were four of them, Bobby O'Shea, Jacob Webster, Ava Wright and Olivia Perez. Callie offered them all a tired smile. "Sorry to get you guys out of bed," she said.

"We're all just grateful that you're okay," Olivia said, her hazel eyes filled with concern. She was relatively new to the lab but was proving herself a valuable asset to the team.

"We got everything we could out of the bedroom," Bobby said. "It's all bagged and tagged. It will just add to the evidence that will put this creep away." Tom walked into the room and grabbed the sheet of plywood. "Need some help with that?" Bobby asked.

"No thanks, I've got it." He picked it up and lifted it to his shoulder, then disappeared back down the hallway and into Callie's bedroom.

"Are you sure you're okay, boss?" Jacob asked.

"I'm fine, really." She forced that reassuring smile to her lips once again.

"I'll be in touch," Greg said as they all headed for the front door.

As they walked outside the sound of hammering came from the back of the house. Callie closed and locked the door after them, then turned out the light in the living room and went down the hallway to her bedroom.

Tom hammered the nails into the plywood to hold it in place, using more force than necessary to set the nails. She watched him work, unable to help noticing the play of lean muscle in his bare back, the bulge of his bicep with each whack of the hammer. He was clad only in a pair of jeans that rode low on his hips and a familiar whisper of desire rustled through her.

"I'll call the glass place first thing in the morning," she said as he finished. "They should be able to repair it tomorrow."

He turned and looked at her. His eyes were dark and dangerous and his nostrils flared slightly, like a wild animal scenting prey.

He set the hammer on the nightstand and advanced toward her with slow, deliberate strides.

Her breath caught in her throat and she took a step backward. She wasn't sure what she expected from him but for the first time in her life he scared her just a little bit.

When he reached her he grabbed hold of her shoulders and held tight, his fingers biting through the robe and into her skin. His eyes bored into hers with an intensity that shook her.

"Don't you ever lock a door between us again." His voice vibrated with suppressed rage. "I don't give a damn what's going on between us on a personal level, if you ever lock a door in this house again I'll make sure you don't have doors to lock. You got it?"

She gave a curt nod of her head. He released her shoulders, turned on his heels and strode out of the room. Callie released a shuddering sigh. She wanted to be angry with him for being angry, but she knew he had a good reason for yelling at her.

His job was to protect her and by locking the door she'd made his job more difficult. Besides, she should know that a locked door would never keep Tom Ryan out of a room if he wanted in badly enough.

She drew a deep, steadying breath, then followed after him. She found him in the living room standing in the dark in front of the window.

She moved to stand inches behind him. "I'm sorry, Tom. That was stupid of me."

He turned around to face her, his features cast in deep shadows that hid his expression. "It was stupid of you, but I'm sorry if I just scared you." He raised a hand and raked it through his hair. "To be honest, this whole night scared the hell out of me."

She couldn't stand it. She had to be in his arms. It was only now with just the two of them alone that the true horror of what had just happened struck her.

"I can't tell you how frightened I was when I woke up and he was on top of me." The composure that she'd hung on to until this moment cracked and a sob attempted to escape her.

He was nothing more than a dark shadow in front of her, but she sensed the movement of his arms opening and she walked into his embrace.

Although his arms wrapped around her he kept himself stiff, unyielding as she melted against him. Then, with a weary sigh, he gave himself to the embrace.

"Callie, Callie," he breathed into her hair. "When I heard you scream I think I lost a hundred years of my life."

She leaned her head against his chest, felt the ridge of his scars beneath her cheek and beneath that the sound of his strong heartbeat. "All I could think of was what Lydia Rose looked like after he got finished with her and I didn't want to end up like that."

He tightened his arms around her, the tight embrace saying all that needed to be said. She matched her breathing to his as she listened to the slow steady beat of his heart.

She didn't know how long they remained there, in the dark just holding each other. It was he who finally called a halt. "We need to get some sleep," he said and dropped his hands from around her.

She nodded, but she didn't want to go back to her bedroom where the smell of John Hawk still remained, where she feared nightmares might find her. She also couldn't ask Tom to sleep with him. She'd made it quite clear to him only hours ago that their relationship should remain professional.

"I think I'll just bunk out here on the sofa for the rest of the night," she said.

He hesitated for a long moment and she thought he was going to invite her into his room, but instead he stepped back from her and murmured a good-night.

Callie spent a restless night on the sofa and was awake just before dawn. As she lay in the predawn light she wondered if she were making a mistake where Tom was concerned.

She was so afraid to believe him, to believe that they might have a chance for a future together. He'd said he intended to quit his job once Del Gardo was again behind bars. But there was no guarantee that another assignment wouldn't come up and he'd be gone, leaving her devastated yet again and him back on the solitary path that was his life.

Her doubts about her decision remained with her throughout Sunday and into Monday morning as she and Tom drove to the lab. "What are your plans for the day?" she asked as he parked the car in their usual spot.

"I'm not sure. I'll check in with Ben and Dylan and some of the other agents and see if anything has broken in Julie's case. Other than that I'm at loose ends until you get off work this evening." He unfastened his seat belt and got out of the car.

She watched as he walked around the front of the car and her heart squeezed in her chest. Yesterday they had shared the same space of her house all day long, but there had been little talk, little interaction at all between them. He'd been cool and professional, making no personal comments and letting her know that for the remainder of their time together he would just do his job.

Wasn't that all she'd wanted from him? From the moment she'd awakened in the hospital after the fire and realized he was going to be her keeper, she'd vowed to keep her heart safe from him. So, why did a million doubts still float through her head? Why did this all feel so incredibly complicated?

The morning passed quickly, filled with the kind of work Callie loved. Questions with answers, tests with results, science at its finest, that's what made her most comfortable.

It was almost four o'clock when Bree came into her office and sat in the chair next to Callie's desk. "Heard you had an exciting night on Saturday."

Callie smiled at her friend. "Probably no less exciting than yours," she replied, then grinned as Bree's cheeks grew pink. "What are you doing here today? I thought you and Patrick would still be enjoying wedded bliss."

"You know us, we're both workaholics at heart. Besides, we've spent most of this afternoon finding out about our boy John Hawk."

"And?" Callie leaned forward in her chair, eager to hear what they had learned about the young man who had attacked her.

"Schizophrenic and off his meds," Bree replied. "He's twenty-two years old and lived on the reservation with his mother—father unknown. Everyone who knew him knew that he was in trouble, but nobody stepped up to do anything about it. Apparently the voices in his head told him those women were evil and only the bear could kill them."

Bree shook her head and continued, "And now he'll spend the rest of his life either in jail or institutionalized. I'm glad to see you no worse for the encounter."

Callie raised a hand to her throat and fought back a shiver. "It's not something I'd want to repeat anytime soon—or ever," she said. "Now, let's talk about something more pleasant. How does it feel to be Mrs. Patrick Martinez?"

Bree's face lit up with a beatific smile. "Wonderful, you should try it."

"You want me to become Mrs. Patrick Martinez?" Callie asked teasingly.

Bree laughed. "Ha, try it and I'll have to show you how good I am with my gun. Marriage. I meant you should try marriage."

Callie leaned back in her chair and tried to ignore the familiar squeeze of her heart. "You and Patrick had quite a history to overcome."

Bree nodded, her smile disappearing from her lovely

face. "We met years ago in Utah and fell madly in love. My parents weren't happy, they wanted me to marry a Ute man. Patrick and I allowed our cultural differences to get in the way and after a terrible fight we parted ways. I eventually married a man my parents thought was suitable and Patrick moved here to Kenner City."

Bree's dark eyes grew even darker. "I was pregnant but my family convinced me not to tell Patrick. They were afraid he'd take the baby from me. So I tried to build a life and unfortunately the man I married was abusive. I got out of the marriage and moved to the reservation here and focused on my job and raising Peter as a single parent. Then Julie got murdered and suddenly Patrick and I were thrown together again. And the rest, as they say, is history."

Callie leaned back in her chair and sighed thoughtfully. "Weren't you afraid to try it again? I mean, if it didn't work between you the first time what made you believe it would work this time?"

"I was terrified," Bree confessed. "I didn't just have my own heart to worry about, but also Peter's. Peter needed his dad and it didn't take me long to realize that my love for Patrick had never died." She tilted her head to one side and gazed at Callie with open curiosity. "Is this about you and Tom?"

Warmth leapt into Callie's cheeks. "What makes you think it's about Tom?"

Bree smiled knowingly. "Because anytime the two of you are together sparks fly and the energy between you is palpable. It doesn't take a rocket scientist to know something is there."

"Something was there…years ago. I thought we were going to have a happily-ever-after, but instead he took a new assignment and left me behind." Callie drew a deep breath. This was the first time she'd ever talked about her relationship with Tom.

"And now?" Bree raised one of her coal-black eyebrows.

"And now he says he loves me, that he's going to quit the FBI and wants to make a life with me." Callie bit down on her lower lip. "And I'm afraid to try it again."

"Ah, Callie. I wish I could tell you what you should do, what's right for you and Tom, but you know that I can't. You have to listen to your heart. Sometimes it takes more than one try to get it right. Sometimes it's a matter of right person, but wrong timing. The lucky ones get the second chance to try it again with someone they love. And speaking of…" she looked at her wristwatch. "I'm supposed to meet my husband five minutes ago."

With a quick goodbye she left the office. Callie leaned back in her chair and wearily rubbed her forehead where a headache threatened to take hold.

Bree had an added reason for wanting to make her relationship work with Patrick—their son. Peter had needed his father and certainly that had played a role in Bree's decision to give love with Patrick another chance.

Callie and Tom had no son. An unexpected fist

reached inside her and grabbed her heart, squeezing with such force it made it hard for her to breathe.

Don't think.

That little voice of protection whispered inside her.

Don't think. Don't feel.

There's no going back. You made the right decision where Tom was concerned.

Keep your secret.

Protect your heart.

The litany went around and around in her head. The only way to do those things was to keep her distance from Tom and be firm in her decision that they would never have a future together.

She hoped Del Gardo was captured quickly. She needed to get Tom Ryan permanently out of her life.

TOM SAT in the conference room alone, waiting for the time to come to take Callie home. The other agents had left the building a few minutes ago, but Tom remained seated at the table, his thoughts going in a million different directions.

As usual, the briefing with Jerry Ortiz had been discouraging. Nothing new to report, no sighting of the man they all wanted to find and no new leads into Julie's murder.

And what bothered him more than anything was that for the first time since the investigation began he was questioning the loyalty of one of the team.

For the last several months there had been whispers

about Ben Parrish. Tom rarely listened to gossip, but lately the whispers had gotten just a little bit louder and the talk was that it was possible he was working both sides of the law.

Ben had been the one to find Julie's body at the remote location where she'd been killed and Tom had never really gotten a good answer as to what Ben was doing there in the first place.

How had he stumbled on her in that secluded area on reservation land? It wasn't a place where Ben would have just been strolling through.

It was the last thing Tom wanted to believe of his friend and coworker, but there was no question that Ben had seemed unusually secretive lately and Tom didn't take anything for granted when it came to his work.

Was it possible that they weren't getting any closer to finding Del Gardo because Del Gardo had a man on the inside? Someone who was telling him where the agents were looking, where was a good place to hide?

Was that man Ben Parrish?

Certainly the temptation to walk both sides of the line was always there, particularly with a man like Vincent Del Gardo who had the kind of money it might take to turn an agent's head.

Although Tom couldn't imagine any price being able to buy Ben, Ben had made some comments throughout the investigation that made him suspect.

Ben had expressed some doubt about Del Gardo murdering Julie. Some of what he'd said had hinted at a sympathy for the mobster. He'd also said that he wasn't sure it was Del Gardo who was behind the attacks on Callie. He was certainly the only agent on the case who held those beliefs.

Tom hoped the whispers and rumors were wrong, that Ben hadn't gone to the dark side. Julie gone. Ben suspect. Things were falling apart and Tom felt as if he had nothing to hang on to.

He leaned his head back and closed his eyes. Yesterday had been the longest day of his life. He and Callie had been in her house, each of them walking on eggshells, carefully navigating the wealth of energy and emotion that existed between them.

He'd given it his best shot. He'd hoped that his love for Callie would be enough to overcome the past, but it hadn't worked.

Tom had never in his life known loneliness. Being alone was what he'd always done best. But yesterday he'd sat on the sofa and watched Callie who was seated in the chair across from him. She was reading a book, but more than that, she was closed off, not engaging him on any level and it was then that, for the first time in his life, he'd felt lonely.

"You going home or are you going to sit here all night?" Dylan spoke from the doorway, his deep voice pulling Tom from his thoughts.

Tom glanced at his wristwatch and shoved back from the long table. "Going home," he said as he stood. "What are you still doing here?"

"Ava thought she'd found a necklace that matched the pattern that was on Julie's neck, but it was a false alarm. Close, but not a match."

The two men walked down the hallway together. "If we could find that necklace or whatever it is that left that pattern, we'd be that much closer to finding the killer," Dylan said, his frustration obvious in his voice.

"All we can do is keep working it, keep trying to figure it all out," Tom replied. Was that what he needed to do with Callie? Keep working it? Continue to try to make her see that they were meant to be together?

He and Dylan parted ways at the lab door. Dylan headed for the bank of elevators and Tom went inside to find Callie.

As usual at this time of day she was at her desk, doing the paperwork that was a large part of her job as head of the forensics lab.

He stood just outside the doorway and watched her, his love swelling in his chest. He loved everything about her, the sweet curve of her jaw line, those amazing blue eyes that could radiate either an incredible warmth or an icy frost that could stop a man in his tracks. He loved the weight of her breasts, the small span of her waist and those shapely legs.

But, more importantly than all that he loved her laugh, he loved her compulsive neatness and how she thought that making macaroni and cheese out of a box was real cooking.

Most important of all he liked the kind of man he was

when he was with her. She made him want things he'd never wanted before, things like commitment and family and forever. Nobody else in his life had ever made him want those things.

Too late, a little voice whispered inside his head. He'd been years too late for her. He shoved his hands in his pockets and jingled some change as a new wave of despair, of loneliness, filled his soul.

Chapter Ten

It had been another week of busy days, silent evenings and lonely nights. Callie was wondering how long Tom would be willing to stay on the assignment as her bodyguard. The tension between them was once again unbelievably uncomfortable and there was no end in sight.

Her home was beginning to feel like a prison and Tom her jailer, a jailer she alternately wanted to escape and whose arms she wanted to fall into.

As they'd left the house that morning for the lab, gray clouds had hung ominously low in the sky and by midmorning there was still no peek of sunshine.

All the weathermen were talking about a huge weather event predicted to hit in the next week. The word *blizzard* had been used more than once.

Just what she needed, Callie thought as she sat at her desk, to be snowed in with Tom. Blizzards in this area of the country were nothing to laugh about. They could cripple the city for days at a time.

The lab had been unusually quiet that day. A double homicide in Durango had called out most of the staff. Callie had found the quiet disconcerting as it allowed her too much time to think and she was tired of thinking about her personal life.

Since the day she'd told Tom that she couldn't forgive him he'd retreated into a shell of cool business-like competence. Still, there were times when she caught him gazing at her with desire, with something that looked remarkably like love in his eyes.

"Callie?"

She turned from the desk to see Elizabeth. "Sheriff Martinez just called. He needs somebody out on the scene of an abandoned car."

"Where?" Callie asked.

"Out near Mexican Hat."

As Elizabeth gave her the specific directions she wrote them down then got up from her desk. She needed a field trip. She needed to get out of the lab. She desperately needed some action that wasn't taking place either in the lab or in her house.

She grabbed her coat and pulled it on, then picked up her field kit that was actually an oversized tackle box, and left her office to go in search of Tom, who she knew would be in the building somewhere.

Olivia Perez and Jacob Webster were the only two in the lab and she gave them the directions to the abandoned car and told them to meet her there. If it was the scene of some sort of accident Jacob was an expert at casting tire tracks and Olivia had a good eye for reconstructing a scene.

There was something going on between the two of them. Callie suspected a secret romance, but both were keeping it tightly under wraps. Patrick and Bree, Jacob and Olivia, romance was everywhere except in Callie's heart, which she told herself remained unforgiving when it came to Tom.

She found Tom in the conference room and he grabbed his coat and rose from the table as he saw her in her coat and with her kit in hand. "What's happened?" he asked when he joined her in the hallway.

"I'm not sure. Patrick called and said he needed somebody on the scene of an abandoned car. I've got Jacob and Olivia meeting me there."

As they walked toward the elevator she gave him the directions that Elizabeth had given her. Within minutes they were in his car and headed toward the Ute reservation land.

"Did Patrick say what the problem was?" Tom asked as he drove. As always his gaze was divided between the road ahead and the rearview mirror.

"No, but something must be wrong. We usually aren't called out to an abandoned car unless there's some suspicion of foul play."

As he drove to the location she tried not to notice the familiar scent of him that hung in the air. Would there come a time when the mere fragrance of him no longer affected her? Eventually would she stop wanting him?

She focused on the work ahead, trying to keep her mind off the faint flutter of regret that whispered through her each time she thought of Tom.

Collect, preserve, inventory, package and transport, those were the tasks ahead of her. She needed to remain focused on her work and not on Tom.

They rode in the silence that had marked their relationship since the night she'd told him there were no do-overs for them.

It was a long drive but finally they reached the scene. It was an old-model sedan, half in a ditch and half out. Patrick and two of his deputies stood near the car. A third deputy was seated in the back of one of the patrol cars.

At first glance, Callie wasn't sure why she was here. The vehicle didn't appear to have been hit, there didn't seem to be any body damage that she could see.

She got out of the car and raised her collar against the cold wind as Tom went to the trunk to retrieve her kit. "What have we got?" she asked Patrick.

"I'm not sure. I got a call of a car off the road and when I came out here to investigate the driver door was open but there was no sign of the driver. Car is registered to one Aspen Meadows."

He paused as Jacob and Olivia pulled up in Jacob's car. Once they had joined Patrick and Callie, Patrick quickly went over everything again.

"Anyone check to see if maybe it was just car trouble?" Jacob asked. "And Aspen went walking for help?"

"I don't know about car trouble. Nobody has been inside the car. I've been waiting for you all to arrive before letting anyone inside. There appears to be something that looks like blood on the driver headrest and on the door, and if that didn't cause me concern, there was a baby boy found in the backseat."

Callie's breath caught in her chest. "Is he…"

"He seems fine." Patrick pointed to the patrol car. "I've got Deputy Connelly on babysitting duty."

"Then let's get to work," she said briskly. "Jacob, you want to start by taking pictures of the scene?" She looked back to Patrick. "Maybe an animal ran across the road in front of her and she stopped abruptly and hit her head on the steering wheel or the side window. You might send your deputies out to look for her. She could be wandering around with a head injury and didn't think about the baby when she left the car."

Patrick nodded. "You might want to take a closer look at the rear bumper. It has a scrape on it, like it's been hit, but I can't tell if it's a fresh mark or not."

Callie nodded. "What are you doing about the baby?"

"We're trying to locate a relative now to come and take him," Patrick said. "And I've already got a couple of men trying to retrace Aspen's movements for the last twenty-four hours."

Callie pulled on her latex gloves. *Don't think about the baby,* a little voice whispered inside her head as she approached the vehicle. Her job at the moment was to collect, preserve, inventory, package and transport any evidence to the lab for further testing. That's what she needed to focus on.

She was aware of Tom joining the two deputies who were headed out to search for the driver who might have been wounded. Callie began to walk slowly around the car and eye it for evidentiary purposes.

There was no question that Patrick had been right to call them out, there were too many questions. Had Aspen simply walked off and left her baby or had she been a victim of some kind of foul play? Had she even been driving the car?

Patrick was right, the rear bumper showed signs of a bump by another car. Whether that had anything to do with the car being in the ditch was yet to be determined.

Callie approached the open driver door and peered inside, immediately seeing the two small dots of what appeared to be blood on the headrest and another smear of a bloodlike substance on the door. Unfortunately, it was impossible to tell how fresh it might be because of the frigid weather conditions.

Once Jacob was finished taking all the photos that they would need, Callie carefully scraped the blood into an awaiting bindle, then labeled what she'd collected and from where in the car.

She no longer felt the cold as she focused solely on her job. All thoughts of Tom and babies and anything else melted beneath her concentration on her work.

She was aware of Olivia and Jacob working the area

around the car. Jacob was casting tire tracks in the area, a tricky feat in the cold weather, and Olivia was finger-printing the passenger door.

Tom and the deputies returned without any luck of finding anyone injured and wandering the area. And they stood nearby as the forensic team worked to provide some answers.

Minutes turned into an hour and a half as the team worked to collect whatever evidence might be present. Although they had no idea what had happened, if a crime had even been committed here, Callie had a bad feeling in the pit of her stomach.

"Aspen Meadows," Patrick said when Callie finally crawled out of the car. "She's a thirty-three-year-old schoolteacher from the reservation. I just contacted her cousin, Emma Richards, who's on her way to come and take custody of the baby until we can figure out what's going on and where Aspen disappeared to."

Callie nodded. "Has anyone checked the baby?"

Patrick frowned. "What do you mean? He seems fine. According to Emma, his name is Jack and he's six weeks old. He's slept through all of this."

"What about the father?" Callie asked.

"According to Emma nobody knows who the father is. Apparently Aspen hasn't told anyone who got her pregnant. Emma also insisted that there's no way Aspen just up and walked away from her baby."

"I need to check out the little guy and make sure there's no blood or any other evidentiary material on him." Although the last thing she wanted to do was see the baby boy, she also knew in order to do her job thoroughly, everything had to be checked, and that included little Jack Meadows.

With feet that dragged with dread, she walked over to the patrol car where Deputy Connelly opened the door and stepped out, the sleeping baby boy in his arms.

"I wish my Joey would sleep like this little guy," he said as he held the baby out to Callie. "Joey still doesn't know what three hours of sleep feels like and neither do me and my wife."

Don't think, the voice in her head screamed as she took the baby from him. Just do your job. Focus on the job.

The bundle of baby fit perfectly in her arms. Clad in a light blue snowsuit, he smelled of powder and sweetness.

Don't think. Don't feel.

She put the boy on the backseat of the patrol car and unzipped his snowsuit, wanting to check him over to make sure there was nothing on or in his clothes that might provide a clue as to what had happened to his mother.

Little Jack Meadows stirred, and stretched with tiny fisted hands overhead as Callie managed to get the snowsuit off his little body.

Beneath the snowsuit he was dressed in a little plaid shirt, jeans and a pair of blue socks and it was the sight of those little blue socks that forced a tide of emotion to swell in her chest.

Blue booties.

She swam in it, her vision blurring as she stared at little Jack Meadows. *Don't think. Don't feel.* The mantra that had always worked before couldn't slice through the grief that suddenly had her by the throat and refused to let go.

The self-control that she'd maintained for two years was gone and she knew she had to get out of here before she completely lost it.

"OLIVIA," Callie called to her coworker from the backseat of the patrol car. Tom watched as the two spoke briefly then Callie handed Olivia the baby and hurried to Patrick. She spoke to him only for a moment then walked toward Tom.

He knew immediately that something was wrong. Her face was as white as the snowflakes that had begun to spit from the overcast skies and she walked with a brittleness that made her appear as if she might shatter at any moment.

"Take me home," she said as she reached him.

"What happened? What's wrong?" he asked. Her eyes were huge and held a wild glaze he'd never seen before. He took her by the arm, irrationally afraid for her—perhaps of her. "Callie?"

"Just please get me out of here. I'm sick. Can't you see that I'm sick?" Her voice rose with an edge of hysteria he'd never heard from her before.

He led her to his car where she collapsed into the passenger seat. As he walked around to the driver door he tried to figure out what had happened. Nothing short of a heart attack would pull Callie off a case in the middle of gathering evidence.

As he got into the car he quickly started the engine. She had her hands up over her face and leaned back in the seat as still as a statue.

Once the fan was blowing warm air he pulled away from the scene, one eye on the road and the other on Callie. She didn't make a sound, but continued to keep her hands across her face.

"Callie, talk to me," he said softly. "What's going on?"

She shook her head vehemently. "Just get me home." Her voice was muffled by her hands, but still held that edge of hysteria.

Tom frowned and stepped on the gas. She'd been fine as she'd collected evidence from the car. She'd been calm and efficient as she went about her work and instructed the others what to do.

Everything had been fine until she'd gone to the patrol car to see the baby. The baby. He clenched the steering wheel more tightly. Babies and blue booties. Visits to an obstetrician. And now this, her uncharacteristic behavior after holding a baby.

She was keeping something from him, something that he had a right to know. And he wasn't going to let her sleep tonight until he had the answer.

It was a long drive back and Callie remained rigid in the seat, her face covered with her hands for the entire trip.

When they reached the house she didn't wait for him

to come around to escort her to the door, but instead bolted from the car and ran toward the house.

Tom cursed under his breath as he hurried after her. By the time he followed her through the front door it was obvious she was headed for her bedroom.

"Callie, wait!" he called after her.

"No, go away."

"We need to talk." He caught up with her, grabbed her by the shoulders and spun her around to face him. He sucked in his breath as he saw the raw emotion that twisted her features.

"I don't want to talk. Please don't make me talk." A sob wrenched from her, sounding like it ripped from her heart, her very soul.

She tried to wrench away from him, but he held tight to her shoulders, his heart beating so fast he felt as if he'd been running a marathon. "Why did holding that baby upset you? No more running, Callie. No more lies. Tell me the truth about those booties."

She stopped struggling to get free from him and stilled. As her gaze met his, Tom wasn't sure he wanted to know what she was about to say.

"You want the truth?" She sucked in a sob that escaped her lips. "The truth is I was pregnant when you left. But our baby died, Tom. Our son is dead."

His hands slipped from her shoulders as her words thundered through his head. With a deep, wrenching sob she turned and ran for her bedroom.

He stared after her, the beat of his heart slowing to

a mournful rhythm. They'd had a baby, a son. And that son had died. As her words sank in a stabbing grief filled him.

He stumbled and leaned against the wall as wave after wave of grief ripped through him. Along with the grief came questions. What had happened? How had this happened? And why hadn't she told him before? Why hadn't she somehow contacted him when she first learned she was pregnant?

But he knew the answer to the last question. She hadn't tried to contact him because he'd walked away from her, because he'd chosen a path that didn't include her. Why would she have told him they were going to have a son when he'd made it clear to her he wasn't a forever kind of man, that he wasn't interested in marriage or family?

Regrets. They nearly sent him to his knees as emotions he'd never experienced before swelled inside him. He could hear the sounds of Callie's deep sobs coming from her bedroom and the sound brought tears to his eyes.

No wonder she hated him. No wonder she couldn't forgive him. She'd gone through the worst possible thing a person could endure all alone, the death of a child, the death of their child.

Tears blurred his vision as the swell of emotion pressed tighter inside his chest. Now he knew why she'd hung on to those little blue booties. They hadn't belonged to the son of a friend of hers. They'd belonged to the little boy she'd lost.

He used the palms of his hands to swipe away his tears. The sound of her crying coming from her bedroom was so painful it resonated inside him.

Go to her, a little voice whispered inside his head. *Don't let her go through this, too, all alone. She needs you.*

It was only as he pushed off the wall to go into her room that he realized the truth of the matter.

He needed her.

Chapter Eleven

For two years Callie had kept her sorrow locked away in a place she had refused to access. But now, there was no hiding from it, no compartmentalizing, as wave after wave of grief crashed through her.

She desperately fought for control and tried to stifle the sobs that welled up inside her, forcing air from her lungs in gasps. But, as her arms remembered the feel of little Jack Meadows, as her head filled with the sweet baby scent of him, she lost it completely.

She cried as she'd never cried before as excruciating pain ripped through her heart, through her very soul. Her baby. She'd lost her baby.

The pain was too intense to bear, the agony ripped through her like nothing she'd ever felt.

There can be other babies, the doctor had said at the time, as if somehow that would make it all right. "You're young and healthy," he'd said as if that would ease the pain of her loss.

There had been nobody to share the grief with her,

nobody who cared about the life-altering trauma of a lost soul.

She didn't know how long she wept before she sensed Tom's presence in the bedroom.

It was only now she realized that the reason she hadn't told him about the baby when he'd first asked wasn't because she hadn't wanted him to know, but rather because she hadn't wanted to face it herself. As long as she didn't talk about it, didn't think about it, she could pretend it hadn't happened.

But now it was too late. Pandora's box had sprung open and the secret of her loss had not only come to the light for him, but for her as well.

She tensed as she sensed him moving closer to the bed where she lay face down, her face buried in her pillow. She had no idea what to expect from Tom, didn't know if he'd come at her with anger or not.

Her crying had eased, leaving behind the kind of dry sobs that racked her body. The bed next to her depressed with Tom's weight and he laid his hand gently on the small of her back.

For several long moments they remained that way, him stroking her back as the last of her dry sobs slowly left her body.

"Callie?" His voice was soft and tender, holding none of the anger she'd feared, but filled with unanswered questions.

She turned over on her back and looked at him, her

heart crunching in her chest as she saw the dark grief that filled his deep brown eyes.

"When I first found out I was pregnant, I was still so angry with you," she began. "And yet I was beyond thrilled that I was going to have your baby. But because I was so angry it never entered my mind to try to get in touch with you."

She paused, remembering that complex mix of emotions that had filled her when the doctor had confirmed that she was pregnant. "Then, when several months passed, I realized that eventually I would contact you to tell you. I knew from personal experience what it was like to grow up without a father and I didn't want to do that to our child. He was going to need his father and no matter what my feelings toward you, I would have let you be a part of his life."

Tom's features were softer than she'd ever seen them and his lower lip trembled, letting her know the utter depth of his emotional pain.

She slid her hands down to her flat abdomen and fought against a new sob that welled up inside her. "I can't tell you how happy I was about the baby, how much I loved him from the moment I learned of his existence. Everything seemed to be going fine. I was healthy, the baby seemed healthy. When I reached four months I bought a crib and began to buy everything he'd need when he came into the world."

Once again grief squeezed her heart, making it difficult to speak, to breathe. "I carried him for six months.

I felt the life inside me and I loved him, Tom. I loved him so much."

He pulled her up and into his arms and she welcomed the embrace. She laid her head on his chest where she could hear the beat of his heart.

"I was six months along when I went to see Dr. Weatherby for my usual monthly check-up. He couldn't hear a heartbeat and I suddenly realized I hadn't felt the baby move for a week or so. I knew then. I saw the truth in Dr. Weatherby's eyes and I knew our baby was dead."

Tom's arms tightened around her as she continued. "Dr. Weatherby put me in the hospital that afternoon and induced labor. Ten hours later I delivered our perfect, beautiful, dead baby boy." She shuddered against him as memories of that terrible moment in her life played out in her mind.

"It wasn't your fault, Callie."

His words pierced through her and found the tiny seed inside her that whispered of an irrational guilt. "Logically I know that," she said against his chest. "I took my vitamins, didn't drink or smoke. I ate well and got plenty of sleep. I did everything I could to assure a healthy baby, but apparently it just wasn't meant to be."

Once again his arms tightened around her and she finally raised her head to look at him, stunned to see tears trekking down his cheeks.

The sight made her start to cry again and they clung together and wept for the baby they'd lost. She didn't know how long they remained in each other's arms, sharing the grief that only two parents could feel for the loss of a child.

It didn't matter that the baby had never drawn breath. It was the promise of what had been dashed, the death of hopes not realized that tore though her and the strange relief of knowing that Tom was the only person on earth who could share those same feelings.

Finally the well of tears was empty and still they remained holding each other. Callie was spent, empty of all the emotion that had been bottled up inside her for the past two years.

She released a tremulous sigh and once again looked up at Tom. His tears were gone as well, but in his eyes she saw a need that shot like wildfire through her, the need to connect, the need to fill the emptiness.

She wasn't sure whether he kissed her or she kissed him, but their lips met and Callie wanted to lose herself in him, in the simple act of affirming life.

His mouth was warm against hers and she opened to him, allowing the kiss to deepen into something more than warm, more than hot.

His hands slid down her back, the sensation filling her with sweet desire. She welcomed it with no thoughts of tomorrow, with no thought of right or wrong. She wanted only this moment with him, a kind of healing that had been a long time in coming.

He murmured her name against her lips as he began to fumble with the buttons of her blouse. She tore her mouth from his and shoved his hands aside impatiently.

As she unfastened her blouse he pulled his shirt over his head and tossed it to the floor.

Within seconds they were both naked and back in the bed. Where before they had come at each other with voracious hunger, this time there was infinite tenderness in each caress, in every kiss.

He touched her as if she were the most precious thing in the world and she responded in kind, stroking across the wealth of scars on his chest with tenderness and caring.

He kissed her just behind her ear, in the place he knew would shoot shivers through her. His hands cupped her breasts as she leaned her head to kiss the scar tissue over his heart.

Time stood still as they touched and kissed and for the first time in almost three years Callie loved him without reservations, without fear.

The trauma they'd just shared made her feel closer to him than she'd ever felt before, bonded her to him in a way she knew would be forever etched into her heart, into her very soul.

He stroked down the length of her body, his hands hot, his movements languid yet pulling forth a fire inside her. She responded in kind, running her hands down the flat of his abdomen, across his lean, muscular hips.

She loved the feel of him, the sinewy muscle beneath warm skin. He was fully aroused, but she didn't touch him there. Instead she caressed his inner thigh and loved the hot gasp he released as she finally moved her hand higher and grasped his hard length.

He allowed her to stroke him only for a minute, then pushed her hand away and reached for his wallet and the condom she knew was inside.

She wanted to tell him to forget about it, that she wanted him inside her without protection, but there was still a tiny piece of rational thought left in her mind, one that reminded her that this wasn't forever. Tom wasn't forever. He was just for now and she couldn't take a chance of history repeating itself.

As he moved onto her, into her, tears once again sprang to her eyes as her emotions reeled wildly out of control.

As he moved his hips against hers he stared down at her and she saw his pain, his love and his desire for her all in the dark depths of his brown eyes.

She closed her eyes and gave herself to the sheer simplicity of physical pleasure and tried not to think about the fact that without her hatred of Tom, without her grief over what had happened, she didn't know what she'd hang on to when this day was over.

ONCE CALLIE WAS SOUND ASLEEP Tom crept quietly out of her bed, pulled his jeans on and went into the living room. He sat in a chair near the window where in the light of a distant street lamp he could see the sparkling snowflakes flurrying in the air.

In the quiet conversation after lovemaking Callie had told him that she'd named the baby Daniel, after one of her mother's boyfriends who had been kind to her as a young girl. Little Daniel was buried in a cemetery just outside of Las Vegas.

A son. Although he mourned what Callie had gone through alone, his grief at the moment was all his own, that of a father whose child had died.

He squeezed his eyes tightly closed against the burn of tears. He'd never known how much he'd wanted a child until now. The idea of being a father had always been alien to him, but now he realized how much he'd wanted to be what he'd never had in his own life…a dad.

His mind flashed with images of what might have been, a chubby little hand hanging tightly to his, little arms reaching out for him.

First day of school, baseball games, popcorn in front of the television, there were so many experiences that would never be, at least not with a baby named Daniel.

Would this have happened if he'd never left her? Was it stress over being alone, heartbreak over his defection that had ultimately caused Daniel's death?

He opened his eyes and stared out the window, recognizing that these were foolish thoughts. It was impossible to question the twists and turns of fate, impossible to know if the outcome would have been any different whether he'd been a good and loving support to Callie or not.

Callie.

Ten hours of labor and all she'd gotten was the agony of making burial arrangements. Alone. She'd gone through it all alone.

Was it any wonder she hated him? Was it any wonder she hadn't been able to forgive him? At the moment she couldn't hate him any more than he loathed himself.

Maybe the kindest thing he could do for her was pull himself off this duty. Surely he was only a reminder of the worst experience she'd ever gone through in her life. Even though the thought of never seeing her again ached inside him, he'd rather get out of her life for good than cause her any more pain.

He must have fallen asleep for it was the touch of her hand on his shoulder that awakened him the next morning. He shot out of the chair in shock, appalled that he'd been sleeping so soundly he hadn't heard her until she'd touched him.

He swiped a hand through his hair as she stepped back from him, her gaze void of all emotion. "Are you all right?"

"Yeah. I just can't believe I was sleeping so soundly I didn't hear you up and about."

"I'd like to get to the lab a little early today, so if you could get ready to go I'd appreciate it." She offered him a cool, detached smile.

"Give me fifteen minutes and I'll be ready," he said. As he headed to the bathroom for a quick shower, she went into the kitchen.

As he stood beneath a hot spray he realized that the closeness they'd shared the night before hadn't made it into the light of dawn.

She was once again closed off, out of reach and

somehow, someway he had to figure out how to get her out of his mind, out of his heart.

True to his word, fifteen minutes later he met her at the front door where she stood wearing her coat and waiting for him. "Ready?" she asked.

He pulled on his coat, grabbed her by the elbow and together they left the house. The snow the night before had left only a light dusting on the ground.

As she slid into the passenger side of the car, Tom noticed a man standing on the sidewalk just a little ways down the street. Even though he was too far away to pose any immediate danger, adrenaline filled Tom and he placed a hand on the butt of his gun as he got into the driver side.

"Problem?" Callie asked, as if sensing something amiss.

"A man standing down there. You know him?" Tom started the car engine and turned to look at the man once again. He was slender, with a red stocking cap pulled over his head and wore dark-rimmed glasses. In all the time that Tom had been transporting Callie from home to work and back, he'd never seen this man before. Although that didn't mean much, they rarely saw anyone outside when coming to and from her house.

"No, but I really don't know any of my neighbors," she replied.

As Tom pulled slowly out of the driveway he kept his focus on the man. What was he doing just standing there in the cold? As Tom watched the man turned around and headed back toward the house behind him. Tom relaxed a bit. Apparently it was just a neighbor.

He couldn't allow his emotions to make him lose sight of why he was back in Callie's life. Somewhere out there was Del Gardo, the man who wanted her dead, the man who had possibly killed Julie. Tom had to stay alert at all times to potential danger.

He headed down the street and as he glanced in his side mirror he saw that the man hadn't gone into the house but instead was headed for a car parked along the street.

A neighbor headed to the store or off to work?

Or something else?

Somebody watching Callie's house?

Tom knew better than to jump to conclusions. Still, it all felt odd and Tom definitely didn't like odd.

He shot a glance to Callie. She looked no worse for the emotional maelstrom she'd experienced the day before. The pale blue blouse that peeked out of the top of her coat emphasized the ice blue of her eyes, eyes that held no hint of the river of tears they'd cried the day before.

It was obvious she had no intention of talking about what had happened yesterday. She kept her gaze focused ahead, as if eager to get to the lab and back to the work that kept her from feeling, from thinking.

"I wonder if they found Aspen Meadows yet," she said, breaking the silence that had built between them.

"Who?" he asked absently.

"The woman who owns the car we processed yester-

day. The mother of little Jack Meadows." The only indication that the mention of the baby boy caused her any
stress was the whitening of her knuckles as her fingers
clasped together in her lap.

"Hopefully they've found her and there's a logical
explanation for the car and the baby being abandoned
on the side of the road," he replied.

The rest of the drive into the lab she talked about the
cases she was working and even though he wanted to
talk to her about what they'd shared yesterday, even
though he wanted to tell her about his decision to pull
himself off her case, he didn't. He merely listened to her
and let her have the peace of the drive.

When they reached the lab they parted ways. Tom
went down the hall to the conference room and found
it empty. Officially he wasn't on the Julie Grainger
murder case, although the agents had welcomed any
help, any thoughts he could add to the puzzle. He sat in
one of the chairs at the table and wondered where
everyone was this morning.

He eyed the telephone in the center of the table. With
the touch of a button he could be in contact with Jerry
Ortiz and ask him to send somebody else out for the protective duty of Callie.

Jerry and the rest of the team would probably
welcome him as a full-time participant in the
Grainger/Del Gardo investigation. He reached up and
grabbed the medal hanging around his neck.

He knew the medal, along with the one Ben Parrish

had received, were key pieces of evidence, but they hadn't been able to figure out what they meant, where they fit in their pursuit of Vincent Del Gardo and Julie's murder.

Red stocking cap and dark-framed glasses. A vision of the man standing on the street staring down at Callie's place filled his mind.

A neighbor? Or somebody more ominous?

He wasn't going to make the call to Jerry until he found out who that man was and what he'd been doing standing on the sidewalk on a cold February morning staring in the direction of Callie's home.

He got up from the table and headed for the door but before he could reach it he nearly collided with Agent Sam Salinger.

"Hey, Tom," Sam said in greeting. "Crappy weather out there today."

"Yeah, and it's supposed to get worse before it gets better," Tom replied.

"I heard on the way in the weathermen are still forecasting a big snow event in the next week."

"Where is everyone?" Tom asked.

"Out and about, chasing down the leads we don't have." Sam stuffed his hands in his pockets and shook his head. "Why? You got something? I'm at loose ends." The young agent couldn't hide his eagerness at the possibility of some action, any action.

"I saw a man this morning standing on the sidewalk just down the street from Callie MacBride's house. Something about him being there struck me as wrong."

Tom frowned. "I was thinking of taking a drive back there and seeing if he lives at the house he was standing in front of."

"I could take the ride with you," Sam offered.

Tom hesitated only a moment and then nodded. "Okay, let's do it."

Tom stopped in the lab to tell Callie he was leaving the building and then together he and Sam made their way to the elevators.

"You think it was Del Gardo?" Sam asked once they were in Tom's car and headed back to Callie's neighborhood.

Tom frowned and tried to summon a picture of the man in his head. "I don't know. He was about the right height and weight, but we both know Del Gardo is average in both those characteristics so that's no real help. He had on a red stocking cap so I couldn't tell if he had hair or not and he was wearing dark-rimmed glasses."

Tom sighed. "I don't know, I might be overreacting to the whole thing, but it just felt wrong." He told Sam about the man starting toward the house as they drove by, then, the moment they had passed, heading for a car parked on the street.

"So, you think he was just pretending to go to the house in case you saw him?" Sam asked.

"It's a thought," Tom agreed. "Or it might have been one of Del Gardo's thugs doing surveillance work for him." Once again Tom sighed. "Or it could have just been a man who likes the cold and the snow who stopped for a long breath of winter air before getting into his car and going to work."

"You and Julie were close, right?"

As Tom thought of his fellow agent a band around his chest grew tight. "Yeah, we were close. Acevedo, Parrish and Julie and I all went through the academy together. Despite our different assignments we stayed tight through the years."

"This whole Del Gardo thing put a big black eye on everyone," Sam said.

"You got that right. It's not often a mobster just sentenced to prison manages to escape from the courthouse."

"And manages to stay undercover all this time," Sam added.

"Nobody ever said Del Gardo was a stupid man, but sooner or later he's going to make a mistake and we'll get him." Tom tightened his hands on the steering wheel as he thought of the man who had killed a woman he cared about and now threatened the woman he loved.

Tom pulled his car in front of the house where he'd seen the man standing in the driveway. The car the man had gotten into was gone, but Tom hoped whoever might be in the house would have a logical explanation and an identity for the man. This was probably nothing more than a wild goose chase, but Tom knew he wouldn't rest easy until he checked it out.

He and Sam got out of the car and approached the front door. The frigid wind threatened to slice right through him as he knocked on the door.

He kept a hand on the butt of his gun, unsure what to expect and he was grateful to have Sam next to him as backup. He knocked again and heard a faint feminine voice tell him to hold his horses.

The door was opened a moment later by a little gray-haired woman in a pale blue duster. "May I help you?" she asked as she eyed them suspiciously and kept a firm grip on the door.

Tom and Sam identified themselves as FBI agents and showed her their badges. Tom said, "We'd just like to ask you a couple of questions, Mrs...."

"Tandy. Grace Tandy. Questions about what?"

Tom told her about seeing the man in front of her house that morning. "Was that your husband?"

"Now that would be some kind of miracle because my Henry died two years ago, God rest his soul. I don't know what that man was doing in my driveway, but I can tell you he didn't belong here."

It was the same answer they got at each and every house on the block. Nobody knew the man in the red stocking cap and with dark-rimmed glasses.

With each house they visited Tom's anxiety grew and he cursed himself for not paying closer attention, for not noticing the make and model of the car the man had headed for, for not stopping and questioning his presence on the street.

One thing was certain, as they headed back to the lab Tom knew he wasn't about to make that phone call to Jerry Ortiz and be pulled off his duty with Callie. If Del

Gardo was that close, if one of his henchmen had her in his sights, then no matter how uncomfortable things got between them, no matter how difficult it was on him, there was no way Tom was walking away from her again.

Chapter Twelve

Aspen Meadows was still missing. Callie was greeted with the news first thing that morning and by four o'clock in the afternoon nothing had changed.

Callie and the members of her team had all worked throughout the day to process the evidence they'd collected from Aspen's abandoned car.

Olivia had lifted a dozen fingerprints and had catalogued them and was sending each of them through the AFIS—automated fingerprint identification system—database to see if they found a match. Unfortunately, unless the people who had left the fingerprints behind had been arrested before or worked for the government, their prints wouldn't be in the system.

Jacob was working on trying to match the tire prints he'd taken to an appropriate vehicle model and type and Callie had been running DNA tests on the blood found on the headrest and the door of the car.

Patrick had brought her a hairbrush from Aspen Meadows's home and she was also getting DNA from the hair to use to match against the blood. Soon they'd know if that blood belonged to the missing mother.

Patrick had also told her that the last person who had seen Aspen had been Jack's babysitter, who had told him that Aspen had picked up Jack about an hour before her car had been found in that ditch. What had happened to Aspen in that hour between picking up her son and her vehicle and baby being found on the side of the road?

Callie felt particularly driven to help find Aspen Meadows. Little Jack Meadows was a baby without his mother, and Callie was a mother without her baby. What she wanted more than anything was to aid in the reunion that would bring Aspen and baby Jack back together again.

It was almost time for Tom to arrive to pick her up and take her back to her house when Bree came into Callie's office. As usual, she flopped into the chair next to Callie's and expelled a long deep sigh.

"According to everyone I spoke to today who knows Aspen Meadows, there's no way she forgot or just walked away from that car and left her baby in the backseat," Bree said with a frown. "I've got a bad feeling about this, Callie."

Callie nodded. "I hate to admit it, but so do I. I've got Bobby working on a crash scene re-creation. We didn't get any scraping of paint off the fender from contact with any other vehicle, but with the tire marks on the road and the ding on the bumper, I wonder if maybe she was forced off the road," Callie said.

"But why? That's what we can't figure out. She's a schoolteacher. As far as we can tell she didn't live a high-risk lifestyle, she was devoted to her job and that baby. If somebody forced her off the road, why didn't they take the car?"

"Her purse wasn't in the vehicle. Maybe it was a robbery," Callie offered.

"Then where is Aspen?"

Neither of them spoke and the silence held an ominous portent. It was finally Callie who broke the silence. "We're doing everything we can here, Bree. It all takes time."

"I know." Bree released another sigh. "I'm just worried that this isn't going to have a happy ending."

"Some of them don't," Callie said softly.

Bree stood. "I'm hoping the weather holds. Even though we searched the area yesterday, Patrick and I would like to do a wider search around the car today. By the way, how are you feeling? Patrick said you had to leave the scene yesterday because you weren't feeling well."

"I'm fine today," Callie said and tried not to think of that moment the day before when she'd known she was losing control, when she'd known the grief that she'd refused to face was suddenly in her face and refusing to be ignored. "Guess it was just a touch of flu or something, but I'm fine now."

"Good. We can't have you go down now. Between the Julie Grainger murder and now this thing with Aspen Meadows, we're going to depend on you to make forensic sense of things."

"That's what we try to do," Callie replied. "Unfortunately I've got nothing for you on the Meadows scene right now."

"I figured it was too soon for you to have any definitive answers."

"You know I'll let you know the minute anything pops," Callie promised.

After saying goodbye, Bree left the office and Callie returned her attention to her computer screen, although her thoughts were miles away.

She'd awakened unusually early that morning, probably because she'd fallen asleep early the night before after the intense explosion of emotion she and Tom had shared.

When she'd opened her eyes this morning she'd been empty of all emotion. She could no longer find it in her to be bitter or angry with Tom and the overwhelming grief that had once festered inside her was gone as well. She was just numb and on autopilot.

She hadn't realized until now how much energy she'd expended hating Tom and avoiding thoughts of the baby she'd lost. It was what had gotten her up in the mornings and kept her focused solely on work.

She'd been hiding in her anger, hiding from life by working long hours and refusing to make any real, meaningful bonds with anyone. She'd lived in her home for a year and didn't even know her neighbors. She was still a young woman and yet she didn't date, she didn't do anything socially.

The baby was gone and nothing she did could change the facts of her past. What she had to figure out was what she wanted in her future.

But, not now, not today with Aspen Meadows's whereabouts heavy in her mind. As always it was easy for her to lose herself in her work and she was seated at a microscope when Tom walked in.

As she looked up and saw him standing in the reception area, she couldn't help the quickening of her heartbeat. She thought a million years could pass and she'd still feel Tom's presence in the acceleration of her heartbeat, in that tiny flutter of anticipation he'd always managed to pull forth from her.

Sexual attraction, she reminded herself. There were some men good at lovemaking and Tom Ryan was certainly one of those men. Surely that's the only reason her heart still responded to him. Surely that's the only reason his very presence alone managed to slice through the numbness that had gripped her all day.

She put away what she'd been working on and went back to her office to get her coat. She'd told Bree that some stories didn't have happy endings and she had a feeling she and Tom were one of those stories.

Even though she loved him, he still scared her. Love without trust would never work and she just wasn't sure she could trust him to choose her over another assignment. She didn't trust that she wouldn't wind up alone again.

"What are we doing for supper?" she asked once they were in his car and headed home.

"Ah, the burning question that plagues us at the end of each day." He shot her a quick glance. "Why don't we stop by the Morning Ray Café and grab a bite to eat there?"

She looked at him in surprise. "You wouldn't mind eating out instead of in?"

"The café is small, I can sit facing the door. I think we'll be fine for a quick meal."

He probably didn't want to spend any more time alone with her than necessary. Although she didn't sense any anger radiating from him, she wondered if maybe after the grief over their baby was gone he wouldn't somehow blame her for what had happened, for not contacting him the moment she found out she was pregnant.

He'd had to wait two years after the fact to grieve and maybe he now hated her for that. She wasn't sure how she'd react if the tables were turned.

It took only minutes for them to arrive at the café. As usual, he escorted her inside and the warmth and hominess of the Morning Ray Café felt welcome.

They sat at the table toward the back, with Tom facing the front door and Callie opposite him. Nora Martinez approached them with her usual bright smile and a couple of menus.

"Word is old man winter is going to hit us hard," she said, her blue eyes sparkling.

"That's what they say," Tom agreed.

They visited for a few minutes, talking about the

wedding, about the weather and about the daily special, then she left them alone with the promise that a waitress would be right over to take their orders.

Callie shrugged out of her coat and hung it on the back of her chair. Tom did the same with his outer coat, but kept on his sports jacket that she knew hid the gun he wore in his shoulder holster.

"Nora's meatloaf is always good," Callie said as she looked down at the menu.

"Some of the other agents have told me you can't get any bad food at the Morning Ray Café," he replied.

"That's true. Nora is a terrific cook." Callie reached for her water glass and took a sip. "Anything exciting happen for you today?" she asked as she set her glass back on the table.

As the front door of the café whooshed open, Tom's gaze shot over her shoulder. She could tell by the lack of tension in him that whoever had entered wasn't a threat.

He directed his brown eyes back to her. "That man we saw this morning standing on the sidewalk just up the street from your place? I talked to almost everyone on the block and he didn't belong there."

She frowned and felt a whisper of new fear seep through her. "You think it was somebody watching my house?"

"I think it's possible."

Callie took another sip of her water as her throat went dry. She leaned back in the chair and drew a deep breath. "There have been times over the last couple of months that I've felt like somebody was watching me, but I chalked it up to my imagination. I figured if Del Gardo or one of his men was that close to me I wouldn't get the chance to feel their presence, I'd just get a bullet to the back. Why hasn't he already killed me, Tom?"

"I don't know." Tom frowned and sat up straighter as the waitress arrived to take their orders.

When they were left alone again, Tom continued. "It's possible that Del Gardo has been too busy keeping hidden to worry about you right now. It's also possible that the man on the street this morning was watching us to get a feel for our routine and find out where there might be a weakness in security."

"Which is why you changed the routine by coming here," she replied.

"That's part of it," he agreed. "The other reason why I brought you here was because I thought we both could use a break. I thought it would be nice to share a meal and talk."

She eyed him warily. "Talk about what?"

"About nothing, about movies or books or politics and religion." His gaze lingered on her, a tiny wistful-ness in the brown depths. "I'll talk about whatever you want to, Callie. But for tonight, just for this meal, I'd like us to be two ordinary people enjoying a meal together without any baggage between us."

Relief rushed through her. "That would be nice," she agreed. They both needed a break from the emotional roller coaster ride they'd been on for the past couple of days. "So, what are we going to talk about?"

"I can tell you that your neighbors seem like nice people." As he told her about the people he'd spoken to in her neighborhood, Callie felt herself relaxing beneath the non-threatening conversation.

He told her about the widow, Grace Tandy, and a divorcee who lived with her two children on the right of Callie. There was a doctor, a sanitation worker and several stay-at-home moms on her block.

When their food arrived the pleasant conversation continued. They talked about winter weather and the kinds of things they enjoyed when it snowed. Callie was a hot-cocoa-and-roaring-fire kind of girl, while Tom liked snowboarding and skiing, but he admitted that at the end of an afternoon in the snow he was a fire-and-hot-cocoa kind of man.

He shared with her some of the funny stories from his childhood in foster care and she returned the favor, talking about life with a showgirl mother.

"I'm surprised you didn't become a showgirl like her," Tom said.

Callie laughed. "If there was one thing my mother impressed on me it was that she'd disown me if I followed in her footsteps. She wanted more for me and encouraged me to get all the education I could and pick a career that would last. Apparently my father left enough money for me to go to college."

"And she never told you who he was?" Tom asked.

"Never and I asked more than once, but she definitely gave me the feeling that he had died and it was just too painful for her to discuss."

They lingered over coffee after the meal, as if each of them were reluctant to call an end to this time of peace between them.

It was Tom who brought things back to the reality of their situation. "We should probably go," he said as he glanced toward the café front door. "It's dark and I'd like to get you home safe and sound."

She smiled at him. "I'd like that, too."

It was almost eight by the time they got back into his car and headed to her house. The warm glow the good food and easy conversation had created in her continued.

"I thought about pulling myself off your case today," he said as he drove.

She looked at him in surprise and then released a small sigh. "Things have been complicated between us, haven't they?"

He offered her a small smile. "I'd say that's an understatement."

"Tom, I'll be honest with you, I'm not overly eager to have anyone else protecting me, but I also don't want you to stay if you don't want to be here." She was surprised that the idea of him leaving filled her with such dread and yet she wasn't prepared to offer him more. She wasn't in a place to offer him a more permanent place in her life, wasn't even sure he wanted one with her anymore.

"I'm not going anywhere, Callie," he said in return. "I'll see this through to the end." He pulled up into her driveway and shut off the car engine. Unfastening his seat belt, he turned to look at her. "I think we've both been experts at running away when things get difficult. I'm not running this time, Callie. If you want me out of your life this go around, you're going to have to tell me to leave."

He got out of the car and she watched as he came around to the passenger door to get her. He was right. When he'd gotten scared of their relationship he'd run to another assignment. When she'd been afraid to face her grief, she'd run to her work and hidden in her anger, burying herself in both and keeping any other real life at bay.

Maybe it was time they both stopped running.

"Why don't you make a nice fire while I go change my clothes," she suggested when they got inside the house. She smiled at him, a real smile that came from her heart.

His eyes glowed as he nodded.

As Callie went down the hallway to her bedroom she wondered if when they'd been together before it had simply been the right man at the wrong time. Was this the right time for them?

There were no more secrets and no matter how hard she tried she couldn't summon any anger toward him. In fact, as she entered the bedroom, she realized she loved him as much now as she had before.

All she really had to decide was if she was willing to trust him again with her heart, if she could believe that he was her future.

TOM LAID THE FIRE and set it to burn, then watched the flames as they flickered and danced. Somehow while they'd been in the café a tiny glimmer of hope had appeared in his chest, the hope that maybe, just maybe, they had a future together after all.

Callie had been different during the meal. Softer, warmer, she'd once again become the woman he'd fallen in love with, the woman he still loved.

When he'd looked into her eyes over dinner he'd thought he'd seen not just forgiveness but also acceptance and that's what had stirred the hope that filled his heart.

He didn't turn on any other lights in the house. He liked the warm glow of just the fire lighting the room. What he'd like to do was make love to Callie in the flickering golden radiance of the flames.

The first time they'd made love they had come at each other with wild hunger and passion. The second time they'd come together it had been in shared pain and grief. He'd now like to make love to her with nothing but joy between them.

But, he'd take his cues from her. He didn't want to do anything to upset the delicate balance that existed between them at the moment.

He shucked his jacket and threw it over the back of

the sofa, then removed his gun and holster and set them on the coffee table. He eased into the sofa cushions to wait for her. And he felt as if he had been waiting for her for a lifetime.

Leaning his head back against the sofa cushions he thought of his childhood. He'd been shuffled from family to family, never having a room to call his own, a place that felt like home.

In the space of a month, this house, Callie's house, felt like home. No, it wasn't the house, it was the woman herself. Callie was home.

He sat up as she came into the living room. She was dressed in her nightgown and robe and she smiled as she saw the fire. "Hmm, nice," she said. "Since we didn't have dessert after dinner, how about some cheese and fruit?"

"Sure, that sounds good," he agreed and started to get up.

"Sit, I'll take care of it." She disappeared into the kitchen, leaving only that evocative scent of hers behind.

He leaned back once again, hoping the mood wouldn't be broken, hoping that tonight would mark a new beginning for them both.

She returned a few minutes later with a plate. In the center was a slab of cheese pierced with a small paring knife. Plump green and purple grapes surrounded the cheese.

Placing the plate on the coffee table, she sank onto the sofa next to him. The fact that she sat next to him instead of in the chair across from the sofa told him that he hadn't misread her signals, that for the first time since they'd reunited she was open to him.

"Darn, I meant to get a glass of wine," she exclaimed.

"I'll get it," he said and got up from the sofa. At that moment the telephone rang. "I'll get the wine, you get the phone."

She stood and reached for the cordless on the end table as he headed toward the kitchen. "Hello? What?"

Tom turned back to face her as he heard the frantic tone to her voice. In the flickering firelight he met her gaze. Her eyes widened as she looked just over his shoulder. "Tom, look out!"

He started to whirl around, but before he could complete the act, something hard slammed down on the back of his head.

He crashed to his knees, darkness swimming around him. As he careened forward to his face, the last thing he heard was the sound of Callie's scream.

Chapter Thirteen

Callie dropped the phone and screamed in terror as Tom hit the floor and remained unmoving. Was he dead? She barely had time to process what had happened when the big man wearing a ski mask rushed toward her.

She turned to run, but he tackled her from behind, slamming her down to the floor next to the coffee table with a thud.

She kicked her legs and flailed her arms, her breaths gasps of fear as she tried to get away from him. He grunted as her foot managed to catch him in the thigh.

He momentarily loosened his grip on her and she got to her feet but took only another step before he had her on her back once again. She didn't try to shove him off, knew he was too big, too heavy. Instead she tried to poke at his eyes through the tiny slits in his mask as she continued to buck wildly beneath him.

He muttered a curse as her knee connected with his midsection, but he held tight and as they wrestled he wrapped his big hands around her throat and began to squeeze.

This was the moment she'd feared would come when Del Gardo had escaped from the courthouse. She'd always known somehow in the back of her mind that he'd find her and that he'd get to her when he was ready.

And yet, it didn't make sense. She knew it wasn't Del Gardo who was squeezing the life from her. She knew it with certainty.

She bucked and kicked beneath him as his hands squeezed tighter, cutting off her airflow. She needed air. She needed to breathe.

She beat on his back with her hands and desperately grabbed his wrists in an effort to break his hold. Pulling and yanking, she felt her strength ebbing.

Oh, God, she needed air and he was too strong and she couldn't breathe! In an act of sheer desperation, she raked her fingernails on his wrists, knowing that when somebody found her body they would scrape her fingernails and would at least be able to get DNA that would hopefully, eventually identify her killer.

Her killer. She was going to die and she'd never get an opportunity to tell Tom that she loved him, that she forgave him and wasn't afraid to trust him anymore.

For all she knew Tom was dead. Tears blurred her vision as darkness edged in around her. A weary acceptance filled her as she looked into the masked face of her attacker. Although in the dim light of the room she couldn't make out the color of his eyes, she saw the glitter of success they contained.

It enraged her, that this man had gotten into her house, that he'd killed the man she loved and now thought he'd be successful in killing her. And with her rage came the memory of Tom's gun on top of the coffee table.

If she could just reach the gun before she fell unconscious. As the darkness encroached, she reached for the top of the coffee table. Desperate, fighting the dark, she scrabbled her hand on the wooden top.

Find the gun.

Find the gun.

The words screamed in her head as she felt her life draining away. Instead of the cold hard medal of the gun she found the platter of cheese and grapes. She wanted to sob in despair, but then her fingers found the knife stuck into the top of the cheese.

She pulled it out and with a firm grip drove it into the back of the man who was squeezing the life out of her. He screamed in a combination of pain and rage, but he took his hands from her neck.

Gasping and choking, Callie pulled in large gulps of air as the darkness that had threatened to consume her retreated. The respite was short-lived. With a new brutality, he fell on her again and grabbed her throat, obviously not mortally wounded by the small paring knife.

We'll get you, you bastard, she thought. He might kill her, but her team of forensic scientists would get the skin from beneath her nails, they'd check her for any hairs that didn't belong and hopefully that wound in his back would leak a couple drops of blood.

Eventually her team at the lab would identify him and he'd end up in jail. It would be a hollow victory, she thought.

Once again the darkness drew near, threatening to overtake her as her lungs burned from lack of oxygen. Within moments it would all be over and her decision to get on with her life, to embrace all the joy and love she could find would be for naught.

A roar filled the air and suddenly the man was magically lifted off her body. As Callie coughed and gasped, she saw Tom, alive and well, throw the man against the wall.

The masked man rushed Tom, and as the two struggled with each other, gigantic shadows darted across the walls. Neither of them said a word as they fought, swinging fists and punching like prize fighters.

Callie scurried out of the way, still choking as tears streaked down her cheeks. Tom slammed his fist into the lower jaw of the masked man, then followed up with another punch. He reeled away from Tom and without warning ran for the kitchen.

Tom followed. Callie was vaguely aware of a whoosh of cold air as the back door opened, then silence. With a sob, she pulled herself up off the floor and collapsed into the sofa.

She was vaguely aware of the spit and sizzle of the

fire as she curled up and continued to gasp for air. Her throat burned but she was scarcely aware of it as she waited for Tom to return.

Where was Tom? Had the fight continued into her backyard? *Let him be okay,* she prayed. *Please keep Tom safe.*

She was still trying to catch her breath when Tom returned and she gasped in relief. "I lost him in the dark," he said, his own rapid breathing filling the room. "Are you all right?" He hurried to her side and sat on the sofa next to her.

She nodded and tears began to fall once again as Tom pulled her into his arms. "I thought you were dead," she cried.

"You know how hard-headed I am," he replied with a teasing tone. "It definitely takes more than one hit in the head to do any real damage."

An unexpected laugh burst out of her, then she was crying again as he held her tight and murmured words of assurance.

"I'm going to make some calls," he said when he finally released her and stood. "We need to get Patrick out here, and some of your lab people. I also need to contact some agents and let them know Del Gardo just made a move on you."

Callie shook her head. "No, it wasn't Del Gardo."

Tom turned on the overhead light and looked at her in surprise. "Then it was one of his goons."

"No, it wasn't. I don't think he had anything to do

with what just happened." She swallowed and placed a hand against her burning throat. "It was Del Gardo on the phone. He told me to get out, to get out of the house immediately." She could tell she'd stunned Tom. "I'm sure it was him on the phone, Tom. I'd know his voice in my sleep. Why would he warn me, Tom?"

"I don't know." Obviously troubled, he picked up the phone from the floor where she'd dropped it earlier and he began to call the law enforcement who would respond to the crime.

IT WAS ALMOST DAWN by the time everyone was ready to leave Callie's house. Callie had sat patiently as Olivia scraped beneath her fingernails into the awaiting evidence envelopes. Jacob had kept busy in the living room where several drops of blood had been found. With the blood and the scrapings they would easily be able to identify DNA from the attacker.

Tom had explained everything that had occurred not just to Patrick and his men, but also to two FBI agents who had arrived with the hopes of learning something about Del Gardo.

"Are you sure it was his voice you heard on the phone?" Sam Salinger asked her for the hundredth time over the course of the night.

"I'm positive," Callie had replied. "He's called me before. I know his voice and it was definitely Vincent Del Gardo who called and warned me to get out of the house."

Everyone agreed that it didn't make sense, but Callie remained convinced that it had been the mobster on the phone. Phone records would be checked to see if the call was traceable, but Callie knew Del Gardo was too smart for that.

The intruder had gotten into the house through the back door. The lock had been sprung and the theory was that when Callie had gone to the kitchen to prepare the cheese and fruit the man had hidden in the pantry closet.

It had given Callie the chills to think that while she'd pulled cheese and grapes out of the refrigerator a killer had been hiding in her pantry.

Finally everything that could be done had been done and Callie and Tom stood side by side at the front door as they said goodbye to everyone. "It's starting to snow," Tom said.

Callie nodded and for a moment remained standing and watching the glittering flakes drift down from the sky. She finally closed the front door and leaned against it.

"You okay?" Tom asked. His eyes darkened as they lingered on her bruised throat.

"I'm tired, but I'm overwhelmingly grateful to be alive," she replied. "What about you? How's that hard head of yours?"

He reached up and touched the back of his head where she knew he had a goose egg. He'd been hit with her electric can opener and even though he'd been knocked unconscious he'd insisted he didn't have a concussion and didn't need any medical care. "It's a little sore, but I'm fine," he assured her.

For a long moment their gazes remained locked, then he opened his arms to her and she immediately stepped into the embrace.

She closed her eyes as she melted against him, into him, allowing the familiar scent of him to fill her head, the solid beat of his heart to comfort her. "I thought I was going to die," she said.

He tightened his arms around her. "Not on my watch," he replied.

"When his hands were wrapped around my throat, I truly thought it was the end of the line for me." She shivered and he reached up and stroked her hair. She raised her face to look at him. "We got through this, but it's not over, is it?"

He hesitated, then shook his head. "No, it's not over. It won't be over until Julie's murderer is in prison and it won't be over until Del Gardo is back in custody."

"Why would he call me and warn that I was in danger?" she asked.

"I don't know. I have a feeling we aren't going to have answers anytime soon. If we're lucky the man who attacked you tonight has a record and once we've got his DNA pinned down we can get him. We'll get him, Callie. I'm not going to leave you until I know for sure that you're out of danger."

She looked up at him and her heart expanded with all the love she'd been afraid to feel, afraid to accept.

She wanted to tell him what was in her heart. She broke away from the embrace and took him by the hand. "Come sit with me, Tom. We need to talk."

He stiffened slightly as if anticipating something bad, but allowed her to lead him to the couch where they both sat.

She took his hand in hers and gazed at him with loving eyes. "I've spent a long time being angry with you. As long as I could hang on to my anger, I wouldn't have to face the grief over losing Daniel."

He squeezed her hand and waited for her to continue.

"When I held Jack Meadows in my arms, all my grief came crashing in on me and no amount of anger I could summon toward you could keep it away. And after that sorrow was spent I realized I wasn't angry with you anymore. But, I was still so afraid to trust you, to believe that we have a future together."

"Callie," he began, his eyes burning with need.

"Wait." She held up a hand to still whatever he was about to say. "Then tonight, as that man was squeezing the life out of me, I realized that if I died, the one thing I would regret would be allowing fear to keep us apart. I would die with the regret that I hadn't given us a second chance to get it right. I love you, Tom Ryan. I've never stopped loving you and if you still want me, then I'm yours."

"If I still want you?" His eyes widened. "Callie, I've never wanted anything more than I want to make a life with you, build a future together." He pulled her back into his arms and kissed her, a kiss of promise, of joy.

When the kiss ended he stood and held out his hand to her. "I want picket fences and babies, I want to go to sleep in the same bed every night with you beside me. I want to be your bodyguard for life, Callie, because more than anything I want you."

At the moment, the mystery of Del Gardo's warning phone call and the terror of the attack that just occurred seemed like a lifetime ago. She was captured by the light in Tom's eyes, by the smile that curved his lips and she knew without any scientific reasoning that this time they were going to get it right.

* * * * *

KENNER COUNTY CRIME UNIT
continues next month when the predicted blizzard finally hits, putting an unfortunate hold on the investigation.

Mills & Boon® Intrigue
brings you a sneak preview of…

Rachel Lee's A Soldier's Homecoming

When he learns the truth about his father, military
man Ethan Parish is determined to reunite with his
long-lost family in Wyoming. On his way into town, he
clashes with policewoman Connie Halloran, whose
captivating beauty entices him. Together they begin
to uncover the dangers of family secrets…

Don't miss this thrilling first story in the
CONARD COUNTY: THE NEXT GENERATION
mini-series, available next month from
Mills & Boon® Intrigue.

A Soldier's Homecoming
by
Rachel Lee

Deputy Constance Halloran drove along the U.S. highway toward Conard City, taking her time, keeping an eye on traffic, glad her shift was almost over.

Spring had settled over the county, greening it with recent rains, filling the air with the fragrance of wildflowers and the scent she thought of as *green*. With her window rolled down, the aroma wafted into her car, earth's special perfume.

Today had been a lazy day, an easy shift. She'd had only one call about a minor theft at one of the ranches; then she'd spent most of the day patrolling her sector. She hadn't written any speeding tickets, which was unusual. Even the traffic seemed to be enjoying a case of spring fever.

Maybe she would light the barbecue tonight and make some hamburgers. Sophie, her seven-year-old daughter, loved grilled hamburgers beyond everything, and loved the opportunity to eat outside at their porch table almost as much. Of course, the evenings could still get chilly, but a sweater would do.

The idea pleased her, and she began to hum a lilting melody. A semi passed her from the opposite direction and flashed his lights in a friendly manner. Connie flashed back, her smile broadening. Some days it felt good just to be alive.

Another mile down the road, she spotted a man standing on the shoulder, thumb out. At once she put on her roof lights, gave one whoop of her siren and pulled over until he was square in the view of her dash camera. He dropped his arm and waited for her.

A couple of cars passed as she radioed dispatch with her position and the reason for her stop.

"Got it, Connie," Velma said, her smoke-frogged voice cracking. "You be careful, hear?"

"I always am."

Glancing over to make sure she wouldn't be opening her door into traffic, Connie climbed out and approached the man.

As she drew closer, she realized he looked scruffy and exotic all at once. Native American, she registered instantly. Long black hair with a streak of gray fell to his shoulders. He also had a beard, unusually thick for someone of his genetic background. Dark eyes looked back at her. The thousand-yard stare. She'd seen it before.

For an instant she wondered if he was mentally ill; then her mind pieced together the conglomeration of clothing he wore, and she identified him as a soldier, or maybe a veteran. His pants were made of the new digitized camouflage fabric, but his jacket was the old olive drab. As she approached, he let a backpack slip from his shoulder to the ground, revealing the collar of his cammie shirt, and she saw the black oak leaf of a major.

At once some of her tension eased. "I'm sorry, sir," she said courteously, "but hitchhiking is illegal."

He nodded, his gaze leaving her and scanning the surrounding countryside. "Sorry, I forgot. Been out of the country."

"I guessed that. Whereabouts?"

His inky gaze returned to her. "Afghanistan. I'll just keep walking."

"No," she said impulsively, breaking all the rules in an instant. "I'll drive you to town. How come you don't have a car?"

Something like amusement, just a hint, flickered swiftly across his face. "I need to be home a while longer before I'll be comfortable behind the wheel."

She let that go, sensing the story behind it wasn't something he was about to share. "Well, hop in. I'm going off shift, so unless something happens, I'll have you in town in twenty minutes."

"Thanks."

He hefted his backpack and followed her to the car. Breaking more rules, she let him sit in front with her, rather than in the safer backseat cage. Even in the large

SUVs the department preferred, he seemed too big. Over six feet, easily, and sturdily built.

She reached for her microphone and called the dispatcher. "I'm back on the road, Velma, on my way in. I'm giving someone a ride."

Velma tutted loudly. "You know you shouldn't."

"It's a special case."

"Whatever." Velma sounded disgusted in the way of a woman used to having her good advice ignored.

Connie signed off and smiled at her passenger. "Velma is the department's mother."

He nodded, saying nothing. A few seconds later they were back on the road, heading down the highway toward town. They passed a herd of cattle on a gentle slope, grazing amicably alongside a group of deer. In places the barbed-wire fences were totally hidden in a tangle of tumbleweed. Indian paintbrush dotted the roadside with scarlet and orange, as if the colors had been scattered by a giant hand.

"It's beautiful country," Connie remarked. "Are you staying or just passing through?"

"A bit of both."

"You have friends here?"

"Sort of. Some folks I want to see, anyway."

She opened her mouth to ask who, then swallowed the words. He didn't seem to want to talk much—maybe with good reason, considering where he'd been. She thought of Billy Joe Yuma, her cousin Wendy's husband, and the problems he still suffered sometimes from Vietnam. This guy's wounds had to be fresher.

When she spoke again, it was to ask something less invasive. "Ever been here before?"

"No."

Well, that gambit wasn't going to work. Stifling a sigh, she gave her attention back to the road and tried to ignore the man beside her. If he stayed in town for more than twenty-four hours, someone would learn something about him and word would pass faster than wildfire. The county had grown quite a bit in the past fifteen years, but it hadn't grown much. People still knew everything about their neighbors, and strangers still attracted a lot of curiosity and speculation.

However, it went against the grain for her to treat a stranger with silence. Around here, folks generally made strangers feel welcome.

"I can take you to a motel if you want."

"Sheriff's office is fine."

"Okay." A scattering of houses near the road announced that Conard City now lay less than ten miles ahead. "My uncle used to be sheriff here," she said by way of keeping a friendly conversation going.

"Yeah?"

At last a sign of curiosity. "He retired a couple of years ago," she explained. "He and my aunt are in South America and are later going on a cruise to Antarctica. It blows my mind to even think of it."

That elicited a chuckle. "It wouldn't be my choice."

"Mine, either, right now. Maybe when I retire I'll see things differently."

"You never know."

She tossed him another glance and saw that he appeared a bit more relaxed.

"So," he said after a moment, "you followed in your uncle's footsteps?"

"Eventually. I grew up in Laramie. Then I moved to Denver."

"How'd that work out?"

"Well, I got my degree, got married, got divorced, decided I didn't like the big bad world all that much and came back to be a deputy."

"What's that like?"

"I love it." She glanced at him again, wondering what had suddenly unlocked the key to his mouth. But he seemed to have gone away again, looking out the windows, watching intently. So on guard. Expecting trouble at any instant.

And there were no magic words to cure that. Nothing but time would do that, if even that could succeed.

"I worked as a cop in the city," she said after a moment. "It's better here."

"Why?"

"Less crime. More helping people."

"I can see that."

She reckoned he could.

"So do you like your new sheriff?"

"Gage Dalton," she supplied. "Yeah. He can be hard to get to know, but once you do, he's great. He used to be DEA, then he came here and my dad hired him as a criminologist. We never had one before."

"That is small-town."

She smiled. "Yeah. It's great."

They reached the edge of town, and soon were driving along Main Street toward the courthouse square and the storefront sheriff's office. On the way, she pointed out the City Diner.

"Eat there if you want rib-sticking food. Despite the sign out front, everyone calls it Maude's diner. You won't find high-class service, but if you're not worried about cholesterol, sugar or salt, there's no better place to get a meal or a piece of pie."

"I'll remember that."

She pulled into her slot in front of the office and turned off the ignition. Before he climbed out, she turned in her seat to face him directly. "I'm Connie Halloran," she said.

"Ethan. Thanks for the ride."

© Susan Civil-Brown and Cristian Brown 2008

0810/46a

 **INTRIGUE**

Coming next month

2-IN-1 ANTHOLOGY

SNOWED IN WITH THE BOSS
by Jessica Andersen

Millionaire Griffin and his secretary Sophie are under threat
at his mountain retreat. And relying on each other for
survival could mean giving in to their deepest desires.

CRIMINALLY HANDSOME
by Cassie Miles

A terrifying vision sends frightened psychic Emma into the
protective arms of sceptical – *and oh-so-sexy* – CSI Miguel
as they struggle to catch a killer.

2-IN-1 ANTHOLOGY

THE HIGH COUNTRY RANCHER
by Jan Hambright

When detective Mariah draws the attention of a killer,
reticent rancher Baylor, a suspect under her investigation, is
determined to keep her safe – *and satisfied*!

A SOLDIER'S HOMECOMING
by Rachel Lee

Falling in love with Connie was never part of dark and
damaged Ethan's plan. Yet the beautiful deputy and her
adorable daughter brought out all his protective instincts.

On sale 20th August 2010

Available at WHSmith, Tesco, ASDA, Eason and all good bookshops.
For full Mills & Boon range including eBooks visit
www.millsandboon.co.uk

INTRIGUE

Coming next month

2-IN-1 ANTHOLOGY

SECRET AGENT, SECRET FATHER
by Donna Young

Left for dead, spy Jacob had no recollection of who he was or who had tried to kill him. The only thing he responded to was Grace – and her seriously sensual touch!

THE CAVANAUGH CODE
by Marie Ferrarella

Private investigator JC finds detective Taylor's tough-as-nails demeanour a turn-on. And her stubborn refusal to accept his help makes him want her even more.

SINGLE TITLE

HUNTING DOWN THE HORSEMAN
by BJ Daniels

Stuntman Judd has never given a thought to marriage, yet he starts to reconsider when adventurous trick-rider Faith catches his eye.

2 FREE BOOKS
AND A SURPRISE GIFT

We would like to take this opportunity to thank you for reading this Mills & Boon® book by offering you the chance to take TWO more specially selected books from the Intrigue series absolutely FREE! We're also making this offer to introduce you to the benefits of the Mills & Boon® Book Club™—

- **FREE home delivery**
- **FREE gifts and competitions**
- **FREE monthly Newsletter**
- **Exclusive Mills & Boon Book Club offers**
- **Books available before they're in the shops**

Accepting these FREE books and gift places you under no obligation to buy, you may cancel at any time, even after receiving your free books. Simply complete your details below and return the entire page to the address below. You don't even need a stamp!

YES Please send me 2 free Intrigue books and a surprise gift. I understand that unless you hear from me, I will receive 5 superb new stories every month, including two 2-in-1 books priced at £4.99 each and a single book priced at £3.19, postage and packing free. I am under no obligation to purchase any books and may cancel my subscription at any time. The free books and gift will be mine to keep in any case.

Ms/Mrs/Miss/Mr _____ Initials _____

Surname _____

Address _____

_____

_____ Postcode _____

E-mail _____

Send this whole page to: Mills & Boon Book Club, Free Book Offer, FREEPOST NAT 10298, Richmond, TW9 1BR

Offer valid in UK only and is not available to current Mills & Boon Book Club subscribers to this series. Overseas and Eire please write for details.. We reserve the right to refuse an application and applicants must be aged 18 years or over. Only one application per household. Terms and prices subject to change without notice. Offer expires 31st October 2010. As a result of this application, you may receive offers from Harlequin Mills & Boon and other carefully selected companies. If you would prefer not to share in this opportunity please write to The Data Manager, PO Box 676, Richmond, TW9 1WU.

Mills & Boon® is a registered trademark owned by Harlequin Mills & Boon Limited. The Mills & Boon® Book Club™ is being used as a trademark.